ALFRED HITCHCOCK'S TALES

Large Print Alf

Alfred Hitchcock's tales to
be read with caution

WITHDR

ALFRED HITCHCOCK'S TALES TO BE READ WITH CAUTION

Chivers Press ● Thorndike Press
Bath, Avon, England ● Thorndike, Maine USA

This Large Print edition is published by Chivers Press, England, and by Thorndike Press, USA.

Published in 1995 in the U.K. by arrangement with Dell Magazines, a division of Bantam, Doubleday Dell Direct, Inc.

Published in 1995 in the U.S. by arrangement with Dell Magazines, a division of Bantam, Doubleday Dell Direct, Inc.

U.K. Hardcover ISBN 0–7451–3096 8 (Chivers Large Print)
U.K. Softcover ISBN 0–7451–3097 6 (Camden Large Print)
U.S. Softcover ISBN 0–7862–0380–3 (General Series Edition)

The text of this Large Print edition is unabridged.
Other aspects of the book may vary from the original edition.

Set in 16 pt. New Times Roman.

Printed in Great Britain on acid-free paper.

British Library Cataloguing in Publication Data available

Library of Congress Cataloging-in-Publication Data

Alfred Hitchcock's tales to be read with caution / edited by Eleanor
    Sullivan.
        p. cm.
    Stories previously published in Alfred Hitchcock's mystery magazine.
    ISBN 0–7862–0380–3 (lg. print : lsc)
    1. Detective and mystery stories, American. 2. Large type books.
I. Sullivan, Eleanor. II. Alfred Hitchcock's mystery magazine.
III. Title: Tales to be read with caution.
[PS648.D4A347 1995]
813.'.087208—dc20
                                                    94–41624

COPYRIGHT NOTICES
AND ACKNOWLEDGMENTS

CONTENTS

INTRODUCTION

Fair warning. Even if you are naturally cautious it would be remiss of me not to advise prudence as you proceed from story to story in this new death-and-defiance-filled anthology. If you heed this admonition, your discretion will be rewarded—with shock-absorbing revelations and dark insights. So do go chary into this good collection and you will rage against the dying of your reading light.

A few words of special interest about this anthology. It is enhanced by stories from both the best-selling Patricia Matthews and her distinguished husband, Clayton Matthews. The story by Stephen Wasylyk, 'The Loose End,' represents the first mystery he ever wrote and published. And 'Frightened Lady,' by C. B. Gilford received a scroll from the Mystery Writers of America as one of the best mystery short stories published in 1972. And none of the twenty-four stories in this book have appeared previously in print any later than 1972.

A MELEE OF DIAMONDS

E. D. Hoch

The man with the silver-headed cane turned into Union Street just after nine o'clock, walking briskly through the scattering of evening shoppers and salesclerks hurrying home after a long day. It was a clear April evening, cool enough for the topcoat the man wore, but still a relief at the end of a long winter. He glanced into occasional shop windows as he walked, but did not pause until he'd reached the corner of Union and Madison. There, he seemed to hesitate for a moment at the windows of the Midtown Diamond Exchange. He glanced quickly to each side, as if making certain there was no one near, and then smashed the nearest window with his silver-headed cane.

The high-pitched ringing of the alarm mingled with the sound of breaking glass, as the man reached quickly into the window. A few pedestrians froze in their places, but as the man turned to make his escape a uniformed policeman suddenly appeared around the corner. 'Hold it right there!' he barked, reaching for his holstered revolver.

The man turned, startled at the voice so close, and swung his cane at the officer. Then,

1

as the policeman moved in, he swung again, catching the side of the head just beneath the cap. The officer staggered and went down, and the man with the cane rounded the corner running.

'Stop him!' a shirt-sleeved man shouted from the doorway of the Diamond Exchange. 'We've been robbed!'

The police officer, dazed and bleeding, tried to get to his knees and then fell back to the sidewalk, but a young man in paint-stained slacks and a zippered jacket detached himself from the frozen onlookers and started after the fleeing robber. He was a fast runner, and he overtook the man with the cane halfway down the block. They tumbled together into a pile of discarded boxes, rolling on the pavement, as the man tried to bring his cane up for another blow.

He shook free somehow, losing the cane but regaining his feet, and headed for an alleyway. A police car, attracted by the alarm, screeched to a halt in the street, and two officers jumped out with drawn guns.

'Stop or we'll shoot!' the nearest officer commanded, and fired his pistol into the air in warning.

The sound of the shot echoed along the street, and the running man skidded to a halt at the entrance to the alleyway. He turned and raised his hands above his head. 'All right,' he said. 'I'm not armed. Don't shoot.'

The officer kept his pistol out until the second cop had snapped on the handcuffs.

* * *

'Damn it!' Captain Leopold exploded, staring at the paper cup full of light brown coffee that Lieutenant Fletcher had just set before him. 'Is that the best you can get out of the machine?'

'Something's wrong with it, Captain. We've sent for a serviceman.'

Leopold grumbled and tried to drink the stuff. One swallow was all he could stomach. The men in the department had given him a coffee percolator of his very own when he'd assumed command of the combined Homicide and Violent Crimes squad, but on this particular morning, with his coffee can empty, he'd been forced to return to the temperamental vending machine in the hall.

'Get me a cola instead, will you, Fletcher?' he said at last, pouring the coffee down the sink in one corner of his office. When the lieutenant came back, he asked, 'Phil Begler's in the hospital?'

Fletcher nodded in confirmation. 'There's a report on your desk. Phil came upon a guy stealing a handful of diamonds from the window of the Midtown Diamond Exchange. The guy whacked him on the head with a cane and started running. They caught him, but Phil's in the hospital with a concussion.'

3

'I should go see him,' Leopold decided. 'Phil's a good guy.'

'They identified the fellow that stole the diamonds and hit him as Rudy Hoffman, from New York. He's got a long record of smash-and-grab jobs.'

Leopold nodded. 'Maybe Phil Begler's concussion will be enough to put him away for good.'

Fletcher nodded. 'Hope so, Captain, but there is one little problem with the case.'

'What's that?' Leopold asked.

'Well, they caught Hoffman only a half-block from the scene, after a young fellow chased and tackled him, and fought with him till a patrol car arrived. Hoffman got $58,000 worth of diamonds out of that window, and he was in sight of at least one person every instant until they arrested him.'

'So?'

'The diamonds weren't on him, Captain. No trace of them.'

'He dropped them in the street.'

'They searched. They searched the street, they searched him, they even searched the patrol car he was in after his arrest. No diamonds.'

Leopold was vaguely irritated that such a simple matter should disrupt the morning's routine. 'Haven't they questioned him about it?'

'He's not talking, Captain.'

4

'All right,' he said with a sigh. 'Bring him down. I'll have to show you guys how it's done.'

Rudy Hoffman was a gray-haired man in his early forties. The years in prison, Leopold noted, had left him with a pale complexion and shifty, uncertain eyes. He licked his lips often as he spoke, nervously glancing from Leopold to Fletcher and then back again.

'I don't know anything,' he said. 'I'm not talking without a lawyer. You can't even question me without a lawyer. I know my rights!'

Leopold sat down opposite him. 'It's not just a little smash-and-grab this time, Rudy. That cop you hit might die. You could go up for the rest of your life.'

'He's just got a concussion. I heard the guards talkin'.'

'Still, we've got you on assault with a deadly weapon. With your record, that's enough. We don't even need the felony charge. So you see, you're not really protecting yourself by clamming up about the diamonds. Even if we don't find them, we've still got you nailed.'

Rudy Hoffman merely smiled and looked sleepy. 'Those diamonds are where you'll never find them, cop. That much I promise you.'

Leopold glared at him for a moment, thinking of Phil Begler in a hospital bed. 'We'll see about that,' he said, and stood up. 'Come on, Fletcher, we're keeping him from his

5

beauty sleep.'

Back in Leopold's office, Fletcher said, 'See what I mean, Captain? He's a hard one.'

Leopold was grim. 'I'll find those damned diamonds and stuff them down his throat. Tell me everything that happened from the instant he broke the window.'

'I can do better than that, Captain. The kid who chased him is outside now, waiting to make a statement. Want to see him now?'

Neil Quart was not exactly a kid, though he was still on the light side of twenty-five. Leopold had seen the type many times before, on the streets usually, with shaggy hair and dirty clothes, taunting the rest of the world.

'You're quite a hero,' Leopold told him. 'Suppose you tell us how it happened.'

Quart rubbed at his nose, trying to look cool. 'I work over at Bambaum's nights, in the shipping department. I'd just finished there at nine o'clock and was heading home. Down by the Diamond Exchange I saw this guy with the cane smash a window. I wasn't close enough to grab him, but as he started to run away this cop rounds the corner. The guy hit him with the cane, hard, and knocked him down. Now, I don't have any love for cops, but I decided to take out after this guy. I ran him down halfway up the block, and we tussled a little. He tried to conk me with the cane too, but I got it away from him. Then he was up and running, but the other cops got there. One cop fired a shot in the air and it was all over.'

Leopold nodded. 'How long was the robber—Rudy Hoffman—out of your sight?'

'He wasn't out of my sight. Not for a second! I went right after him when he knocked the cop down. Hell, I thought he might have killed him.'

'You didn't see him throw anything away, into the street?'

'Not a thing.'

'Could he have thrown anything away as he raised his hands?'

'I don't think so.'

Fletcher interrupted at this point. 'They caught him at the entrance to an alleyway, Captain. Every inch of it was searched.'

Leopold turned back to Neil Quart. 'As you've probably guessed, we're looking for the diamonds he stole. Any idea what he might have done with them?'

The young man shrugged. 'Not a glimmer. Unless ... We were wrestling around some boxes.'

'They were all checked,' Fletcher said. 'Everything was checked. The police were there all night, looking.'

'You still did a good job,' Leopold told the young man. 'You weren't afraid to get involved, and that's what counts.'

'Thanks. I just didn't like to see him hit that cop.'

Outside, Fletcher asked, 'Satisfied,

Captain?'

'Not by a long shot. What about Hoffman's clothes?'

'We went over every stitch, including his topcoat. Nothing there.'

'All right,' Leopold decided, grim-faced. 'Let's go see where it happened.'

*   *   *

The Midtown Diamond Exchange still showed the scars of the previous night's robbery, with a boarded-up window and a little pile of broken glass.

The assistant manager, who'd been on duty the previous evening, was a sandy-haired man named Peter Arnold who looked pained by the whole affair.

'Just tell us how it was,' Leopold told him. 'Everything you can remember.'

'It was just closing time, a few minutes after nine. The other clerk had gone home, and I'd locked the front door. That was when I heard the window smash and saw him scooping up the diamonds.'

'Let's go back a bit, Mr. Arnold. How many diamonds were in the window?'

'Dozens! We had a few large rings mounted on cards giving the prices, and then we had perhaps twenty-five or thirty smaller stones, unmounted. A melee of diamonds, to use the trade term—although that usually refers to stones of less than a quarter carat. Most of these were larger.'

'They were valued at $58,000?'

Peter Arnold nodded sadly. 'I've already heard from our New York office about it.'

'Do you always leave that many diamonds in your store window?'

'Not at all. They're in the window only while the store is open. My first duty after locking the door would have been to remove them from that and the other display windows and lock them in the vault for the night. I had just locked the door and was starting for the window on the other side when I heard the smashing of glass. I looked over and saw this man scooping the diamonds out of their trays. The window alarm was ringing, of course, and as he started away Officer Begler appeared around the corner.'

'You know Phil Begler?'

The jeweler nodded. 'He's been on this beat maybe four or five years. Usually he's right around this corner, but at nine he goes up to direct traffic out of the parking ramp in the next block. It was only a fluke he happened to get back just when that man broke the window.'

'Any idea what he did with the diamonds during his escape?'

'I'm baffled. If he'd dropped them, I should think at least a few would have been found.'

Leopold walked to the boarded-up window,

9

and pulled aside the black velvet drape so he could peer into it. The diamond trays were still there, speckled with broken glass, but there were no gems. 'He got everything?'

'No, there were four rings on cards and six unmounted stones that he missed, but he made a good haul. We estimate $58,000, or even a bit more.'

Leopold let the drape drop back into place. He took out a picture of Rudy Hoffman. 'Ever see him in the store before the robbery, casing the place?'

'I don't remember him, but of course someone else may have been on duty.'

'I'll leave this picture with you. Show it to your manager and the clerks. See if anyone remembers him.'

'You think it was well-planned?'

'He got rid of the diamonds somewhere, and that took planning.'

On the way out, Leopold paused at the little pile of broken glass and bent to examine it.

'Find something, Captain?' Fletcher asked.

'Ever think about how much broken glass and diamonds look alike, Fletcher?'

'Are there any diamonds in that pile?'

'No, just broken glass.'

On the way back downtown, Fletcher said, 'They did an X-ray on Hoffman too, in case you're thinking he might have swallowed them.'

'Never considered it for a moment.' He

10

stared through the car's dirty windshield at the passing scene. Police headquarters was separated from the main Union Street shopping area by some ten blocks of abandoned, run-down buildings—many of them doomed by a much-postponed urban renewal project. Those that still had tenants housed record shops and adult bookstores on their lower levels, renting the rooms above to bearded young people and transient types. It was a shabby section of the inner city, but the crime rate was not as high as might be expected.

'They should tear it all down,' Fletcher commented.

'I suppose they will, one of these days.' Leopold had another thought. 'What about the men who searched the street? Could one of them have pocketed the diamonds?'

Fletcher thought about it. 'We've got some bad eggs in the department, Captain—like any other city—but I'd trust any of the men who were out there last night. I know them all, from Begler on down. They're honest cops.'

Leopold said no more until they reached his office. Then he asked Fletcher to bring him Rudy Hoffman's clothing. They went over each piece together, though the clothes had been searched earlier, and they found nothing.

Leopold frowned and went to stare out the window at the crowded parking lot that was his only view. 'How about a wig, false teeth,

11

something like that?'

Fletcher shook his head. 'Nothing, Captain.'

Leopold turned suddenly. 'Damn it, Fletcher, why didn't I think of it before? There's one thing we've completely overlooked, one thing that's missing from Hoffman's possessions!'

Fletcher looked blank. 'What's that, Captain?'

'The cane, of course! The silver-headed cane he used to break the window and crack Phil Begler's skull! Where is it?'

'I suppose they've got it tagged as the weapon. It would be in the evidence drawer, or else already at the D.A.'s office, for presentation before the grand jury.'

'Find it, Fletcher, and let's take a look at it.'

Lieutenant Fletcher was back in five minutes, carrying a long black walking stick with a silver head in the shape of a ball held by a bird's claw. Leopold snorted and turned it over in his hands.

'Doesn't really go with Hoffman somehow,' Fletcher commented. 'Not his style.'

'No.' Leopold turned it over in his hands, and tried to twist off the top. It seemed solid, as was the shaft of the cane. 'He probably stole it from somewhere. There's certainly nothing hidden in it.'

'Let's think about it,' Fletcher suggested. 'Maybe something will come to us by

12

morning.'

Leopold glanced at his watch and nodded. It was after three, and he wanted to stop by the hospital and see Officer Begler on his way home. 'Good idea,' he agreed. 'See you in the morning.'

'Say, how about coming over for dinner tonight, Captain? Carol was saying the other day that she hasn't seen you since the Christmas party.'

'Thanks, Fletcher. I could use some of your wife's cooking, but let's make it another time. Give her my best, though.'

He drove over to Memorial Hospital and spent a half hour with Begler, who grinned from beneath his bandages and seemed in good enough spirits. Leopold paused in the lobby to chat with a couple of nurses, and then headed home to his apartment, encountering the rush-hour traffic he usually tried to avoid. Driving along Union Street, he remembered the empty coffee can in his office and pulled over at a neighborhood grocery.

The place was cluttered and crowded. He picked up a can of coffee and found a clerk to take his money. 'Anything else, sir?'

Leopold shook his head. 'That's it.' Then he noticed the dark-haired girl who'd entered behind him. She pretended to be choosing a loaf of bread, but she was really watching him. No one takes that long to choose bread, he knew, and when she finally moved up to the

13

clerk with her selection her eyes were still on Leopold.

The clerk slipped the coffee can into a paper bag, and Leopold left the store. Before he could cross the sidewalk to his car he heard the girl's voice behind him. 'You're a detective, aren't you?'

He turned to her with a smile he hoped was friendly. She was a good-looking girl, in her early twenties, but her face seemed drawn and tired at the moment. 'You might say that.'

'Do you want the loot from the Midtown Diamond robbery?'

In all his years of police work, nothing like it had ever happened to him before. He'd spent a full day trying to locate the diamonds that had disappeared by some sort of magic, and now this girl walked up to him outside a grocery store and offered them, just like that.

'Do you know where it is?'

She nodded. 'I can take you there, if you'll promise not to arrest me or my boyfriend.'

'Who is your boyfriend?'

'Names aren't important. He didn't have anything to do with the robbery. Have I your promise?'

'Then how'd he get the diamonds?'

'He's supposed to take them to New York and sell them—you know, like a fence. I don't want any part of it. I want you to take them.'

'How'd you know I was a detective?'

'I followed you from the hospital. You were

visiting that policeman who was injured. I went there to find out how he was, and a nurse pointed you out as a detective.'

'You're concerned about Officer Begler?'

'Certainly. I never knew it would be anything like this when Freddy agreed to handle the stuff. I want out of it, before we all end up behind bars.'

'Can you take me to the diamonds?'

She glanced quickly down the street and nodded. 'Leave your car here. We'll go in mine.'

He followed her to the corner and slid into the front seat of a little foreign sedan, still clutching his pound of coffee. She drove like a demon, weaving in and out of the rush-hour lines of traffic. In five minutes they'd reached the run-down section of Union, where the buildings waited for demolition, and he knew this was her destination. She parked the car and led him up a narrow flight of dimly lit stairs to an apartment above a vacant barber shop. In view of the long-haired residents, Leopold could easily understand why it had been forced to close.

'Is Freddy here?' he asked the girl, shifting the coffee to his left hand so his right would be near his gun.

'Who told you his name?' she asked, startled.

'You did.'

'All right. No, he's not here. If he knew what

15

I was doing, he'd probably kill me!' she prophesied.

She unlocked the door and led Leopold into a drab, dim living room. A large white cat came running to meet her, and she knelt to stroke its fur. 'Where are the diamonds?' he asked her.

'This way. In the kitchen.'

He followed her out, expecting a trap, expecting a seduction, expecting almost anything but the little leather pouch she took from the breadbox and opened before his eyes. She poured them out on the counter—big diamonds, little diamonds, some in rings but most unset. Leopold simply stared, almost at a loss for words. 'These are all of them?' he asked finally.

'Yes.'

'How did Hoffman get them to you? He's in jail.'

'He has an accomplice who brought them to Freddy. Now take them and go, before he comes back!'

But as Leopold's hand closed over the little pouch of diamonds, they heard a sound at the apartment door. It was a key in a lock, and a moment later they heard the door open.

'Is that him?' Leopold whispered.

'Yes, yes! He'll kill us both!'

'Go out and try to stall him.'

She hurried through the swinging kitchen door, her face white, and Leopold looked around for a way out. There was only a door to

16

a dead-end pantry, and a window that looked out onto a back alley. He tried the window and found it painted shut, unbudging. He turned back toward the door to the living room, listening to the muffled voices on the other side, and slipped the revolver from his holster. He stared down at the jewels for a moment and an idea came to him.

Two minutes later, he stepped through the swinging door with his gun drawn. 'Hold it right there, Freddy.'

There was a gasp from the girl and Freddy turned, startled at the voice, but it took him only an instant to realize what was happening. 'You damned little double-crossing tramp!' he shouted at the girl. 'Glenda, I'll kill you for this!' He started for her, but Leopold waved him back with the gun.

'You'll kill no one. I'm Captain Leopold of Violent Crimes, and if anything happens to her I'll have you behind bars.'

'What did she tell you?'

'She brought me here to give me the diamonds, to try and save your skin, but somebody beat us to them. They're gone.'

Freddy was on his feet. He was a little man with mouselike features, and he moved now like a rodent who discovered the trap does not even contain a piece of cheese. 'What do you mean, they're gone? They can't be gone!'

Glenda's eyes had widened in wonder, as she tried to decide what Leopold was up to. 'Look

17

for yourself,' he told Freddy, and lowered his gun.

The little man lost no time in getting to the kitchen. He tore through the breadbox, the wastebasket, the cupboards, while Leopold stood in the doorway. Finally, after ten minutes of searching, he asked, 'Where are they, Glenda? Get them now!'

'It's like he said, Freddy! Honest!'

'You hid them somewhere,' he accused.

'No! Honest!'

'Would she have brought me here if she'd hidden the diamonds somewhere else?' Leopold argued.

Freddy eyed him with open distrust. 'How do I know they're not in your pocket?'

Leopold put away his gun and raised his arms. 'You can search me if you want.' Now that he'd seen Freddy in action, he knew he didn't need the gun to take him, if it came to that.

The little man stepped close, eyeing Leopold, and ran his hands carefully over his body, checking his topcoat and pants, cuffs and sleeves. It was a good search, but he found nothing. Leopold removed his gun to show the inside of the holster, then opened the revolver itself to show that the chambers held nothing but bullets.

'What's in the bag?' Freddy asked.

Leopold smiled. 'A pound of coffee. I was on my way home when Glenda contacted me.'

Freddy took out the coffee can and looked into the bag. Then he replaced it in disgust. 'All right, I believe you—but if the diamonds aren't here, where are they?'

'I'm as anxious to get them as you are,' Leopold assured him. 'It seems to me there's only one other person who could have them.'

'Who's that?'

'The guy who brought them to you in the first place—Rudy Hoffman's accomplice.'

Freddy thought about that. 'Why would he take them?'

Leopold shrugged. 'With Hoffman in jail, maybe he figured he could keep the loot for himself. By delivering the diamonds to you, and then stealing them back, he'd be in the clear.'

'Yeah,' Freddy said, beginning to go along with it. 'That damned double-crosser would pull something like this!'

'Want to tell me who he is?'

Freddy's eyes narrowed in distrust. 'I'll handle it, cop.'

'Look, you're on very thin ice. If I catch you with those diamonds, I could arrest you for receiving stolen property.'

Freddy thought about it. 'No,' he decided, 'I'm not telling you. Maybe the guy didn't take them.'

Leopold sighed and turned to the girl. 'Glenda, who is Hoffman's accomplice?'

'I don't know. I didn't see him.'

19

'She's telling the truth, cop. I'm the only one who knows, besides Hoffman—and he's not about to talk. Even if he gets sent up, it wouldn't be for too long, and when he gets out he can still work his sweet little scheme in other cities.'

'Are you part of his scheme?'

'I was going to fence the gems, that's all. Don't bother taking notes, though, because I'll deny everything.'

'If you won't tell me who the accomplice is, call him up. Tell him you know he took the stuff and get him over here.'

That idea seemed to appeal to the little man. 'Yeah,' he said slowly. 'Maybe I could do that.'

'If I get the diamonds and the accomplice, Freddy, you're off the hook.'

'All right, I'll call him.'

He walked to the phone and Leopold shot Glenda a look that told her to play along with him. Given a bit of luck, he'd have the accomplice and get her off the hook with Freddy.

'Hello? This is Freddy Doyle. Yeah, yeah … Well, something's gone wrong. The diamonds are missing … You heard me, missing! … Well, you damned well better get over here to the apartment … Yeah, right now! And if you've got those stones, you better have 'em with you!'

He hung up and Leopold said, 'That was good. Did he admit taking them?'

'Hell, no! He thinks I'm pulling a double cross, or that's what he said anyway. He'll be here.'

They sat down to wait, and Leopold watched the darkness settle over the city. He felt good, knowing the next hour's work would probably wrap up the case. 'Get me a drink,' Freddy ordered the girl at one point, and she hurried out to the kitchen.

It was just after seven o'clock when the buzzer sounded and they heard someone starting up the stairs. 'Expecting anyone else?' Leopold asked.

'No, that'll be him. Better be careful—he might have a gun.'

'Let him in. I'll be right behind you at the door.'

While Glenda stood terrified in the kitchen doorway, Freddy Doyle opened the apartment door. He peered into the now-darkened hall and asked, 'Is that you...?'

Leopold cursed silently. He tried to step back quickly and pull Freddy with him, but it was too late. Three quick shots came with deafening suddenness from the darkness, and Freddy toppled backward into his arms.

'Stop!' Leopold shouted. 'Police!'

He heard the running footsteps on the stairway, and allowed Freddy's limp body to sag to the floor. Behind him, Glenda was screaming. Leopold made it to the banister and fired a shot down the stairway, but he had no

21

target. The street door was yanked open, and Freddy's assailant was gone. By the time Leopold reached the street there was no sign of him.

He climbed the stairs and went back into the apartment. Glenda was on the floor, kneeling in a widening pool of blood. '*He's dead!*' she shouted, close to hysterics.

'I know,' Leopold said, feeling suddenly old. He walked to the telephone and dialed headquarters.

* * *

Fletcher found him in his office, staring glumly at the wall. 'I came as soon as I could, Captain. What happened?'

'I bungled, that's what happened, Fletcher. I was trying to pull off a neat trick, and I got a guy killed.'

Fletcher sat down in his usual chair, opposite the desk. 'Tell me about it.'

Leopold ran quickly over the events of the evening, from his visit to the hospital, through the shooting of Freddy Doyle. 'I didn't think our man was desperate enough to commit murder,' he admitted.

'Why would he kill Doyle?'

'Because he saw it was a trap. Maybe the bullets were aimed at me, too, but Doyle was in the way. I suppose he suspected something when Freddy called to say the diamonds were

22

missing, because he knew he hadn't taken them.'

'But where were they?' Fletcher asked. 'You said you saw them.'

Leopold nodded. 'They're right here—my one accomplishment for the night.' He took the can of coffee from its paper bag. 'I had only a couple of minutes alone in that kitchen, but I got the idea that Freddy could lead me to Hoffman's accomplice if he thought the accomplice had returned and stolen the diamonds back again. So I used a can opener to open the bottom of this coffee can part way. I emptied just enough coffee into the sink so there'd be room in the can for this pouch of diamonds. Then I bent the bottom shut the best I could, and capped it with this plastic lid they give you, just so no coffee would run out. When Freddy was searching for the diamonds, he actually lifted the can out of its bag, but the top was still sealed and he never thought to examine the bottom.'

Fletcher opened the pouch and spilled a few of the gems onto the desk top. 'A clever trick, Captain.'

'Clever—except that now Freddy is dead and we've got a murder on our hands. Our man isn't one to stand still for games.'

The lieutenant was frowning down at the gems. 'If Hoffman used an accomplice, it had to be somebody who came in contact with him during those few minutes after the robbery. He

23

couldn't have hidden the diamonds anywhere, because the street was searched, and there's only one person he had physical contact with—only one person he could have slipped the jewels to.'

Leopold nodded. 'I've been thinking the same thing, Fletcher. Put out a pickup order on Neil Quart.'

*   *   *

The young man sat uncomfortably in the interrogation room chair, looking from one to the other of them. 'What is this, anyway? You drag me down here at midnight like a common criminal? Just this morning I was a hero!'

'That was this morning,' Fletcher said.

Leopold sat on the edge of the desk, close to the man in the chair.

'Look, Neil, I think it's time you told us the whole story. It's not just robbery now—it's murder.'

'Murder! I don't ...' He started to rise and Fletcher pushed him back in the chair.

'Hoffman passed those diamonds to someone, who delivered them to a fence and later killed the fence. You're the only one who had physical contact with Hoffman after the robbery.'

'But I ran after him! I wrestled with him! I held him till the police got there! You know I did!'

24

'And while you were conveniently holding him, he slipped you the diamonds.'

'No! You're crazy! I didn't...'

Leopold began pacing the room. 'There's no other way it could have been. You have to be the accomplice, Quart.'

'Look, it doesn't make sense! He was getting away! Why should there be this elaborate scheme to pass me the diamonds when he was getting away with them? If I hadn't grabbed him, he'd have made good his escape.'

Leopold thought about that, trying to sort out the facts in his mind. What Neil Quart said made sense, too much sense. 'Where were you tonight around seven o'clock?'

'Working in Bambaum's shipping department, like every night. You can ask them.'

'All right,' Leopold said with a sigh. 'Get out of here. Go on home. We'll check it in the morning.'

Fletcher looked surprised. 'But Captain...'

'It's all right, Fletcher. I was wrong—again. This is my night for being wrong.'

Fletcher followed him back into his office. 'Let me fix you some coffee, Captain.'

Leopold handed over the can. 'I've lost it, Fletcher. I can't even think straight any more. I jump on some poor kid and try to make a murderer out of him. I get some guy killed for nothing.'

'You recovered the diamonds, Captain.'

25

'Yeah.'

Fletcher was filling the coffee pot. 'Well, Hoffman sure did something with those diamonds. He had them when he hit Officer Begler, and he didn't have them when they grabbed him a few minutes later.'

Leopold sat up straight. 'How do we know that, Fletcher?'

'What? Well, hell, he sure didn't crack Begler's skull because he *wasn't* carrying the diamonds.'

'Fletcher,' Leopold said very slowly, 'I think that's exactly what he did.'

*   *   *

They were waiting for Peter Arnold in the morning, when he unlocked the door of the Midtown Diamond Exchange. He glanced up, surprised, and said, 'Captain Leopold! You look as if you've been up all night.'

'I have,' Leopold said, following him inside the store. Fletcher came too, but stayed by the door. 'I've been getting people out of bed, checking on your finances, Arnold. I didn't want to make another mistake.'

'What?'

'It was a damned clever plan, I have to say that. I suppose Rudy Hoffman thought it up, and then got friendly with some jewelers around town till he found one who needed the money.'

26

'I don't know what you're talking about.'

'I think you do, Arnold. You closed the shop at nine o'clock the other night, and quickly removed the diamonds from that window. Rudy Hoffman came by as scheduled, broke the window and ran. You pocketed the diamonds and called the police. Then you took the diamonds to Freddy Doyle, who was supposed to sell them. The plan had a great advantage—Hoffman didn't have to spend precious seconds scooping up the loot in the window, and if he were arrested a block or two away, he'd be clean. No diamonds, no evidence. He probably planned to dump the cane and topcoat and keep on going. Only Officer Begler wasn't where he was supposed to be, directing traffic. Hoffman knew it was too soon to be arrested—right by the window. He didn't have the diamonds and the whole plot would be obvious, so he hit Begler with the cane and ran. That's when he had more bad luck—a young fellow named Neil Quart chased after him. You had the diamonds all the time, but unfortunately Hoffman didn't even have a chance to pretend he'd dumped them. We had an impossible crime on our hands, even though you didn't plan it that way.'

Peter Arnold continued staring at them. He ran a damp tongue over his lips and said, 'I assume you have some proof for all this?'

'Plenty of proof. You're in bad financial trouble, and aiding in the theft of your

27

company's diamonds was an easy way out for you. We've got the gems back, and with you in jail I'm sure Hoffman can be persuaded to tell it like it was.'

'There were witnesses who saw Hoffman at the window, though.'

'Yes, but they only saw him reach inside. He would hardly have had time to scoop up all those loose diamonds, and only you, Arnold, actually said you saw him do that. You said you saw it while you were locking the door, even though there's a velvet drape at the rear of the window that keeps you from seeing anything from inside the store. You didn't see him take the diamonds because he never took them. They were already in your pocket when he broke the window and started running.'

'I don't—'

'You panicked when Freddy called you, and especially when you saw me in the doorway with him. You recognized me, of course, and started shooting. That alone told me the killer was someone I'd questioned in connection with the case.'

Peter Arnold moved then, as Leopold knew he would. It was only a matter of guessing whether the murder gun was in his coat pocket or behind the counter. His hand went for his pocket, and Fletcher shot him from the doorway. It was a neat shot in the shoulder— the sort Fletcher was good at.

Arnold toppled against a showcase, crying

and clutching his shoulder, as Leopold slipped the gun from his pocket. 'You should have dumped this in the river,' he said. 'We could never have made the murder charge stick without it.'

Fletcher locked the front door and called for an ambulance. They had to get Arnold patched up, and booked for murder and robbery, and then they could both go home to bed.

ONE FOR THE CROW

M. Barrett

Ed chose the fast route, the new highway which was engineered to bypass Ozark and go directly into the hills. Had he taken the old road south from Springfield, he probably would have lived a longer and a happier life. He certainly would have enjoyed a more pleasant trip along a more scenic route than the one he elected.

About twenty miles out of town, on the old road, he would have come upon a scene with the misty charm of a French impressionist painting: from the hilltop, grapevines march down the slope in orderly rows; in the valley below, as if protected by the hills from change and blight, lies the clean, sleepy town of Ozark, Missouri.

From his vantage point on top of the hill, Ed would have seen the water tower rising white against the green hills beyond, and the iron-gray smokestack of the cheese factory. Had he then continued downhill, he soon would have come to an official sign: *Ozark, Pop.800* and, on a nearby tree, a less formal but more enthusiastic announcement: *Welcome to Ozark, a good live town.*

Clattering across the Finley River bridge

and passing an abandoned mill with its rusty wheel forever still, he would have arrived at the Ozark square where the red brick courthouse stands in the center.

There are always a few men sitting on shaded benches in front of the courthouse, chewing tobacco and occasionally exchanging a few words about the weather, the crops, chicken feed, pesticides. Any of these local experts could have warned Ed about the risks he was taking, but he might not have listened anyway, or heard what was said to him. He was that kind of guy. Besides, a warning of sudden death in such a setting would be difficult for anyone to believe, for the scene is deceiving. All appears to be peace and rural contentment; but primitive passions and strong hatreds are bred in the hills, and old ideas and old grudges die hard. Just five minutes' conversation with one of the fellows in front of the courthouse would have given him a warning, but to gain a little time, he missed his chance.

The powerful engine of his big rented car purred quietly under the hood as Ed looked out the window with distaste at the scrubby oaks and hickory trees struggling for life in the thin topsoil. He felt a city man's scorn for wasted space and a successful man's scorn for what he saw as failure.

'In this Godforsaken place,' he said to himself, 'the hillbillies will be glad for the chance at a little cash.'

31

Ed had a reputation in Hollywood for always being on top of any job, and he was certainly going to be on top of this one with no trouble; *no trouble at all*, he thought.

He wheeled the car off the highway onto a likely-looking farm-to-market road. It was pitted from the winter freeze, and Ed was forced to slow down. A thin film of dust blanketed the weeds and wild strawberries growing on each side of the narrow road, but no matter. The air-conditioned car was sealed against intrusion by the environment.

Ahead appeared the first sign of habitation—a dilapidated farmhouse with a much-patched roof. One window was covered with cardboard, like a patch over a missing eye. A thin streak of smoke drifted from the chimney. A white hen clucked dispiritedly in the front yard.

Ed turned the car off the road onto dry grass, stopped and stepped out, slamming the car door. He looked around speculatively.

It was a clear, cloudless spring day, and after the steady hum of the car, the silence was startling. Far away, a meadowlark sang its pure notes.

Ed walked toward the house. 'Hello,' he called. 'Anyone here? Anyone home?' There was no answer.

He rounded the corner of the house. There, bent low over the red earth, was a tall, bony man in faded blue overalls. His skin, tanned to leather, was bare to the sun over the bib of the overalls.

'What's the matter with you?' Ed demanded. 'Didn't you hear me?'

The man didn't look up. He said shortly, but with no animus, 'I heard you. Long ways off.'

Ed came closer. 'What are you planting there?'

The man at last stood up. He looked Ed in the eye and said, 'Corn,' the monosyllable discouraging conversation.

Ed tried to remember what he knew about corn. It was very little. He had seen some pictures, though, and they didn't look like this.

'I thought you planted corn in furrows,' he said.

'Some do. Where there's not much rain. Plenty of rain here. Plant corn in hills. Four seeds to a hill.'

'Why four?'

The man explained, matter-of-factly, 'One for the cutworm, one for the crow, one for the dry rot, and one to grow.'

'Oh,' Ed said, unenlightened. 'When will it come up?'

'Tassels out about July,' the man answered. Then, clearly dubious, he asked, 'You thinking to grow corn hereabouts?'

'Oh, no,' Ed said hastily. 'I'm just looking for local color.'

The man looked around at the familiar greens and browns of his landscape, and then inquisitively back at Ed.

'The way people talk,' Ed explained, 'their customs, their folkways. Those things.'

The farmer frowned; whether disapproving or puzzled, it was impossible to tell.

'Reckon you better come inside, then, and talk to Ma. She knows all about folks' ways.' Moving to the back door, he added, 'I'm Luke Anderson. This is our place, Ma's and mine, since we lost our son.'

Ed followed him through a squeaking screen door into the kitchen. It was cool and dark after the bright sun outside.

A woman with gray hair stood at a stained sink, shelling beans.

Luke said, without preamble, 'This fellow wants to know about our ways.'

The woman turned to them, her face expressionless. She wiped her hands on her cotton apron, slowly and deliberately. She inspected the visitor as she might have scrutinized a mule offered for sale. Like her husband, the woman was browned by the sun; and like him, she was economically lean, without an ounce of unnecessary flesh.

She pulled a straight wooden chair up to the kitchen table and put her hands on the oilcloth, palms down, as if preparing for a seance. Luke and Ed sat down too.

'Why do you want to know our ways?' she asked with guarded curiosity.

'We want to make a movie here in the hills,'

34

Ed said. 'The setting has to look authentic. Real, you know.' He was uncertain how much these ignorant people could understand. 'We want to cast local people, in minor roles, of course. And we'll pay.'

The woman was clearly not impressed. She looked at him sharply from startlingly-light blue eyes. 'They done made a movie once, nearby.'

'I know,' Ed said. It had been a disaster. Every possible thing had gone wrong—the entire cast sick, equipment breaking down and even disappearing, and the director actually dropping out of sight, never to be seen again. That had caused quite a stir in the press. It was, in fact, the only thing which saved the movie from being a box-office disaster. No one particularly mourned the loss of the director. He hadn't turned out any good work in years.

The woman said, 'Those other movie folk built cabins and pretend barns from stuff they brought with them. Those things are still there. Maybe you could use them for your movie and not mess up a new part of the hills?'

Ed smiled indulgently. *These people are so naive.* 'I'm afraid that won't do. That old set is much too artificial. We need virgin territory. Of course, we'll improve on it some. But the old site is ruined for our purposes.'

The woman spoke quietly, 'That's how it seems to us, too—spoilt. Spoilt for living. Spoilt for farming. Spoilt for looking at. You think to do that here, on the side of the hill? Spoil it?'

'Not at all,' Ed said impatiently. *Don't these hicks understand anything?* 'We'll bring new life to this place. Lots of tourists will come just to watch us shooting. There'll be new business, new money pouring in, lots of action.'

A glance passed between husband and wife which Ed could not interpret. The woman put both hands on the table and pushed herself to her feet. 'Since you're here, you best stay on for dinner,' she said.

The meal was quickly served. She put the plates on the oilcloth. Ed looked dubiously at the food. There were ham hocks, beans, and hot corn bread, with fresh warm milk. Ed managed to choke down enough not to offend. He thought wistfully of a cold martini and rare roast beef.

'I'll red up the dishes,' the woman said. 'You men go along to the front porch. We can set in the shade and talk awhile.'

Ed followed Luke through the living room. The shades were down, and the room had the dimly lit appearance of being underwater. The faded carpet was worn through to the floor in places. A sofa, tilting on three legs, was covered with an afghan. Ed thought with satisfaction, *We can use this. It certainly looks authentic.*

They stepped out onto the porch. The floorboards were warped, and for a moment the wavy effect made Ed dizzy. They sat down in straight wooden chairs, identical to those in the kitchen. The woman soon joined them.

They looked through the haze of the warm afternoon across the yard to a hill beyond. A wasp buzzed busily at his nest in a corner under the roof.

'That hill over there,' Ed said. 'We could use that in several scenes. It looks easy to climb.'

The woman glanced at him. Her voice was soft but clear.

'Some say that hill should be let be. Most folks won't go there for any reason.'

'Oh?' Ed asked, intrigued.

'It's the Bald Knob,' Luke said, as if that explained everything.

'Bald Knob?' Ed asked.

The woman explained, 'A bald knob is nothing but a hill with no trees growing on top. This one's different, though.'

'It's where the Bald Knobbers met,' Luke said.

The woman leaned her head against the back of her chair and gazed off into the distance. 'Was a time,' she said, 'when roads were bad and town too far away. We hadn't no pertection of the law. No one to see that cows wasn't stolen nor strangers didn't come, causing trouble.' She paused and looked at Ed. If he found any significance for himself in the statement, however, he gave no indication.

She went on: 'Some of the men hereabouts got together to make themselves the law

37

officers. They had their meetings atop that bald knob there. Sometimes at night a person could see their bonfire. It was a good sight. Made a body feel safe, to know someone was there, caring.

'Then real trouble set in. Some outsider come and set to build himself a fancy house on Bald Knob. He liked the view, he said. We never had much truck with outsiders. They never seem to catch our ways of thinking. This man was extra bad, building there on Bald Knob where our men had their meetings, and not understanding why that was wrong. He brought a curse to the hills and to all the folks hereabouts. We knowed 'twas him all right. No one else was new in these parts.

'There wasn't no rain for months on end. The cows went dry. The hens stopped laying. Folks was hungry, and we couldn't see no way out of our trouble. It was the outsider and the strangeness he brought to the hills. The hills don't tolerate no alien ways. Something had to change. So the Bald Knobbers came in the dark one night and killed him where he lay.'

She paused to let the point strike home.

'Then the real lawmen came from Ozark. They heard of what was done, and they said our men had to be punished. The Bald Knobbers came to trial, and the jury said they had to be hanged. One of those was our son.'

The tone of her voice hadn't altered in any degree with that statement, and Ed could almost imagine that he hadn't heard it correctly.

'The real lawmen had trouble, though, when it came to carrying out what they wanted to do. No one hereabouts would do the hanging. Those men were our own, and nobody would have it on his soul to kill their own folks. So the law sent off to Kansas City for a real hanging man.'

Luke prompted, 'Brought his own ropes.'

'Yes. And built the gallows, one for each man, twelve in a row right there on the courthouse square. People come from miles around to watch.

'On the hanging morning, they brought the Bald Knobbers from the jailhouse—some men, and some just boys not yet to razor growed. Our son was one not yet a man.'

The woman was silent for a moment, in tribute to the blindness of justice. 'But then a strangeness come. Seemed like that hanging man just couldn't get his job done. There was something didn't want our folks to hang. Some say the rope he brought from Kansas City was green, and stretched. That's as may be. Maybe it was something else. Anyways, the trap would spring and a man would drop through, stretching that rope with his weight, and dangle there with his feet bouncing on the ground. You can't break no man's neck that way.

'When it was all over, they couldn't hang but

39

two. At last, they just give up and let the others go. No one had the heart for any more. The Bald Knobbers were let go free and told to go away, somewheres else. They never been seen since.'

She gazed at the top of the hill. 'And yet, there's some folks say their spirits never left. Some say that at least one Bald Knobber never went away at all. Sometimes you can see a bonfire on Bald Knob at night. Some say the Bald Knobbers do pertect us yet. From strangers and the like.'

Only the wasp, buzzing, made a sound in the still air.

Ed said, 'That's quite a story. I'm going to climb that hill and see how things look on top.'

Luke said quietly, 'I wouldn't, if I was you.'

The woman said, 'Go, if you want.' There was warning in her tone—and promise.

Across the still afternoon a mournful, cooing sound came from far away.

'Rain crow,' Luke announced. 'Means rain soon, for sure.'

Ed looked up, unbelieving, at the clear sky, and smiled complacently. 'Well, I'd better go take a look at Bald Knob now, before the deluge.'

He set out across the dry, brittle grass. In a few minutes Luke and the woman saw him start up the hill. Then he passed from sight among the oak trees.

The two stood up. 'It'll be all right, Luke,'

the woman reassured, putting her hand on his arm. 'He's there. I know he is. He'll take care of everything. Just like he done before, with that other movie man.'

They went indoors.

Night came. Ed didn't return. A watchful person might have thought that he saw a fire burning on top of Bald Knob as darkness set in.

Then the storm struck. Lightning flickered on the horizon. The first huge, spattering drops of rain fell, bringing the odor of moisture on dry land. A howling wind bent the trees. Then torrents of water poured from the sky. Lightning bolts flashed and thunder bounced from hill to hill.

Luke and the woman looked at one another wordlessly, and went to bed.

The morning sun shone on a world washed clean and shining. Luke and the woman set out up the hill. Ed's footprints were washed away. There was no sign that anyone had been there before them.

Luke found him just below the tree line. Above where Ed lay, the hilltop was bare. The big oak tree which lay on top of him had been split by a lightning bolt. Under it, Ed was crushed like a bug under a man's heel.

The woman spoke softly: 'Get him out from there, Luke. We'll plant him in the hill, where we planted the other man.'

Luke bent to the job.

'It was our son again,' the woman said with pride. 'He lured that man under the oak tree. Any hill man knows better than to go under a tree in a thunderstorm.'

Luke intoned, 'One for the cutworm, one for the crow...'

HAPPINESS BEFORE DEATH

H. Slesar

The psychiatrist's voice, in some ventriloquial effect, seemed to be emanating from his framed diploma over his head. The engraved scrawl lent majesty to his otherwise mundane name: Harold Miller. Studying the splendid loops and swirls, Werther Oaks wondered if Dr. Miller had supplied his own signature to be grandly redesigned by the fine Italian hand—or was it Viennese? He squinted and made out the place of matriculation: New Jersey. Where have all the Viennese psychiatrists gone? Dr. Miller seemed to realize he wasn't listening. Throat-clearing followed.

'I'm sorry,' Werther said. 'I'm having trouble concentrating. What you're saying is—well, I can't really believe what you're saying.'

'I know,' Dr. Miller said, the voice now emanating gravely from its natural source. 'It's not an easy thing to hear about one's own wife. But I honestly believe it's so, Mr. Oaks. That overdose was no accident. As Freud once said, there *are* no accidents.'

'It's just hard to comprehend. I mean, about Sylvia. With all she has.' A wry addition: 'I don't mean to include myself, of course. I haven't been a bad sort of husband, but I don't

43

ask you to accept that.'

'And I didn't ask you here to point an accusing finger either.'

Werther looked at Miller's fingers. They were short and stubby. Werther's hands were exquisite. He had been a hand model when he met Sylvia at the Grosse Pointe Country Club. When she learned of his odd profession, she had smiled insultingly. Later, on the terrace, she had wondered aloud what it would be like to be touched by a pair of famous hands.

'Dr. Miller,' Werther said, 'my wife swore to me that she took those extra pills purely by mistake. Are you telling me that it was deliberate?'

'I'd say it was the expression of an unconscious wish. Because, you see, the fact that your wife has "everything" doesn't mean that she has—*everything*. Do you see what I mean?'

Werther considered slapping Sylvia that night, with one of his famous hands. Instead, he framed her face between his palms and planted a gentle kiss on her lips. The slap would have surprised her less.

Two months later, despite the anguish of her friends, who bluntly called Werther a fortune hunter and worse, they were married. On their honeymoon, she had seized him by the wrists and exulted, 'Now they're mine!' He made a joke about giving his hands in marriage, and Sylvia had laughed. It was the last time he'd

44

heard her laugh.

'Well, she's not exactly a cheerful woman,' Werther told the psychiatrist. 'I knew that from the moment I met her. She has fits of depression, but I never thought of them as being terribly serious.'

'She tells me that she would lock herself in her room for three and four days at a time.'

'Well, yes, she does that now and then. It's her way of getting away from all the pressures.'

'What pressures?'

'Having money doesn't take away obligations,' Werther said, actually parroting Sylvia's financial manager, Vossberg.

'Ah,' Miller said, looking almost Viennese now. 'But having money doesn't always guarantee emotional health.'

'Won't buy happiness?'

'To a psychiatrist,' Miller said in deep tones, 'that cliché is fraught with meaning. And there, I think, is the key to your wife's problem. The silver spoon she was born with is still in her mouth, and now it's choking her. Perhaps to death.'

Werther's eyes blinked several times.

'Money has made her miserable,' Dr. Miller continued. 'Money has made her lead a life devoid of personal satisfaction. She is unable to enjoy simple pleasures, and therefore she experiences *no* pleasure at all.'

'Found *that* out,' Werther murmured. 'But do you really think she's unhappy enough to kill herself?'

'Unless something is done,' Dr. Miller said, 'there may well be another "accident" like the one two nights ago. And this next one may prove fatal.'

When Dr. Miller walked him out of the office, Werther offered one of his famous hands, and it was trembling badly. Miller suggested that he get some rest, too.

Werther left the medical building and was surprised to find that it was still daylight. His XKL was at the curb, overparked by half an hour, but he still took the time to walk around the block and think about what he had just learned.

Sylvia might kill herself.

Sylvia was so miserable that she was going to die of her misery.

The full import filled him up like a wineglass, and the effect was like champagne. If nobody had been watching, he would have leaped in the air with joy.

*   *   *

Velvet knew something was different about him, but waited with catlike contentment to let Werther make his own explanation. She curled up on the floor beside him as he sat rigidly on the sofa, smoking a small brown cigar and inhaling it like the cigarettes he had eschewed. She tugged one sock down to his shoes and

46

rubbed his ankle.

'Thursday night,' Werther said slowly, 'Sylvia swallowed four sleeping pills, maybe five. Said she made a mistake. Thought they were aspirin.'

'Who takes five aspirin?' Velvet asked logically.

'Ah,' Werther said, realizing that he now sounded like Dr. Miller.

'Wushy-mushy-tushy, will you please tell me what's the big deal?'

He winced at the name, but it was something worth living with. Velvet was the highest-paid girl in the Tilford Model Agency. She never earned less than a hundred dollars an hour, which made her personal income higher than Werther's own allowance (dispensed by Vossberg). Under the circumstances, he considered himself lucky to be Velvet's special friend. They had met in the agency several months before his Grosse Pointe encounter with Sylvia. (He had gone to Detroit to perform in a commercial for one of the auto companies. 'Watch these hands on this wheel and learn what's really new in auto engineering!') When he had married Sylvia, Velvet had screamed at him for almost a full hour, ending up with a case of laryngitis that kept her from performing in a Silk-Creme commercial the next day. Every month after that, she sent him a bill for the residuals she wasn't receiving. He had finally paid his debt with a diamond bracelet charged at Tiffany. To this day, Vossberg thought he had presented the gift to Sylvia.

'My wife is going to kill herself,' Werther said. 'That's the big deal.'

'Are you joking? Are you saying that for a *joke*?'

'Vel,' Werther said with pained lips, 'do you think I'd joke about such a thing? Do you realize what it *means*? We don't have to go through with the car business, with the whole chancy *brake* business, with that whole sticky, rotten, scary *murder* business!'

'Oh, Wushy,' Velvet wailed, covering her ears, 'don't say that word here. How can you *say* that word in my house? Who knows who could *hear* you? You know we promised never to say "mm-mm".'

'We've been talking about mm-mm for six months,' Werther said. 'And now poor Sylvia may mm-mm herself.'

'*Poor* Sylvia?'

'Yes,' Werther said. 'She's worse off than I thought—all mixed up inside, hates her own money. That's a laugh, isn't it? Her hating the money I love so much.'

'You got to be crazy to hate money,' Velvet said. 'Maybe that's why she's going to that shrink, because she's crazy.'

'She's unhappy,' Werther said, sighing out a trail of smoke. 'She's always been unhappy. Because the money never meant anything to

48

her—like it does to me, for instance.'

'And me,' Velvet said. 'Look, Werther, look,' jabbing an inch-long nail at the corner of her eyes. 'Look at the crow's-feet starting. In another year, down come the rates.'

'There's no telling when she'll do it,' Werther said. 'No telling when she'll try again. Maybe next week, maybe next year, maybe two years from now.'

'Hey!'

'The psychiatrist couldn't predict, he just doesn't know. It all depends.'

'On how *unhappy* she is? Then make her unhappy, Wushy!'

'Yeah, fine, great.' He frowned. 'And the money, the will, the inheritance? I'm hanging by a thread right now, and don't think Vossberg isn't standing by with a big pair of scissors. No,' he said sadly, 'I don't *want* to make that poor woman unhappy. I like her, Velvet, I really feel sorry for that poor miserable person.'

'That's what I love about you,' Velvet sighed, a soft cheek against his ankle. 'You're a person with heart.'

'So what I have to do,' Werther said, 'is *give* her an overdose of sleeping pills. Dr. Miller will swear she was ready for it, and nobody's the wiser.'

* * *

49

Sylvia's eyes were closed when he entered the bedroom. His heartbeat accelerated as he went up to the satin-sheeted oval bed and put his hand close to her mouth. Her breath fogged his polished fingernails.

'Sylvia?' he whispered.

'I'm not asleep,' she said. Her eyes came open and looked at him directly; her pupils were like black wells filled with unshed tears. 'I was waiting for you. I wanted to hear what Dr. Miller told you.'

'Now who said I saw Dr. Miller?'

'The scratch-pad near the phone. You wrote down his address. Obviously he called you. What did he say about me?'

'About you, nothing.' Werther smiled. 'He just wanted to know what kind of rotten husband doesn't watch what his wife takes out of the medicine cabinet.'

'How dare he call you a rotten husband?'

'But I am,' he said cheerfully. 'Look at the hours I keep. If I had gotten home before ten that night, this wouldn't have happened.'

'I know you work hard,' Sylvia said. Of course, she knew nothing of the kind; she merely assumed that all men worked hard. Her father had made seventy million dollars by never leaving his office except to get his teeth cleaned. Werther, who now worked for the company her father had founded (American Bit & Drill), was actually the most indolent executive imaginable, which suited everyone

50

just fine. An ignorant executive owes his colleagues an avoidance of diligence.

'Tell me the truth,' Sylvia said. 'What did Dr. Miller say about me? Did he tell you all my little traumas?'

'No,' Werther answered. 'He just said that you were a very wonderful person who hasn't been given a real chance to be herself.'

For a moment, the wells of her eyes almost brought in a gusher.

'There must be something wrong with me, Werther. Why can't I *feel* happy? I know I *should* be happy, but all I feel is this emptiness inside. Werther, tell me what to do!'

'Right now, darling,' her husband said, 'just close your eyes and try to sleep. Remember, Vossberg will be here in the morning. You'll need your strength to put up with him.'

'You're my strength, Werther,' she said, and clutched at his beautiful hands.

The gesture choked him up. When her eyes closed again, still tearless, he felt moisture under his own lids. 'Poor Sylvia,' he whispered.

The next day, he flung all six darts at the target in his office, and then picked up the phone with determination.

'Velvet,' he said, 'I've got to talk to you.'

'I'm listening.'

'Not on the phone. Are you going to the shampoo job?'

'All through. Now I've come home to wash my hair.'

51

'I'll meet you there.'

He forced her to sit on the couch while he paced the floor.

'I can't do it,' he said.

'What?'

'Don't get excited.' She wasn't; just baffled.

'I don't mean I've changed my mind. I mean I just can't do it *now*, right now. It wouldn't be right.'

'What wouldn't be? Mm-mm-ing her?'

'Yes. Mm-mm-ing her. Not now, Velvet, I just can't.'

'But you said now would be the best time, Wushy, on account of her psychiatrist *knows* she's suicidal, and he'll blame it all on *her*, not on you.'

'I know what I said.'

'Then why wait? I mean, if she's miserable now, that's the time when she'd *do* it.'

'But that's also the reason I *can't* do it, Vel. Because she's miserable. Because that poor lady hasn't known a day of really being happy in her whole life. Choking on that silver spoon.'

'What spoon?'

'Never mind,' Werther said. 'The point is, she's had nothing to be happy about. Not even me.'

'But she loves you.'

'I'm her strength,' Werther said, now sounding like Sylvia. 'That's all I am to her. But I haven't made her happy, and that isn't right. It isn't fair, Velvet, to take all her money

52

without giving her *something* in return.'

'Gee, you're a funny sort of person,' Velvet said, not without admiration.

'So what I was thinking,' Werther said, 'was that I might try to make her happy—really happy—before she dies.'

'Huh?'

'I don't know if I can succeed. I don't know if this Dr. Miller really knows what he's talking about, whether his theory is right—that money's spoiled her so bad she can't enjoy the simple things.'

'What simple things?'

'You know. Like the things in nature. The sky when the clouds are getting together to discuss the rain...'

'Oh, Werther, that's beautiful!'

He had read it on a calendar. 'The sky when it's really worth looking at, and the way the ocean rolls, and the way the grass feels when you lie down on it after walking a little too far...'

'Yes,' Velvet nodded, 'yes, I know what you mean, Wushy. I enjoy those things, too, but it's even nicer if you have money.'

'No,' he said. 'It's doing these things *without* money, without *paying* for them, without buying a *ticket* to everything and feeling you've got to enjoy them just because there was a price tag attached ... Don't you see what I mean?'

'Wushy, will you please tell me what you're going to do?'

'I'm going to take Sylvia on a trip—a special trip—no first-class arrangements, no fancy hotels, nothing that money can buy. I'm going to see if she can be happy the way poor people can be happy, not giving a damn about tomorrow, just happy to be alive, and with each other, man and woman, sky, ocean, grass. I know it sounds crazy, maybe *she'll* think I'm crazy, but I'm going to suggest it. She's got it coming to her, Vel. A little happiness before the end. You know?'

'Yes,' Velvet said, looking at him in awe. 'And you know what else I know, Wushy? You're going to make me a wonderful husband.'

* * *

Sylvia was incredulous at first. 'A trip without money? What on earth do you mean?'

He laughed. 'I knew you'd have that reaction, darling. But I mean every word of it. Oh, not that we'd be completely flat broke. We'd take maybe four, five hundred dollars with us. But we won't go to any of *those* places, we won't stop at hotels, we won't hire cars or do anything else that a couple of crazy kids couldn't afford to do.'

'Werther, I can't believe you're serious. We've always spent a fortune on our trips—'

'And how much fun did you ever have? Face it, Sylvia, how much have you enjoyed them?'

54

'But where would we go?'

'Where do Gypsies go? Anywhere, everywhere! No destination. Off on the open road.'

'In a wagon?'

'How about a bicycle? How about our feet? Or our thumbs, for that matter?'

'You mean hitchhike?'

'Why not? You've got a very pretty thumb; did I ever tell you that?'

'Coming from you, Hands, that's a compliment.'

He laughed like a boy. 'We'll be hoboes, darling. We'll be vagrants, tramps, wanderers, nomads! If we're lucky, maybe we'll even get ourselves arrested—'

'No thank you!'

'We'll eat hamburgers in roadside stands and pick blueberries in the woods. We'll stay at the cheapest motels and sign the register Mr. and Mrs. Smith so that no one will suspect that we're legitimately married...'

She was actually smiling.

'Werther, I think you're just a little mad.'

'But I want us to be completely mad, Sylvia. I want us both to know what it feels like to breathe unconditioned air, and swim in unchlorinated water, and drink cheap wine and eat Mrs. Nobody's food and maybe beat the check if we're running out of cash...'

'I really think you mean this.'

'I want us to leave tomorrow—tonight—this

minute—and not tell anyone where we're going, not even Vossberg; just grab whatever cash that's lying around and take off for parts unknown. No letter of credit, no word to the bank, no suitcases—'

Sylvia gasped.

'Well, all right, one small suitcase, *small*, just very necessary things.'

'Werther, it's the silliest idea I ever heard in my whole life. I don't think we'd last more than a week doing such a thing.'

'If we feel like it, we could stow away on a ship going to Europe. We could probably bum our way across the entire continent.'

'I've never seen you like this, Werther!'

'And I've never seen you really enjoy life, Sylvia,' he said, taking her into his arms. 'And that's why I want you to say yes.'

'And you're sure we shouldn't tell Vossberg?'

Werther beamed with a sense of victory.

'We'll send him a postcard,' he said jubilantly. 'We'll send him a card from some tacky gift shop, and we'll write—"having a wonderful time! Glad you're not here!"'

For the second time since he knew her, Sylvia laughed.

*　　　*　　　*

Velvet received Werther's letter two months later. She had almost abandoned hope of ever hearing from him again, and her subsequent depression had taken its toll. Three more crows had marched across her face in the interim, and like an augury, the agency received (and accepted in her name) an assignment to pose in a beer ad for ninety dollars an hour—ten percent downgrade.

She tore open the letter with such excitement that she lost half a dozen words on the second page.

The remains of the letter read as follows:

Darling Vel,

Sorry I haven't written, but the circumstances made it impossible. Sylvia and I have just returned from Big Sur, where we were staying in a commune which was notable for the fact that it was impossible, literally impossible, to tell the boys from the girls, at least through visual acuity. This was because the male half of the commune (I'm assuming there was a male half) had all decided that beards were 'out' this year, even though long hair was still 'in'. As for myself, however, you will be interested to know that I have a luxuriant brown beard which makes me look a bit like Walt Whitman, I think, only younger and handsomer, if you'll pardon my vanity. Sylvia herself looks entirely different from the woman who left with me on our wild adventure two months ago. She hasn't worn one iota of makeup since the first week (she took half a dozen cosmetics with her when we started out, but she soon threw them away). Just the same, she never looked better. Her skin is brown as a walnut but as unwrinkled as a peach. She's lost at least ten pounds which I thought would make her into a scarecrow, but somehow it suits her very well. She's terribly pleased about her svelte new figure but oddly enough she doesn't think of it in terms of what clothes she'll drape it in. She has simply stopped caring about Halston and Yves St. Laurent and Madame Gres and about ever going back to fashionable restaurants or appearing at fashionable parties. In fact, most of the things that Sylvia thought were necessary to the so-called 'good life' no longer hold the slightest interest for her. But the important thing I wanted you to know is that Sylvia is *happy*. I mean she's *happy*, Vel, she's never been happier or more contented in her entire life. From the day we left (with exactly four hundred and twelve dollars in our pockets, and the solemn resolution to make it last two months) she found a whole new personality hiding inside that body of hers, a prisoner who was dying to come out and see the world as it really was. I can't possibly tell you what these two months have been like. Can you imagine eating goat as a main course for dinner, or sleeping in a haystack for two nights in a row, or riding in

58

a boxcar with three drunken tramps who played the harmonica all night long in terrible cacophony, or getting a job picking apples and eating so many of them that you never wanted to see an apple again, or making friends with a gang of rock-and-roll musicians who took us on their bus all the way to Charlotte, North Carolina, a distance of sixty miles? Vel, I can't tell you everything, but then we've got lots of time for you to hear the whole story. All you need know for now is that I did what I thought was right, that I did what I knew I had to do, and now it's all over and finished, and Sylvia and I are coming back home. She's a changed person, Vel, and a much happier person, but I wanted you to know that I haven't changed, not about the things that are important to me. I'm sure you know what I mean. So don't expect me to be in touch with you for several days. You'll know why in just a little while. Meanwhile, all my love, and don't forget to burn this letter.

Werther

P.S. I told you to burn this letter. What are you waiting for?

Velvet burned the letter.

*   *   *

It was a week to the day that she read the news about Sylvia Oaks' tragic death. Only one newspaper, the *News*, considered the story important enough to relate outside of its obituary columns, but in all the papers which reported it, she was described as an 'heiress.' The *Times* ran her picture, one obviously taken before her days of nut-brown skin and no makeup. Most of the obituary was devoted to her father, not her; it was a sad, gratuitous insult, Velvet thought. The cause of her death was listed as an overdose of sleeping pills. She was survived by her husband, Werther. The article in the *News* said she had been 'depressed.'

When Werther didn't show up the next day, or the day after, Velvet started getting anxiety attacks. She didn't want to phone him at home; there might still be mourners around who would raise eyebrows. However, when she still hadn't heard from him by the end of the week, she decided to risk a call. A maid answered, said that he was in conference, and Velvet hung up, more anxious than ever.

That night, Werther called and explained.

The conference was with Vossberg, the man Werther was always mentioning with huge bitterness: He had something to do with money. There were questions about the estate, about probating of the will, questions that Werther couldn't get answered. He sounded troubled. Velvet understood, of course. People who committed mm-mm would have to be troubled.

Finally, Werther called and said he was coming over. He sounded funny.

'You sounded funny,' Velvet told him.

She looked at him and added, 'You *look* funny.'

'It's the beard,' Werther said. 'I shaved it off. My skin under it was white. The rest of my face is tan. That's why I look funny.' He sat heavily on the couch, staring straight ahead.

'Wushy, you didn't learn to take *drugs* or something in that commune, did you?'

'No,' Werther said, shaking his head, without moving his eyes.

'Then what is it? Why do you look that way?'

'I made her happy,' Werther said dreamily. 'I did what I said I'd do, Vel. I made Sylvia happy before she died. Then I gave her those pills, and she went to sleep, and she was smiling. I swear she was smiling when they found her.'

'Is that why you're like this?' Velvet asked.

'No,' Werther said. He looked down at his exquisite hands. He noticed that there were wrinkles on the back, like the tracks of a bird. Then he looked at Velvet.

'I just came from the lawyer's office,' he said. 'I found out what Sylvia did when we came back from our trip. She changed her will, Velvet.'

'She *what*?'

'She gave it all away. All her money. She gave it all to charity. She wanted to be poor, because that's what made her happy.

'Happy,' Werther repeated, the word sounding like the beginning of a dirge.

THE LETTERS OF MME. DE CARRERE

O. Schisgall

Monsieur Georges d'Armentil,
Attorney-at-Law,
23 Rue Bouget, Paris.

Monsieur:

Three days ago, just before his death, my friend Paul Surat summoned me to his bedside. He asked me, as *notaire* of this village, to write to you on his behalf so that you might understand what prompted him to do what he did. Once you understood his position, he felt, you would forgive him and make his journey to the Hereafter somewhat easier to negotiate.

I hope you will grant him such forgiveness, Monsieur, for he was not a bad man. Indeed, in all his 70 years he never cheated a soul, and in consequence he died penniless. This I know only too well, for as the undertaker of this village I had the sad duty of burying Paul Surat, and he could give me no advance payment for these services except this gold watch. I assure you it was scarcely of sufficient value to compensate for my expenses. But this I will pass over, forgiving Paul as I trust you too will forgive him.

To begin with, allow me to say that I retain a very pleasant and clear impression of you, Monsieur. Whenever you visited our village to call on young Madame de Carrere, you drove by my café. You may remember it as the largest of the three in Cobline-sur-Aisne—the one facing the church across the Place de Ville. On those occasions when you stopped for an *apéritif*, it was an honor to have so distinguished a guest at my tables.

I realize your own recollection of me, if it exists at all, may be unfortunate. Perhaps Mme. de Carrere at some time mentioned to you that when I advanced her a few thousand francs—she was awaiting the settlement of her husband's estate and insurance at the time—she considered my interest rates unreasonable. Yet I give you my solemn word, Monsieur, that I charged her no more than I charge others; and I have lent money to a great many of my neighbors, always helping them in times of distress. I also regret that when Madame finally paid off the debt she chose to denounce me rather than to thank me. It was most unfair. But all things pass, Monsieur, as did my own resentment of her anger.

Let us, however, talk now of our late and lamented friend, Paul Surat.

Think of him kindly, Monsieur. You must know that he spent his entire adult life, 52 years out of his 70, in service to the family of Mme. de Carrere. He started as a stable boy and he rose to the position of major domo, in complete charge of the villa.

Possibly you know too that Paul never received much pay. The Carrere family, though comfortable, was not rich or over-generous with its servants. But Paul—the quiet, stout, pleasant little man—was gentle and loyal, content with having a good home. Though he was never able to save enough for his old age, he had every expectation—and rightfully so, would you not agree—that after his lifetime of service, the family would take care of him in his twilight years.

Hélas, Monsieur, how fate tricks us! After the war, when young Mme. de Carrere was left a widow, she had the villa but little money with which to maintain it. Still, she was young and attractive, and there was every reason to anticipate that she would some day marry again—and marry well.

Paul was delighted when, after a few years of widowhood, she began to travel to Paris, to Cannes, to Nice, in the hope of meeting the right man. It was on one of these trips, I understand, that she met you. Paul informed me that though you were considerably older than Mme. de Carrere, your interest in her was deep. And he was pleased you were so clearly a gentleman of substance. He welcomed your frequent visits to Mme. de

Carrere at her villa and he was equally delighted to notice, with the arrival of the daily post, that you and Madame were in constant correspondence.

Her untimely death last year must have been a severe shock to you, Monsieur, as it was to all of us in Cobline-sur-Aisne. There are many who insist she should never have driven her car on an icy mountain road at night, but surely Heaven must have its reasons for what we mortals call accidents. I myself supervised the funeral—a service for which, I may add, I have not been able to collect my full fee. It was a blow to us all to learn that Mme. de Carrere had died almost destitute.

It was particularly trying for poor Paul Surat, you will understand, who had counted on being supported in his old age by Madame. Now he discovered that he had nothing at all—except those few trifles he picked up in the villa, like her packets of letters.

He explained to me that when you hurried to the villa after the funeral and sought those letters which *you* had written to Madame, he had already put them away in a safe place. And he could sympathize with your fear that they might become public or come to the attention of your wife.

Monsieur, do not judge Paul too harshly, I pray of you. He was human. He was old.

He had no employment, no money, nothing. He needed some way of living out the rest of his life, and that was why he offered to keep the letters hidden if you sent him but a pittance to live on—a mere 5000 francs a week. And you had the generosity finally to agree. He sought only a way of staying alive, and he hoped before his death that you would not bear his memory too bitter a grudge. Think of him, Monsieur, as unfortunate, not as evil.

Most respectfully yours,

Armand Bezac.

P.S. Since I have the letters now, I shall be glad to keep them hidden on the same terms you gave Paul—5000 francs per week. Please enclose the first payment with your reply.

Monsieur Armand Bezac,
Cobline-sur-Aisne.

Monsieur:
Your effrontery is beyond words. Do you not know the laws pertaining to blackmail? I refuse even to discuss this matter.

Georges d'Armentil

Monsieur Georges d'Armentil,
23 Rue Bouget, Paris.

Monsieur:

67

I regret to note the explosion of your temper. Nevertheless I shall remain calm, assuring you again that if you agree to send me 5000 francs per week, the letters will never be revealed. If you decide to refuse, however, I will take whatever steps I regard as most effective.

Armand Bezac

Monsieur Armand Bezac,
Cobline-sur-Aisne.

Monsieur:
Some weeks before his demise Paul Surat wrote me a letter. He left it with friends, instructing them to mail it to me after his death. It has just arrived. Let me quote a passage from its pages. Surat wrote:

'All my life I have loved this village and its people. Now that I am alone, I find they are my truest friends. Though I have little money—having managed to save just enough to meet my simplest needs—they all welcome me to their homes; and though many of them have as little as I, they share it with me generously.

'And many of these friends of mine—so many of them—live in misery and wretchedness because of the town usurer, Armand Bezac. He came to Cobline-sur-Aisne some five years ago, and in five years he has managed to fix a strangling hold on their lives. In one way or other he manages, indeed, to drain the blood and happiness of almost everybody in the village. The man is a ghoul. He proved it to me—and I hated him for it—when he victimized Mme. de Carrere in her worst hour of need—immediately after her husband's death. Everyone in this community, everyone I love, would be happier if he were in prison, where he belongs.

'Monsieur, he had his own ideas about your visits to Mme. de Carrere. He even said to many people that I must be living on the proceeds of what I know and am concealing—a lie about Mme. de Carrere and you which made me furious. But now I shall take advantage of his lies. I will make him feed on them.

'Forgive me, Monsieur, but I intend to give Bezac a fanciful story about certain letters. Knowing him as I do, I am confident that when I die he will attempt to blackmail you. Obviously he will not have any letters, since they are non-existent, but he will *believe* they exist, and he will try to make you believe he has them.

'You and I know, Monsieur, that though you were fond of Mme. de Carrere, you saw her only as her lawyer. Since you never sent her a single love letter you have nothing to fear from Bezac's empty threats. But he will be unaware of this, and I am sure that

69

whatever the scoundrel writes you will be sufficient to put him in jail for attempted blackmail. I hope you will do all the good people of Cobline-sur-Aisne a service by transporting this evil creature to the place where he belongs—behind bars.

'I am asking my friends to hold this letter until some time after my death, so that whatever actions you take against Bezac will be the result of your own honest indignation, not of collusion with me. May the usurer get a long prison term—this is the legacy which I, a poor man, leave to all my good friends of the village in memory of Madame de Carrere.'

This is what Paul Surat wrote to me, and I thought, Monsieur, you would be interested in this excerpt from his letter.

Georges d'Armentil.

P.S. Yesterday—a full day before I received his letter—I turned your blackmail correspondence over to the Prefecture of Police.

70

LINDA IS GONE

P. C. Smith

The young woman remembered a small town and long-ago winter snow, or did she? She remembered it now but would not tomorrow. She remembered a family and a young man in a house on a tree-lined street; a yesterday memory almost gone today. She remembered a summer picnic—noise, games, laughter, and cars on the highway in the distance...

'What's your name, chick?' asked the guy in the shiny new 1963 convertible.

'Linnette,' she had said, knowing it was not exactly that, but liking the sound of it on her tongue, so that she repeated the name, 'Linnette,' with its soft roll and decisively final click.

'Linnette. Yes, it fits you,' he had said, and she felt the name wrap around her narrow shoulders and hold her small waist with comfort. She looked at the sound of it with big blue eyes and smiled at the sight of it with too-thin lips painted to provocative inducement.

She caught the name and held its reality within the unreality of that which surrounded her.

*   *   *

At one time or another on that day in the park almost everyone claimed to have seen Linda, but no one could remember at which time or other she had been seen. Who counts hours of a summer day at an all-out picnic?

The rolling, heavily wooded park was thoroughly searched and the hobo jungle at its very edge, down by the muddy river, 'was gone over with a fine-tooth comb,' the police chief said. 'We can't find hide or hair of her,' and admitted he didn't know what to do next.

Who gets lost in a town like this with nothing but prairies and farmland on each side? Who? *Only Linda, wouldn't you know, who thinks she's so much, acting like she's better than anybody else. Newly married, too...*

How about her husband? Maybe he killed her and buried the body.

Kenneth? Kenneth Borchard? That'd be like killing the goose that laid the golden eggs. Anyway, he was crazy about her. Where would he bury the body?

Oh, there's a million places for a kid like that with a car.

Perhaps there were, especially a kid who'd come from trash. After all, his father had killed his mother in a drunken rage and turned the shotgun on himself. You can't get around that kind of blood.

Kenneth seems a nice sort of kid.

72

Sure he is, as long as things go along all right.
Maybe things didn't go along all right and he did
to his wife what his old man did to his mother.
Oh! Maybe so ...

They grilled Kenneth; but first they talked to Linda's father, Leland Krebs, city councilman and owner of the feed store.

Up to that point, the father's secret thought had been that Linda had gotten peeved or hurt about something and hightailed it to the highway to hitch a ride to nowhere, and he was scared. His daughter, such a pretty, shy, sensitive and usually tractable little doll had hightailed it off twice before—not that anyone else knew about those times, of course. The first was when she was twelve and got a shameful D on her report card, and again when she was sixteen and wasn't invited to a party of her peers. He had found her, the first time, down the railroad yards waiting for a freight; and the second, on a country road hoping for a hitch. Both times she had returned home peaceably as soon as her father assured her that he would force the teacher to raise her grade and would throw a party for her equal to two of the one to which she had not been invited.

When the police chief sounded out Leland Krebs he did so carefully, with one eye on Krebs' civic importance and the other on his own career. 'You know we've done all we can, Mr. Krebs,' he said, spreading his hands helplessly. 'We've combed the county and

73

alerted the agencies. We've been thinking ...' using the editorial 'we' in order to spread the blame around, 'we've been thinking, how about your son-in-law, Kenneth Borchard?'

'How about him?' Krebs answered thoughtfully, and wondered, indeed, how about Kenneth Borchard?

It was right after Linda had graduated from high school that she had proclaimed, 'Now I want only to marry Kenneth Borchard.'

'*What?*' Krebs exploded.

Linda's mother, Minnie Krebs, quivering protoplasm of inadequacy, folded her hands over her breasts and breathed fast.

'Kenneth Borchard?' boomed Linda's father. 'He's just a kid, and scum to boot. You're too young to get married anyway.'

Leland Krebs was wrong on two counts and right on one. Kenneth was a kid chronologically only, having lived twice as long as his years in order to establish a reputation out of nothing, making him probably less scum and more of a man than most of the so-called men in town. That Linda was too young to be married was the truth. Linda was too young for almost anything.

She withdrew. The moment her father dared to bring forth argument, her lips closed tight so that only the lipstick peaks were left, her eyes went blank and her face took on a hightail-escape look.

'Well, let's talk it over,' suggested her father,

and her mother let her hands drop from her breasts.

Kenneth was, really and truly, very crazy about Linda. She was what he aspired to, having the diffidence, modesty, lovely purity and aloof dignity he worshiped, yet felt he could never attain. He almost fell out of his 1950 heap the night she primly proposed. 'We'll be married,' she announced as if she were planning an afternoon tea. 'Right away.'

'How can we, for Pete's sake? I haven't even got a job except for that piddlin' boxboy job down at the market. I was thinking of using that scholarship I got and going to State—'

'You won't have to,' Linda said, offering him a substitute for education. 'Daddy'll give you a job in the feed store. A *good* job. And we can live with my folks until you work yourself up. Daddy said so.'

Kenneth was overwhelmed, first by the fact that his life was being arranged, then by the one who was doing the arranging. 'Linda,' he choked, and kissed her somewhat less chastely than he had ever before kissed her.

They had been married a little less than two months that August 17th, 1963, the Saturday Linda disappeared from the park picnic.

'I never saw her again after I left the house that morning to go to my job at the feed store,' Kenneth explained, remembering the morning following the night before that had tied him up in knots. What did Linda think other married people did in bed—sang hymnal duets? Played word games? Held hands? It was another of those times that she called him a beast and coldly withdrew herself to the far side of the bed as if he were scum, and yes, she had told him he was that, too.

'I left at eight,' related Kenneth, remembering the cold, white face on the pillow, eyes closed against him, folded hands holding the sheet tightly shut like a veil of purity. 'She went to the park with her folks—early. I didn't get away to go until five.'

'After you got there,' the chief of police asked, 'didn't you see her?'

'No,' Kenneth said. Nor had he looked, but he wouldn't tell that part. It was his sin of omission that he hadn't looked for her. He hadn't wanted to. He still felt the words 'beast' and 'scum' like insulting handprints on his sensitive face, loving her, loving her on his knees, loving her abjectly and loving her with a tentative passion. It was the last that made of him a scummy beast and sent him, in the park, to the beer keg, not to search out his wife.

'Didn't you look?' asked the police chief, making the question an accusation.

'Well ...' and Kenneth said sure he looked, too loudly, as if he were lying. 'But I didn't see her. And, gosh, she could have been anywhere. You know how it was. There were all those games and people milling around ...'

So then the police chief questioned the

picnickers as to whether or not they had seen Linda's husband. Most people had, or thought they had, at one time or another, late that day; but no one could remember at which time or other, between five and eight o'clock when it began to get dark, that they had seen him, if at all.

'It was eight o'clock when I began looking,' Kenneth said. 'Everybody began to look then.'

Between five and eight, the chief of police reasoned cannily, during that time the people didn't know when or even whether or not they had seen Kenneth, he could have taken his wife from one of the wooded areas off in his car and killed and buried her. Or he could have found her alone, killed her on the spot, dragged her away and buried her.

What else? She couldn't be found, so she must be dead and covered

Kenneth was formally charged and took up residence in one of the four cells in the jailhouse.

*　　*　　*

The young woman was accustomed to the slipping away of things, ideas and memories, to leave her on ankles of air, so now that winter was here with no change in the climate, she was not really surprised. She remembered only now and then a small town with winter snow, but was that memory from out of her past or

77

something she might have read?

There was a new man here in the house where she was living. At least she thought he was new, and remembered another house, a family, another man, and wept for she knew not what.

'The trouble with you, Linese, is you're always crying,' she heard from somewhere, with the name her only reality, or almost reality, and not the speaker.

Was it her name or was it *nearly* her name? Her hands reached up to catch and hold the name tight. She *must* hold something tight, but she wanted not to be held herself.

She remembered, in subliminal flash, a picnic and noise and games, and immediately lost the memory, to weep again.

*   *   *

The snow was thick in drifts around the courthouse during Kenneth Borchard's trial, where the town judged him guilty and innocent, whichever way the wind blew, looking upon him with delighted excitement for the publicity he had produced, and with suspicious reserve just in case he actually was a killer.

The chief of police took a neutral no-comment stand, causing everybody to know that he thought Kenneth Borchard guilty as hell because, after all, a live girl had not been found, had she, even though he, in his wisdom, had led the search? So, there must be a dead girl somewhere and Kenneth Borchard killed her.

Leland Krebs' mind was fixed from the very first instant the idea had been placed there. *I should have watched her more closely. She had the closed-in, ready-to-hightail-it look that morning.* 'Sure he did it,' he told sympathetic listeners. 'I take him into my home, give him a job, let him marry Linda and he kills her.'

Minnie Krebs said nothing. Minnie Krebs never said anything about anything.

The trial was a farce, but played seriously and with solemnity, since it offered the defense attorney an opportunity to practice criminal law and allowed the prosecution to prosecute more than vandalism and theft. By their combined inept efforts, Kenneth was convicted of murder two and sentenced to twenty years.

*   *   *

The man in the room with the palm fronds at the window asked the young woman where she had been that day.

'What day?' she countered quickly.

'Yesterday. Dammit, Linese,' he cried in frustration, 'Wednesday, August 17th. The year is 1966, in case you've forgotten, and you probably have. So, where were you? I come home from work and you're off someplace.

Where in hell were you?'

Blankly, she gazed at and through him. 'I was looking,' she said, 'for a park filled with trees, and a picnic.'

'Oh, man,' he moaned, 'it's always that. You're forever looking for something. Some damn park ... some damn street ... snow in winter ... and in California. You get these streaks and you're off in limbo. I've had it. You understand? Another time ... just one more time you're not here when you're supposed to be ...'

'Where is here?' she asked.

*   *   *

On August 17th, 1966, there in the state penitentiary, Kenneth Borchard had completed the work necessary for his B.A. degree and looked forward to earning his master's. He rarely thought of Linda—after all, they had been married less than two months three years ago, hardly long enough to remember and too long ago to conjecture upon.

Leland Krebs erected a granite memorial to his daughter in the park while he privately wondered where she really was.

Minnie Krebs never did see the memorial, for she rarely left the house. 'In deep mourning,' her husband described her seclusion, but the general opinion was that she was locked up in the house because she was just plain crazy ... 'Always was a little nutty, you know.'

* * *

The young woman felt as if the carpet of grass beneath her feet bent and swayed more than usual, much more than usual. She staggered over sliding carpet, arms outstretched for balance, feet running for safety, and reached the bench to throw herself down upon it and laugh with triumph at outwitting this slippery world.

She smiled and nodded the hours away, catching at thoughts that flickered in her mind, catching and losing them, chuckling at their passing, amused by the kaleidoscope of color and butterfly-wing movement of these scampering pictures in her brain.

People strolling by noticed and remarked upon her.

'Maybe she's high on something.'

'A drunk, more than likely.'

'Hey, what's with her?'

'She's a kook. This park collects 'em.'

Only two old gentlemen, chess opponents, saw her from the beginning and observed her through the hours. 'Look at that woman, drunk as a coot,' one said to the other as her steps stuttered toward the bench. 'Don't like to see women drink.'

'This is 1968. Women drink all the time,' declared the other, moving his knight three squares forward and two squares sideways while his friend's eyes were off the board.

They watched her between moves and commented on her condition, and after several hours of inattentive chess, came to the conclusion that the woman on the bench was not drunk at all, but had some wires crossed.

'So what do we do?' one asked the other.

'Call someone, I suppose.'

'Call who?'

'The police, maybe.'

They folded their board and boxed the chessmen and walked across the palm-tree-lined park to stand on the curbing and await a prowl car that regularly patrolled this downtown street. While they waited, they discussed the significance of their discovery, building stories, each topping the other, that caused their old eyes to gleam with inventive delight.

'Maybe she murdered someone and went off her rocker,' came the final pinnacle of suggestion, and they stood there in double horror, sure that one should have stayed to see that the killer remained where she was while the other went for help.

Neither had offered to return and stand watch by the time the patrol car came slowly down the street. Both leaped to attention, arms upraised, voices squeaking with age and self-importance.

The two officers walked across the park with the two old men who were frantic now with fear that the woman might be gone and they would be tagged as a couple of imaginative old idiots. But no, she was still there, still smiling and nodding, still talking to her thoughts with little trills of sound.

One officer stood, the other knelt on a knee before her, getting no answer to his questions until he asked her name. She looked back at him. She caught a thought. Her lips thinned to a fine line of contemplation. 'Linn ...' Dissatisfied, she shook her head. 'Linn,' and shrugged, accepting this new narrow view of a horizon which had done nothing but fluctuate for as long as she could remember, though she could not remember long nor accurately.

'Where do you live?' she was asked, replying that she did not live at all, and spoke of a park, peering through the frame of the kneeling officer's bent arm.

He rose up from his knee and looked at his partner who offered a slight nod. He leaned down and gently touched the woman's shoulder. 'Come with me. Would you come with me, please?' he asked.

Linn nodded. She stood and staggered, clutching at the officer's arm, glad of the support. 'Oh, yes,' she said, 'it is very slippery in the world in which I live.'

When, in 1968, Kenneth Borchard was turned down for parole, he plunged back into his education. After his master's, he started studying law, never thinking of Linda now that he had become maturely introspective enough to realize he had lost nothing, through her, but his freedom.

That year, Leland Krebs retired from active participation in the feed store and gave some thought to hiring a private detective to investigate the disappearance of his daughter. Then, on second thought, he decided to let the situation lie quietly for fear she might be found, and Kenneth freed.

It had been so long since anyone had seen Minnie Krebs, they had all forgotten her existence.

*   *   *

The day-room attendant stood at the window watching two male patients in their daily attempt to carry a trash barrel from a spot by the fence to a pick-up junction fifty yards away. Each being obsessively righthanded, one grabbed a side handle with his right hand and walked forward, following the other in a continuous frustrated circle.

The attendant turned her back on the window, knowing the argumentative fury that would ensue, also knowing it would not be resolved, and stepped to her desk that was placed so as to offer a wide-swept observation point to include all the patients in the day room, the four at a card table playing a spirited no-rule game, the catatonic in steady gaze of the ceiling, the furious knitter making knots of her work, and the young woman who wrote the letter.

She was always writing a letter which, when finished, she folded, placed in an envelope, licked closed and addressed to nobody.

The day-room attendant was emotionally interested in these letters, probably because she would like to write letters too, and also had no one to whom she could write. 'You're new here,' a nurse told her. 'Everyone new gets interested in her. Each new doctor pores over the letters. He compiles them, compares them, trying to figure out whether hers is a process schizophrenia or a reactive schizophrenia, and tries to talk to her and gets nothing back and the letters pile up, all of them pretty much the same, about a picnic in the park and snow in the winter; and finally he throws them all away. Then another doctor comes along and the same things happen. Sure, it's interesting at first, but then . . .' and the nurse shrugged. She had watched the woman for three years, ever since her admission to this California State Mental Hospital in 1968. She had seen the gradual slide from tractable noncommunication, with only occasional flashes of useless memory, to moody isolation filled with letter-writing—the letters all signed with the name 'Linn' finally shortened to 'Lin.'

'Who is she, really?' the attendant asked.

'Who knows?' the nurse said. 'Even she doesn't know who she is.'

* * *

By 1971, Kenneth Borchard knew enough law so that he was in great demand by his fellow inmates for the drafting and submission of writs of habeas corpus and certiorari. He considered his eight years in prison as well-spent and never once thought about whose absence it was that had put him there and whose continued absence kept him there.

Leland Krebs had, long since, eased his slightly shifting conscience with the excuse that since Kenneth Borchard must have put the withdrawn, ready-to-hightail-it look on his daughter's face that August morning of 1963, he could rot in prison for all of him.

Minnie Krebs sat vacant-eyed and non-moving in her room.

* * *

On that summer day of 1971, no one member of the mental hospital staff could be absolutely sure what it was that had brought Linda out of her darkness and into identity. The doctors gave credit to psychotherapy; technicians to shock treatment; the nurses thought, of course, their chemotherapy had turned the trick; but the day-room attendant knew it had been the letters—the letters that had retained her interest, if not that of the nurses or doctors—those blank envelopes handed her each day, which she discussed in monologue, asking the questions, 'Who is it you write to?' and 'Where do you write each day?'—always unanswered until today, August 17, 1971, when 'Lin' handed her the envelope addressed to Kenneth Borchard in a small Midwestern town, with the name, Linda Borchard, written in the upper left-hand corner.

*　　*　　*

The chief of police answered the station-house phone and was startled into frozen silence at what he thought he heard. Finally, unlocking his tongue from the roof of his mouth, he stammered in repetition that, yes, a Kenneth Borchard did live in town, or used to, and yes, he was married to a girl by the name of Linda, who ... *The hell you say* ... and the police chief fished for a handkerchief to wipe away the sweat that poured down his brow from the significance of the words he was hearing.

Five minutes later, he was explaining to Linda's father why he didn't think it was his daughter whom they said was in that asylum way out there in California—how could it be, with the Borchard kid in prison for killing her, and her buried somewhere nobody'd found yet?

Leland Krebs *knew* it was Linda, his joy at the miracle of having her restored to him so pure that he forgot Kenneth Borchard, her husband, in prison for her murder. He flew off to California to claim his child, with the firm resolution that he would anticipate her future moods and wishes and always endow her with, and surround her with everything her heart desired so that never again would she get the hightail look on her lovely face and leave him bereft.

Minnie Krebs, unroused by news of her daughter, continued to survey the wall of her bedroom that she had so catatonically surveyed for almost eight years, and the chief of police said it certainly went to prove he sure couldn't find a dead body when there wasn't any dead body to find, so nobody could blame him, could they? He was just glad Mr. Krebs had his daughter back ... oh - damn - now - the - state - authorities - would - have - to - be - notified - and - they'd - find - out - it - had - been - his - recommendation - to - keep - that - kid - locked - up - and - throw - away - the - key - because - he - was - a - killer - like - his - father - before - him ...

Kenneth, notified that he was no murderer

after all, immediately submitted his own writ of certiorari as well as habeas corpus, along with a judgment against the state for wrongful detention and cruel and inhuman treatment. He became so involved with the legal processes of gaining his freedom, establishing his full civil rights and acquiring a profitable return on his time of incarceration, he forgot to think of Linda until, once the legal red tape of the Midwestern penitentiary was untangled and the institutional bureaucracy of the California State Mental Hospital bogged down to exhausted simplicity, he saw her again and knew damned well that she hadn't been worth a minute of those eight years in prison.

'This is Kenneth, my dear,' Leland Krebs said to his daughter, clicking the consonants and rounding the vowels to form a clear and understanding statement. 'Kenneth Borchard, my dear, your husband,' the last said with a flicker of remorse.

Linda knew who Kenneth was, she knew with immediate and total recall that completely eradicated the past eight years from her life. It was summer, there had been a picnic in the park ... 'Such a nice picnic,' she said, her voice a childish treble, and Kenneth, remembering his eight-year-long picnic, hated her.

Minnie Krebs stared at the wall of her room without knowing of her daughter's absence or return, and the town was shot through with guilt, each individual townsperson feeling his own particular pang of conscience, wanting to make it up to Kenneth, so that when he set up his law practice they flocked to his office with their real and imagined troubles—and he took care of them and prospered.

With the money he received from his suit against the state (the largest sum ever paid for wrongful detention), he built a house above the wooded park, a showplace, an estate.

The townspeople pointed it out to each other, pridefully and with comments.

He deserves it. If anybody deserves success, it's him.

Who would have thought, ten years ago ...

Even two years! With him still in prison then and her out there in California. How he could have been so forgiving, I'll never know—not letting us dump the chief off the police force or Krebs off the council, and taking back that wife who caused it all and treating her like a queen ...

Yeah. Beats me. But then, you don't find many like Mr. Borchard.

That you don't. He's a prince.

Kenneth Borchard walked through the park every day, his law office being at one side of it and his home on the other. Sometimes he walked across the close-cropped lawns and cement walkways to approach his house from the front. Other times, he went around and through the woods and climbed the hill, entering his house through the rear. He learned

90

much about the park and its growing things and felt the firmness of the ground under his feet after a dry spell, its sponginess after rain. He learned how much rain could cause it to muddy and cling soggily to a stick thrust into it and how a lesser rain made it so friable that the stick entered easily and the soil broke away cleanly. The soil was just right after this September rain in 1973. The time was right too, after two years of freedom, success and public respect. At five-thirty in the evening, the woods were deeply shadowed; by six, the hill would be in dusk; and by six-thirty, it should be quite dark.

He entered the lighted kitchen, whistling. Linda turned from the stove and lifted her cheek, withdrawing it the moment he had brushed it with his lips. She spoke of the chops she was frying to inedibility, blaming the butcher. She spoke of her daddy, who had visited her that day as he did each day, but she did not speak of her mother whom she had forgotten, as had everyone else in town. She spoke of the gardener who had been rude, and the house being too much to care for...

Her world, now so small and solid, with snow in the winter and a park to be seen from her windows, that she must pick at it for its small solidity, its park and its snow in season, with her solidly small mind that had dwelt upon parks and snow for eight lost years.

Kenneth promised to speak to the butcher

and gardener. He fervently promised to install a housekeeper, this last a promise he planned to keep for himself.

He looked at his watch—almost six—and glanced through the kitchen windows, now nearly dark beyond the light. With abortive gestures of assistance, he attempted to hurry Linda's dinner preparations and, typically obstinate, she put barriers in the way.

First, she asked him to mix martinis; she who rarely drank. 'You don't have to get to that chamber of commerce meeting until eight,' she pointed out in childish treble, which was true.

Then she decided to serve the dinner in the dining room instead of conveniently in the kitchen.

She set the dining table, drank her martini, and burned the chops until 6:30. He could have killed her then, and felt his fists tighten. He should have been in the act of doing so, according to his timing.

Perversely, while he was consulting his watch and refiguring his time, Linda decided on another martini before sitting down to the table. Fifteen minutes for the drink, a half hour for dinner, fifteen minutes to clear the table and get the dishes done—that meant it would be 7:30 before he could kill her, and he sure as hell couldn't kill her, drag her down to the woods, bury her, get back to the house, call Krebs and leave for the chamber meeting by a quarter of eight...

So he reached across the martini pitcher, folded his hands around her long slim neck and pressed tight.

Kenneth Borchard was sure that she was definitely dead by 6:37, and dropped her body to the kitchen floor. He stood still for one moment of recapitulation, mentally adding the tasks that she should have done to those he had so meticulously planned for himself, changed the order of his schedule and raced upstairs to her closet, where he lifted out the new fall coat. He carefully closed the door and walked slowly down the stairs, catching his breath.

In the kitchen, he knelt to thrust Linda's limp arms into the coat sleeves. He memorized her clothing, brown slacks, tan sweater. It was 6:50 and he began to smell the chops that had burned dry. He jumped up, turned off the flame, stuffed the chops down the garbage disposal and filled the pan with water to soak. While the disposal was running, he dumped the limp salad and looked around wildly for any more food that should have been eaten during an ordinarily composed dinner, scraped a pan of green beans and turned back to Linda.

In death, her eyes were wide and blue, with no less expression than they had held in life, her thin lips drawn back and parted. Kenneth was devoutly glad that she was dead at last.

It was seven o'clock and this part of the operation was but a mechanical replay of plans long in the making—the gardener's boots and gloves, the wheelbarrow and shovel from the tool shed out back—hoisting the body from the kitchen floor to the wheelbarrow to trundle it through the dark, and down the grassy hillside to the edge of the woods that fringed the park. A softly cool wind blew through the trees and clouds collided in the sky, denoting another rain, which was good, provided it did not start for a couple of hours.

The soil was exactly as he knew it would be, easy to slice through, just compact enough so that he could lift out shovelfuls of sod and lay them aside, friable so that he could work quickly. He began to sweat in the cool breeze and pulled off his suit coat, laying it across the body, and worried—would he have enough time to change his shirt—what time was it now? He couldn't make out the digits or the hands of his watch in the dark of the trees and the overcast of the sky.

He worked quickly, digging the grave narrow but deep, regularly measuring its depth by the handle of the shovel, the sod on one side, soil on the other, until he was satisfied.

He laid down the shovel carefully and fanned his arms to dry his shirt of perspiration. He picked up his suit coat from the body, put it on, shrugged it in place, then tipped the wheelbarrow so that the body fell into the trench he had dug. He bent, careful not to kneel in the soft earth, and straightened her

94

out, then he shoveled in the soil, tramping it with the gardener's boots. When the grave was filled within three inches, he fit the clods of sod over it, tramping these down, and using the shovel, scattered the soil that had been displaced by her body, so that it fell in small secret heaps under the trees and in the turf.

He placed the shovel in the wheelbarrow and pulled it after him up the hill. The kitchen windows provided a path of light to the tool shed. He looked at his watch: 7:30. He'd done a beautiful job! He upended the wheelbarrow, hung up the shovel, placed the gloves on the workbench, toed off the boots and placed them exactly as he had found them. He shook his trouser legs into their impeccable crease, closed the door of the shed and walked to the kitchen.

There were the dirty pans! At 7:32!

He walked to the hall, lifted the phone and dialed the Krebs' number. He put a hearty note into his voice. 'What say I pick you up a little before eight and we go on together to the C. of C. meeting? No point in using two cars.' He hung up and raced to the kitchen and groaned. He took off his coat again and tossed it to a chair, then he unbuttoned and rolled up his shirt sleeves and tackled the pans.

He finally found a box labeled 'scouring pads' and was finished by 7:45—all the pans put away, the kitchen in order. He stacked the dishes in the dining room, tossed the silverware into a drawer, whisked off the tablecloth,

95

folded and put it away, remembering to put the centerpiece back on the table. It was 7:48. He looked at his hands, rolled down his shirt sleeves. He wouldn't have time to change.

He hurried to the living room, turned on the TV set, piled the pillows at the end of the divan, and punched them as if a head had rested there. He left only one lamp burning.

He turned off the lights in the dining room, grabbed his suit coat from the kitchen chair and put it on, buttoning one button, and took a quick look around the tidy kitchen, glancing at his watch: 7:52. He turned off the kitchen lights, slammed the door, made sure it was locked and ran for the garage.

He picked up Krebs at 7:59 and arrived at the meeting by 8:10 where he maintained an attentive attitude without hearing a word of the business, so intent was he upon listening for hopeful rain against the windows. With rain, even a gentle rain, the trampled grass of the grave would spring up again and the scattered soil would sink into the ground...

Had the meeting been a long one, Kenneth would have suggested to Krebs, with a light and teasingly conspiring chuckle, that he come home with him to explain the lateness of the hour; but since the meeting was over at nine o'clock, he opened the car door for his father-in-law and offered his alternate suggestion. 'Sir,' he said, 'it's still early. I'll drive you up to the house first, we'll have a nightcap and then

Linda and I'll both take you home. She can use the fresh air after an evening in front of the TV set—at least, that's where she was when I left and I'll bet she's still there...'

The rain began just as he unlocked the back door and opened it to the sound of a familiar commercial tune. He laughed with relief and called, 'Hi, honey,' telling Krebs to go on in while he mixed the drinks.

He waited then, in an ecstasy of frozen excitement. Through the patter of quickening raindrops against the windowpanes, it came at last, the 'Linda' cry, a confusion of sound within the sound of the commercial, and Kenneth loosened his muscles, eager for activity, and loped to the living room to stand and stare at the dented pillows, then at the television set that rolled its picture.

'Linda,' he bawled up the stairs, and took them, two at a time. He made a purposeful clatter, charging from room to room, turning on lights and slamming doors. He raced down the stairs, snapped off the television set and brushed Krebs aside as he searched the downstairs rooms, closets, cupboards, even the furnace room beneath the house.

He ran from the kitchen, slammed the door of the tool shed, turned on the garage lights and came back in, soaked. He walked to the hallway, shoulders slumped, dialed a number and ordered the police in a voice carefully broken. 'The chief of police,' he added with a sob.

Then he turned toward his father-in-law and said, 'She's gone. It is happening again, just as it happened before,' watching him, watching the dawning realization on Leland Krebs' round father-face as the sudden knowledge assailed him that Linda was gone and it was indeed happening again, but not as it had before. This time, he could not accuse Kenneth Borchard of the crime that he had committed, having once accused him of the uncommitted crime.

The police chief, there in minutes, eager to rectify rash conceptions and past misjudgment, solemnly listed the clothing worn by the missing woman: brown slacks, tan sweater, new brown fall coat, no handbag, therefore no identification. The chief shook his head. 'Well, about all we can do is put out an APB on her,' he said, as Kenneth Borchard was sure he would, 'and concentrate on the asylums between here and California,' with an apologetic and somewhat resentful glance toward Leland Krebs, to whom he didn't owe one damn thing.

*   *   *

The townspeople now had not only a hero and a prince, but a romantic martyr. Minnie Krebs continued to stare at the wall of her room unaware that her daughter had gone and returned, only to go again. Leland Krebs sat with her much of the time.

Kenneth Borchard knew at last that Linda had been worth every minute of his eight years in prison, now that he had paid her back for them...

WHICH ONE'S THE GUILTY ONE?

E. Wellen

Waiting for the door to open, Mort Seymour sat slumped as if he felt the weight of all his years. At times he closed his eyes for an instant against a flash of pain, but always opened them quickly and fixed them on the door. He heard footsteps and tried to remember the police sergeant's name. He felt a minor panic as he tried to recall it before the sergeant entered.

He fell back in his chair in relief; he paid with one more flash of pain—for relaxing too suddenly—but that was all right, for he'd remembered that the sergeant's name was Young. Mort Seymour made it a point to learn and use the name of everyone he met, not merely because he knew it flattered a customer or prospective customer, but because he knew everyone had an identity and wanted others to be aware of that identity, that unique identity, in a world that more and more swallowed it up, reduced it to slots in a business machine card.

The door opened and Mort Seymour heard the blunt instruments of thick fingers pecking away at a typewriter, heard the rasp of a voice grating away at a telephone, and Sergeant Young entered. Sergeant Young had been youthful once; now he was as gray as Mort

Seymour. In spite of all their differences, all their spites, that was one thing all men had in common, they shared the passing of time.

Mort Seymour started to his feet, but Sergeant Young waved him down.

'Take it easy,' the sergeant said.

'Thank you, Sergeant Young,' Mort Seymour said. He was glad to sink back; he hadn't thought his legs would be so shaky.

Sergeant Young lifted the desk lamp to the top of the filing cabinet and aimed the shine at the blank wall as though lighting a stage setting. Then he leaned out into the corridor and beckoned and six men filed in and lined up against the blank wall. Sergeant Young eyed Mort Seymour and stretched out his right hand toward the men, palm up, as if serving them to him on a platter.

Mort Seymour screwed up his eyes and scrutinized the six men. They were all the same general size, but there were differences; it was by the differences that he would know the man for whom he was looking. The first was too sandy; the second was too fleshy; the third was too dark; the fourth—

Mort Seymour pushed himself to his feet. He stood there unsteadily, but he stood there. He stared into the eyes of the fourth man. The man stared back boredly. Mort Seymour glanced at the fifth and sixth men, but his gaze came back to the fourth. Mort Seymour moved nearer to the light. On the unillumined side of his head, a patch of gauze and tape gave back pale light coming off the wall behind him; on the inside of his head there was something of the fear that lingered from the time men lived in caves and fell back in terror from a flash of lightning. Mort Seymour disregarded the pain and pointed.

'That's the man.' He tried to hold his finger steady.

'Which one?' Sergeant Young sounded hopeful.

'That one. Fourth from the end.'

Sergeant Young sighed. Mort Seymour turned to see the sergeant grimace and shake his head sadly.

'I was afraid of this,' the sergeant said. 'Sorry, Mr. Seymour, you're still too shook up to give us a good make. Maybe later.' But his voice said he doubted it.

Mort Seymour knew he was gaping, but he could not help it. He swallowed hard and said, 'What do you mean? I tell you that's the man.'

Sergeant Young canted his head and the six men started to file out. The sergeant said, 'Muller, you stay.'

The fourth man stepped aside and waited. Mort Seymour eyed him thinking, *That's the man. That's the man. I know that's the man. What's wrong with Sergeant Young?*

Sergeant Young had been on his feet all day. He sighed profoundly. 'I was hoping you meant the third man. He was our hottest

102

suspect.'

Mort Seymour pointed again to the fourth man, almost touching him. 'This is the man who came into my store and hit me on the head and robbed me.'

Sergeant Young looked as if he wanted to make a face, but he said patiently, 'Mr. Seymour, this man is Officer Muller. He's a plainclothesman. When we put up a suspect for a witness to identify, we make it a practice to put him up alongside plainclothesmen who come near fitting the same description. That way the suspect gets a fair shake and can't go crying in court that we practically told the witness it was him.'

Mort Seymour stared at Officer Muller, who stared back boredly. He shook his head stubbornly, disregarding flashes of pain. When, in half the world, crime not only put on the mask of innocence but threw about itself the robe of the law and forced the victim to stand before the bar, why was it so strange to uncover a policeman-bandit? He was about to say something of the sort, but Sergeant Young was speaking.

Sergeant Young seemed to be trying to be gentle, but sounded as if there was something he was angry about. 'Look, Mr. Seymour, we all get old. None of us can sidestep it. The legs get weary; the hands get shaky; the eyes get blurry. Nothing to make you feel ashamed; we all get old. Muller, take Mr. Seymour home.'

Mort Seymour wanted to cry out, make loud protest; the sergeant didn't know what he was doing, sending him off alone with the man Mort Seymour knew had come into his store and hit him on the head and robbed him. But pain blinded him; by the time he could see and speak again, he saw that Sergeant Young had left him alone with Officer Muller.

Officer Muller, still seeming bored, slowly took the lamp down off the filing cabinet and put it back on the desk, the shadows changing on his face, forming menacing wedges. Mort Seymour read into the cuneiforms a warning to leave. So while Officer Muller was adjusting the shade, he edged toward the doorway, meaning to make off before Officer Muller could follow him.

Mort Seymour, hearing no footsteps behind him, felt he was making it and quickened his step. But Officer Muller caught up with him. He said nothing as they walked together through the detective squad room. The man typing and the man phoning did not glance up as they passed.

At the parking spaces adjoining the station house, Officer Muller stopped and pointed to a long black sedan.

Mort Seymour shook his head, saying, 'That's all right, I'll take a taxi.'

Officer Muller said, 'I'll take you.' His voice was quiet but firm.

Mort Seymour said, 'I don't want to put you

to any trouble.'

Officer Muller said, 'The Sergeant told me to take you.'

'Can't you tell him you took me?'

For the first time, Officer Muller lost his bored look. He said with a half smile, 'Still think I'm the man?'

Mort Seymour eyed Officer Muller. If only he had heard the bandit speak. But beyond a grunt of surprise, he was pretty sure the bandit had made no sound. If he had said anything—say a muttered comment on the amount of the loot—in Mort Seymour's unconscious hearing it struck no note now when Officer Muller spoke. Officer Muller's smile grew and Mort Seymour suddenly felt like an old man.

Officer Muller offered a hand, but Mort Seymour forced himself to straighten. He said, 'I'll make out all right.' He smiled sheepishly. 'About that identification, a man—you know—hates to admit he's growing old and can't see good anymore.'

Officer Muller nodded. He steered Mort Seymour to the long black sedan and they got in. 'Where do you live?'

Mort Seymour said tiredly, 'I'm not going home. I'm going to open the store.'

Officer Muller gazed at the bandage and at Mort Seymour's pale face and shrugged. 'Okay.'

He shot the car out onto the street and turned left.

Mort Seymour's heart began to make a hollow thumping sound he feared Officer Muller would hear. If Officer Muller was innocent, he wouldn't know where the store was. Why then had he turned left? Mort Seymour's heart quieted. It was a one-way street; Officer Muller had to turn left. Now Mort Seymour remained silent and waited. Before they reached the corner, Officer Muller said, 'Where's the store?'

'Keep heading this way,' Mort Seymour said, 'till you reach Eccles, then turn right. It's near the end. Twelve, number twelve.'

Officer Muller nodded. It had grown suddenly dark and he switched on the headlights. It was strange and terrifying, Mort Seymour thought, to be riding in this long black car through this sudden darkness, that made familiar streets flashing by unfamiliar. He had an urge to make light of it with small talk, but instead kept eyeing Officer Muller's face.

All at once Officer Muller clapped his massive hands on the black wheel and laughed thunderously; the noise sent a bolt of pain through Mort Seymour's skull.

Officer Muller glanced sidewise at the man beside him and said, 'Be funny if it was me, wouldn't it now?'

Mort Seymour smiled feebly.

'You're lucky it ain't me,' Officer Muller said with another sidewise glance. 'Know why?

106

If it was me, and I thought you really believed it was me and was gonna do something about it, I'd make short work of you. Know how? Another blow on the same spot. They'd just think it was delayed shock from the first blow killed you.'

Mort Seymour smiled even more feebly. He stared at the flickering face. Was Officer Muller really the man, and therefore threatening him obliquely? Or was he merely having fun getting back at Mort Seymour for having wrongly identified him?

Officer Muller laughed again. 'That would be funny.'

Mort Seymour made an effort to seem amused. 'Yes, it would.'

Whatever the truth might be, he did not want to think about the whole thing. He was almost glad for the times the pain would not let him think. But he made himself think. Fingering the bandage on his head, he lived again the moment that led up to the assault. Probably suspecting a gun under the counter, the bandit had timed it so Mort Seymour was away from the counter, his back to the open door, reaching up to arrange the bottles on the shelves. Mort Seymour wouldn't even have heard the soft swift approach, if the man's toe had not stubbed on the warped plank the landlord was always fixing to fix, but never got around to fixing. Mort Seymour whirled, but had had time for only a fleeting look at the man before the blow landed.

A flash of pain reminded him of Sergeant Young's painful words; especially painful because they were true. The years had crept up on him. The legs were weary; the hands were shaky; the eyes were blurry.

He had to come to terms with life. He sighed. And he smiled, when Officer Muller glanced at him. It was not Officer Muller's fault that he looked—to the old eyes of Mort Seymour—so like the bandit. Mort Seymour felt a deep gratefulness that it had not been some other innocent man he had pointed out, someone without Officer Muller's official standing, someone without an alibi. He shivered; he, Mort Seymour, might have borne false witness.

Officer Muller was swinging the long black sedan to the curb. 'This it?'

Mort Seymour looked around with a start; there was the sign, Seymour Wines & Spirits. He nodded. It was an embarrassing moment for him. He didn't quite know how to apologize and thank and bid good-bye all at the same time. He eyed Officer Muller; it was hard to tell if he had hurt the man's feelings so deeply, that trying to make up for it by offering him something would in itself add to the hurt feelings.

He found his voice. 'Yes, this is it.'

Officer Muller appeared impressed by the window display. 'Nice place you got here.'

'Thanks,' Mort Seymour said. 'Small, but it's a good neighborhood for a package store. I make a living.' He thought he would crack a joke. 'But it's too small for both me and the bandits to make a living out of.'

Officer Muller said, 'Yeah,' indifferently.

The mistaken identification was between them again. Mort Seymour was more than ever anxious to make amends. 'Let me at least offer you a bottle of something,' he said. 'Whatever you like.'

This did not seem to hurt Officer Muller's feelings; he seemed pleased, in fact. They got out of the car. Mort Seymour drew out his keys and opened the door of the store and flicked on the lights and the rows of bottles shone. He went behind the counter to be ready with the wrapping paper and string. Officer Muller stood in the doorway staring around at the bottles. Mort Seymour waved a hand. 'Whatever you like.'

Officer Muller, his eyes fixed on a bottle, started forward for it. Unthinkingly, automatically, he sidestepped the warped board, and stopped.

Mort Seymour eyed Officer Muller and thought, *He's the man*. Officer Muller eyed him and knew that he knew. They faced one another for a frozen instant. Then Officer Muller made a move toward the blackjack at his hip.

But Mort Seymour's hands reached swiftly

and surely under the counter and gripped his gun firmly and swung it up and pointed it at Officer Muller. Mort Seymour's feet were planted and his hand was steady and his eyes were bright.

He said, 'If you don't want to get older, make another move.'

He stood straight; he had his man. But had he? A flicker of panic unsteadied him. Sidestepping the board had shown that Muller was guilty, but you needed more than that, and a flash of guilt in a man's eyes, for conviction. You needed solid evidence.

His hand wavered. But then, in the very next instant, his hand was steady again. There might be a trace of Mort Seymour's flesh or blood or hair on the blackjack; there might be a sliver of wood, from the warped plank, deep-driven into the toe of one of Muller's shoes; there might be traces of dust from Mort Seymour's cash drawer, dust peculiar to a liquor shop, clinging to bills in Muller's wallet. But this was a job for Sergeant Young to do, and there was no doubt about it now that he would do it.

FRIGHTENED LADY

C. B. Gilford

Noel Tasker learned about the murder when he arrived home from the office. That was about five-forty-five on Tuesday. He drove through the entrance of Camelot Court and took the left drive. The right drive was his own, but he often took the left in order to pass by Gaby's apartment. Not that he would ever dare to stop in during daylight hours, but perhaps only to see if her car were there, or maybe, as had happened once, to see a man escorting her out the door. Despite the fact that he didn't own Gaby—and she had reminded him of that often—the experience had caused him a pang of jealousy. Masochistically, he continued to check on her now and then.

The sight which greeted him on this Tuesday, however, was not of Gaby's being escorted to a shiny new foreign sports car. There were four vehicles parked before her door today, three police cruisers and a white ambulance; and there was a crowd on the green lawn.

Noel Tasker braked to a quick stop, not wisely perhaps, but instinctively. That was Gaby's door standing wide open, with a policeman just outside it to fend off the crowd.

111

He leaped from the car, then realized it was not his place to show such concern, and sauntered over to join the crowd.

'What's going on?' he asked the nearest man.

'There's been a murder.'

Noel began to shake. He hoped the fact wasn't noticeable to his neighbor. The next question was infinitely more difficult. 'Who was it?'

'A woman. I think her name was Marchant.'

Gabrielle Marchant! His Gaby!

He was sick. He wanted to run, to find a private corner somewhere where he could let go, but also he wanted to stay there. He wanted to find out ... the answers to a million questions. What had happened? Who had done it? A crazy thought ran through his head, of going up to the policeman at the door and saying, 'Let me in, Officer. I was the dead woman's lover; one of her lovers, I mean.'

Now his thoughts went pell-mell. *One* of her lovers! That guy he had seen picking up Gaby, taking her out in his fancy, expensive, foreign car. He ought to tell the police about that guy. He was probably the one who killed her! Describe the guy, describe the car ...

'I hear she was good-looking.' The man beside him was continuing the conversation.

'Yes ...' Noel answered absently.

'You knew her?'

'Well, I ...'

He stopped. Another thought was seeping

112

into his reeling brain. If Gabrielle Marchant was suddenly murdered, *all* her lovers would be suspect, wouldn't they? Not that Noel Tasker was in any way implicated in her death; but now that she was dead, he didn't want to be implicated in her *life*.

'You knew her?'

'Well, I—I knew who she was.'

'You've seen her?'

'Well, yes.'

'Good-looking?'

'Well, depends. Depends on what you like. I guess she was, sort of.'

He walked away from the man, who could have been a plainclothes detective, or a busybody sort who might report to the cops that he was talking to someone who acted very upset and nervous. So Noel returned to his car and drove away because now he was no longer mourning for the loss of Gaby, or shocked at her death. He was frightened.

He wheeled around the police cars and the ambulance, trying to go slowly, trying not to attract attention. He drove all the way to the far end, then back again on his own street, and parked in his own carport. The adjacent spot was empty. Leona hadn't arrived yet. He was thankful for that.

Once inside his own apartment, he felt a little better, but he was still shaking. He fixed himself a drink, heavy on the bourbon, easy on the soda. His hands trembled through the

113

operation. He took a long swallow, then carried the rest of it into the bedroom. There he yanked off his jacket and tie. Afterward, though he didn't want to, he walked to the window.

There was only one thing out there on the rear lawn to suggest that there might be something wrong in Gabrielle's apartment—a cop; a uniformed cop standing at the rear door—just standing there. Maybe he was guarding the door, but there was no crowd in the rear; all the activity was out front.

Noel sipped at his drink, hoping to quiet the trembling in his hands. The view out this window was too painfully familiar, but he stayed there nevertheless, staring.

It had been while standing at this window that he'd first seen Gaby. She had moved in last spring, and on the first sunshiny day she had appeared. What was the distance between the two buildings, between the window where he stood now, and Gaby's back door? Two hundred feet? Maybe a little more, but the view had been good.

Gaby had come out that day to begin her summer tan, wearing one of the tiniest bikinis Noel Tasker had ever seen. Gaby had the figure for it: legs long, graceful, so aware of their own perfection that they seemed to be posing; a slim waistline that emphasized the curves above and below; a bust that bulged out of the little bra. She arranged herself on a chaise longue, and Noel Tasker stared.

Through the months of May and June, he continued to stare, whenever Gaby was out there on the lawn and Leona was absent from the apartment. He even bought binoculars to achieve a more intimate view, and hid the instrument in his briefcase, a place where Leona never peeked. During May and June, the sunbather's skin changed from creamy ivory to creamy golden.

In July, Noel became Gaby's lover.

It hadn't been easy to manage—nor difficult. He had observed her living habits, clocked her movements, and so was driving by one morning when she'd had car trouble and was able to give her a lift downtown. Afterward there'd been a 'chance' meeting at the office where she worked, followed by cocktails the same afternoon; then two dinner dates, and finally, by appropriate degrees and the passage of time, home to bed.

All very discreet. His job had always demanded his being away a few evenings, calling on clients, attending a meeting now and then. The evenings out had become merely a bit more frequent. Leona had something of an after-dark life of her own. She was a secretary, and a very good one, with an income that topped Noel's whenever his sales slipped, as they often did. So she had nightwork occasionally, and the business-women's club she belonged to, and her duplicate bridge.

Thus it hadn't been too hard for Noel to see Gaby a couple of evenings a week.

Poor Gaby, so beautiful and yet so undemanding; though a divorcée, she hadn't been looking for a husband, or even strings. Because she was beautiful, she had plenty of men. All Gaby had ever seemed to want was a good time. Who could have wanted to kill her?

Noel finished his drink and fixed himself another. It was six-fifteen now and Leona wasn't home yet. Was she supposed to be on time tonight or was she staying downtown? His mind was blank.

Miserable, he drank and waited. He couldn't quite believe or accept the new fact yet. Gaby was dead. Her beautiful body had been ... what? Shot? Strangled? Knifed? Did it really matter? The beautiful body was dead, destroyed. There would be no more of those stolen hours together, no more excitement, no more ecstasy. It wasn't fair! He'd had such a good thing going, and someone ... someone ...

The sound of a key in the door lock spun him around. He mustn't be caught staring out this window! Force of habit, as if poor Gaby were out there sunning. He ran from the window and was back in the living room when Leona walked in.

He guessed instantly that she already knew about the excitement in the neighborhood. She was pale, flustered, which was unusual for her. She stared at him. She was even trembling.

116

That was fortunate in a way. Perhaps she wouldn't notice his symptoms.

'A woman was murdered on the other street,' she announced.

Not seeming to care whether or not he already knew, she passed him and marched into the bedroom. He watched her go. She always marched. She'd grown stout and matronly, and the martial stride seemed to fit her. He followed her after a moment. There she was, at *his* window, the window through which he had watched Gaby.

'A woman named Gabrielle something...'

He said nothing. He wasn't going to be so foolish as to furnish the last name.

'It must have been pretty terrible. They say it was a maniac. She was all cut up.'

He bit hard into his lower lip, and steadied himself against the door-jamb. The images pounding into his brain were red and horrible, but somehow he had already guessed. Gaby was no ordinary woman. She would have been murdered in no ordinary way. Cut up! He who had known her body so intimately could visualize the grimmest interpretation of those words.

'It must have been a sex maniac,' Leona said. Suddenly she turned from the window and confronted him. 'She used to sunbathe out there. Did you ever see her?'

He sensed the danger and reacted. Gaby was dead. He had to protect himself. Every man

117

who had a window overlooking that lawn must have seen her. Not to have noticed her would be suspicious in itself. 'I remember a sexy gal, if it was the same one. A brunette?'

Leona nodded. 'I think she was a brunette.'

He swallowed hard. He could scarcely change the subject and ask what was for dinner. 'Cut up, you say? You mean...?'

'Sliced. With something real sharp. Maybe a razor.' She staggered suddenly to the bed and sat. 'A sex maniac, Noel,' she whispered. 'There's a sex maniac loose in this neighborhood.'

* * *

That night was a strange one. The August dusk was redolent with the scents of chrysanthemums and of terror, full of the sounds of cicadas and soft human conversation. The inhabitants of Camelot Court gathered outside in groups, which seemed safer than being alone inside, and rumors were rife.

The corpse had been taken away, thoroughly sheeted, of course, but covered, as everyone knew, with ghastly wounds. The crime had been discovered by a woman named Maxine Borley, who lived across the hall and who'd been, apparently, Gabrielle's only female friend. Maxine had heard the TV playing inside the Marchant apartment, had

118

knocked, received no reply, had opened the unlocked door and walked in. Whether or not Maxine was supposed to give out details, she had: blood all over the place, the body nude, lying in the doorway between the bedroom and the living room; so many cuts that she couldn't count, and so much blood that it was hard to see where the cuts were. One detail was certain, however. There'd been a man's old-fashioned straight razor beside the body.

The news was passed in hushed tones up and down both streets of Camelot Court. Men shivered, women visibly trembled, and they all said what Leona had said.

'There's a sex maniac loose around here.'

Leona didn't want to go back into the apartment, not yet at least. The streets and walks of Camelot were well-lighted, and for the moment there seemed to be safety in numbers outside. She hung tightly onto Noel's arm as they walked about. Women generally stayed close to their husbands. Mostly there were couples living in Camelot. If there were other single women like Gabrielle Marchant, they weren't in evidence on this night.

Whenever neighbours met, they always talked about the same things. Gabrielle Marchant had had boyfriends, lovers. A disappointed lover could have killed her. *Could* have. But why, then, the butchery? If he'd had to use a razor, one slice across the throat would have been sufficient—unless he were insane.

119

Had Gabrielle Marchant been beautiful enough to drive one of her lovers insane? Possibly. She'd been sexy, all right, and she'd displayed herself pretty freely out on the lawn and by the pool. So the murder could also have been committed by a stranger. Why necessarily a stranger? Why not some frustrated guy who lived in Camelot? A maniac *inside* Camelot? That, of course, was the most frightening possibility of all, because, as every woman seemed aware, a maniac might kill again.

Eventually the impromptu group discussions had to break up, people had to get their sleep. The maniac wouldn't strike again tonight. The place was crawling with cops. The Marchant apartment was sealed off, guarded by the police. Police cruisers came and went frequently. Somebody said plainclothesmen were roaming. Certain of Gabrielle's immediate neighbors had already been questioned. There were reporters around, too, who also asked questions. Too many alert people were around tonight; not a good night for a murderer to prowl.

Noel and Leona went home together. Noel had a drink while Leona locked windows, closed venetian blinds, tucked draperies around their edges, wedged chairs under doorknobs front and back. In their bedroom finally, they performed the rituals of retiring.

Noel glanced covertly at his wife during the process. She was realistic enough at least not to affect slinky, transparent nightgowns. Her lavender pajamas ballooned over her heavy breasts, thick waist and generous haunches. He discovered that he couldn't even remember what she'd looked like when they were married thirteen years ago.

Could a woman like Leona really be in danger from the same 'sex maniac' who had murdered Gaby? It seemed impossible. Sex maniacs would have certain standards. They obviously enjoyed murdering women, but judging from the choice of Gaby, such maniacs must prefer murdering beautiful women.

When Noel and Leona climbed into bed, with Noel suddenly wondering why after all these years they still slept together in a double bed, Leona snuggled up close. 'Noel,' she whispered, 'I'm scared,' and she proved it by trembling violently. 'You will protect me, won't you, Noel?'

'Yes,' he promised, though he didn't mean it even then. 'I'll protect you.'

The next morning Lieutenant Kabrick of Homicide arrived. He was a squat, square man, powerful-looking as a bear. He didn't smile, merely nodded and showed his identification. 'You must be Mr. Tasker.'

'Yes.'

'May I come in?'

Noel stepped aside.

'Mrs. Tasker at home?'

'She just left for work.'

'Maybe I can catch her later. While I'm here, I'd like to ask you a few questions.'

'Questions?' Despite gritted teeth and clenched fists, Noel's trembling started again.

'About the murder of Gabrielle Marchant.' The lieutenant seemed not to notice the trembling. 'Did you know Miss Marchant?'

The question Noel had realized would come eventually, the question he dreaded; he had thought of a dozen answers, none of which he liked particularly, but he had to say something. 'Not exactly know...'

'What does that mean, Mr. Tasker?'

'Well, I can't say that I knew her. But I ... Well, I guess like everybody else, I—I knew who she was.'

'How was that?'

'Well, I—I saw her ... from a distance ... outdoors ... several times, I guess.'

The lieutenant stared enigmatically, then nodded.

'Can I look around?'

'You mean ... search?'

The stare continued, unblinking. 'I just wanted to see what view of the Marchant apartment you have from here.'

'Oh.' Noel didn't know whether to feel relieved or not. He led the way into the bedroom, pulled up the blind.

The lieutenant stood at the window for a long time. 'Good view you had here,' he said.

'Yes, my wife and I appreciate the open

122

space.'

'They tell me Miss Marchant was a sunbather.'

Noel made no comment.

'Those several times you said you saw her, Mr. Tasker, must have been when she was sunbathing.'

'Yes, I guess so.'

'You don't remember that well? They tell me she was rather spectacular.'

'Well, it's some distance . . .'

'A couple hundred feet, I'd say.' The lieutenant turned away from the window. 'I suppose you read about the case in the paper this morning.'

'Yes.'

'Well, like it said, although the body wasn't discovered until Tuesday afternoon, we're certain that the crime was committed on Monday evening. Between nine and eleven P.M. is what the doc says. There was no forcible entry. The murderer just rang the doorbell; probably the front door, but maybe it was the back door. That's why I'm here, Mr. Tasker. I wanted to find out whether you or your wife saw anything strange in the vicinity of the Marchant apartment on Monday night.'

'I wasn't here!' Noel was bursting to reveal his alibi. Even if they connected him with Gaby otherwise, they couldn't pin the murder on him. 'I didn't come home at all. Monday. I mean, I didn't come home until real late. It was a lot later than eleven. Maybe one or one-thirty. We had a dinner and a sales meeting, and afterward I had some drinks with a couple of guys.'

Lieutenant Kabrick nodded slowly. 'Okay, Mr. Tasker, so you didn't see anything. How about your wife?'

'I don't know.'

'Was she home?'

'She didn't say. Sometimes when I'm not going to be here for dinner, she eats out, too. I think maybe that's what she did. But I don't know what time she got home.'

'If she had noticed anything peculiar, she'd probably have mentioned it to you, I guess. Everybody around here has been very cooperative. They want to find the killer.'

Noel tried to stay calm. It wasn't easy. 'I don't know what we could have seen if we'd been home,' he said. 'It's pretty far away, and it was dark.'

The lieutenant nodded. 'But you never can tell,' he said. 'That's why we're asking everybody here in the complex. And of course, maybe we ought to be interested in other times besides Monday night. The fact there was no forcible entry into the apartment doesn't prove anything, but it's possible that the murder was committed by someone known to Miss Marchant. This will come out in the papers maybe later today, Mr. Tasker, but the medical examination didn't indicate rape.'

124

Noel started. 'Then it wasn't a sex murder?'

'I didn't say that. There are all different kinds of sex murders. But it doesn't seem to have been a rape-murder. I've got a little theory on it myself. Maybe it was a revenge murder.'

'Revenge?' Noel stuffed his hands into his pockets to hide their trembling.

'Like, maybe, a jealous lover. Or a rejected lover. Miss Marchant was attractive. We don't know how many men there were in her life. So that's why I'm asking you about other times besides Monday evening. Did you ever notice what people came and went over across the way? We're trying to find out what men hung around Miss Marchant.'

The guy in the expensive foreign car! Would it be smart to mention that incident? To admit that he had deliberately driven down the other street and noticed the guy? Stay out of it, Noel told himself. Stay far out.

'Can you give us any information along that line, Mr. Tasker?'

'No, I'm afraid I can't.'

The lieutenant shrugged. 'Well, thanks, Mr. Tasker,' he said on his way out. 'Tell your wife I may stop by. And also tell her not to worry. We'll catch the guy. We've gone over the place for prints, and we've lifted quite a few. Some of them may have been left by the murderer.'

When the lieutenant had gone, Noel sank onto the sofa. Fingerprints! He hadn't thought

125

about fingerprints. His own would be all over Gaby's apartment...

He spent the day worrying about fingerprinting, and then that evening his worries were suddenly over. The story appeared in the newspaper, either deliberately leaked by the police for purposes of their own, or uncovered by an enterprising reporter. A most important fingerprint had been found in the Marchant apartment. Since the print did not belong to the deceased, it had to belong to the murderer. Who else but the murderer, since it was imprinted on the murder weapon, and in blood?

So whatever other strange prints they found around the apartment, they wouldn't even bother to check them, would they? Everybody's apartment must be full of fingerprints. People come and go. Even in and out of bedrooms? Of course, innocently. But it didn't matter. The police had a print of Gaby's murderer now, and that would be the only one they'd check out thoroughly, through the F.B.I. files in Washington, or however they did it.

Noel felt so relieved that he wanted to talk about the case now, and the only person he had to talk to was Leona. He showed her the newspaper the moment she arrived home.

'They'll catch that maniac now,' he announced. 'The police found a bloody fingerprint on the razor.'

Leona grabbed the paper and read it without bothering to sit down. Was she actually frightened by all this murder business? Or was she pretending? Do unattractive women like to pretend they're desirable, even to a homicidal maniac?

'Well,' she said finally, 'they'll catch him now. They've got a fingerprint of him. Then we can all relax.' She went to the kitchen, transferred TV dinners from the freezer to the oven, and afterward retired to the bedroom. He didn't follow her there. After Gaby, the sight of Leona's changing clothes had become rather an obscene spectacle.

Then, just before the TV dinners were ready, Lieutenant Kabrick arrived, and it was a different Noel Tasker who received him this time. Gaby was gone, the moments of ecstasy would be no more; but Noel Tasker was alive and safe, and now he was confident.

'Lieutenant,' he fairly bubbled, 'you came to see my wife, didn't you? Honey, the detective's here! Sit down, Lieutenant. Read all about it in the paper—the bloody fingerprint on the razor. Have you located the matching print in your files yet?'

Kabrick sat down, tentatively, on the edge of a chair. 'No, I'm afraid not,' he said.

Leona came in, wearing Bermuda shorts. She didn't look good in them. Kabrick rose politely, anyway, and introduced himself.

'Mrs. Tasker, were you at home Monday

127

night? We're canvassing to see if any of the neighbors noticed anything or anybody around the Marchant apartment that night.'

'I wasn't home,' Leona answered quickly, and by remaining standing made the lieutenant stand too.

'When did you get home, Mrs. Tasker?'

'It must have been midnight.' She trembled. 'And to think I drove in here, and parked my car, and walked to my door ... and there was a maniac hanging around ...'

'We think he was gone by then, Mrs. Tasker.'

'Lieutenant,' Noel interrupted, 'sit down. Care for a drink? Cup of coffee?'

Kabrick refused both, but he did sit down. Leona sat on the sofa.

'I guess if you're still asking questions,' she ventured softly, 'that means you haven't caught the man yet.'

'Not yet.'

'Then no woman is safe.'

The lieutenant shrugged. 'We go on the assumption,' he said, 'that no woman is ever safe. The world is full of nuts. But that doesn't mean that this murderer will strike again. He may have been a friend of Miss Marchant, you see, and may have killed for revenge or jealousy.'

Again Noel was tempted to mention the guy with the foreign car, but he resisted. He was out of it now, and he wanted to stay out.

'There was no rape involved,' Kabrick pointed out, 'and probably not even attempted rape. You see, we're convinced that Miss Marchant was attacked from behind.'

'Behind?' Noel echoed, really curious. 'With a razor?'

'Very simple,' Kabrick explained. 'Miss Marchant was a small woman, short, about five-one. That made this method of attack easy. The murderer was right-handed, we believe. Standing behind Miss Marchant, he reached over her left shoulder, cupped her chin in the palm of his left hand, forced her chin upward, bringing her head back, and tightened her neck. Then with his right hand he reached across her right shoulder and simply drew the razor across her throat. Somehow that M.O. suggests deliberation to me. I don't go with the maniac theory. So the other women around here may be safer than you think, Mrs. Tasker.'

Leona didn't give up. She wanted to feel that she was in danger, Noel felt certain, because she wanted to feel desirable. 'He cut her all up, though,' she argued. 'Only a maniac would do that.'

'The body was mutilated after she was dead,' Kabrick said. He sat back farther in his chair and surveyed both his listeners. 'I could be wrong, of course,' he went on. 'I'm always theorizing, but in Homicide you have to. There's this matter of the blood. You know what M.O. means, Mr. Tasker?'

'*Modus operandi*,' Noel answered confidently.

'That's right. The criminal's method of operation. The way he commits the crime. Now, what are the advantages of attacking the victim from behind in a razor murder?'

Noel thought. 'Surprise?'

'Maybe. And the victim has less chance to protect herself with her arms. You can get right to the vital spot. But there's another advantage. The murderer doesn't get too much blood on himself.'

'Really?' Noel asked in admiration.

'That's a very important advantage. It minimizes the problem of disposal of bloody garments. Which can be quite a problem. Plenty of murders have been solved by the discovery of bloody clothes.'

'But Miss Marchant was cut up,' Noel objected. 'The woman who discovered the body said there was blood all over the place.'

Lieutenant Kabrick slouched in the depths of the chair and smiled. 'There was and there wasn't,' he said. 'Now, let's say Miss Marchant is dead from a cut throat. She's lying more or less face up on the floor. Only one cut so far. There's a lot of blood, mostly on the front of the corpse. And on the razor and the murderer's hands, of course. But now the victim is dead, quiet, easy to cut on. From here on, the murderer can proceed very carefully, avoid getting blood on himself. You see, there was one very peculiar fact. Although there's blood on the carpet in nearly every direction, there are no footprints in the blood. Wouldn't you say the murderer was being very, very careful?'

'Seems so,' Noel admitted.

'Now tell me,' Kabrick pursued, 'what kind of maniac do we have, then? One seized with blood lust, who wants to cut and cut, who wants to mutilate, to butcher? Yes, all that. In a sense, every murderer is a maniac. But this is one who has other things on his mind, too. Like the problems of disposal of bloody clothes and bloody shoes.'

Noel was calm now, completely absorbed. 'What about the bloody fingerprint on the razor?' he demanded.

'Two explanations. Remember, no killer is completely sane. Explanation one, then: he deliberately wanted to leave a clue to his identity for the thrill of the risk involved. Explanation two: he saw something, heard something, got scared, and ran, before he was quite finished. Although there were plenty of slashes, incidentally, the job did look a little unfinished. Maybe that sounds strange, but I've seen quite a few of these cases—' Kabrick broke off suddenly, glanced at his watch, and stood up. 'Maybe I got too graphic,' he said to Leona. 'What I really wanted to do was to make you feel a little better, a little safer maybe. Because I think that killer was interested in only one woman.'

He walked to the door. 'If at any time either of you does remember any little item about Miss Marchant, whether it seems important to you or not, I hope you'll let us know.'

The detective was gone, but Leona continued to sit there, pale, shivering, staring at nothing.

'What's the matter?' Noel asked. Perhaps he was beginning to enjoy her fear, now that his own was past.

'I'm afraid,' she said.

He smiled indulgently. What reason did she have to be afraid? Who would want to murder her? Only himself, her husband, and even he didn't have any special reason to do it at the moment.

* * *

Life, however, has a way of changing. The best-laid plans and all that. For Noel Tasker, who didn't have any plans, best-laid or otherwise, things could still go awry.

Lieutenant Kabrick and his cohorts did not bring the murderer of Gabrielle Marchant to justice. The police, it was said, did a thorough job on the Marchant apartment, ripping, so the rumor went, the paper from the walls and the carpeting from the floors, to no avail. They gave up finally, and disappeared from the scene. The management of Camelot Court didn't try to rent the redecorated apartment apparently. They were too busy trying to fill their other vacancies. Nervous renters drifted away when leases expired. Other nervous renters stayed, among them Leona Tasker, seeming to enjoy the little tremors of apprehension which went up and down their spines whenever they had to walk through the dusk and night of advancing autumn. The tremors all the more enjoyable being experienced in safety. The killer did not strike again.

Noel Tasker, who possessed enough masculine animal vitality to have interested the likes of Gabrielle Marchant, somehow lacked the moxie to achieve very much in the world of commerce. His business career went from bad to worse. His customers fell to the blandishments of competitors. His boss kept him on, but cut his drawing account and issued vague threats. Noel considered trying to find another mistress to fill the emptiness in his life, but discovered with dismay he couldn't afford the luxury. He remembered Gaby, who had never demanded much, and he brooded.

To Leona, however, although she might continue to cringe in mock terror at the thought of the lurking maniac, life down at the office was kinder. She received a promotion, a minor executive title, rather unusual for a female.

'Do you get a company car?' Noel sniped at her when she told him the news. His own company car, he knew, might be taken away from him any day.

'No,' she admitted, 'but my other fringe benefits have been increased. I've got fifty thousand dollars' worth of company-paid life insurance now.'

It became only a matter of time, therefore, before Noel Tasker steeled himself to the obvious decision. Time, meanwhile, was running out.

He didn't know how long he could hang onto his own job. An unemployed man with a wife insured to the tune of fifty thousand bucks might look just a little too suspicious. Then also, his job, with all the night work it entailed, was his only source of alibis.

The 'maniac' had not been as obliging as he might have been. When he failed to commit further crimes, Lieutenant Kabrick's theories of revenge and jealousy gained strength. Even worse, the women of Camelot Court were ceasing to be terrified, Leona included.

Oh, they played the little game as long as they could, especially when a bunch of them were together; half a dozen thirtyish and fortyish females, some past their prime, some never having had any, all cackling about how the killer could be hiding in any shadow, ogling their charms, and lusting to slice those charms like so much baloney. Baloney indeed!

So it would be a favor to those old hags to give a new little boost to their adrenalin production. Actually, the hags were rather important to Noel's plan. They would be sure to testify, when the time came, that Leona Tasker had been for months deathly afraid of the fate which eventually befell her.

M.O. Noel had it memorized. Lieutenant Kabrick had been most obliging; the newspapers too. Everybody knew the M.O., and they'd recognize it when they saw it again. Too bad about the lieutenant's theories. He'd have to change his mind.

The straight razor was easy to obtain. Noel picked one up on an out-of-town trip. There'd have to be one difference about the razor, though. There'd be no bloody fingerprint on it this time. But then the M.O. is not always precisely the same, is it? A criminal, even a maniac, learns as he goes along.

The worst risk involved the alibi. What it amounted to was simple: he had to be in two places at the same time. Not easy, perhaps, if one is supposed to be at dinner with a single customer and at home with one's wife simultaneously. But what about a larger social occasion, where one might slip away for a few minutes without the absence being noted, and yet where a dozen half-inebriated witnesses might swear that, 'Sure, old Noel was here with us all evening'?

Life cooperated with Noel Tasker on this

135

one score. A business convention was coming to town.

'Are you going to be home on Thursday night?' he asked Leona.

'Why shouldn't I be?' she asked him. Her persistent terror had reduced her out-alone-after-dark activities. 'I suppose you'll be at your old convention party. Well, I'll be here watching TV.'

Thursday night it would be, then.

Qualms? Still? Right down to the wire? Oh, yes, indeed, but the choice was inevitable—and bitter.

On the one hand, he could continue as he was. Losing his present selling job, he might of course get another; such as selling encyclopedias from door to door, for instance. Leona could support him—and become more and more possessive of him, more and more demanding. Ever since the Marchant murder, under the pretense of being afraid, she had required more affection, snuggling a bit closer every night in bed, and on Saturday and Sunday mornings lingering there for a bit of dalliance. After Gaby, he could endure Leona even less.

But with fifty thousand, plus their joint savings account, he could go somewhere else, start over. Maybe fifty thousand wouldn't last forever, maybe he'd eventually be back in the same bind he was in now; but fifty thousand would buy a lot of time, and somewhere along the route he might pick up another Gaby. Hell, he didn't have to plan all the way to his old age. More important was to enjoy the little bit of youth he had left.

Was there really any choice? Thursday night it had to be.

*　　*　　*

At the convention-opening banquet on Thursday evening, Noel Tasker tried to impress his presence upon as many conventioneers as he possibly could. He slapped backs, pumped hands, told jokes. Also he pretended to drink—but only pretended. He stayed cold-sober.

The dinner dragged on, his nerves frayed, but nobody noticed such details. He hung on grimly. Afterward there were cigars, and much milling about. Then, finally, the time he was waiting for: the chairs and seating arrangements all got a bit confused because the lights went out, a special forty-five-minute film on new developments in the industry. He had forty-five minutes, therefore, of invisibility.

Only a waiter or two could have observed his exit. He didn't use an elevator. He had parked in the street, so no parking attendant was involved. He drove home in twelve minutes. No one, he was fairly certain, observed his arrival in Camelot Court. Now that it was autumn, people stayed indoors, never noticed the comings and goings of their neighbors.

Only Leona welcomed him, rather amazed. She was attired in nightie and robe, with her dyed black hair in curlers—but she smiled at him.

'What are you doing home so early?' she asked.

'It was boring,' he said.

She didn't question that.

He went into the bedroom and disrobed. When he emerged again, stark naked, with one hand, the right hand, the razor hand, behind his back, she did have a question.

'Noel, what on earth?'

He smiled. He shrugged. 'I told you it was boring at the dinner. I thought there might be something more interesting here.' He had to get her off that sofa, to maneuver her into the required position.

'Noel! You've had too much to drink!'

He shook his head.

'A girl must have jumped out of the cake—'

'And gave me ideas? Maybe that was it.' The seconds and minutes were ticking away, and she was playing coy, taking her time. 'How about it, Leona?'

'I just put my hair up...'

'Take it down.'

She slowly placed the bookmark in her book, laid the thing carefully aside—and smiled. 'Noel,' she said. 'You're positively wicked tonight.'

'Yes, I am,' he admitted. 'I'm waiting.'

She rose slowly, ever so slowly. Then she paused, in the very middle of the room, and slowly ... slowly undid the belt of her robe.

'Take it off,' he invited. 'The draperies are closed.' They were. He had made sure of that.

She shrugged out of the robe and stood there, just in the nightie. 'Shall I take this off too?' she asked, simpering.

'Why not?'

She started—and he started to slip around behind her. *How glad I am*, he thought, *that Gaby wasn't raped that night. That would have been a most difficult M.O. to stick to.*

She was halfway out of the nightie—a good situation, he decided impatiently—when he stepped to a position directly behind her, grabbed her hair, curlers and all, pulled upward and backward, and gritting his teeth in a supreme effort of will, pulled the razor across her throat.

Oh, the blood! He hadn't dreamed how far it could spurt, and he hadn't dreamed, either, how powerful a woman Leona was, or how powerful any woman, in the very process of bleeding to death, could be. She lunged sideways, trying to escape. He hung onto her hair. She fell toward the sofa, and he hung on. She grabbed for the coffee table, and he hung on. She reached for a heavy ashtray there, her hands and arms all covered with blood now. She reached for the tray ... for a weapon? He

139

hung on. He weighted her body down with his own. He couldn't allow her to turn on him, couldn't let her swing on him with that tray. He couldn't afford a lump on his head.

Then, when he was afraid she would never, ever succumb, she suddenly sagged. They stayed together for a moment, her head and arms on the table, he riding on her back, her life's blood pouring out, reddening the table, the ashtray, and the floor beneath. Finally—he knew it somehow—she was dead.

He wasted a precious minute, perhaps two, before he could bring himself to the next, and the most difficult, phase of the project. He'd had no appetite at the banquet, had eaten as little as possible, but now he felt ready to vomit. A horrible thought bounded around in his brain; could his vomit be analyzed and compared with the menu served at the banquet?

He rallied. The M.O. Follow it or fail. Impersonate the maniac, or let it look like a rational crime, a husband murdering his wife for a rational motive, fifty thousand dollars.

So he dragged the now inert body away from the table, laid it face up on the floor. Blood still gurgled from the throat wound. The razor was bloody, his own hand was bloody—but he hadn't stepped in the stuff.

He went to work with his eyes closed, then realized he might cut himself, which would never do. Follow the M.O. He'd heard the story about precisely what had happened to Gaby. Maxine Borley, who had discovered Gaby's body, had authored the story, so it had been an eyewitness account. Now, he hoped that Maxine had gotten it straight.

Finally he was finished—except for that one item, the one slight difference in this second crime. The murderer must not leave his fingerprint on the razor. Noel could have worn gloves, of course, but then he would have had to dispose of bloody gloves. No, his way was simpler. Using a corner of Leona's nightie, he rubbed blood off the razor, dropped the weapon into a red pool, then soaked the nightie in the same pool. No crime lab could ever lift a print now off that mess.

Finally, there was himself. Lieutenant Kabrick had been so right. This particular M.O. didn't splash much blood on the murderer. His clothes were in the bedroom, of course. There were no bloody footprints; just hands and arms.

To make totally certain, he took a shower; not a leisurely shower, but thorough, including his hair. The night air would dry it. Afterward, he climbed back into his clothes. When he walked from the bedroom back through the living room, he didn't glance at the body on the floor.

He locked the door as he went out. Nobody saw him return to his car, get in, and drive off. In twelve minutes he reached the hotel. He was

141

even able to park in the same spot he had vacated earlier.

The movie was just ending when he rejoined the conventioneers. Now he drank for real, slapped more backs, pumped more hands, told more jokes than he had before, but he was thinking all the time. He solicited comments about the film, and his obliging companions told him everything about the film he needed to know. Kabrick wasn't going to trick him that way.

It was late when he left the hotel. He didn't really want to leave. He would have preferred to stay there with some of the out-of-town guys, sleep on the floor or something, but he chose to go home, like a faithful, loving husband should.

He drove more slowly this time, taking about twenty minutes. He parked, walked up the path, opened the door with his key. He had left the light on, so he didn't need to flip the switch. There was Leona, lying just where he had left her. Good, faithful, dependable Leona.

He dialed the number of the police, and in a broken voice reported the crime.

*   *   *

Noel Tasker did spend the rest of that night in a hotel, after all, at Lieutenant Kabrick's suggestion, so the police investigation team

142

could have the apartment.

Noel slept fitfully. His emotional condition was no act for the police. He really was in a state almost of shock. Committing the murder had been no easy thing.

The lieutenant found him at the hotel at eleven on Friday morning. He hadn't stirred. The lieutenant knocked, and Noel opened the door willingly.

'Leona had a right to be terrified, didn't she?' he began. 'It was that same maniac, wasn't it?'

The lieutenant shrugged and sidled to a chair. 'Same?' he echoed after he had sat.

Noel stared. 'Wasn't it? I saw the razor.'

'No prints on the razor this time,' Kabrick informed him. Deep inside, invisibly, Noel smiled. *One thing done right.*

'There were bloody prints on the coffee table and on an ashtray though.'

'The killer's?'

'No, your wife's.' The lieutenant glanced up. His eyes were hard, implacable. 'Funny thing. We caught it right away. A print of your wife's, on the table and on the tray, matched the print on the razor in the Marchant apartment.'

Noel sat on the edge of the bed, slowly, carefully. Things were beginning to spin.

'Let's talk, Mr. Tasker,' the lieutenant said. 'We've got a lot of things to talk about. Like maybe how your wife was the one who killed Marchant. And why she killed her. And then, finally, if your wife killed Marchant, who killed your wife? Now, Mr. Tasker, I've got a theory...'

Noel stopped listening. Why, why should Leona have cut Gaby's throat? He couldn't think of a reason—but perhaps it would occur to him later.

THE FOLLOWERS

B. Deal

There were three of them and he was one man alone—and he was carrying money that didn't belong to him. Bryan had first spotted the three men when he got off the bus in the residential section where he lived. They had risen from their seats in the rear and followed him. He had known immediately that they didn't belong there; their habitat was on the other side of town where, during the day, he taught school.

The PTA money was in an envelope in his breast pocket—two hundred and fifty dollars that he had collected as treasurer at the meeting tonight to buy uniforms for the school band. He could feel the envelope weighty with small bills and his heartbeat quickened as he surveyed the danger. It was late, too late, and the street was completely deserted. Here there was light, but they were following. Following and waiting. He walked on, feeling the tremor in his legs, trying to keep his back straight and brave.

Bryan knew them. Not these three individually, but he knew this new and dangerous breed. For six years now, he had tried to penetrate their armor of group indifference and group arrogance. Their hair was draped long and sleek in a ducktail cut and all three wore exactly the same kind of jacket, with identical turned-up collars rubbing the lobes of their ears. The one in the middle was tall, another was heavy and short, and the third was nondescript. But, somehow, they looked and acted like identical triplets. They walked close together in the middle of the sidewalk, their steps an intricate, patterned, off-beat rhythm.

He was afraid. Perhaps they wanted money; perhaps they just wanted the thrill of beating a grown man into the ground. They won't be expecting two hundred and fifty dollars, Bryan thought. When they find that, maybe they'll forget about beating and killing. Maybe that will save me.

But he pushed the thought away. It wasn't his money ... only five dollars of it, that he had contributed to start the collection off tonight. It belonged to people just like him, five dollars here and five dollars there, who had given it into his care because they trusted him.

And not to just those who gave, he thought. It belongs to the kids who have instruments and pride in their band, but no uniforms to go along with the pride they feel. They need those uniforms.

The school band had never been a success. His school was in a poor district and money was scarce. The instruments were battered and worn through years of pawn-shop travel—he

146

knew, for he'd helped to buy them. So the kids hadn't turned out for band, in past years, the way they should. Not until this year. Not until he had stood up in Assembly and promised them that the PTA would provide new and beautiful uniforms.

He quickened his step. All that activity for uniforms had been before he had decided to leave the school, to leave teaching, after this term. But that was just another, more urgent, reason to come through on his promise. It would be the one thing he could leave behind him out of his years of trying. A little pride, a little sense of belonging; he could at least give the kids that, for the first payment on the uniforms rested in his lefthand breast pocket right now.

He wondered why the three followers were delaying; the streets here were lighted, but they were completely still and deserted. Soon he would be home, off the dangerous streets, and he could call the police. He turned at the intersection and crossed the street, seeing from the new-angled vision that they were closer now. If they just waited a few more blocks...

Then he almost stopped in the street, the remembering striking sharp and vital into him. He knew why they were waiting. Just last week he'd read it in the newspaper ... a man had been followed home and held up on his own doorstep just as he turned the key in his lock. They had forced their way into the house, and

147

Bryan remembered the picture of the man's wife and daughter, the horror of shock and violence still in their faces.

They're waiting, he thought, *knowing I'll lead them home*. He made himself keep on walking, the decision agonizing in him, his footsteps dragging into a leaden gait. Sanctuary had been so near for a moment, and now it was so far away. If I turned and went to them, he thought. If I thrust the money into their hands, maybe...

But he wouldn't. He wouldn't go home—and he wouldn't give up the money. I've got to keep going, he thought. I've got to keep walking and keep thinking. For there's no sanctuary, there's no safety except in my own strength and thought.

He had reached the next corner. It took an effort of will to turn his footsteps away from home. But he did it, and he was going down a street he had never traveled in his tight little round between home and school. As he turned, he saw them coming on out of the corner of his eyes, three abreast, moving in a deadly precision of purpose. They were not hurrying to catch him yet; they were still waiting, staying a careful half-block behind him all the way.

In the moment he was out of sight around the corner, he felt a desperate compulsion to run. He steeled his nerves against the desire, keeping his gait down to the same steady plodding as before. I've got to think it out, he told himself grimly, pushing down the smothering fear inside him. They could outrun me within a block, for they're young and strong.

He wished then, wistfully, for the youthful strength he had known as an artillery captain during the war. Then he had been hard and lithe, sure in command and movement. But now he was stocky, with the beginnings of a paunch, and in a block of running, in the sudden pounding turmoil of a fight, his lungs and legs would give out on him, leaving him gasping and helpless.

He walked on, hoping for the sight of a police car. Vividly he could see himself running into the street, flagging it down, and placing himself in their protective custody. That was his only chance now, that or a friendly throng of people. They wouldn't wait and follow forever—soon they would decide he wasn't going home. And then...

He hesitated at the next corner, then turned too quickly in a random direction. It was a mistake, for within another block the street was much darker and the three linked footsteps came closer behind him. There's no escape, he told himself despairingly. The least I can hope for is a beating, then be left lying in an alley somewhere with my face like raw meat and my pockets empty. *And the uniform money gone.*

With the money in his pocket, he should have gone home directly from the PTA meeting. But two of his old buddies from the 89th had called him at school, wanting him to take in a musical, with dinner and a drink afterward. He agreed to go, after the meeting, for they lived out of town and didn't come to the city but once or twice a year.

Plodding on, hoping against hope for a patrol car, people, an open service station, he thought of his old war-time buddies. We were young then, and strong, he thought. And even brave, he added, thinking of the not-too-common medal in his cuff-link box at home. Now I'm middle-aged and too fat around the waist and I know that a man, even with all his trying and desire, can't teach the way he thinks of teaching before he goes into the practice of it.

He was thinking now, not just feeling, and in the movement of his mind his stark fear was briefly submerged. *Surely you've learned something about them, even in your failure.* But suddenly, in the middle of the thinking, his mind whispered an enticing thought: *you can buy them off with the money. You can always try that.*

He listened to the thought this time before pushing it away again with a revulsion of his mind. I'll turn and walk toward them, he told himself. Maybe they'll part and let me through. But he knew immediately the trap could not be escaped so easily. They're so close together, he thought, I could never walk through them. Not ever in this world. I can't break the chains that bind them into a common action, a common purpose. No more than I could in the classroom.

They were not individuals; they were a group, to be described and characterized and thought about only as a group. Group mind, group thought, group body ... only three, he thought. But more than enough...

He knew, then, that he would have to face them. The patrol cars went swiftly and unpredictably about their business. And here in this unfamiliar section he would find no open store or service station where he could enter and be safe. Soon, now, they would tire of following and close in on him.

It was up to him—his own knowledge, his own courage, his own luck. He was a single man, an individual, against the group. And luck and courage were outnumbered, three to one.

He saw the alley ahead of him, on the same side of the street, with the nose of the truck sticking out on the sidewalk where it had been parked for the night. The buildings were tall and dark here, looking like warehouses, and he did not know where he was. At the moment he couldn't have turned and walked straight home.

Nearer the alley now, he saw the truck did not quite fill the space. There was a narrow gap along one side between the truck and the wall, just wide enough for a body to slip through. The look of it triggered a recollection in him, a beating he had seen in the schoolyard once. He knew suddenly now, as he had not known before, that that beating was tied up with his final recognition of failure and his firm decision to leave teaching.

There was one boy, frightened and defiant, in a circle made by the others. His jacket was already torn and his face was bleeding. In the instant of seeing, Bryan had started walking toward the scene to break it up. But he didn't have a chance. His voice, his stern words, were ignored. There was no visible signal. But the entire circled mass closed in at the same instant, responsive to the common radar of the group. When they finished, their victim was a mangled hunk of unconscious flesh.

That same afternoon, alone in his office checking papers, the decision to leave teaching had firmed in his mind. He had known, at last and inevitably, the extent of his failure. He had seen that the teacher is outnumbered in the classroom and, in the cohesiveness of the group he faces, he can penetrate and teach only at their will. Consent was rarely and capriciously given and Bryan knew no way to control it. That wasn't the kind of teaching Bryan had prepared himself to do and so he decided he would quit at the end of the term. He didn't know, yet, what he was going to do; but it would be something that depended on him alone for the results and the success.

He stopped at the truck fender and turned, slowly, looking back at them. They were very near now, but he could not see their faces. Only their three forms bulked large and together in the darkness. They're through waiting for me to lead them home, he thought. He knew it as well as if they had told him. So now I must decide...

He turned and stepped into the alley, squeezing his way past the truck into the darkness. He didn't want to do it. His instinct was to flee blindly toward light and people. Here it was cold and dark and he was alone, and the truck reeked of fish, stirring a knot of nausea in his stomach. He put a trembling hand into his pocket, touching the inadequate penknife. But he drew it out and opened the blade, even knowing the kind of knives they would be carrying.

There was a flurry of movement on the street. 'Hurry,' a voice said. 'He'll be out the other end before we...'

They were squeezing past the truck.

'I'm right here,' Bryan said. 'I'm not running any more.'

He was surprised at the steadiness of his voice. It was strong and clear, without the fear he knew to be in him, and it shocked the three followers, stopping them. He could feel the sudden silence of their surprise.

'You might as well come out, mister,' one of

the voices said. 'Give us your money, and we'll let you go.'

He put his right hand inside his coat, touching the envelope, feeling the heavy wadded weight of the small bills. They were crumpled and grimy and worn from many hands. They had been given to him to hold and to keep, to turn into the new uniforms the band-kids needed because their instruments were so battered and worn.

It was not really a decision. There is no bargaining possible with a group-force; the individual can only fight it. In the same instant of the temptation, he knew that he could not trust them, could not believe in them.

His voice was still steady when he spoke; there had been scarcely a pause between the offer and his answer. 'I'm a schoolteacher,' he said. 'You know I don't have any money.'

It was the right answer—but it was wrong, too. He realized it immediately in the way the voice confronting him changed.

'So you're a teacher,' it said. 'I'm glad you told us that. Come on out!'

'I'm not coming out,' Bryan said. 'You'll have to come in and get me.' He could feel the freezing chill touch his backbone.

They didn't answer. But he could hear their low voices, the scuffle of their feet. He waited, tense in the darkness.

'We're coming in after you, teacher,' another voice said. 'If you don't come out and

154

take it.'

'It's not going to be that easy,' Bryan said. 'Because I'm safe now, as safe as I'd be in my own home.' He stopped, but they did not answer. 'I haven't seen your faces,' he said. 'But I know you. On the street, you'd kill me. But here I'm safe. You know why?'

He waited. There was a shuffle of movement, but that was all.

'Because you must come alone,' he said softly. 'You must come one at a time, between the truck and the wall.' He could hear the sound of his breathing, but his voice was controlled, for he knew the sudden truth and understanding in him that he had never realized through six years of failure at his job. 'And you can't do that. Because there isn't a leader among you. You're all followers and your leader is the common will of the group.' He listened. Silence.

'One of you must make up his individual mind. He's got to come through the darkness and face me alone, just as if he didn't have a gang to back him up.'

He listened, but there was still silence. Nothing but silence. He felt a waver of fear in him, but he quieted it by his confidence. Then he heard a scraping sound behind him and he whirled.

There was a dim light at the far end of the alley and he could see the two figures silhouetted against it as they advanced into the darkness upon him. They're smarter than I thought, his mind groaned. While I talked, two of them ran around the block to the alley entrance behind me. They've trapped me in my own trap. And I must still face them together.

He shrank back against the truck, the useless penknife in his hand. The money wouldn't help now. Even that slim reed of chance was gone. He watched them walk toward him, moving steadily and purposefully, expecting no mercy. Not after they knew he was a teacher; not after the truth he had told them about themselves.

Then he remembered. One was guarding the exit by the truck. Without hesitation he turned and pressed his body between the truck and the wall, pushing toward the sidewalk.

'You out there,' he said. 'I'm coming out. And you're alone. You're all alone.'

He could hear the breathing of the lone boy in front of him. He glanced over his shoulder to check the other two.

'It's me and you,' he said. 'One man against one man. And I'm coming.'

He was almost to the sidewalk before he heard the hasty run of footsteps. He hurried, then, but he was too late; the sidewalk was empty. *He ran away*, Bryan thought with elation. I was right. They can't ever stand alone, for they're only followers.

He turned back toward the alley. 'I'm on this side of the truck again,' he said clearly, his voice challenging. 'Come on. Come on and take me. But you'll have to take me one at a time. Come on.'

He listened. And soon the stillness was so deep that he knew they were gone, that they had been unable to pass through the individual decision of truck and alley wall to reach him.

He stood still on the sidewalk, looking into the dark, deserted alley. I was wrong too, he thought. In school I was wrong. I looked at them, after awhile, only as a group, always as a group, never as they are broken down into individuals. And that's a mistake. That's the biggest mistake of all…

He turned and started walking home. He felt wonderfully free of fear and uncertainty.

NEVER SHAKE A FAMILY TREE

D. E. Westlake

Actually, I have never been so shocked in all my born days, and I seventy-three my last birthday and eleven times a grandmother and twice a great-grandmother. But never in all my born days did I see the like, and that's the truth.

Actually, it all began with my interest in genealogy, which I got from Mrs. Ernestine Simpson, a lady I met at Bay Arbor, in Florida, when I went there three summers ago. I certainly didn't like Florida—far too expensive, if you ask me, and far too bright, and with just too many mosquitoes and other insects to be believed—but I wouldn't say the trip was a total loss, since it did interest me in genealogical research, which is certainly a wonderful hobby, as well as being very valuable, what with one thing and another.

Actually, my genealogical researches had been valuable in more ways than one, since they have also been instrumental in my meeting some very pleasant ladies and gentlemen, although some of them only by postal, and of course it was through this hobby that I met Mr. Gerald Fowlkes in the first place.

But I'm getting far ahead of my story, and

158

ought to begin at the beginning, except that I'm blessed if I know where the beginning actually is. In one way of looking at things, the beginning is my introduction to genealogy through Mrs. Ernestine Simpson, who has since passed on, but in another way the beginning is really almost two hundred years ago, and in still another way the story doesn't really begin until the first time I came across the name of Euphemia Barber.

Well. Actually, I suppose, I really ought to begin by explaining just what genealogical research is. It is the study of one's family tree. One checks marriage and birth and death records, searches old family Bibles and talks to various members of one's family, and one gradually builds up a family tree, showing who fathered whom and what year, and when so-and-so died, and so on. It's really a fascinating work, and there are any number of amateur genealogical societies throughout the country, and when one has one's family tree built up for as far as one wants—seven generations, or nine generations, or however long one wants—then it is possible to write this all up in a folder and bequeath it to the local library, and then there is a *record* of one's family for all time to come, and I for one think that's important and valuable to have even if my youngest boy Tom does laugh at it and say it's just a silly hobby. Well, it *isn't* a silly hobby. After all, I found evidence of murder that way, didn't I?

So, actually, I suppose the whole thing really begins when I first came across the name of Euphemia Barber. Euphemia Barber was John Anderson's second wife. John Anderson was born in Goochland County, Virginia, in 1754. He married Ethel Rita Mary Rayborn in 1777, just around the time of the Revolution, and they had seven children, which wasn't at all strange for that time, though large families have, I notice, gone out of style today, and I for one think it's a shame.

At any rate, it was John and Ethel Anderson's third child, a girl named Prudence, who is in my direct line on my mother's father's side, so of course I had them in my family tree. But then, in going through Appomattox County records—Goochland County being now a part of Appomattox, and no longer a separate county of its own—I came across the name of Euphemia Barber. It seems that Ethel Anderson died in 1793, in giving birth to her eighth child—who also died—and three years later, 1796, John Anderson remarried, this time marrying a widow named Euphemia Barber. At that time, he was forty-two years of age, and her age was given as thirty-nine.

Of course, Euphemia Barber was not at all in my direct line, being John Anderson's second wife, but I was interested to some extent in her pedigree as well, wanting to add her parents' names and her place of birth to my family chart, and also because there were some

160

Barbers fairly distantly related on my father's mother's side, and I was wondering if this Euphemia might be kin to them. But the records were very incomplete, and all I could learn was that Euphemia Barber was not a native of Virginia, and had apparently only been in the area for a year or two when she had married John Anderson. Shortly after John's death in 1798, two years after their marriage, she had sold the Anderson farm, which was apparently a somewhat prosperous location, and had moved away again. So that I had neither birth nor death records on her, nor any record of her first husband, whose last name had apparently been Barber, but only the one lone record of her marriage to my great-great-great-great-great-grandfather on my mother's father's side.

Actually, there was no reason for me to pursue the question further, since Euphemia Barber wasn't in my direct line anyway, but I had worked diligently and, I think, well, on my family tree, and had it almost complete back nine generations, and there was really very little left to do with it, so I was glad to do some tracking down.

Which is why I included Euphemia Barber in my next entry in the Genealogical Exchange. Now, I suppose I ought to explain what the Genealogical Exchange is. There are any number of people throughout the country who are amateur genealogists, concerned primarily with their own family trees, but of course family trees do interlock, and any one of these people is liable to know about just the one record which has been eluding some other searcher for months. And so there are magazines devoted to the exchanging of some information, for nominal fees. In the last few years, I had picked up all sorts of valuable leads in this way. And so my entry in the summer issue of the Genealogical Exchange read:

BUCKLEY, Mrs. Henrietta Rhodes, 119A Newbury St., Boston, Mass. Xch data on *Rhodes, Anderson, Richards, Pryor, Marshall, Lord.* Want any info Euphemia *Barber*, m. John Anderson, Va. 1796.

Well. The Genealogical Exchange had been helpful to me in the past, but I never received anywhere near the response caused by Euphemia Barber. And the first response of all came from Mr. Gerald Fowlkes.

It was a scant two days after I received my own copy of the summer issue of the Exchange. I was still poring over it myself, looking for people who might be linked to various branches of my family tree, when the telephone rang. Actually, I suppose I was somewhat irked at being taken from my studies, and perhaps I sounded a bit impatient when I answered.

162

If so, the gentleman at the other end gave no sign of it. His voice was most pleasant, quite deep and masculine, and he said, 'May I speak, please, with Mrs. Henrietta Buckley?'

'This is Mrs. Buckley,' I told him.

'Ah,' he said. 'Forgive my telephoning, please, Mrs. Buckley. We have never met. But I noticed your entry in the current issue of the Genealogical Exchange—'

'Oh?'

I was immediately excited, all thought of impatience gone. This was surely the fastest reply I'd ever had to date!

'Yes,' he said. 'I noticed the reference to Euphemia Barber. I do believe that may be the Euphemia Stover who married Jason Barber in Savannah, Georgia, in 1791. Jason Barber is in my direct line, on my mother's side. Jason and Euphemia had only the one child, Abner, and I am descended from him.'

'Well,' I said. 'You certainly do seem to have complete information.'

'Oh, yes,' he said. 'My own family chart is almost complete. For twelve generations, that is. I'm not sure whether I'll try to go back farther than that or not. The English records before 1600 are so incomplete, you know.'

'Yes, of course,' I said. I was, I admit, taken aback. Twelve generations! Surely that was the most ambitious family tree I had ever heard of, though I had read sometimes of people who had carried particular branches back as many

163

as fifteen generations. But to actually be speaking to a person who had traced his entire family back twelve generations!

'Perhaps,' he said, 'it would be possible for us to meet, and I could give you the information I have on Euphemia Barber. There are also some Marshalls in one branch of my family; perhaps I can be of help to you there, as well.' He laughed, a deep and pleasant sound, which reminded me of my late husband, Edward, when he was most particularly pleased. 'And, of course,' he said, 'there is always the chance that you may have some information on the Marshalls which can help me.'

'I think that would be very nice,' I said, and so I invited him to come to the apartment the very next afternoon.

At one point the next day, perhaps half an hour before Gerald Fowlkes was to arrive, I stopped my fluttering around to take stock of myself and to realize that if ever there were an indication of second childhood taking over, my thoughts and actions preparatory to Mr. Fowlkes' arrival were certainly it. I had been rushing hither and thither, dusting, rearranging, polishing, pausing incessantly to look in the mirror and touch my hair with fluttering fingers, all as though I were a flighty teen-ager before her very first date. 'Henrietta,' I told myself sharply, 'you are seventy-three years old, and all that nonsense is well behind you now. Eleven times a grandmother, and just look at how you carry on!'

But poor Edward had been dead and gone these past nine years, my brothers and sisters were all in their graves, and as for my children, all but Tom, the youngest, were thousands of miles away, living their own lives—as of course they should—and only occasionally remembering to write a duty letter to Mother. And I am much too aware of the dangers of the clinging mother to force my presence too often upon Tom and his family. So I am very much alone, except of course for my friends in the various church activities and for those I have met, albeit only by postal, through my genealogical research.

So it *was* pleasant to be visited by a charming gentleman caller, and particularly so when that gentleman shared my own particular interests.

And Mr. Gerald Fowlkes, on his arrival, was surely no disappointment. He looked to be no more than fifty-five years of age, though he swore to sixty-two, and had a fine shock of gray hair above a strong and kindly face. He dressed very well, with that combination of expense and breeding so little found these days, when the well-bred seem invariably to be poor and the well-to-do seem invariably to be horribly plebeian. His manner was refined and gentlemanly, what we used to call courtly, and he had some very nice things to say about the appearance of my living room.

Actually, I make no unusual claims as a housekeeper. Living alone, and with quite a comfortable income having been left me by Edward, it is no problem at all to choose tasteful furnishings and keep them neat. (Besides, I had scrubbed the apartment from top to bottom in preparation for Mr. Fowlkes' visit.)

He had brought his pedigree along, and what a really beautiful job he had done. Pedigree charts, photostats of all sorts of records, a running history typed very neatly on bond paper and inserted in a loose-leaf notebook—all in all, the kind of careful, planned, well-thought-out perfection so unsuccessfully striven for by all amateur genealogists.

From Mr. Fowlkes, I got the missing information on Euphemia Barber. She was born in 1765, in Salem, Massachusetts, the fourth child of seven born to John and Alicia Stover. She married Jason Barber in Savannah in 1791. Jason, a well-to-do merchant, passed on in 1794, shortly after the birth of their first child, Abner. Abner was brought up by his paternal grandparents, and Euphemia moved away from Savannah. As I already knew, she had then gone to Virginia, where she had married John Anderson. After that, Mr. Fowlkes had no record of her, until her death in Cincinnati, Ohio, in 1852. She was buried as Euphemia Stover Barber, apparently not having used the Anderson name after John Anderson's death.

This done, we went on to compare family histories and discover an Alan Marshall of Liverpool, England, around 1680, common to both trees. I was able to give Mr. Fowlkes Alan Marshall's birth date. And then the specific purpose of our meeting was finished. I offered tea and cakes, it then being four-thirty in the afternoon, and Mr. Fowlkes graciously accepted my offering.

And so began the strangest three months of my entire life. Before leaving, Mr. Fowlkes asked me to accompany him to a concert on Friday evening, and I very readily agreed. Then, and afterward, he was a perfect gentleman.

It didn't take me long to realize that I was being courted. Actually, I couldn't believe it at first. After all, at *my* age! But I myself did know some very nice couples who had married late in life—a widow and a widower, both lonely, sharing interests, and deciding to lighten their remaining years together—and looked at in that light it wasn't at all as ridiculous as it might appear at first.

Actually, I had expected my son Tom to laugh at the idea, and to dislike Mr. Fowlkes instantly upon meeting him. I suppose various fictional works that I have read had given me this expectation. So I was most pleasantly surprised when Tom and Mr. Fowlkes got along famously together from their very first meeting, and even more surprised when Tom came to me and told me Mr. Fowlkes had asked him if he would have any objection to his, Mr. Fowlkes', asking for my hand in matrimony. Tom said he had no objection at all, but actually thought it a wonderful idea, for he knew that both Mr. Fowlkes and myself were rather lonely, with nothing but our genealogical hobbies to occupy our minds.

As to Mr. Fowlkes' background, he very early gave me his entire history. He came from a fairly well-to-do family in upstate New York, and was himself now retired from his business, which had been a stock brokerage in Albany. He was a widower these last six years, and his first marriage had not been blessed with any children, so that he was completely alone in the world.

The next three months were certainly active ones. Mr. Fowlkes—Gerald—squired me everywhere, to concerts and to museums and even, after we had come to know one another well enough, to the theater. He was at all times most polite and thoughtful, and there was scarcely a day went by but what we were together.

During this entire time, of course, my own genealogical researches came to an absolute standstill. I was much too busy, and my mind was much too full of Gerald, for me to concern myself with family members who were long since gone to their rewards. Promising leads from the Genealogical Exchange were not followed up, for I didn't write a single letter. And though I did receive many in the Exchange, they all went unopened into a cubbyhole in my desk. And so the matter stayed, while the courtship progressed.

After three months, Gerald at last proposed. 'I am not a young man, Henrietta,' he said. 'Nor a particularly handsome man—' though he most certainly was very handsome, indeed '—nor even a very rich man, although I do have sufficient for my declining years. And I have little to offer you, Henrietta, save my own self, whatever poor companionship I can give you, and the assurance that I will be ever at your side.'

What a beautiful proposal! After being nine years a widow, and never expecting even in fanciful daydreams to be once more a wife, what a beautiful proposal and from what a charming gentleman!

I agreed at once, of course, and telephoned Tom the good news that very minute. Tom and his wife, Estelle, had a dinner party for us, and then we made our plans. We would be married three weeks hence. A short time? Yes, of course, it was, but there was really no reason to wait. And we would honeymoon in Washington, D.C., where my oldest boy, Roger, has quite a responsible position with the State Department. After which, we would return to Boston and take up our residence in a lovely old home on Beacon Hill, which was then for sale and which we would jointly purchase.

Ah, the plans! The preparations! How newly filled were my so-recently empty days!

I spent most of the last week closing my apartment on Newbury Street. The furnishings would be moved to our new home by Tom, while Gerald and I were in Washington. But, of course, there was ever so much packing to be done, and I got at it with a will.

And so at last I came to my desk, and my genealogical researches lying as I had left them. I sat down at the desk, somewhat weary, for it was late afternoon and I had been hard at work since sun-up, and I decided to spend a short while getting my papers into order before packing them away. And so I opened the mail which had accumulated over the last three months.

There were twenty-three letters. Twelve asked for information on various family names mentioned in my entry in the Exchange, five offered to give me information, and six concerned Euphemia Barber. It was, after all, Euphemia Barber who had brought Gerald and I together in the first place, and so I took time out to read these letters.

And so came the shock. I read the six letters, and then I simply sat limp at the desk, staring into space, and watched the monstrous pattern

170

as it grew in my mind. For there was no question of the truth, no question at all.

Consider: Before starting the letters, this is what I knew of Euphemia Barber: She had been born Euphemia Stover in Salem, Massachusetts, in 1765. In 1791, she married Jason Barber, a widower of Savannah, Georgia. Jason died two years later, in 1793, of a stomach upset. Three years later, Euphemia appeared in Virginia and married John Anderson, also a widower. John died two years thereafter, in 1798, of stomach upset. In both cases, Euphemia sold her late husband's property and moved on.

And here is what the letters added to that, in chronological order:

From Mrs. Winnie Mae Cuthbert, Dallas, Texas: Euphemia Barber, in 1800, two years after John Anderson's death, appeared in Harrisburg, Pennsylvania, and married one Andrew Cuthbert, a widower and a prosperous feed merchant. Andrew died in 1801, of a stomach upset. The widow sold his store, and moved on.

From Miss Ethel Sutton, Louisville, Kentucky: Euphemia Barber, in 1804, married Samuel Nicholson of Louisville, a widower and a well-to-do tobacco farmer. Samuel Nicholson passed on in 1807, of a stomach upset. The widow sold his farm, and moved on.

From Mrs. Isabelle Padgett, Concord, California: in 1808, Euphemia Barber married

Thomas Norton, then Mayor of Dover, New Jersey, and a widower. In 1809, Thomas Norton died of a stomach upset.

From Mrs. Luella Miller, Bicknell, Utah: Euphemia Barber married Jonas Miller, a wealthy shipowner of Portsmouth, New Hampshire, a widower, in 1811. The same year, Jonas Miller died of a stomach upset. The widow sold his property and moved on.

From Mrs. Lola Hopkins, Vancouver, Washington: In 1813, in southern Indiana, Euphemia Barber married Edward Hopkins, a widower and a farmer. Edward Hopkins died in 1816, of a stomach upset. The widow sold the farm, and moved on.

From Mr. Roy Cumbie, Kansas City, Missouri: In 1819, Euphemia Barber married Stanley Thatcher of Kansas City, Missouri, a river barge owner and a widower. Stanley Thatcher died, of a stomach upset, in 1821. The widow sold his property, and moved on.

The evidence was clear, and complete. The intervals of time without dates could mean that there had been other widowers who had succumbed to Euphemia Barber's fatal charms, and whose descendants did not number among themselves an amateur genealogist. Who could tell just how many husbands Euphemia had murdered? For murder it quite clearly was, brutal murder, for profit. I had evidence of eight murders, and who knew but what there were eight more, or

172

eighteen more? Who could tell, at this late date, just how many times Euphemia Barber had murdered for profit, and had never been caught?

Such a woman is inconceivable. Her husbands were always widowers, sure to be lonely, sure to be susceptible to a wily woman. She preyed on widowers, and left them all a widow.

Gerald.

The thought came to me, and I pushed it firmly away. It couldn't possibly be true; it couldn't possibly have a single grain of truth.

But what did I know of Gerald Fowlkes, other than what he had told me? And wasn't I a widow, lonely and susceptible? And wasn't I financially well off?

Like father, like son, they say. Could it be also, like great-great-great-great-great-grandmother, like great-great-great-great-great-grandson?

What a thought! It came to me that there must be any number of widows in the country, like myself, who were interested in tracing their family trees. Women who had a bit of money and leisure, whose children were grown and gone out into the world to live their own lives, and who filled some of the empty hours with the hobby of genealogy. An unscrupulous man, preying on well-to-do widows, could find no better introduction than a common interest in genealogy.

173

What a terrible thought to have about Gerald! And yet, I couldn't push it from my mind, and at last I decided that the only thing I could possibly do was try to substantiate the autobiography he had given me, for if he had told the truth about himself, then he could surely not be a beast of the type I was imagining.

A stockbroker, he had claimed to have been, in Albany, New York. I at once telephoned an old friend of my first husband's, who was himself a Boston stockbroker, and asked him if it would be possible for him to find out if there had been, at any time in the last fifteen or twenty years, an Albany stockbroker named Gerald Fowlkes. He said he could do so with ease, using some sort of directory he had, and would call me back. He did so, with the shattering news that no such individual was listed!

Still I refused to believe. Donning my coat and hat, I left the apartment at once and went directly to the telephone company, where, after an incredible number of white lies concerning genealogical research, I at last persuaded someone to search for an old Albany, New York telephone book. I knew that the main office of the company kept books for other major cities, as a convenience for the public, but I wasn't sure they would have any from past years. Nor was the clerk I talked to, but at last she did go and search, and came back finally with the 1946 telephone book from Albany, dusty and somewhat ripped, but still intact, with both the normal listings and the yellow pages.

No Gerald Fowlkes was listed in the white pages, or in the yellow pages under Stocks & Bonds.

So. It was true. And I could see exactly what Gerald's method was. Whenever he was ready to find another victim, he searched one or another of the genealogical magazines until he found someone who shared one of his own past relations. He then proceeded to effect a meeting with that person, found out quickly enough whether or not the intended victim was a widow, of the proper age range, and with the properly large bank account, and then the courtship began.

I imagined that this was the first time he had made the mistake of using Euphemia Barber as the go-between. And I doubted that he even realized he was following in Euphemia's footsteps. Certainly, none of the six people who had written to me about Euphemia could possibly guess, knowing only of one marriage and death, what Euphemia's role in life had actually been.

And what was I to do now? In the taxi, on the way back to my apartment, I sat huddled in a corner, and tried to think.

For this *was* a severe shock, and a terrible disappointment. And could I face Tom, or my other children, or any one of my friends, to whom I had already written the glad news of my impending marriage? And how could I return to the drabness of my days before Gerald had come to bring gaiety and companionship and courtly grace to my days?

Could I even call the police? I was sufficiently convinced myself, but could I possibly convince anyone else?

All at once, I made my decision. And, having made it, I immediately felt ten years younger, ten pounds lighter, and quite a bit less foolish. For, I might as well admit, in addition to everything else, this had been a terrible blow to my pride.

But the decision was made, and I returned to my apartment cheerful and happy.

* * *

And so we were married.

Married? Of course. Why not?

Because he will try to murder me? Well, of course, he *will* try to murder me. As a matter of fact, he has already tried, half a dozen times.

But Gerald is working at a terrible disadvantage. For he cannot murder me in any way that looks like murder. It must appear to be a natural death, or, at the very worst, an accident. Which means that he must be devious, and he must plot and plan, and never come at me openly to do me in.

176

And there is the source of his disadvantage. For I am forewarned, and forewarned is forearmed.

But what, really, do I have to lose? At seventy-three, how many days on this earth do I have left? And how *rich* life is these days! How rich compared to my life before Gerald came into it! Spiced with the thrill of danger, the excitement of cat and mouse, the intricate moves and countermoves of the most fascinating game of all.

And, of course, a pleasant and charming husband. Gerald *has* to be pleasant and charming. He can never disagree with me, at least not very forcefully, for he can't afford the danger of my leaving him. Nor can he afford to believe that I suspect him. I have never spoken of the matter to him, and so far as he is concerned I know nothing. We go to concerts and museums and the theater together. Gerald is attentive and gentlemanly, quite the best sort of companion at all times.

Of course, I can't allow him to feed me breakfast in bed, as he would so love to do. No, I told him I was an old-fashioned woman, and believed that cooking was a woman's job, and so I won't let him near the kitchen. Poor Gerald!

And we don't take trips, no matter how much he suggests them.

And we've closed off the second story of our home, since I pointed out that the first floor

177

was certainly spacious enough for just the two of us, and I felt I was getting a little old for climbing stairs. He could do nothing, of course, but agree.

And, in the meantime, I have found another hobby, though of course Gerald knows nothing of it. Through discreet inquiries, and careful perusal of past issues of the various genealogical magazines, the use of the family names in Gerald's family tree, I am gradually compiling another sort of tree. Not a family tree, no. One might facetiously call it a hanging tree. It is a list of Gerald's wives. It is in with my genealogical files, which I have willed to the Boston library. Should Gerald manage to catch me after all, what a surprise is in store for the librarian who sorts out those files of mine! Not as big as surprise as the one in store for Gerald, of course.

Ah, here comes Gerald now, in the automobile he bought last week. He's going to ask me again to go for a ride with him.

But I shan't go.

HERE LIES ANOTHER BLACKMAILER

B. Pronzini

My Uncle Walter studied me across the massive oak desk in his library, looking at once irascible, anxious and a little fearful. 'I have some questions to ask you, Harold,' he said at length, 'and I want truthful answers, do you understand?'

'I am not in the habit of lying,' I lied stiffly.

'No? To my mind your behaviour has always left much to be desired, and has been downright suspect at times. But that is not the issue at hand, except indirectly. The issue at hand is this: where were you at eleven-forty last evening?'

'At eleven-forty? I was in bed, of course.'

'You were not,' my uncle said sharply. 'Elsie saw you going downstairs at five minutes of eleven, fully dressed; she told me about it when I questioned her this morning.'

Elsie was the family maid, and much too nosy for her own good. She was also the only person who lived on this small estate except for myself, Uncle Walter, and Aunt Pearl. I frowned and said, 'I remember now. I went for a walk.'

'At eleven P.M.?'

'I couldn't sleep and I thought the fresh air

might help.'

'Where did you go on this walk?'

'Oh, here and there. Just walking, you know.'

'Did you leave the grounds?'

'Not that I recall.'

'Did you go out by the old carriage house?'

'No,' I lied.

My uncle was making an obvious effort to conceal his impatience. 'You *were* out by the old carriage house, weren't you?'

'I've already said I wasn't.'

'I saw you there, Harold. At least, I'm fairly certain I did. You were lurking in the oleander bushes.'

'I do not lurk in bushes,' I lied.

'*Somebody* was lurking in the bushes, and it couldn't possibly have been anyone but you. Elsie and Aunt Pearl were both here in the house.'

'May I ask a question?'

'What is it?'

'What were *you* doing out by the old carriage house at eleven-forty last night?'

Uncle Walter's face had begun to take on the unpleasant color of raw calf's liver. 'What I was doing there is of no consequence. I want to know why you were there, and what you might have seen and heard.'

'Was there something to see and hear, Uncle?'

'No, of course not. I just want to know—

180

Look here, Harold, what did you see and hear from those bushes?'

'I wasn't *in* them in the first place, so I couldn't have seen or heard anything, could I?'

Uncle Walter stood abruptly and began to pace the room, his hands folded behind his back. He looked like a pompous old lawyer, which is precisely what he was. Finally he came over to stand in front of my chair, glaring down at me. 'You were not out by the carriage house at eleven-forty last night? You did not see anything and you did not hear anything at any time during your alleged walk?'

'No,' I lied.

'I have no recourse but to accept your word, then. Actually it doesn't matter whether you were there or not, in one sense, because you refuse to admit it. I trust you will continue to refuse to admit it, to me and to anyone else.'

'I don't believe I follow that, Uncle.'

'You don't have to follow it. Very well, Harold, that's all.'

I stood up and left the library and went out to the sun porch at the rear of the house. When I was certain neither Elsie nor Aunt Pearl was about, and that my uncle had not chosen to pursue me surreptitiously, I slipped out and hurried through the landscaped grounds to the old carriage house. The oleander bushes, where I had been lurking at eleven-forty the previous night after following Uncle Walter from the house—I *had* gone for a short walk, and had noticed him sneaking out—were located along the southern wall of the building. I passed along parallel to them and around to the back, to the approximate spot where my uncle had stood talking to the man whom he had met there. They had spoken in low tones, of course, but in the late-evening summer stillness I had been able to hear every word. I had also been able to hear the muffled report which had abruptly terminated their conversation.

Now, what, I wondered, glancing around, *did Uncle Walter do with the body?*

The gunshot had startled me somewhat, and I had involuntarily rustled the bushes and therefore been forced to run when my uncle came quickly to investigate. I had then hidden behind one of the privet hedges until I was certain he did not intend to search for me. Minutes later I slipped around by the carriage house again; but I had not been able to locate my uncle and I had not wanted to chance discovery by prowling through the darkness. So I returned to the privet hedge and waited, and twenty-five minutes later Uncle Walter had appeared and gone directly back to the house.

A half hour or so is really not very much time in which to hide a dead man, so I found the body quite easily. It was haphazardly concealed among several tall eucalyptus trees some sixty yards from the carriage house, covered with leaves and strips of aromatic bark which regularly peels from the trees. A rather unimaginative hiding place, to be sure, although it was no doubt intended to be temporary. Uncle Walter had obviously given no prior consideration to body disposal, and had therefore hidden the corpse here until he could think of something more permanent to do with it. If he arrived at a decision by this evening, he would then, I reasoned, return here for the purpose of removal and ultimate secretion.

I uncovered the dead man and studied him for a moment. He was small and slender, with sharp features and close-set eyes. In the same way my uncle looked exactly like what he was, so did this person look like what *he* was, or had been—a criminal, naturally. In his case, a blackmailer—and not at all a clever or cautious one, to have allowed Uncle Walter to talk him into the time and place of last night's rendezvous. What excuse had my uncle given him for the unconventionality of it all? Well, no matter. The man really had been quite stupid to have accepted such terms under any circumstances, and was now quite dead as a result.

Yet Uncle Walter was equally as stupid: first, to have put himself in a position where he could be blackmailed; and second, to have perpetrated a carelessly planned and executed homicide on his own property. My uncle, however, was impulsive, and much less bright than he seemed to most people. He also apparently had a predilection for beautiful blonde show girls, about which my Aunt Pearl knew nothing, and about which I also had known nothing until overhearing last evening's conversation. This was the reason he had been blackmailed. He had committed murder because the extortionist wanted considerably more money than he had been getting for his continued silence—and Uncle Walter was a notoriously tightfisted man.

It took me the better part of two hours to move the body. I am not particularly strong, and even though the dead man was small and relatively light, it was a physical struggle to which I am not accustomed. At last, however, I had secreted the blackmailer's remains in what I considered to be quite a clever hiding place—one that was not even on my uncle's property.

Across the dry creek which formed the rear boundary line was a grove of densely-grown trees, and well into them I found a large decaying log, all that was left of a long-dead tree felled by insects or disease. At first glance it seemed to be solid, but upon careful inspection I discovered that it was for the most part hollow. I dragged the body to the log and managed to stuff it inside; then I carefully covered all traces of the entombment. No one venturing into this grove, including my unimaginative uncle, would think of investigating a seemingly solid log.

Satisfied, I returned unobserved to the house, had a bath, and spent the remainder of the day reading in my room.

Uncle Walter was apoplectic. 'What did you do with it?' he shouted at me. 'What did you *do* with it?'

I looked at him innocently across his desk. It was shortly past eight the following morning, and he had summoned me from my room with furious poundings on the door. I was still in my robe and slippers.

'What did I do with what?' I asked.

'You know what!'

'I'm afraid I don't, Uncle.'

'I know it was you, Harold, just as I knew all along it was you in the oleander bushes two nights ago. So you heard and saw everything, did you? Well, go ahead—admit it.'

'I have nothing to admit.'

He slapped the desk top angrily with the palm of one hand. '*Why* did you move it? That's what I fail to comprehend. Why, Harold? Why did you move it?'

'The conversation seems to be going around in circles,' I said. 'I really don't know what you're talking about, Uncle.'

'Of course you know what I'm talking about! Harold—what did you do with it?'

'With what?'

'You know—' He caught himself, and his face was an interesting color bordering on mauve. 'Why do you persist in lying to me? What are you up to?'

'I'm not up to anything,' I lied.

'Harold...'

'If you're finished with me, I would like to get dressed. This may be the middle of summer, but it's rather chilly in here.'

'Yes, get dressed. And then you're coming with me.'

'Where are we going?'

'Out to look for it. I want you along.'

'What are we going to look for?'

He glared at me malevolently. 'I'll find it,' he said. 'You can't have moved it far. I *will* find it, Harold!'

Of course he didn't.

*   *   *

I knocked on the library door late that evening and stepped inside. Uncle Walter was sitting at his desk, holding his head as if it pained him greatly; his face was gray, and I saw that there were heavy pouches under his eyes. The time, it seemed, was exactly right.

When he saw me, the gray pallor modulated into crimson. He certainly did change color often, like a chameleon. 'You,' he said. 'You!'

'Are you feeling all right, Uncle? You don't look very well at all.'

'If you weren't a relative of mine, if you weren't—Oh, what's the use? Harold, look,

186

just tell me what you did with it. I just want to know that it's ... safe. Do you understand?'

'Not really,' I said. I looked at him steadily. 'But I seem to have the feeling that whatever it is you were looking for today *is* safe.'

He brightened. 'Are you sure?'

'One can never be sure about anything, can one?'

'What does that mean?'

I sat down and said seriously, 'You know, Uncle, I've been thinking. My monthly allowance is really rather small, and I wonder if you could see your way clear to raising it.'

His hands gripped the edge of his desk. 'So that's it.'

'What's it?'

'What you're up to, why you keep lying to me and why you moved the ... *it*. All I've done is trade one blackmailer for another, and my own nephew at that!'

'Blackmailer?' I managed to look shocked. 'What a terrible thing to say, Uncle. I'm only asking politely for an increase in my monthly allowance. That's not the same thing at all, is it?'

His face took on a thoughtful expression, and he calmed down considerably. 'No,' he said. 'No, it isn't. Of course not. Very well, then, you shall have your increase. Now, where is it?'

'Where is what?' I asked.

'Now look here—'

187

'I still don't know what it is you're talking about,' I said. 'But then, if I weren't to get my increase—or if I were to get it and it should suddenly be revoked—I suppose I could find out easily enough what is going on. I could talk to Aunt Pearl, or even to the police...'

My uncle sighed resignedly. 'You've made your point, Harold. I suppose the only important thing is that ... *it* is safe, and you've already told me that much, haven't you? Well, how much of an increase do you want?'

'Triple the present sum, I think.'

'One hundred and fifty dollars a month?'

'Yes.'

'What are you going to do with that much money? You're only eleven years old!'

'I'll think of something, Uncle. I'm very clever, you know.'

He closed his eyes. 'All right, consider your allowance tripled, but you're never to request a single penny more. Not a single penny, Harold.'

'Oh, I won't—not a single penny,' I lied, and smiled inwardly. Unlike most everyone else of my age, I knew just exactly what I was going to be when I grew up...

THE MISSING TATTOO

C. Matthews

The carnie night was a kaleidoscope of psychedelic colors and a riot of sound, the whoosh of the rides, the braying voices of concession-joint men and sideshow barkers, and over and under it all the merry tinkle of the merry-go-round calliope.

Bernie Mather, the front talker for the Ten-in-One freak show, was just beginning his bally, beating on a gong to attract attention, his voice pouring into the hand mike. 'Hi, lookee, hi, lookee! Gather down close, folks, for a free show. Hi, lookee, this is where the freaks are!'

I stood on the edge of the gathering crowd before the freak show bally platform. It was going to be a big tip. Montana's Wonder Shows was playing at a fair, and the crowds were satisfactorily large along the midway.

A passing carnie tapped me on the shoulder. 'Hi, Patch. I see you're still with it.'

'Yeah, I'm still with it.'

That's me—Patch. Real name, Dave Cole, but to everybody on the Montana carnival I was Patch. To a carnie, a patch is exactly what the name implies. A fixer, the guy who greases the local fuzz, if grease is needed, to allow the games to operate openly and to permit the broads in the girlie shows to strip down to the buff. Oddly enough, considering the insular carnie world's dislike of any and all fuzz, I also operated as a sort of law on the lot, keeping the peace, seeing that the game agents didn't get too greedy, arbitrating disputes, whatever. In short, a carnie patch is a troubleshooter. In some ways I had more power around the carnie than Tex Montana, the owner, who paid my salary.

In fact, Kay Foster, the cook-tent cashier, had once accused me of just that. 'You know why you stay a carnie, Dave, when you could probably set up a private law practice somewhere? You like the power you have here. Big frog in a little puddle.'

Kay and I had a mild thing going, and she hated carnie life. I had practiced law briefly some years back, had run into a spot of trouble, not enough to get me disbarred but close to it.

Anyway, Kay thought I should marry her, quit the carnie and return to being a townie. I was willing to marry her, but wasn't yet prepared for the other. I resented the frog-in-the-puddle crack. I enjoyed the life of a carnie, and the job I had. It had its compensations.

I noticed that Bernie had spotted me in the crowd. He winked and turned with a flourish of his cane.

'All right, folks, I'm going to bring out the

freaks now, give you a free sample of what you will see inside for the small price of an admission ticket!'

The freak show had ten acts. For each pitch Bernie brought out three freaks, usually different ones. Those that were mobile, that is. Sally, the Fat Lady, for instance, weighed in the neighborhood of seven hundred pounds, and it would have taken a hoist to get her onto the bally platform.

This time Bernie brought out Sam, the Anatomical Marvel, Dirk, the Sword Swallower, and May, the Tattooed Lady. Some freaks are natural, born that way, others are gimmicked. The Anatomical Marvel was natural, the Sword Swallower gimmicked, and May would have to be placed somewhere in between. I had been with Montana's Wonder Shows for three seasons and had made myself familiar with all the carnies, the Ten-in-One freaks included, but I was still fascinated by May's tattoos. Bernie, who'd been a freak show operator for twenty years, once told me she had the most thoroughly tattooed body he'd ever seen. Bernie was also the inside talker during each performance, so May was right under his nose, in a manner of speaking.

May was thirty, give or take, and had a lovely face. That was all you could see of her on the bally platform. She wore a long robe covering her from neck to toe. I'd seen her on exhibition inside any number of times, wearing

191

briefs and a halter. The rest of her, every visible inch, was covered with marvelously designed tattoos, like a painting you have to study a long time to get its full meaning. Religious sketches, hunting scenes, profiles of famous men, the American flag, and across her abdomen sailed a two-masted schooner, which she could cause to pitch and toss with contortions of her stomach.

Wise old Bernie only tantalized with May now, flicking at the folds of her robe with the tip of his cane and giving the crowd a teasing peek at a leg tattooed up out of sight.

As I walked away, Bernie had already turned away from May and was pointing at double-jointed Sam, the Anatomical Marvel, who also knew just how much exposure a bally called for. He waggled each ear in a different direction and held one hand straight out while he rotated each finger separately.

It was close to midnight now, and the crowd was beginning to thin out as I strolled to the cook tent. The people remaining were mostly clotted around the show tents as the talkers did their last bally of the night.

The cook tent was beginning to fill up as some carnies had already packed it in for the night. At the cash register Kay was busy, so I flipped a hand at her and went on back for coffee and a midnight sandwich.

I took my time, having a second cup of coffee, waiting for all the shows and rides to close down, so I could prowl the midway and see that it was buttoned up for the night. It wasn't my job to do guard duty—we had two night men for that—but I liked to check things out for myself.

Soon, everything was closed but the cook tent. Many of the carnies lived in house trailers or tents on the lot and could cook there, but most of them came to the cook tent to lie about their night's grosses. I was about to get up and start my tour of inspection when I saw a man I recognized as a canvasman from the Ten-in-One hurrying toward my table. 'Patch, Bernie needs you right away!'

I stood up. 'What's the trouble?'

'It's May. She's dead!'

'Dead?'

'Murdered, looks like!'

I remembered where I was and glanced around, but it was too late. Those close to me had fallen silent, and I knew they'd overheard. The word would spread like a tent blaze. I waved the canvasman quiet and hustled him out.

We hurried toward the Ten-in-One, feet crunching in the fresh wood shavings already spread along the midway for tomorrow's crowds. The midway was deserted now, all the lights off except a string of bulbs down the center. The concession tent flaps were down, like greedy mouths satiated and closed, and the rides were still, like monsters of various shapes and sizes slumbering under their night hoods.

Bernie was waiting for me in front of the show tent. A slender, dapper man of indeterminate age, he leaned against the ticket box, a glowing pipe stuck in a face as narrow as an ax blade.

'What's happened, Bernie? Somebody kill May?' I asked.

'I can't see what else,' he said in his raspy voice. 'We turned a small tip for the last show and May said she had to ... Well, she had something to do, so I told her to go ahead, the marks wouldn't miss one tattooed lady. After we sloughed it for the night, I went back to her trailer. The lights were on, but she didn't answer my knock. I found the door wasn't locked, so I opened it and went in. May was lying there, a knife in her back.'

'Was the knife from Dirk's trunk?'

Bernie looked startled, at least as startled as he ever looked. 'You know, I never thought of that, but it could be, it just could be.'

I was silent for a moment, thinking. Before becoming a sword swallower, Dirk had had a knife-throwing act and May, before she'd been tattooed, had been his assistant. Knife-throwing acts are old hat, not much in demand anymore, so Dirk stopped throwing knives and started swallowing them, and May got tattooed. What was giving me pause for thought was a memory surfacing. Dirk and May had also once had a thing going, a

194

romance that had dissolved when May met Vernon Raines, who talked her into becoming a tattooed lady. Vernon was a charmer and a crook. Not a crook in the carnie sense of a flat-joint operator, but a heist artist, a man with a gun. He had used the carnie as a cover-up, committing townie crimes, such as holding up banks. We hadn't known that, of course—Tex Montana wouldn't have stood for it. Last season, however, Vernon had held up a bank in a town called Midfork, killing a guard, and got away with a hundred grand. He was caught before he could spend any of it. That was when we learned Vernon had a record. Because of that record, and his killing the bank guard, he got life, with no possibility of parole.

The money was never found.

'Well ...' I sighed heavily. 'I guess we'd better go have a look.'

We started around the tent to where May's trailer was parked. Bernie said nothing about my calling the police. I would have to do that eventually, of course, but the carnies wouldn't call them on their own initiative if the midway was stacked knee-deep with corpses.

As we rounded the corner of the tent and came in sight of the Ten-in-One freaks clustered before the trailer, Bernie stopped me with a hand on my arm. 'Before you go in there, Patch, there's something you should know ...' He hesitated.

'Well?'

'It's kind of a queer thing ... and I've seen some queer things in my years of carnying.'

'What's the queer thing? Get on with it, man!'

'One of May's tattoos is missing.'

'What?' I gaped at him. '*What's* missing?'

'Somebody peeled a piece of skin off her back, about two inches square.'

I closed my mouth with a snort and began plowing my way through the gathered carnies. The trailer lights were on, and I opened the door and stepped inside. May lay face down on the floor in the living area, still in the halter and shorts she'd worn for the shows. The brown handle of a long knife protruded from her back just below the left shoulder blade, and lower down on her back, just as Bernie had said, a piece of skin, roughly two inches square, was missing.

There was very little blood, only a little oozing, which meant she had been dead, the heart had stopped pumping, when the skin had been cut away.

Bernie stepped inside, and I asked him, 'What tattoo is missing?'

'How the hell should I know? With all the tattoos May had, how can I tell which one is missing?'

'I don't suppose any pictures were ever taken of her tattoos?'

'None that I know of.'

196

'Somebody should know what one is missing. Vernon maybe—he had her tattooed, but he's in jail.'

'Not anymore he ain't.'

I stared at him. 'What do you mean?'

'He escaped sometime last night. Didn't *you* know?'

'No, I didn't know!' I snarled. 'How did *you* know?'

'May told me,' Bernie said calmly. 'She *said* Vernon called here, wanted to see her. That's what she was so upset about.'

'Did he show up?'

'He could have, but I didn't see him.'

'He could have killed her, too! I don't suppose it occurred to you to tell the police an escaped con was on his way here?'

Bernie just looked at me.

'All right! Sorry I asked. You could have told *me*, at least.'

He shrugged. 'I didn't think it was any of my business.'

'It figures,' I muttered, then sighed. 'I hope you don't mind too much if I call the police now, but I'd like to talk to Dirk first. I didn't see him outside.'

'I imagine he's in his tent getting bombed. You know he still had a thing for May and the stupid broad told him that Vernon was out.'

'Seems everybody knew Vernon was out but me.'

'No reason for you to know, Patch. Who'd

197

have thought he would kill her? What reason did he have?'

'*If* he did,' I muttered, walking out of the trailer.

Neither of us put it into words, but I knew the same thought had to be in Bernie's mind. Obviously May had been killed for the two-by-two tattoo, and if Vernon had killed her, it could only be for one reason. The tattoo was a map of where the bank loot was hidden. That was ironic in a way. For over a year May had been walking around, on exhibition before thousands of people, with directions on her back where to find a hundred grand, except nobody could have recognized it as such. Yet, if Vernon had killed her, why would he do it for that reason? To save splitting the loot with her?

I told Bernie to stay behind and keep everyone out of the trailer. He was filling his pipe from a cavernous leather tobacco pouch as I left him.

Dirk's tent was up the line about thirty yards. Dirk had been hitting the booze, all right. I could smell it when I pushed the tent flap back and went in. I fumbled overhead for the light cord.

When the light came on, Dirk, lying fully clothed on the cot, stirred and sat up, which meant he couldn't be too drunk. He threw an arm up to shield his eyes from the light and said blearily, 'Huh? What is it?'

Dirk was in my age bracket, around forty.

Nobody knew his real name. Around a carnie, you don't ask that question. He was over six feet, thin as a board, with an emaciated look. As a part of the act he swallowed a lighted neon tube—you could see it through the outer wall of his stomach. It was pretty weird, watching that tube of light travel down inside his skinny frame.

'Oh ... it's you, Patch.' He blinked at me. 'What's up?'

I decided to use shock treatment.

'May's dead, Dirk. Murdered.'

'May's what ...?' He started away from the cot, staggered and almost fell. 'Murdered?'

I snapped the questions at him. 'Were you in May's trailer tonight, Dirk?'

'No ... Of course not. Right after my last turn I came in here for a drink or two. May left earlier.'

'Were you still in love with her?'

'No ... Well, yes, but May ... The marriage was over, Patch, you knew that.'

I should explain that a carnie 'marriage' is often without benefit of license or clergy and could last anywhere from a week up to a lifetime. A carnie doesn't consider this as illegal or immoral. If it works, who's hurt? If it doesn't work, it's much less trouble to dissolve, one or both parties deciding it's over. Carnies did this long before the hippies did, proving there's little that's new. But understand, many carnie marriages, probably the majority, *are* legal in every sense of the word.

'Did you know Vernon was on his way here to see May?'

Dirk hesitated a moment before replying. 'Yes, May told me.'

'Did you see him tonight?'

'No ...' He took a step toward me. 'Did Vernon kill her?'

'I don't know. Did *you*?'

He literally staggered, reeling as from a blow. 'I wouldn't kill May, Patch!'

'Let's see your knife case, Dirk.'

'Why?'

'She was killed with a knife, a throwing knife.'

'And you're thinking—?'

'Dirk, let's see it!'

'Okay, okay!'

Dirk pulled a trunk from under his cot, from which he took a special case, flat like an attaché case and slightly larger. He put it on the cot and opened it.

I stepped closer. The case, lined in velvet, held two rows of knives in graduated sizes and shapes, all fitted into niches in the velvet and held in place by leather straps. There were twenty ... No, eighteen. Two were missing.

Dirk gasped. 'Two are gone!'

'And I know where one is. In May's back.'

'Patch, I swear ...'

'How long since you've looked in the case?'

'Oh, weeks, I guess. I open it now and then to

clean and polish them, keep them from rusting.'

'Were any missing the last time you looked?'

'No, they were all there.'

'All right, Dirk. Don't suddenly decide to take off. It's time I got the law in on this thing.'

'I'm not going anywhere, Patch,' he said steadily.

I went up the midway to the office wagon. Tex Montana, a huge man of sixty-odd, flamboyant in his cowboy garb, boots, Stetson, and the rest, was waiting for me. The nearest Tex had ever been to either Texas or Montana was western Missouri, when his carnie played a fair date there once. I briefed him on the situation, and he agreed I should call the town fuzz.

We were in Iowa, high corn country, and I expected a hick. Consequently, I was surprised by my first look at Sheriff Ray Tomlin. He wore a conservative suit, dark tie and white shirt—all business, with no manure on his shoes. It wasn't long before he showed the usual townie wariness toward, and distrust of, carnies. Then, when he learned that the murder victim was a tattooed female member of a freak show, with a piece of tattooed skin missing...

I was sure I could read his thoughts: *Who cares if one carnie freak killed another? Why put myself out? Two more days and they'll be gone from my bailiwick.* Then his second thought, when I'd told him about Dirk and Vernon: *An escaped convict and a sword swallower, either one could have done it and who cares which one lands in jail?*

Naturally his first choice would be Vernon. The capture of an escaped con, a murderer as well, could gain him a headline or two—but Vernon wasn't available, so Dirk would have to do.

After May's body was taken away, and the technicians had left, Sheriff Tomlin settled down to questioning a sullen Dirk. I eased out of the Ten-in-One tent, lit a cigar and strolled the midway, deep in thought.

The midway was totally deserted now. The only light, aside from the single string overhead, came from the cook tent up front. I paused in front of the House of Mirrors. I was uneasy over the second knife missing from Dirk's case. Yet, if Vernon had been on the lot, had killed May, he'd be long gone by this time.

I dropped the cigar butt into the damp shavings and ground it out under my toe. Abruptly the front of the Glass House behind me blazed with light, the clown heads on each side of the entrance opening and closing enormous, hinged mouths, idiotic, recorded laughter pouring from them. A Glass House, ours called the House of Mirrors, is a structure of complicated glass corridors through which a paying customer wanders trying to find a way out. What he thinks are doors turn out to be mirrors, and vice versa. Most carnivals have one, for even though Glass Houses are usually a losing proposition, they are as traditional as Ferris wheels and merry-go-rounds.

I squinted against the glare of light, peering into the glittering mirrors. A wanderer in the glass maze is reflected again and again and can be seen as he blunders nose-first into mirror after mirror, providing a hilarious and free spectator sport.

Now I saw, somewhere in the center of the maze, what seemed to be the figure of a man in a kneeling position, as though in prayer. If you're familiar with the maze, you can walk all the way through and out again without faltering. I'd never mastered it. I was as much without a sense of direction inside as any mark. I thought of calling out, but I knew I couldn't be heard over the insane laughter, and I didn't know where the switches were.

With a sigh I tentatively stepped inside the House of Mirrors and was immediately lost in the glass maze. I stumbled and blundered, bumping my nose against solid glass until it began to throb like a sore tooth, and all the while I could see the crouching figure, now behind me, now ahead, never any closer. All the while, the canned laughter issuing from the speakers hidden in the hinged clown mouths assailed my ears until I wanted to scream.

After an eternity I made the right choice and stood beside the kneeling figure. I squatted and touched a finger to the back of the neck. Cold as ice. At the pressure of my finger the figure slowly toppled, falling on its side. It was Vernon Raines, his darkly handsome face contorted in death.

I had found Dirk's other missing knife.

Both of Vernon's hands were wrapped tightly around the knife handle, which was driven to the hilt just below the rib cage. Blood was thick and dark on the floor. From the position in which he'd been kneeling, he could have fallen on the knife, or committed suicide. He was in the typical hara-kiri position. Except Vernon wasn't Oriental, and I wouldn't have thought...

I frisked him quickly. I didn't find the strip of skin from May's back. I went through his pockets a second time, looking for signs of dried blood and finding none.

Without warning the canned laughter shut off. I jumped to my feet, shocked by a sudden silence that was almost painful.

Then a voice came over the loudspeakers. 'Patch, is that you in there? We can see you...'

I couldn't see out, of course. I nodded several times.

'All right, stay there. We'll be right in.' It was Bernie's voice.

It took them only a few minutes to reach me—Bernie, Sheriff Tomlin, and two of his men. There wasn't room enough for all of us in the small corridor formed by the mirrors, and the two deputies were stacked up around the turn. Their images were repeated endlessly in the mirrors, and I had the smothering sensation of being surrounded.

Bernie said, 'We heard the laughter and wondered . . .' He stopped, staring at the body. 'It's Vernon. Is he dead?'

'He's dead.'

Sheriff Tomlin said alertly, 'Vernon Raines? The escaped convict?'

I nodded. 'None other, Sheriff.'

'That seems to be it then,' the sheriff said with satisfaction. 'He came back, killed the woman, then killed himself.'

I started to comment, then changed my mind and said instead, 'It's too close in here. Let's go outside.'

The sheriff turned to one of his men and told him to get the medical examiner back. The man started out and crashed face-on into a mirror. He retreated, cursing and rubbing his nose. Bernie took the lead and guided us out. I drew a grateful gulp of fresh air and busied myself lighting a cigar.

I felt the sheriff's hard stare. 'Like I said inside, that seems to wrap it up.'

I sighed heavily. 'It leaves a lot of questions that way, Sheriff.'

'Such as?'

'Such as, why did he kill May?'

'Jealousy. She was playing around with this other guy, this knife swallower.'

'That was long over, as I understand it. And

it was long over with Vernon and May, too. At least as far as she was concerned. It was over when she learned Vernon was a bank robber.'

'But she was still keeping in touch with him. Otherwise how did he know where to find her so quickly, the way you carnies jump from town to town, week after week?'

'That's easy. The carnie bible.'

He stared. 'The carnie bible?'

'The magazine, *Amusement Business*. It lists show dates and locations of all carnivals. All carnies read it religiously, even one in prison like Vernon.'

The sheriff subsided, grumbling.

I went on, 'Why did Vernon kill himself, *if* he did, in about the hardest way possible?'

'How should I know? Remorse, any number of reasons.'

'And what happened to the piece of skin from May's back?'

'I don't think anybody can answer that one.' He snorted laughter. 'Maybe one of your carnie freaks is a cannibal.'

It wasn't at all funny, but I let it pass. 'I think I know what happened to it.'

'Do you, now? Well, I'd be right interested in hearing.' His slow voice dripped sarcasm.

'That square of skin is some sort of map showing where Vernon hid the loot from the Midfork bank holdup. He was going to prison for the rest of his life, but he wanted a permanent map showing where the loot was

206

hidden in case he ever managed to escape.'

'So? He came back and killed her for it.'

'He doesn't have it on him. I happened to look for the thing.'

'What right did you ... All right, you didn't find it. So?'

'So, somebody, knowing Vernon had escaped and was on his way here for May and the map, killed May, peeled the skin off, then waylaid Vernon and killed him as well. That's why *two* knives were taken from Dirk's case instead of one. Two murders were planned all along. Now the murderer has a clear path to the hundred grand.'

'*Who's* got a clear path? Do you know?'

'I think so, yeah. Bernie?'

Bernie, standing beside me and silent all the while, jumped. 'Yes, Patch. What is it?'

'What did you do with the tattoo, Bernie?'

'Me ...? You're out of your mind, Patch!'

'Not the way I've got it figured.' I dropped the cigar butt and ground it out. 'You told me you didn't know what tattoo was missing. I don't believe that. You'd know if a freak in the Ten-in-One had so much as a hangnail. And with May right under your nose day after day ... You knew, Bernie. You may not have known what it meant at first, but you found out. Either May told you or you guessed. It's possible May knew what the tattoo meant and told you. She was conscientious that way and figured she could trust you. You were biding

207

your time, probably until we played Midfork this year, but suddenly you couldn't wait any longer. With Vernon out of the pen and on his way here, you had to act...'

One thing about Sheriff Tomlin, his reflexes were good. As Bernie broke away at a dead run, the sheriff tackled him and brought him down not twenty yards away.

They found the tattoo rolled up in Bernie's tobacco pouch, with tobacco shreds stuck to it.

The sheriff showed me the tattoo. At first glance it appeared to be a beautifully detailed pastoral scene, a clutch of farm buildings, a grove of trees and a pasture with grazing animals. Closer inspection disclosed faint figures etched in. They could only be longitude and latitude markings. Beside one tiny tree was an x, so small as to be almost invisible to the naked eye. I returned it to Sheriff Tomlin. 'I hope you find the loot.'

'We'll find it, never fear,' he said grimly.

I stood and watched them take a stubbornly silent Bernie away, the deputies towing him along between them up the deserted midway. It appeared everyone was bedded down now, but I knew this wasn't true. They were watching from various points. One carnie—I doubted I would ever know which one—had turned on the lights in the House of Mirrors so I would find Vernon's body. They would never have told the fuzz, but they wanted me to know.

Now, as the sounds of the siren died away in

the distance, the midway was silent and peaceful, at long last buttoned up for the night. I sighed and started up the midway to the office wagon. I knew Tex Montana would be waiting for my report.

I learned later that Bernie finally confessed to both murders and was convicted.

When we played the Midfork Fair a few weeks later, I asked around. They had found the bank loot buried at the base of a tree on a farm a few miles outside of town, exactly where the tattoo had indicated.

THE FALL OF DR. SCOURBY

P. Matthews

Ms. Gladys Grumly, stout thighs pistoning powerfully, left hand sliding along the banister, purposefully pounded her way up the cement stairs of the Administration Building Tower. Her eyes fixed straight ahead, she climbed close to the left side of the stairs. She was more than a little afraid of heights, and if she walked to the right, the terrifying vortex formed by the spiral staircase seemed to suck her eyes downward, until her mind crashed against the cold, hard square of concrete at the bottom.

Breathing deeply—good for the lungs—she approached the landing of the seventh floor. As she paused a moment to get her breath, she became aware of a sound from above her. She raised her eyes to a blur of motion. Before her nearsighted gaze could register what she was seeing, something plummeted past her line of vision. It took a moment for her mind to identify the 'something' as a human body. As her mind registered this fact, it also registered the sound of a heavy object hitting the cement square, seven floors below.

Ms. Grumly prided herself on the fact that she was a strong, healthy woman, who had never fainted in her life. Ms. Grumly fainted now.

*   *   *

It was 1:15 P.M. Mark Cassidy, chief investigator for the campus police at State University, looked at the report in front of him and sighed wearily. He pulled out his desk drawer and rummaged for cigarettes, before he remembered that he had quit the nasty habit. He slammed the drawer shut, and took a roll of candy out of his pocket. Putting one of the candies in his mouth, he pulled the report toward him: a motorcycle stolen from Lot B; obscene words on the walls of the men's room in the Science Building; a doodle-dasher in the library, and some minor vandalism at the Martin Hall escalator—a usual day's activities.

He became conscious of the sharp sting of heartburn in the pit of his stomach. He should not have had the enchiladas at the cafeteria; or maybe, as his doctor had suggested, it was the job. There were certainly enough aggravations to ruin a man's digestion.

The door to his office slammed back loudly, and he looked up as Sue Collins, the desk clerk, burst in and then stood white-faced in his doorway, as if unable to go farther. She opened her mouth, but it was a moment before the words came out.

'Mr. Cassidy! Mr. Cassidy! Someone has . . .

Someone is...'

Cassidy got up from his desk quickly and pushed past the girl, who now seemed incapable of movement as well as coherent speech.

As he entered the other room, he saw the rest of the staff hovering over and around a stout, pained-looking woman, who seemed familiar to him.

Sergeant Walters stepped forward. 'This is Miss Grumly, Mark. She works in Accounting. She was returning from lunch, going up the tower stairs, when she saw a man fall from the eighth-floor landing.'

Cassidy felt his gut tighten. He was already moving toward the door, giving orders. 'Walters, get a blanket and come with me. Sue, you and Margaret stay with Miss Grumly. Don't let her leave until I talk with her.'

Cassidy had seen more than a few dead bodies in his time, but that had been a few years back. Campus police work had left him strangely unprepared for the sight of this one. With something of an effort, he made himself look at the body professionally. The body was male, Caucasian, with thinning brown hair worn just past collar length, and bushy sideburns. He was wearing cream-colored pants, a white shirt with Mexican-designed trim, brown sandals and red socks. The man had landed on his back, and Cassidy recognized Dr. Daniel Scourby, head of the

Drama Department.

Suddenly Cassidy became conscious that a vast, cumulative whisper was coming down from above him, like the susurration in a giant seashell. Looking up, he could see tier upon tier of white faces peering over the banisters of the stairway as it coiled up to the eighth floor.

'Put the blanket over him,' he said to Walters. The other man lifted the blanket and gingerly placed it over the body.

*   *   *

Lt. Leo Moreno, of Homicide, sat on the edge of Cassidy's desk as if he belonged there. He was a stocky man, with a smooth, tanned face, and sharp, blue eyes. 'Hi, Cassidy. Your chief tells me that you've got a little trouble here. I understand that one of your profs took a dive from the eighth floor of the stairwell.'

Cassidy nodded. 'That's about it.'

'Jumped, fell, or pushed?'

Cassidy sighed. 'I don't know yet, Leo. I was just going to talk to the only witness.'

'Want us to take over? You know, this is a little different than somebody ripping off a bicycle, or demonstrating in the dean's office.'

Cassidy tried to keep his voice calm. 'I know that, Leo. After all, I do have some experience with this type of thing. You never seem to remember, but I spent ten years on a city police force.'

213

'Yeah. I do keep forgetting that. Well, suit yourself. But if you find you can't handle it, don't forget to give us a call. We're pretty busy right now, but we can always find time to help out a brother officer.'

Cassidy watched Moreno leave the room. He sure had the needle out. Cassidy knew that the city police had a patronizing view of the campus force. There *had* been a time when campus police were little more than traffic cops and guards, but now they had a real force, and men with good backgrounds in law enforcement who were authorized to handle any crime that occurred on campus, and Cassidy, as investigator, was involved in almost all of them.

Cassidy hesitated a moment. He was anxious to talk to the witness, Gladys Grumly, but maybe he should talk to his chief first.

Chief Baker was a big man, heavy-shouldered and crag-faced. He looked up from his desk as Cassidy entered the room.

'Oh, hello, Cassidy. I heard that you've been talking to Moreno. That son-of-a-gun is like a genie, the way he pops up. I still don't know how he found out about this thing so fast.'

'The lieutenant has good connections,' Cassidy said, 'but listen, I want first crack at this. I know this case is a little bigger than the ones that usually come up on campus, and I know Homicide will start putting pressure on us if the case isn't tied up quickly, but first give me a couple of days on my own. All right?'

Baker looked at him and shrugged. 'All right, Cassidy. You're a good man. Take your best shot.'

Cassidy left his office to question Ms. Grumly.

She was determined to be a good witness. Cassidy could tell by the determined look in her eye, and the controlled set of her face. Only a slight tic in her right eyelid, and the pulse throbbing in her sturdy throat, indicated her nervousness.

Cassidy leaned toward her, trying for the right blend of respect and solicitude.

'Now, Miss Grumly, I know it's difficult for you to talk about what has happened, but—'

'*Ms.* Grumly, if you please, Mr. Cassidy.' Ms. Grumly's tone was cool, and so were her eyes.

'Of course,' Cassidy said smoothly. 'Ms. Grumly. Now, we need your help. As the only witness, your testimony is very important.'

Ms. Grumly's stern expression softened a bit.

'I will do my duty,' she said.

'Good. Now, tell me just what you saw and heard before Dr. Scourby fell.'

'I was just coming to the seventh-floor landing. I stopped for a moment to rest, and as I stopped, I heard this funny sound above me.'

'A funny sound? Just what kind of a sound was it?'

215

A frown creased Ms. Grumly's ample forehead. 'Why, just a sound, a noise.'

'Think about it. What was it like?'

Ms. Grumly's gaze turned inward. 'Well, it sounded a little like a cough, or a grunt. I'm sorry to be so vague, but it was not a sound I am accustomed to hearing.'

'And after you heard the sound?'

'I looked up to see where it came from. I saw something on the eighth-floor landing; a movement.'

'A movement?'

Ms. Grumly's wide cheeks pinked. 'I don't see very well without my glasses, Mr. Cassidy. All I could see was what appeared to be two people moving about on the landing, and as I looked up, one of them went over the railing.'

Her face went pale at the memory, and for an instant she lost her composure. Cassidy realized he could get nothing more from her at the moment.

'Thank you, Ms. Grumly. You've been a big help. If you remember anything else, about the sound you heard, for instance, let me know at once, will you?'

She nodded, and the color began to come back into her face.

'Oh, there is one thing more. How did you happen to be using the stairs instead of the elevator?'

She looked at him with great disdain. 'I always take the stairs. Exercise! If more people

216

around here used the stairs, and their legs, they'd be in much better condition.'

Not Scourby, Cassidy thought wryly, and she must have read his mind, because her face flushed a dark and unbecoming red.

Dr. Daniel Scourby, Cassidy soon discovered, had not been the best-liked member of the drama faculty. A flamboyant and volatile man, long on temperament, and short on good manners, he managed to alienate most of his colleagues and a good number of his students with his egotism and cruelty. Despite these traits, however, he had been quite a man with the ladies, and was well known on campus for his numerous love affairs.

Cassidy learned that Dr. Scourby had been in the accounting office on the eighth floor shortly before his death. He had gone there to pick up a travel check. The check had not been ready, and with his usual patience and charm, he had caused a scene. His visit to the accounting office was well remembered. Elsie Smith, who had waited on him and borne the brunt of his anger, verified that he left the office at 1:00 P.M. She remembered the time, because he had kept her fifteen minutes past her lunch break.

Ms. Grumly had seen Scourby fall at about 1:10 P.M. Cassidy was unable to turn up anyone who had seen Scourby during those last ten minutes. Too, Cassidy wondered why

217

Scourby had taken the stairs. He thought about the eighth-floor landing. He had found nothing there to help him, no physical clues that might show him what had happened there. The railing was sturdy, and approximately waist-high. Scourby was not a tall man, but he was heavy-bodied and broad-shouldered. It would not be an easy job to force a man of his size and weight over the railing.

Cassidy sighed. There simply was no physical evidence to go on. On the other hand, he had more than enough suspects. Almost everyone on campus had disliked Scourby, and more than a few people actively hated the man.

Cassidy was acutely conscious of the passage of time. He could almost feel Moreno leaning over his shoulder, waiting for him to admit that he couldn't get it all together. Well, damn Moreno! He *would* get it together.

He ran his mind down the list of people who might have the best reason to hate Scourby. Cassidy had determined that Scourby had two ex-wives, but they were both remarried, and lived out of state. There were no children, and evidently no other living relatives. That pretty much ruled out his family.

From what Cassidy had been able to learn, the man had few friends outside of the campus community. Like many academicians, the main thrust of his life seemed to revolve around the campus. Despite his general unpopularity, he was very active in the life of the university in general, and in his own department in particular.

Since the incident had occurred on campus, it seemed logical to Cassidy that whoever had been with Scourby on that landing was also from the campus. It also seemed logical that the most likely suspects were in Scourby's own department: Dr. Linus Martin, the man whom Scourby had climbed over in his race for the chairmanship of the department; Ben Aldon, student, actor, who had publicly stated that he hated Scourby's guts because of a coed's suicide and would like to see him hanged from a certain portion of his anatomy; Melissa Jackson, student, actress, part-time student assistant. It was general knowledge that she'd had an affair with Scourby. It had ended badly, and she had taken it hard. There must be others, too, who hated Scourby, but whose reasons were not public knowledge.

       *   *   *

Cassidy sat in the fifth row of the darkened theater, his eyes fixed on the two young people on stage. The young man was tall, athletic-looking, and ruggedly handsome. The girl was also tall, and very beautiful.

Ben Aldon and Melissa Jackson were starring in the Drama Department production of *Picnic*, which was being directed by Linus Martin. The kids were good.

A slight figure entered stage right. Cassidy knew this was Jimmie Breen, Scourby's girl Friday in the drama office. Cassidy had not been able to find out how she felt about Scourby. From all accounts, she did her job well, and stood up under Scourby's little attacks of sadism with commendable aplomb. She was an excellent actress. Cassidy, who usually attended all of the drama productions with his girlfriend Maryann, had seen her in many other productions. She was a thin, childlike girl, with pale androgynous features.

Thinking of the other productions he had attended made Cassidy think of Maryann. If Scourby hadn't gotten himself killed, Cassidy would be with her right now, in her comfortable apartment, having a nice cold bourbon, and a good warm meal, and a little comfort, instead of here, in a stuffy theater, in the dark.

Ben Aldon was his first target during a break. Aldon's young face was flushed, and his eyes were hot.

'Yes!' he said. 'I hated Scourby, and I had good reason. Cindy Purdom was one sweet kid, before he got his hands on her. Scourby messed up her mind with pot and fast talk. Told her he would make her a big star. Of course I resented his taking her away from me, but that wasn't the reason I hated him. I hated him because when he had used her, he threw her out. She was never the same after that. It

220

was only a month later that she took the pills. Yeah, I felt like wasting him, but I didn't, and I have an alibi. I was with Melissa. Neither of us has classes on Tuesday afternoons, and we were over at her pad going over our lines until about 3:00 P.M.'

Cassidy looked at him mildly. 'I don't suppose you have any other witnesses. Someone at the apartment house who saw you together?'

Aldon looked back at him sullenly, but his eyes were uneasy.

'No, at least I don't think so. You check it out. You're the cop!'

'I will, son, I will.'

Aldon muttered something under his breath and moved away. Cassidy sighed. If the regular police got little respect from today's youth, a campus policeman got less.

Melissa Jackson corroborated Aldon's story. She admitted that she still hated Scourby, and was glad that he was dead, but she had been with Ben Aldon at the time, and under the circumstances he had described.

Cassidy looked at her appraisingly. She was a big girl; tall, lithe, and strong. Was she strong enough to have pushed Scourby over the stair railing?

After talking to Melissa, Cassidy talked with Dr. Linus Martin, a tall, narrow-shouldered man, with pale, defenseless-looking eyes. He rubbed at them wearily as he talked to Cassidy.

'Sure, I hated Scourby. I and several dozen other people. But kill him? He's done enough to me without my letting him drive me to murder. I was in my office from 12:00 noon until 1:30 P.M. Jimmie Breen, the drama secretary, can verify that. We've been having some rather late rehearsals, and I was bushed.'

Cassidy talked last with Jimmie Breen. Her large, waif's eyes looked much too big for her narrow little face.

'Yes, Dr. Martin was in his office from 12:00 noon until about 1:00 P.M. and I was in the office until 2:00 P.M. No, I don't think anyone else saw me. At least I didn't see anyone myself. It was pretty quiet around here during the middle of the day.'

Cassidy studied her child's face. 'How did you feel toward Dr. Scourby, Jimmie?'

She lowered her eyelids, but her face did not change expression.

'Like everyone else, I suppose. He wasn't a very likable man. He was hard to work for; a real male chauvinist. Then, after what he did to Cindy ... We were roommates, you know, Cindy and I. After what happened to her, I could never feel friendly toward him.'

'Why did you stay in this job?' Cassidy asked gently.

She shrugged her narrow shoulders. 'I have to work to get through college. This job is convenient, being right here in the department. I could put up with Scourby. I just didn't let him get to me.'

Cassidy resisted a desire to pat her shoulder. As he left, he was thinking that Scourby had certainly gotten to someone, and that someone had in turn, really gotten to him.

Cassidy returned to the office. Only young Thompson was there; the rest of the night shift were out making rounds. Cassidy waved a weary greeting to Thompson, and went into his inner office.

He picked up the coffeepot and shook it. There was some left, but it smelled strong and stale. He decided that, at the very least, he deserved some fresh coffee. He cleaned the pot and filled it with fresh water. It had been a long day, and his mind was growing sluggish with fatigue.

The faces of the people to whom he had talked kept passing before his mind's eye like the faces in a police lineup. Any one of them had sufficient motive, and none of them had an ironclad alibi. If only Ms. Grumly had been wearing her glasses ... If only she could better describe that strange sound heard on the landing above her...

The thought of that sound tantalized Cassidy. He could do nothing now about Ms. Grumly's nearsightedness, but if he could discover what the sound was, or who had made it, he might be on his way to Scourby's murderer.

He unwrapped the sandwich he had

purchased from the vending machine, and poured a cup of the fresh coffee. He really ought to relax for a moment. His mind was going over the same things again and again.

He reached over and turned on the small television set that he kept on the corner of his desk.

There wasn't anything decent on. It was summer, and all that was playing, even during prime time, was reruns. He switched through an ancient variety show, an even older mystery, a Japanese Western, with lots of violence and bad dubbing, and a space opera. He moved his fingers to turn off the set, then switched around the dial once again as he suddenly realized what he had just seen and heard. He watched the program he had turned to for several minutes, tapping his fingers thoughtfully on the arm of his chair. Again he turned off the set. He had a plan.

The Personnel Office was closed, but Cassidy simply let himself in. He knew where the faculty records were kept, and it did not take him long to locate Dr. Linus Martin's file. He read the material thoroughly, replaced the file, then called the Records Office.

*   *   *

Mrs. McIntosh, the assistant registrar, was none too happy when Cassidy arrived at her office a short time later.

224

'You just caught me,' she snapped. 'I was about to go home. Been working late every night. This quarter system is murder.'

'I won't be long,' Cassidy soothed. 'I need to see the schedules of classes for three students: Ben Aldon, Jimmie Breen, and Melissa Jackson.'

Mrs. McIntosh grumbled, but she brought the records quickly enough, and sat watching Cassidy as he went over each of them carefully.

When he was finished, he smiled at her. 'Thanks.'

'Well, I hope that you found what you were looking for.'

He smiled again. 'I think maybe I did.'

He waited until Mrs. McIntosh had locked the office, then left the administration building and headed back toward the theater.

He had looked at four sets of records, including Dr. Martin's. Only one of them had the information for which he had been looking. Alone, it didn't mean a thing. Just a hunch, but maybe, just maybe, he could use that hunch as leverage.

The light was still on in the theater, and when he went inside, he saw that rehearsals were still going on. Both Ben Aldon and Melissa looked tired, and Linus Martin, sitting in the back of the theater, looked up wearily as Cassidy came in.

'Almost through,' he said softly. 'Along about this stage of the game, you begin

225

wondering how it will ever come together, but it does. It does. Do you want to ask more questions? If you do, I warn you that we are all too tired to make sense.'

Cassidy shook his head. 'No more questions. At least not tonight. I'm just going to nose around a little.'

Martin nodded tiredly, and slumped back into his seat. On stage, the two young people had finished their scene. Cassidy walked through the door at the side of the stage, and made his way over the ropes and props to the back.

Jimmie Breen was there, busily painting a portion of a picket fence. She turned at the sound of Cassidy's footsteps.

'You're working late tonight, Jimmie.'

She looked up at him seriously. 'So are you, Mr. Cassidy. But I guess there's no law against that, for either of us.'

'None at all. Jimmie, I wonder if you would come with me to Dr. Scourby's office?'

She looked at him warily.

'Why?'

'I'll tell you when we get there.'

She put down the paintbrush, wiped her hands on her jeans, and turned toward him. Cassidy turned his back to her and began leading the way toward Scourby's office. When he had gone about ten feet, he whirled, as quickly as he could, raised his arm, and lunged toward the girl.

226

He had a vision of round, startled eyes, a white face, and then a good picture of the ceiling, as he landed hard on his back, dazed but intact.

He could hear the sound of running footsteps, and the sound of the girl's ragged breathing, but before that, he had heard something else—the sound for which he had been listening; a funny sound, like a cough, or a grunt, or a judo *kiai*; the sound made as part of a judo move...

It was hard to hate her for it, Cassidy decided. Sitting there in the chair in his office, she looked more like a war orphan than a murderess.

'How did you know it was me?' she asked softly.

'I didn't know for sure. We have a witness who heard a strange sound, a sound that could have been a *kiai*. I checked Dr. Martin's, Melissa's, Ben's and your records. Yours were the only ones that showed any experience in the martial arts—two years of judo classes.'

She shook her head. 'I didn't mean to do it. I mean, I didn't plan it. After Cindy, I promised myself that I would get even with him some way. But I didn't plan it. It just happened.'

She looked up, her dark eyes wide. Her hands fumbled in her lap like two lost things.

'Cindy and I were... We were very close. He just the same as killed her, you know.'

Cassidy said softly, 'What happened? What

happened today, Jimmie?'

She swallowed, and made an attempt to focus on his questions. 'He asked me to call about his travel check. Accounting said that it wasn't ready. He gave me a bad time about that, as if it were my fault. He said he was going over there himself, and straighten things out.

'After he left, I found the papers on his desk. He hadn't submitted them, and that's why the check wasn't ready. I thought I had better get them over to the accounting office before he tore the place apart...'

'So you left the office, and went to the Administration Building.'

'Yes. I was in a hurry, so I went around back of the cafeteria. I didn't meet anyone I recognized. I took the elevator up to the eighth floor, but I was too late. Dr. Scourby was already coming out of the accounting office. He started swearing at me, and suddenly I just couldn't handle it. I ran for the stairs, but he followed me. I ran down the steps to the first landing and turned. He was coming down the steps toward me. All I could think of was how much I hated him. He kept on coming toward me and I...'

In one fluid motion, she rose from the chair and twisted her upper body as she lifted her right shoulder. Cassidy had a vivid mental picture of Scourby pitching over her shoulder into the stairwell.

There was a long silence, broken finally by

228

the sound of a strident, feminine voice in the outer office, then the sound of Walters' baritone attempting to override it.

Walters opened the door and stuck his head in. 'It's Ms. Grumly, Cassidy. She says she's got to talk to you.'

Cassidy looked at Jimmie. Then he reached over and patted her shoulder.

In the outer office, Ms. Grumly stood, pink-cheeked and glowing with self-satisfaction.

'I told him that you said to contact you if I thought of anything else, and I have,' she said triumphantly. 'That sound, the sound I heard on the landing? Well, tonight, I was watching an old movie on television...'

Cassidy sighed wearily as his stomach twinged painfully.

WITHIN THE LAW

J. Lutz

I have an orderly mind. Loose ends bother me a lot, especially when I have a personal interest. Everybody should pay the piper—an eye for an eye, a tooth for a tooth, that sort of thing. Nobody believes in capital punishment more than I do. That's why I follow Jack Hall.

A little over a year ago Hall killed my wife. Nobody can prove it, not the best lawyers alive, because there just isn't any proof. Hall saw to that before he killed her. Adelaide was having an affair with him that was getting out of hand, that threatened to break up his marriage. Hall couldn't have that happen for financial reasons, so he carefully arranged things and strangled Adelaide, and witnesses swore that he was a thousand miles away at the time.

I knew differently because I followed Adelaide that night and saw her meet Hall. He killed her, and I'll see that he pays. Oh, she was having an affair with him, but she *was* my wife, and he *did* kill her. A man ought to love his wife.

I'm walking behind Hall now in Denver. He travels all over the country on his job, and I follow him on my savings account. He'll go into that cocktail lounge, I know. He frequents places like that.

I go into the lounge too, and find a booth where I can watch him sitting at the bar. He knows I'm there. I'm always careful to let him see me. His handsome, beefy face is red as he catches sight of me for a moment in the bar mirror as he orders his drink. It's beginning to bother him more and more lately, me following him.

Hall will probably come over and try to talk again, try to bring things out in the open where he can deal with them, but I see to it that our conversations never take the pressure off him. I know what's bothering him, and he has real reason to fear.

He's standing over me now, his drink in his hand, paunchy but athletic-looking in his dark slacks and tailored gray sport coat. Quite a lady's man.

'When are you gonna give it up, Brewster?'

'I think you know by now, Jack, that I'll never quit.' I always call him by his first name. It annoys him.

He sits down across from me, uninvited. 'But I don't get it! What do you think you're gonna accomplish by followin' me all over the country?'

I keep my voice calm. 'You're going to pay for killing my wife.'

'But I didn't kill your wife!' Hall looks at me with angry puzzlement, trying to convince himself that I'm just a harmless nut. 'Besides,' he says, 'that's a closed issue as far as the police are concerned. I was a suspect and I was cleared.'

'As far as the police are concerned, not I.'

He gives a hollow laugh. 'It's the police that count, buddy boy. I was cleared and there's not much you can do about it.' He raises his glass and takes a big swallow. 'Just between you and me, Adelaide was going to leave you anyway. Why waste your time eatin' your heart out over a dead broad that hated your guts?'

'You wouldn't understand.'

'Oh, yeah? Well, what you don't understand is that the whole thing is over. You can follow me till the cows come home and it won't change a thing. If you so much as even threaten to harm me I'll have you arrested, and if you did kill me you'd fry for it.'

'I know, the letter.' Hall had informed me earlier that he'd left a letter with his lawyer to be opened in the event of his death. The letter explained how I'd been following him and named me as his probable killer. Besides, I had a good motive; it was no secret that I thought he killed Adelaide.

'You can't prove anything,' Hall says. 'You *know* you can't prove anything.'

'Do I?' I sip my drink slowly. 'I think you should get the electric chair, Jack. I think for killing Adelaide you should spend the long months on death row while your appeals all come to their predictable deadends, while you count your days, your meals, your minutes, your steps to the execution room. I think you should count your seconds while they fasten the metal cap to your shaved head.'

'Knock it off!' Hall is sweating and his knuckles are white where he grips his glass.

I shrug. 'As you observed, I can't prove anything.'

His dark brows knit in anger as he stares hard at me. 'Then why keep followin' me?'

'I just happen to go where you go.'

He clenches his jaws, still staring at me, then stands and walks out. I wait a few seconds, then I get up and follow him.

Hall is right, of course. I can't prove he murdered Adelaide, or I would have a long time ago. Still, I know a way to make him pay. Justice demands that a murderer pay for his crime.

I'm staying at the same hotel that Hall is. I always do it this way so I can keep a closer eye on him. Not that it's necessary anymore. He doesn't bother to try to get away from me. He knows that even if he does manage to lose me I'll just pick him up at his next stop. I know his business itinerary and I know all his clients. If worse came to worst, I suppose I could just wait by his home until he showed up and then start following him again. But it's never come to that.

As I follow Hall back to the hotel I think

about the letter. I don't doubt for a moment that he wrote one and that it is in the possession of his lawyer. He thinks it protects him from harm, and in a way I guess it does. I smile as I walk behind him into the lobby. I wouldn't have the stomach to kill him anyway. That would be breaking the law.

We hit Saint Louis that month, and Indianapolis and Chicago—then on to Detroit. I know his route so well I could almost fly ahead and meet him there. But that would be defeating my purpose, so I stay close to him, almost always within sight, while I wait for him to crack—and he's close to cracking. In Indianapolis he came over to me in the hotel bar and threatened to hit me, but I told the bartender to call the police. That calmed him down.

I stay very close to Hall now, and it doesn't surprise me when I overhear him ask on a lobby telephone for a reservation on the afternoon flight to Miami. Still, I think my heart skips a beat, and I'm not an emotional man. Miami is not on Hall's itinerary.

I call the airline he uses and book a seat on the same flight he's on. Usually I do that. I like to sit in front of him on the plane so he can see the back of my head. We both know he can't give me the slip on an airplane.

Hall rents a car at the Miami airport and drives to a big motel out on the edge of the city in a fairly secluded area; but this time I don't stay where he's staying. I check in at one of the biggest hotels I can find, with a private beach and recreation area. The place is thronging with people, and I take a room on the middle floor with a window overlooking a busy street. It's a small, well-furnished room, quiet but surrounded by activity. Perfect. After placing a phone call to Hall to irritate him and let him know where I'm staying, I settle down to wait.

Hall shows up that very night, as I thought he would. He can't afford to waste time. When I open the door he seems ready to force his way in, and it kind of surprises him when I smile and stand back to let him enter.

'To what do I owe the honor?' I ask.

Hall looks around him, as if checking the room. The blinds are closed. He draws a gun from a pocket of his uncharacteristic drab brown suit.

'I take it you're going to kill me,' I say.

'That's right,' Hall says, and he grins, but his small eyes are angry.

'You asked for it. It's the only way I can get you off my back.'

'But aren't you afraid you'll be caught?'

'That argument won't save you,' Hall says, his grin widening. 'I traveled here under a different name, and I'll return the same way tonight. Nobody'll even know I was in Miami. Even if they suspect, I bought me a nice alibi in Detroit. I'm back there playin' poker in a hotel room.'

'You were at the races when Adelaide was murdered, weren't you?'

'Sure,' Hall says. 'I even had the torn tickets to prove it—mailed to me special delivery from Louisville.'

'Clever,' I say with admiration.

'Too clever for you, buddy boy. This time you outsmarted yourself, flyin' here like a regular pigeon, so fast you couldn't even have had time to tell anyone where you were going or why. By the time they find your body I'll be back in Detroit. And the best part is, as far as the police are concerned, I don't even have a motive to kill you.'

'There's one thing,' I say. 'Suppose I lured you here to kill you?'

Despite himself, Hall's florid face suddenly goes pale. Then he regains some of his composure. 'You won't harm a hair on my head, pal. Remember the letter?'

I swallow and nod.

'Into the bedroom!' His voice is higher now as he gets up his nerve for the actual business of killing me.

'You'll get the electric chair,' I say to him as he jabs the gun barrel into the small of my back and pushes me into the bedroom. 'You'll be counting those last seconds.'

'You got it backwards, buddy boy.' He picks up a pillow and folds it around the gun.

I don't even hear the shots as I feel the bullets rip into my chest and I fall backward onto the bed. I'll bet he wonders why I'm smiling when I die. I bet that will bother him.

He doesn't know yet about the recorder in my pocket. Or about the letter I left with *my* lawyer.

ACT OF VIOLENCE

A. Gordon

Long after he had banished it from his conscious mind, the scene kept coming back to him in dreams, kept coming back with appalling clarity, as if burnt into his memory by some searing psychic process. There it always was: the beach white as ivory in the moonlight, and the little waves creaming warm around his feet, and the crumpled figure face down in the gleaming water. And he would wake with a muffled cry of terror and protest...

It had all started out as a casual holiday weekend, nothing more. He had finished his business in Jamaica and was ready to fly back to Miami. But Paxton, the manager of the Kingston office, had dissuaded him. 'Why not give yourself a break, Johnny, old boy? Hop across to the cool side of the island and spend a weekend at Haddon Hall before you go home. Their station wagon meets all the planes at Montego Bay. It's a grand spot: good food, horses, tennis, everything. Best beach on the island. No reason why a gay bachelor like you shouldn't find a pretty girl, either...'

He had found the girl, all right. He found her in the station wagon that met him, as

238

promised, when his plane landed. It had already collected three passengers from the Miami plane. Two were young, selfconscious, hand-holding—obviously honeymooners. The third was this girl.

Following the driver who carried his bags, he saw her profile framed in the station wagon window, and his first odd impression was that she was waiting for something, waiting with a kind of controlled intensity. And this was strange because she *was* waiting, they were all waiting for him, and the fact that they were waiting should not have been quite so noticeable.

Then, as he approached, she turned her head, and he felt the impact of chestnut hair and sun-warmed skin and eyes the color of sea-water, eyes that looked at him appraisingly and did not seem displeased by what they saw. He came up to the car through the hot white sunshine and held out his hand. 'I'm John Aiken,' he said. 'Hope I haven't kept you waiting long.'

The girl's hand felt cool and strong in his. 'I'm Jan Livingston,' she said. 'No, not long.' Her voice was pleasant, friendly, but again for half a second he had the strange intuitive impression of calmness stretched tight over tension. Then it was gone. The bride said, 'We're the Nesbitts,' and gave him a shy smile, and blushed. The driver said, 'All ready now, sar,' and opened the door.

Aiken folded himself up and slid in beside the girl. He glanced once at her left hand. It was ringless. He said, keeping his voice more casual than he felt, 'Your first trip to Jamaica?'

She nodded, but did not reply, so he tried again. 'They tell me this place has everything: riding, tennis, sailing, swimming—what's your preference?'

They were moving, now, through the airport gate, along the winding coastal road. To their left was the incredible jade-and-turquoise sea. The girl was watching it. 'Swimming, I think. Definitely swimming.'

He glanced at her bare brown arms, her lithe body. 'You look as if you might be a good swimmer.'

'Yes,' she said, 'I am. That sounds immodest, but it's the one thing I know I do well.'

He leaned back, careful not to touch her, amazed at the power of the impulse he felt to do just that. 'My swimming's pretty rusty, I'm afraid. Maybe you could give me a few lessons.'

A furrow appeared in her smooth forehead, as if somehow the suggestion did not please her. But it was gone instantly. 'Why, certainly,' she said. 'I'd be glad to, Mr. Aiken.'

The formality did not please him. 'If you're going to be my swimming teacher, can't you just call me Johnny?'

Her mouth curved faintly. His nostrils
240

caught a whiff of the perfume she was wearing: subtle, fragrant, feminine. 'All right,' she said. 'Johnny.'

For an hour, then, they drove steadily eastward. In the back seat, the honeymooners chattered happily. Everything delighted them: the cane fields, the banana trees, the great Jamaican vultures swinging silently in the luminous air. Once a mongoose flashed like a big weasel in front of the wheels. Jan Livingston sat quietly, hands folded in her lap. Now and then, as the station wagon swung around the turns, her shoulder touched Aiken's lightly. He was always aware of the contact, and he had the feeling that she was too, but she gave no sign.

An hour of this, and then ahead of them they saw Haddon Hall, high on a promontory above the sea. A former sugar plantation, converted now to an exclusive guest house with its own palm-fringed beach and a magnificent view. They turned off onto a dusty road that climbed steeply, and Aiken was aware suddenly that the girl's face was pale and that her hands were no longer folded loosely; they were clenched tight. He said to her, softly, 'What's the matter? Is something wrong?'

She shook her head; her hands relaxed. The station wagon swung into a courtyard filled with sunlight and silence and drunken splashes of color from hibiscus and bougainvillaea. A white-coated servant opened the door.

241

'Welcome,' he said in his sing-song, Anglo-African voice. 'Welcome, ladies and gentlemen, to Haddon Hall!'

The place was everything that Paxton had said it would be: wide verandas, cool white-plastered walls, big dim rooms where polished silver gleamed. The proprietress was a sensible Scottish woman named Mackie. She showed Aiken to his room, urged him to ring for anything he wanted, suggested he might like a swim before tea-time. The beach, she said, was a quarter of a mile away by road. The station wagon would be leaving in ten minutes for anyone who wanted to go.

Aiken said, staring out of the window at the distant mountains, 'Do you have many guests here now, Mrs. Mackie?'

'Just a handful; the season's about over, you know.'

'And will everybody be going down to swim?'

'Oh, no! Some are playing tennis; that's what our newlyweds want to do, I believe. Some are out riding. But Miss Livingston wants to swim. And Captain Davis usually does. He's from South Africa—you'll like him. There are bath houses at the beach where you can change.' She looked at him quizzically. 'That Miss Livingston's a pretty girl, isn't she? Quite unusually so.' She gave him her pleasant smile and went out quietly, not waiting for a reply.

Aiken unpacked quickly, wrapped his

swimming trunks in a towel, went down the broad, curving stairs. The big room that served as a lounge was empty, and while he waited he looked through the leather-bound guest-book that lay on the center table. Some of the names were familiar: socialites from New York, celebrities from the entertainment world. But it was the next-to-last entry that caught his eye. *Mr. & Mrs. Ace Murdock, Miami.* And under that a single name: *Antonio Capa.* Both entries were dated the previous day.

Aiken closed the book with a faint grimace of distaste. He did not know Ace Murdock, but he knew who he was. Everyone in Miami knew who he was: a gambler, a connoisseur of race tracks and of women, a fixer of things, a big-time operator. Not outside the law, necessarily; at least, not on the surface. But wherever big money moved, Ace Murdock moved also. If you wanted to put on a championship fight in Miami, or sell a multi-million dollar hotel, Ace was always involved. There were men who hated his guts, and it was said that he was never without a bodyguard. It was also said that women—some women— found him as irresistible as he found them. All in all, an American type: the worst. And here he was, at Haddon Hall...

Behind Aiken, a British voice spoke suddenly, 'Hullo, there.'

He turned and saw a tall rangy man in a khaki shirt and knee-length shorts, blue eyes

243

frank and friendly. 'Davis is the name. Mrs. Mackie says you're for a swim. Mind if I join you?'

'Why, no,' said Aiken. 'Of course not.' He did like the man; there was something solid and direct about him.

'Station wagon's waiting,' Davis said. 'And Miss Livingston's in it. My word, do you have many in the States like her?'

Aiken smiled. 'A few.'

'Enough to make a chap change his nationality! Come on; there's only an hour till tea-time. They're damnably prompt about meals and such.'

* * *

The beach was a scimitar of flawless sand, backed by coconut palms that hissed and rustled in the wind. The two men changed quickly, then walked down to the water's edge. Aiken stared at the sea, emerald where it flowed over the shallows, then shading to amethyst and indigo, peaceful, beautiful...

Davis read his thoughts. 'It's a lovely spot, no question about that. And a little of it's all right. But I wouldn't want to live here. Fine for a vacation, like this. But the flowers are too ruddy big, and the stars are too bright; the sun's too fierce, and the sea's too blasted blue. Your emotions are affected, too. If a man annoys you, you want to kill him. And if you

244

see a pretty girl ... Well, I've got a perfectly good fiancée back in Capetown, but ...'

He stopped in mid-sentence; Jan Livingston had come out of the other bath house. She was wearing a black bathing suit with no ornamentation. It was designed for maximum freedom in the water, and it fitted her like a second skin.

Davis gave an almost inaudible whistle. Aiken knew why, and he didn't blame the South African, but he felt a flash of anger so vivid that it startled him. He did not have to analyze it. It was pure, male-animal jealousy. He did not want Davis or any other man appraising this girl, admiring her.

She came up to them, fitting a white cap over her chestnut hair. She stood there for a moment, arms raised, the lines of her body sharp and clear against the aching blue of the sky. Then she plunged through the first waves, hit the water in a shallow dive, and disappeared.

They waited. Fifteen seconds. Thirty. Forty. Davis said, uneasily, 'D'you think she's all right? She's been under a ...'

Abruptly the white cap reappeared, fifty yards beyond the breakers. A brown arm beckoned them to follow; then the cap disappeared again.

'My word,' Davis said, 'she's a ruddy seal! Go ahead, join the lady. I stay where I can touch bottom if I have to.'

Aiken swam out slowly through the sun-flecked water. Beside him, without warning, Jan Livingston's glistening face appeared. 'Oh,' she said, 'it's wonderful down there. Come on; I'll show you.' She held out her hand. 'Take a deep breath. Take several; it puts oxygen into your bloodstream.'

He did as she ordered, then let her draw him under. They slanted down until Aiken could feel the thrust of pressure against his eardrums. The water was incredibly clear; it was like being led by a mermaid into some silent, silver world. A reef slid slowly beneath them. Near it, on the sand, Aiken saw a giant conch shell. His companion pointed and tugged at his hand, but he shook his head. They were deep enough; already he needed air.

For a moment her fingers tightened; then she let him go. He saw her spiral down, arms and legs glimmering, as he drove for the surface. He made it, lungs bursting, and sucked in great gulps of air. He was still breathing hard when the girl appeared.

'Got it!' She held up her trophy.

'You're amazing,' Aiken told her. 'What do you use for air?'

She laughed. 'Just a matter of practice. I've been swimming since I was three ...' Her voice changed suddenly. 'We seem to have visitors.'

Aiken swiveled himself around. A pair of horses were picking their way down the road that led to the beach. The riders were a man and a woman—the woman's hair flamed like brass under the slanting rays of the sun. A third horseman appeared. Behind Aiken, the girl spoke. 'They must be the Murdocks. Mrs. Mackie said they were out riding. Think I'll swim in and say hello.'

Aiken stared at her. 'You know Ace Murdock?'

'No,' she said softly, 'no. But I've heard of him.' She tossed the conch away and started back, driving through the water with a powerful, six-beat crawl. Aiken watched her walk out onto the beach, nod in response to Davis' introduction, then reach up and stroke the nose of the horse that carried the first male rider. The man leaned down and spoke to her, and even at that distance there was something about him that made Aiken's scalp tighten. Something cold, something arrogant, something—predatory. And evidently Murdock's wife resented something too, for suddenly she wheeled her horse around, gave it a cut with her riding crop, and went galloping back up the road that led to Haddon Hall.

Slowly Aiken swam back to the beach. As the distance narrowed, he saw that Murdock was a younger man than he had expected—and handsome, if you cared for the type. His black hair gleamed; his light, almost colorless eyes contrasted oddly with his suntanned face. He barely nodded when Davis introduced Aiken. He was looking down at Jan Livingston's bare shoulders and the warm, ivory column of her throat. She was smiling up at him, and Aiken had the queer impression that she was completely aware of Murdock's interest, was inviting it, was offering herself in a deliberate way for his inspection and approval.

Behind them, the other rider pulled up. He dismounted awkwardly, and Murdock laughed, straightening in the saddle. 'What's the matter, Capa? Getting a little saddle-sore?' It might have been a good-humored jibe, but it was not. There was a jeering note in Murdock's voice, as if he felt a secret contempt not only for Capa, but for the whole human race.

Capa hunched his shoulders and said nothing. Watching him, Aiken felt surprise. He had expected a bodyguard to be the gorilla type. This was a small man with slender, fragile hands and a face that looked almost babyish until you glanced into his eyes.

Swift and silent, a shadow raced across the beach. Looking up, Aiken saw a great vulture soaring over them, wings rigid, head out-thrust. Murdock nodded at it. 'Twenty bucks says you can't do it again, Capa.'

The little man said softly, 'You must like to lose money.' He seemed to coil himself inward in one smooth indescribable motion, and suddenly there was a gun in his hand, a long-barreled automatic that looked like a small-bore target pistol. It coughed three times, not loud, and overhead Aiken heard two sickening

248

little slaps as bullets met feathers. The vulture staggered, lost altitude, then recovered and began to climb. The gun coughed again. The great bird went into a whirling dive and plunged into the sea.

For five seconds, nobody spoke. Then Murdock said carelessly, 'So all right. So you win your twenty bucks.' He leaned forward and spoke to the girl. 'How about a drink in the bar when you're through playing mermaid?'

She hesitated. 'I'll think about it.'

He straightened up. 'I'll look for you.' He reined the horse around. 'Come on, Capa.' He drove his heels into the animal's sides. The little man re-mounted and followed.

Jan Livingston stood looking after them. Then, with a twist of her shoulders that might have been a shrug or a shudder, she walked over to the bath house, opened the door, went in.

Aiken glanced at Davis. The South African's face looked grim. 'A couple of pretty repulsive types, if you ask me. That Capa is a sadist, he enjoys senseless killing. As for Murdock, the fact that he has a wife doesn't seem to bother him at all.'

Aiken said, 'Does it bother her?'

'His wife?' Davis rasped the back of one big hand across his chin. 'The fair Elaine is not very good at concealing her feelings. You'll see.'

*   *   *

Tea was a ritual at Haddon Hall. They served it on a flagstone terrace that was roughly triangular, with an old bronze cannon at the apex, tranquilly pointing to the sea. Beyond the cannon, a footpath dropped steeply to the beach. Mrs. Mackie sat in an arbor covered with flame-vine and poured tea for those who wanted it.

Elaine Murdock did not appear at first. Her husband came, still in riding clothes, with Capa silent and watchful behind him. He glanced around at the other guests with his cool, contemptuous stare, then went straight up to Jan Livingston. 'The bar's not officially open yet,' he said. 'But I can probably persuade the barman to give us something better than tea.'

She looked up at him, the late sunlight gilding her skin, making her eyes a tawny color. From where he sat, Aiken could see a pulse throbbing faintly in the hollow of her throat. She nodded, and stood up. Murdock put his hand under her elbow. They moved away together. Everyone watched them. In the sudden silence, Davis cleared his throat, a sound eloquent of disapproval. Aiken heard a step behind them and turned. Elaine Murdock had come out onto the terrace.

He saw instantly that once she must have been a beautiful woman. But now the hollows in her cheeks were too deep, the lines around her mouth too bitter—and the erosion, Aiken felt, had not been caused by age so much as by frustration and jealousy and anger.

The French doors closed behind Murdock and the girl. Elaine Murdock stood rigid, gazing after them. Capa went up to her, offered her a cigarette, lit it for her. She moved to the far end of the terrace and stood by the cannon; Aiken could see the tip of the cigarette tremble. After a few moments she turned, crushed the cigarette under her foot as if trying to obliterate it altogether, crossed over to the French doors, went through them.

Aiken stood up suddenly, moved by anger. Why should Murdock be allowed to humiliate his wife in this way? Why was Jan Livingston acting like a cheap little pickup? Abruptly, he became aware that Capa was watching him with eyes as expressionless as the eyes of a shark. He stared back, not trying to conceal his animosity, until the other looked away. Then he went into the big house.

In the bar, a white-jacketed attendant was filling two tall glasses. Ace Murdock sat sideways on his bar stool, one hand resting with casual possessiveness on Jan Livingston's arm. He was looking up at his wife with a kind of sardonic enjoyment. 'I thought you'd had your quota, my dear. But if you really need another drink, take mine. No doubt it'll enhance your fatal charm.'

251

With one convulsive movement, Elaine Murdock picked up the glass and hurled it into the big mirror that backed the bar. The mirror splintered into fragments that sprayed all over the astounded barman.

For a long moment, nobody moved. The barman ducked and came up with a towel. Jan Livingston pushed back her stool. Her face was pale. She went out of the bar quickly, but she did not go alone. Aiken was three steps behind her. He caught up with her quickly. 'Wait a minute!' His breath came heavily, almost as if he had been running. 'What do you think you're doing? What are you trying to do?'

She looked at him levelly. 'What do you mean?'

'You know what I mean! You've known Murdock for less than two hours. You know what kind of a man he is. Yet you—you sit there and let him paw you! You—'

Her eyes blazed suddenly. 'What I do is my business, isn't it?'

'Not if it affects other people! You're humiliating Mrs. Murdock. You're embarrassing all of us. You're—'

She turned away from him without a word. He watched her move up the stairs, out of sight. He heard a slight noise behind him and swung around. Capa was lounging against the wall, watching him. Aiken said, furiously, 'What do you think you're staring at?'

The little man hunched his thin shoulders.

'Nothing much,' he said. 'Just you.'

* * *

Dressing for dinner, Aiken told himself that Jan Livingston was right: what she did was her own affair. If her idea of a holiday adventure was a sordid entanglement with a man like Murdock, then obviously she was not worth worrying about. He had misjudged her, that was all. From now on, the best thing to do was ignore her.

But this was not easy. At the long, narrow dinner table she sat opposite him, wearing a dress of pale yellow that left her shoulders bare. Her hair was brushed straight back and tied with a yellow ribbon, like a little girl's, and the combination of innocence and sophistication was devastating. Every time he looked at her, Aiken felt the impact of it, and he knew Ace Murdock did too.

Beyond her husband, Elaine Murdock sat tense and silent, eating almost nothing, crumbling bits of bread with thin, nervous fingers. Her face was flushed; it was obvious she had been drinking heavily. Across the table Davis tried, not very successfully, to engage her in conversation. Beyond Davis, Capa watched everything with his blank, empty eyes.

The moon rose out of the sea, orange, enormous. After dinner, there was coffee in the lounge. Aiken was asked to make a fourth at bridge, but declined. In spite of all his resolutions, he was watching Jan Livingston. She was being friendly with the other guests, talking with them, laughing with them. But the focus of her attention—Aiken was sure of it— was Murdock. She kept him constantly aware of her.

A calypso band appeared on the terrace. The young honeymooners went out and began to dance, dreamily, in the silver light. Ace Murdock moved indolently across the room, said something to Jan Livingston. She smiled and nodded, and they went out together.

Through the open doors, Aiken saw the girl move into Murdock's arms. The music was soft and tender and she danced close to him, her dress a pale smear in the semi-darkness. Elaine Murdock was watching too; Aiken saw her drive her fingernails into the palms of her hands.

Other guests were drifting out on the terrace, and Aiken went with them. Near the far end he saw Murdock and the girl, still dancing, but so slowly that it was more like an embrace. Abruptly, the revulsion and fury he felt was more than he could stand. He turned, went rapidly down the flight of stone steps that led to the courtyard. He went blindly through it, out into the road.

Behind him, the muted music went on mockingly. Ahead of him, the road sloped away, white as chalk in the moonlight. He began to walk along it, taking the fork that led to the beach. His shoes kicked up little puffs of silvery dust; his footsteps sounded loud in the listening night. He stopped abruptly, a hundred yards from the house, shoulders hunched, fists jammed into pockets. Why should he care what this girl did? Until twelve hours ago he hadn't known that she existed. What was it to him if she chose to behave like a tramp? *What was it to him?*

Just off the road was a great banyan tree, the coiled roots like twisted serpents in the dark. He moved over to it, sat down, lit a cigarette. Overhead the moon sailed, placid and indifferent. Somewhere back in the hills, a dog howled. The cigarette burned down until it scorched his fingers. He flipped it away in a shower of sparks.

He heard their footsteps before he saw them. They came around the bend, walking fast and close together, the man's shirt-front and the girl's dress luminous in the moonlight. They passed within twenty feet of Aiken without seeing him, so close that he could distinguish the yellow ribbon that Jan Livingston wore in her hair, could see on Murdock's face the arrogant, satisfied look of a man on his way to a lonely beach with a pretty girl, a pliant girl...

'So what if she did see us,' Murdock was saying, 'so who cares? She'll have a little tantrum, and then drink herself into her usual...'

The words trailed away. The footsteps receded, were gone. Back in the hills, the dog howled again. Then silence.

Aiken sat still, trying to keep his mind a blank, trying not to let his imagination follow the two figures down to the shadowy beach. But it was no use: he felt an anger, a sense of outrage so strong that when he tried to light another cigarette, the match trembled in his fingers. What was it Davis had said about this place? *Your emotions are affected, too. If a man annoys you, you want to kill him. And if you meet a good-looking girl . . .*

He made himself sit there until the fine, rapid tremor subsided. He took a deep breath, stood up, moved back onto the road. He would not stay here any longer than was necessary. He would go back to his room now, pack his bag, leave early in the morning.

He started walking back up the road to Haddon Hall. The anger seemed to have burned itself out; he felt drained, exhausted. Let them go, he thought wearily, let them keep their moonlight secrets. Let them walk the beach together, let them swim in the quicksilver dark, let them . . .

The impact of the idea was like a blow. He stood there, rigid, remembering the silent underwater world he had shared with the girl, the grip of her strong fingers as she drew him deeper, her fantastic ability to swim under water, to *remain* under water . . .

He made a strangled sound of protest, deep in his throat. It was all clear now: the tension he had sensed in the girl, her brazen behavior were all part of a plan, a carefully conceived and executed plan to lure Ace Murdock to the beach, alone and at night, and from the beach into the water. She was going to kill Murdock in the one way that would be both easy for her—and unprovable.

She was going to drown him.

Aiken whirled and began to run, back down the dusty road, back toward the beach. He had no interest in Murdock, dead or alive. But whatever her motive, whatever her reason, he did not want Jan Livingston to become a murderess, and ruin her life.

Under his feet, he felt the hard surface of the road change to soft sand. He raced through the grove of palm trees that backed the beach and halted, fighting for breath. For a moment he saw nothing; the beach seemed deserted. But then something moved against the moonpath, and he saw the silhouettes of Murdock and the girl at the water's edge. Jan Livingston was wearing her black bathing suit and white cap; Murdock was in swimming trunks. A wave broke white around their ankles, and Aiken saw Murdock draw the girl close and kiss her.

He took a step forward, but before he could move out of the shadow of the trees he saw Elaine Murdock run across the sand from the footpath that dropped in a steep zig-zag from

257

Haddon Hall's terrace. Straight toward her husband she ran. He turned to face her, and as he did Aiken heard something cough, a harsh, metallic sound, and he saw Murdock fall, face down in the gleaming water.

Jan Livingston screamed, the sound high and shrill as Aiken raced across the beach. Water swirled around his ankles as he caught Murdock by the shoulders and dragged him up on the sand. He looked once at the ruined face, then rolled the body over while the dark smear widened. A shadow moved, and looking up he saw Capa.

'You fool!' said Aiken hoarsely. 'Why did you give her the gun?'

'Because she asked for it,' Capa said. 'And because he had it coming to him.'

*   *   *

The police had come and gone, the long questioning was over; they were alone. Outside, the first hint of sunrise tinted the eastern sky with a gentle beauty.

'Yes,' the girl said dully, 'I planned to kill him. He was a blackmailer, an extortionist.'

Aiken nodded.

'If it hadn't been for him, my husband would be alive today. But—Do you want to hear all this?'

'If you want to tell it,' Aiken said. 'Might be good for you to talk it out, at that.'

258

'What makes it all so horrible is that my husband was really innocent. Yet this man framed him. Then drove him relentlessly, viciously until he—until he took his own life. I told myself killing Murdock wouldn't be murder. It would be justice. And besides I didn't want this terrible sort of thing to happen to anyone else.'

Aiken said, 'Do you think you would have gone through with it?'

'Yes,' she said. 'The way you go through a nightmare.'

'I still don't think you'd have done it,' Aiken said.

'I had every intention to. I found out Murdock was here. I made a reservation in my maiden name. And I played up to him, and if I could do that I could have—I could have—'

She turned away from him suddenly and covered her face with her hands.

Aiken stood looking at her. He wanted to console her, but he didn't know what he could say. For the time being it might be best if he just kept quiet.

THE LOOSE END

S. Wasylyk

The tall, baggy-suited, black-haired kid carrying the lightweight briefcase was making too many trips in the automatic elevators to be up to anything legitimate, especially since he was Nipsy Turko, a small-time thief with a long record of losing.

The only person in a position to notice or pay much attention was me, Mark Stedd, a one-armed ex-detective operating a newsstand in the lobby of the building where the elevators were located, and to tell the truth I don't know why I bothered.

The only reason I was inhabiting that cramped hole behind the newsstand was as a personal favor to Manny, an old friend who at the moment was living it up in Florida. Manny's request had been heartily seconded as good rehabilitation by the doctors who had removed what remained of my left arm after the psycho with the shotgun had ripped it to shreds three months before.

I moved out from the cramped hole behind the newsstand to keep an eye on the jack-in-the-box movements of Nipsy. That hole was tailored to fit Manny, six inches shorter and fifty pounds lighter than I, even without a left arm, and I was happy to get out of it.

At the lobby doors I glanced at my watch. Within five minutes the building would begin to empty for lunch and Nipsy could get lost in the crowd. At the other end of the empty lobby glass doors revealed the writing counters of the bank on the first floor of the adjacent building. Friend Nipsy suddenly barged out of an elevator, walked through to the bank, stopped at one of the writing counters, and dropped his briefcase at his feet. Then the lunch crowd hit and the lobby filled rapidly.

I began to push my way forward, almost reaching the doors, when a short, older type with a narrow face hurried through the bank, stopped alongside the kid, busied himself for a moment, then took the kid's briefcase while the kid picked up the one Narrow Face had brought. Narrow Face, another loser in Nipsy's class named Slow Harry Fisher, went out the far bank door in a hurry, and the kid headed back through the glass doors, angling for the nearest elevator. I caught his eye above the crowd and Nipsy, stony-faced, paused for a moment, then stepped into the elevator, pushed a button, and the doors slammed in my face.

Now I heard the wailing of police sirens, which sighed to a halt outside the bank. I reached out and caught the nearest arm. An attractive dark-haired woman, on her way to lunch, turned, looked at me with narrowed

261

eyes.

'Take it easy.' I grinned at her. 'I'd like you to go out there and bring back a policeman, any policeman. Will you do it?'

I'd always gotten along pretty well with women and this one turned out to be no exception. Her face softened, she smiled, nodded, and headed out through the bank, surprising me because local citizens weren't noted for their willingness to become involved in police business.

She brought back one of the older patrolmen, a sensible type named Tompkins.

'Mark,' he said, 'glad to see you up and around.'

I nodded at the crowd outside the bank. 'What goes?'

'Someone took the jewelry store next door.'

'I think I saw your man switch briefcases. Even if you pick him up, I don't think you'll find the jewels on him. They're somewhere upstairs with a kid named Nipsy Turko.'

'You sure?'

'I'm not sure of anything. I'm telling you what I saw and think. Who's in charge?'

Tompkins shrugged. 'Barnes, probably. Your friend here collared me before I had a chance to find out.'

'Then let's get Barnes in here and let him worry about it.'

Tompkins moved. 'I'll get him.'

I shook my head. 'No, thanks. Nipsy is big

enough to handle a one-arm like me if he comes down while you're gone. My battling days are over. I'd rather you took the bank end of the lobby while I stay here. We'll let our beautiful friend get Barnes.' I turned to the woman. 'What's your name, beautiful friend?'

'Diane Waverly.'

'Look, Miss Waverly, will you go to the jewelry store, find the officer in charge, tell him we have some information concerning the robbery, and bring him in here?'

She looked at me coolly. 'Shall I lead him by the nose or the hand?'

I watched her walk away and grinned at Tompkins. 'If I were Barnes, I'd follow her just to follow her.'

Tompkins grinned back. 'Why do you think I came?'

We separated and waited. The lobby was still crowded and I hoped Nipsy wouldn't show. It would be no big chore for him to come down and take off before Tompkins or I could get to him through all those people.

The woman brought Barnes more quickly than I anticipated. Cold-eyed and dapper, Barnes looked more like an advertising executive than a detective-lieutenant, but he was smart. Younger than I, he was a loner, cool and hard, and had moved up through the ranks fast, acquiring a reputation I'd always felt was a little inflated. I never did like him very much.

'Mark, you look good.'

Smooth, I thought admiringly. I know how I looked after three months in that hospital, but he stands there telling me I look good and sounding as if he meant it.

'Joe,' I told him, 'I might have something for you here. You have a make on the guy who knocked off the store?'

He shook his head. 'Small build, thin face, middle-aged; that's all I have.'

'How does Slow Harry Fisher sound?'

'Slow Harry taking a jewelry store? By himself?' Barnes looked at me in amazement.

'Description fits, doesn't it?'

'Sure, but it fits a lot of other guys too.'

'How many other guys come running into a bank, switch briefcases with a loser like Nipsy Turko just a minute or two after the robbery, and take off in the noonday crowd like he just welshed on a big bet?'

'You saw this?'

'Joe,' I said patiently, 'losing your left arm doesn't affect your eyesight. Naturally, I saw it. I also saw Nipsy take off with the briefcase, hit one of the elevators here, and disappear upstairs. So far as I know he's still up there, unless he knows a way out that doesn't come through this lobby, and all this after Nipsy spent a half hour riding each elevator in the building before he met Slow Harry.'

'Slow Harry and Nipsy, there's a combination for you. They'd be in over their heads taking a corner candy store.'

264

'How much did they get?'

'Maybe about two hundred grand in cut and uncut stones, nothing mounted.'

'No sense standing here gabbing about it. You going to look for Nipsy?'

'I guess I'll have to. I'll put an all-points out on Slow Harry, too. If you saw it, you saw it, although I still don't believe it.'

In no time at all there was a uniform at each entrance, one in each elevator, and the superintendent was explaining the building to Barnes.

It was also no time at all before they brought Nipsy down. The trouble was, Nipsy no longer carried the briefcase. Barnes looked at me and I nodded, laughing to myself. Since Nipsy no longer had the briefcase, he'd passed it off or stashed it somewhere. Now Barnes had to go look for it.

Standing alongside the newsstand, my beautiful friend asked, 'What's going on? As official messenger, don't you think I'm entitled to know?'

I explained the situation. 'Just putting two and two together,' I nodded toward Barnes, 'it appears we've come up with zero.'

Two policemen led Nipsy away as Barnes came up. 'Well, he knows his constitutional rights. Not saying a word. I'm booking him on the basis of what you saw but unless we find that briefcase we don't have a thing.'

'Then find the briefcase.'

His eyebrows went up. 'You're a real bundle of joy. Fourteen floors, who knows how many closets, rooms, rest rooms, offices and people. It will take us all afternoon.'

I grinned. 'I'll make a deal with you. For ten percent of the take, I'll search the building for you. Payable only if I find it, of course. I tell you the kid took the briefcase up. It hasn't come down yet.'

Barnes shook his head. 'I still don't get it. Two losers like Nipsy Turko and Slow Harry Fisher, who couldn't plan their way out of a subway concourse even by reading the signs, coming up with something like this. Ordinarily, if either got his hands on two hundred grand worth of anything, he'd be moving in a straight line so fast he'd be a blur. But not this time. They take it slow and easy like a couple of pros. One hits the store during the noonday rush, passes the stuff to the other, who ditches it so that if they get picked up they're both clean. Someone set this up for them. The question is who? Someone from this building?'

'I doubt it,' I said. 'Nothing here except corporation offices, lawyers, advertising agencies, insurance companies, that sort of thing. I'd guess it would be someone from outside. This is a public building. Anyone can walk in. The only thing you can do is find the briefcase before he does.'

Barnes scratched his ear and shrugged.

266

'Well, I don't have any better ideas. Might as well follow yours.' He lined up the super and a half-dozen men and gave them their instructions. With a man at each end of the lobby, no briefcase would leave that building without being examined.

I remembered Diane. 'If you were on your way to lunch, I'm sorry I held you up. What's your boss going to say? Anything I can do to help?'

She half-smiled. 'I won't have any trouble. My boss is away and I'm pretty much on my own. How about you? What were you going to do for lunch?'

'Never gave it a thought.'

'Suppose I bring something back for you?'

'Would you mind? Just coffee will do.'

'On one condition. You look tired. Get behind that counter and get some rest.'

'Lady, you have a deal.'

I gratefully sank onto the stool Manny kept behind the counter. Things were quieter now in the lobby, most of the building crowd back from lunch. I could imagine Barnes' men working their way down, office by office, floor by floor, looking for that briefcase.

Twelve years of my life had been spent in situations like this and now they were gone with nothing but a small pension to show for it. I smiled grimly. I could have been dead, but all I lost was an arm. I didn't intend to stop living because of it. There were plenty of ways for a one-armed man with twelve years of police experience to get along. All it would take would be a little thought and some hard work. One thing sure, I wasn't giving up on Mark Stedd.

Glancing up, for the second time that day I saw a man taller than myself. This one, a complete contrast to Nipsy, was expensively dressed, well-built and distinguished looking in a dissipated sort of way, and carrying a briefcase. He motioned imperiously at Barnes, spoke to him for a few minutes, then paced back and forth impatiently until an elevator appeared.

A soft voice said, 'Here's your coffee.'

I looked up at Diane. 'Beautiful friend, you look more beautiful than ever.'

'You didn't say how you like it, so I guessed black, one sugar.'

'Someone told you,' I lied. Actually I liked plenty of cream and sugar.

She smiled. 'Nope. You just look the type.'

I used my thumb to pry up the lid of the plastic container, rotating the cup slowly as I gradually worked it loose. I noticed she didn't offer to help and liked her for it. The lid gave with a sudden pop.

'You two have anything more to contribute?' Barnes asked, leaning against the counter.

'Not a thing, Joe. Who was the big guy with the briefcase?'

'He's the poor victim,' Barnes said dryly. 'The owner of the jewelry store. Going up to see his insurance company to report the loss. Doesn't waste any time, does he?'

'Looks more the type to get on the phone and yell for his insurance man to come to him, especially for a couple of hundred thousand dollars.'

'They won't pay until we tell them the jewels are gone,' said Barnes. 'No sense rushing.'

'Those jewels aren't gone,' I said. 'They're somewhere in this building.' I grinned to myself. Why not give Barnes something to think about? 'How's this for a theory? He's your outside man. He hires the two to rob the store, has the kid plant the jewels here in the building right next door, comes in supposedly to see his insurance company, files his claim and picks up the jewels at the same time. That way he doesn't lose a stone, yet collects the insurance. Be pretty safe. You'd never check his briefcase. Even if you did, you wouldn't know if any stones he had in there were the stolen ones or not. Be a nice way to get out of money trouble if he's been living it up too much, and he sure looks like he has.'

Barnes looked down into the coffee cup. 'You could be right, but what are you drinking? It has to be more than coffee to come up with a wild one like that.'

'Okay.' I grinned. 'Put a man on him or don't. From now on come up with your own theories.'

I finished my coffee and flipped the cup at the wastebasket behind the counter. It missed and I muttered under my breath.

As I picked it up, I turned it over in my fingers and the idea came, went, came again and I grinned. Why not? I moved past the woman, motioning Barnes to come with me, headed toward the elevators, and punched the call button. One of the elevators hit the lobby floor and opened its doors. I stepped inside, looked up, and found what I was looking for, the usual service door in the ceiling. I reached up and pushed. The door moved. With two good arms, I could have thrown the door open, grasped the edge and taken a look at the elevator roof.

Barnes looked at me strangely and whistled softly. I gave him credit for catching on quickly.

'Now you know what Nipsy was doing in the elevators,' I told him. 'Each of these service doors has a catch that needs a half turn with a screwdriver or coin before it can be opened. Not knowing which elevator he would get after the switch, Nipsy took no chances. He opened them all. Probably pushed the briefcase up through the door the minute the elevator was empty. Want to bet that briefcase isn't riding on the roof of one of these elevators?'

'No bet, Mark.' Barnes motioned to one of the men in the lobby. 'See if there is anything up there.'

The detective leaped up, poked his head through the opening, then dropped down.

'Nothing but grease and dirt,' he reported.

The fifth one had the briefcase resting on the roof.

'Get it down,' Barnes ordered.

'No, hold it, Joe,' I said slowly. 'There's no hurry. Nipsy left it here for some reason. As you said, if *he* was supposed to keep the ice, he'd have kept going through the lobby. He left it here for someone. Why not play it cool and see what happens?'

Barnes stroked his chin. 'Why not? With someone on the roof of the elevator and a couple of plainclothesmen at the lobby doors, I can wait to see if someone picks it up.'

I grinned. 'Good luck. I think I'll go sell some papers. That's what Manny's paying me for.'

Diane was still waiting.

'Sold any papers for me?'

'Not even a magazine.'

'Manny better not spend too much in Florida. At this rate, he'll be broke when he gets back.'

She laughed. 'Is the action over now?'

'All except the grand finale. Barnes will take care of it from here on.'

'In that case, I'd better get back to work. I've enjoyed every minute.'

'I owe you one coffee. Settle for a dinner

271

tomorrow night?'

'Now that's what I call a fair offer. Accepted.'

'Fine. I'll be waiting for you here.'

I watched her swinging hips move away— regretfully. I wouldn't be here tomorrow night. By then, I'd be well on my way out of the country.

The lobby was practically empty now. I told Barnes I was going to the men's washroom on the second floor. Once there, I removed the jewels from the paper towel dispenser where Nipsy had left them for me, locked myself in one of the stalls, and carefully began to stow them in the pocketed belt I was wearing under my shirt.

Two hundred thousand dollars; little enough payment for my left arm, and quite adequate payment for the three weeks it took me to plan the operation, talk Manny into taking his vacation, and browbeat Nipsy and Slow Harry into pulling the job for a small fee. They couldn't refuse since I had plenty on both that the syndicate boys would like to know. Besides, they were safe enough. The only thing the police had on Nipsy was my testimony and I wouldn't be around; as for Slow Harry, they'd have only a simple eyewitness account and no substantial evidence.

Two hundred thousand dollars. I laughed. I owed the department this little job for passing me up for promotion twice and for sending me into that house with a rookie partner who froze instead of firing when the psycho swung the shotgun my way. If I hadn't moved fast, he would have nailed me dead center instead of catching my arm.

Too bad Barnes hadn't bought that story about the jewelry store owner. It would have been good for a big laugh. The only touchy part of the operation was when he wanted to bring the briefcase down. For a quick moment, until I talked him out of it, I regretted showing him where it was. I had expected him to figure it out himself, especially after telling him about Nipsy riding the elevators before the switch, but he didn't pick it up. As I thought, he wasn't as smart as they said he was, so I had to hurry things along.

I had long relished the thought of walking out with those jewels around my waist while somebody guarded that empty briefcase on the elevator roof and I didn't want to be cheated out of it.

Sure, I could have set it up in a half-dozen other ways a lot safer, but this was the way I wanted it—right under their noses—and Bright Boy Barnes getting the assignment was the cake's icing.

I carefully checked the belt to make sure it didn't bulge, buttoned my shirt and coat, unlocked the stall and stepped out into the washroom.

Arms folded, Barnes was leaning against a
273

wash basin, looking at me with his cold eyes. 'You going to make trouble, Mark? We don't want to hurt you. We know that arm isn't quite healed yet.'

I could have killed him, not because I was caught, but because he had absolutely no business being there. With two good arms ... But I didn't have two good arms.

'No trouble, Joe.'

We walked out of the washroom and took the elevator to the lobby.

'Search him,' Barnes told one of his men. He found the belt with no trouble.

'You want to know why, Mark?' he asked gently.

I nodded, although I really didn't care. All I could think of was the two hundred thousand dollars in that belt the detective was holding, the two hundred thousand that really was mine.

'The odds,' Barnes said. 'I figured the odds of you being here in the lobby, of seeing the kid Nipsy, of seeing the briefcase switch, of knowing where to look for the briefcase. The odds were tremendous, Mark. You always were a hard-luck cop, a good man to have around but no big brain, yet you were always one step ahead of me today and that just didn't figure. The percentages say I should have been one step ahead of you. As far as I was concerned, until the whole thing was wrapped up, you were a loose end and I never liked loose ends. Watching you was just something I had to do.'

I'd given him a neatly wrapped package that any sensible man would have bought with no questions asked. All he had to do was watch that briefcase. It was the right thing to do, the logical thing to do, but here he was babbling about odds, percentages, loose ends.

I started to laugh. *Some* detective. And they passed *me* over twice for promotion.

THAT SO-CALLED LAUGH

F. Sisk

Captain Thomas McFate, the man in charge, turned from the swimming pool and came back to the patio. Again he looked down at the body which lolled in a redwood lounge chair and was obviously clothed in nothing but the terrycloth robe.

A purple bubble above the right eye marked the bullet's point of entry and a little cloud of gnats behind the left ear indicated where it had come out. Big blue-winged flies were exploring the toes of the bare feet. McFate leaned over a half-filled glass of tepid liquid on the redwood table beside the chair—gin and tonic, about an hour old. An ashtray contained a self-consumed cigarette, a cylinder of gray. It was then that he noticed the powder-blue envelope protruding from the pocket of the robe.

Crumpled, as if it had been shoved into the pocket with undue force, the envelope was addressed in a somewhat immature feminine hand to *Norman Markham*. There was no further address and the flap was not sealed. Inside were several pages of powder-blue paper compactly covered with lines of writing that sometimes formed a grammatical sentence.

'Dear Norm,' read McFate, 'even knowing

it's useless I am still fool enough to give you one more chance, a showdown, whether it's me or Michele, only I want you to look me right in the eye this time and say it with your own lips and not thru some third party. And if it's Michele as it seems to of been these last few lousy months, well then it's curtains for me, Norm, and this time I mean it so help me.

'I've suffered enough in the name of "love" to be an old decreepit hag, Norm, and here tomorrow I'm going to be just 24 years of age if I live that long. Maybe you'll be able to check it out in the obits, my real age.

'I'm penning these words by your swimming pool, the same pool that once upon a time was going to be ours. Remember? If you can force your mind back a million years maybe you can remember and how you used to tell me I was the brightest star on your horizon. It must of been at least a million years ago because I was young enough then to believe every word you said. I was going on 22, Norm.

'Don't laugh. I know these are mere words on paper and you are 10 miles away at the studio but I half expect you to laugh as if you were right here looking over my shoulder. Like you had ESP or that Yoga thing. And I can't stand that so-called laugh again, Norm.

'Funny how I once thought that laugh was the freakiest thing, good freaky I mean, and I used to admire how you spooned it out on a bad shooting day to the actors and prop men

277

and the sourballs behind the cameras but I was only a script girl then and I couldn't tell a mask from a pancake job, hardly. Then you gave me those three lines to say in that western pilot, the floperoo of the TV season, and I got to know the laugh better, the off-duty side, and the way it could cut a girl's heart to ribbons as easy as any knife.

'You employed it the day you pulled the rug out from under our wedding plans. Remember? Friday nite Sept. 29th, a day I won't ever forget, never. We were supposed to drive to Vegas and have dinner on the way but when I arrived at the office you were leaving with two two-suiters and a flight ticket to New York, a big-money emergency, and when I asked how long you'd be gone you said "Long enough, Sara, just long enough," and then you made with that so-called laugh which you might as well have throwed a glass of ice water in my face.

'What was it supposed to mean, what was I suppose to figure?

'Well, I found out later the hard way, didn't I, Norm, when you came back a week later with that so-called redhead, a third lead in a second-rate musical from summer stock, and you didn't so much as give me a buzz and probably wouldn't have looked me up at all if I hadn't taken that overdose of sleeping pills. So then you came to the hospital with flowers and a smooth story how the redhead was simply a new face for the variety pilot and I believed you hook, line and sinker until the next time ...'

'What is it, Skipper—a love letter?'

McFate glanced at the man who had just wandered through the French windows. 'I'd classify it more a suicide letter, Sergeant.'

The sergeant looked at the body. 'Suicide? You must be kidding, Skipper.'

'... it was that slinky dame you picked up on location in Mexicali,' McFate resumed reading. 'I warned you it was she or me, this life wasn't big enough for both of us, but you came on with that laugh of yours. Even when I told you I'd kill myself you gave me the laugh again. "Have a big sleep," you said. Well, I almost did, Norm, and you know it. If that extra hadn't left his bike in the garage and come to get it when he did, I'd have slept forever on the front seat of the car with gas purring out of the pipe.

'The story of my life, one imported witch after another, and this time it's a so-called Frenchy but this time I got a peculiar feeling it's a little different. This time you're talking marriage again, like you did with me long long ago, and though I don't believe you have any real "follow-thru" in your makeup, I never the less have to confront you with the $64 question. Are you serious about Michele or not? If the answer is yes then, Norm, I am really going to kill myself and no near misses this time, no pills, no gas pipe, no razors on the wrists. This time I got a gun with bullets in it—that cute little 2-shot derringer you gave me in an ivory case, so that I could defend myself from all the wolves but you. Ha ha. And I'm going to make you a witness Norm, like it or not, because if it's Michele instead of me I'm going to stand right in front of you and pull the trigger so that you'll remember this moment the rest of your life, what you done to an honest girl whose worst fault was loving you. And I don't think you will laugh this off in a hurry, Norm, wait and see. Always your Sara.'

'If it's suicide, Skipper,' the sergeant was saying, 'where the hell's the gun?'

McFate put the letter in his pocket. 'A girl named Sara took it with her, one of the deceased's girlfriends.'

'You mean this guy Markham shot himself and some girlfriend swipes the gun?'

'Not exactly, Sergeant. The girl intended to shoot herself but Markham laughed at her. Notice there's still a slight smile of sarcasm on the face.'

280

A VERY SPECIAL TALENT

M. B. Maron

'But he used to hit me,' Angela explained, rubbing her shoulder in memory of past bruises. 'What else could I do?'

'You could have divorced him,' I said firmly.

'He wouldn't let me. You know what the grounds for divorce were in this state then. Don't you care that he beat me?'

Of course it enraged me that that brute had hit my lovely, fragile-looking wife, even if it had been before I'd met her. 'Nevertheless,' I said, 'it's the principle of the thing. It just isn't done.'

'It was his own fault,' she insisted. 'I told him it was dangerous to have the radio that close to the bathtub when he'd been drinking but that was like waving a red flag at a bull. He would have done it then or died.'

She giggled suddenly, remembering that he had, indeed, died.

I was appalled. What does a man do when, after seven blissful years of marriage and two lovely children, he discovers that his adorable little fluff of a wife is a cold-blooded murderess who goes around killing people who aren't nice to her?

'I am *not* a cold-blooded murderess,' Angela

281

flared indignantly, 'and I would never, *never* kill anyone who wasn't nasty to a whole lot of other people, too.'

At this point the back screen door banged and Sandy, my five-year-old replica right down to a cowlick of red hair and a faceful of freckles, burst into the room and angrily demanded, 'What's the matter with you guys? Can't you hear Matt crying? Georgie hit him and he's all bloody!'

Angela whirled and followed Sandy from the room at a trot, with me just behind them.

Four-year-old Matt sat sobbing on the back doorstep. Blood trickled from a split on his lower lip onto his white T-shirt while Sandy's best friend, Chris Coffey, awkwardly patted his shoulder.

One of the things I love about Angela is her absolute cool whenever one of the boys is hurt. I tend to panic at the sight of their blood, but she remains calm and utterly soothing.

She swooped Matt up in her arms, assessed the damage and cheerfully assured him that he wouldn't need stitches. In the kitchen, she applied a cold cloth to his swollen lip and soon had him tentatively smiling again.

The screen door banged again and Jill Coffey, our next door neighbor and Angela's closest friend, came charging in. 'That Georgie! I saw it all! Matt hadn't done a thing to him and Georgie just hauled off and socked him!'

'Yeah, Dad,' Sandy chimed in. 'He won't let us swing, and it's our jungle vine. Chris and me, we built it.'

Matt started to cry again, Jill raged on, Angela began to shoot sparks, and Sandy's shrill indignation pierced the chaotic din.

'Hold it!' I shouted. 'One at a time.'

With many interruptions, a coherent story finally emerged.

When our development was built, the creek which used to cut through our back yards had been diverted, leaving an eight-foot gully overhung with huge old willows which the developers had mercifully spared. With so much of the area bulldozed into sterility, the gully lured kids from blocks around.

Depending on the degree of danger, various stretches of it attracted different age groups: the pre-adolescents usually congregated a block away, where the banks were somewhat steeper and the old creek rocks larger and more jagged. In the section between our house and the Coffeys', the bank was more of a gentle grassy slope and there were fewer rocks, so the pre-school set usually played there.

It seemed that Sandy and his cronies had tied a clothesline rope to one of the overhanging willow branches and had been playing Tarzan, swinging out over the gully as if on jungle vines, experiencing a thrill of danger more imaginary than real. Then Georgie Watson had come along and, as usual, destroyed their fun by taking over the rope swing and hitting Matt.

An overweight nine-year-old, Georgie was a classic neighborhood bully, afraid of boys his own age and a terror to everyone under six. No neighborhood gathering was complete without a twenty-minute discussion of Georgie's latest bit of maliciousness and a psychological dissection of his motives which usually ended with, 'Well, what can you expect, with parents like that?'

I suppose every suburban neighborhood has its one obnoxious family; it seems to be written into the building code. At any rate, the Watsons were ours: loud, vulgar, self-righteous, and completely heedless of anyone else's rights and desires.

They gave boisterous mid-week parties which broke up noisily at one in the morning, or they would come roaring home at two from a Saturday night on the town and Mr. Watson would lean on the horn to bring the baby-sitter out.

After such a riotous night, you'd think the man would have the decency to sleep in on Sunday morning nursing a king-size hangover, but no. There he'd be, seven o'clock the next morning, cranking what must be the world's noisiest lawn mower and carrying on a shouted conversation with Mrs. Watson in the upstairs bedroom.

Mrs. Watson was just as bad. Georgie had

been born after they had given up all hope of having children and she doted on him. Though quick enough to complain when any boy Georgie's age or older picked on him, she was completely blind to his faults.

If confronted by an angry parent and bleeding child, Mrs. Watson would look the enraged mother straight in the eye and say blandly, 'Georgie said he didn't do it and I find Georgie to be very truthful. Besides, he *never* provokes a fight.'

'That kid is a menace to the neighborhood!' Angela fumed, after the three boys had settled down in front of the TV with a pitcher of lemonade.

We had moved out to our screened back porch and Angela was still so angry that her paring knife sliced with wicked precision as she frenched the string beans for dinner.

'But the doctors must love him,' Jill said wryly. 'Five days into summer vacation and he's drawn blood at least four times that I know of.'

She stopped helping Angela with the beans and ticked off the incidents on her fingers. 'Dot's boy had to have three stitches after Georgie threw a rock at him; he pushed little Nancy Smith onto a broken bottle; my Chris got a cut on his chin when Georgie tripped him yesterday, and now your Matt. How we'll get through this summer without having all our kids put in the hospital, I don't know.'

'Somebody ought to do something about him,' Angela said, giving me a meaningful look.

'Not me,' I protested. 'The last time I complained to Watson about Georgie, he waved a monkey wrench in my face and told me adults ought to let kids fight it out among themselves.'

'I know!' Jill exclaimed brightly. 'Let's hire a couple of twelve-year-olds to beat him up!'

'The Watsons would sue,' said Angela glumly.

'Maybe they'll send him to camp or something this year,' I offered hopefully.

'Not a chance,' Angela said. 'Mrs. Watson couldn't be separated from him that long.'

She finished the beans, wiped the paring knife on the seat of her denim shorts, then gazed out through the early evening twilight toward the gully, absentmindedly thwacking the handle of the knife on the palm of her hand.

'Think positively,' she said suddenly. 'Maybe Georgie did us a favor just now.'

Jill and I looked at each other blankly.

'Maybe that rope isn't safe to swing on,' she said.

'But it's good and strong, Mrs. Barrett,' Chris volunteered from the doorway. Their program over, the three boys had drifted out to the porch.

'Yeah, Mom,' Sandy added. 'I tied it with a square knot, just like Dad showed me.'

286

'He did,' echoed Matt with all the assurance of one who hadn't even mastered a granny knot yet.

Angela grinned at him and tousled his hair, a gesture he hated. 'Just the same, I'd feel better if your father and I took a look at it.'

So out we all went, across the already dew-dampened grass to the gully, and while I examined the rope for signs of fraying, Angela swung her lithe hundred pounds up into the willow tree with catlike grace. Naturally, Matt and Sandy are the envy of their peers with a mother who thinks nothing of dropping her work and her dignity to shinny up a tree for a tangled kite or to clamber onto a roof to get a ball lodged in the rain gutters.

'It seems strong enough,' I said. 'What about the knot, Angela?' Between the leaves and the fading light, I could barely see her.

She poked her neat little pointed face through the willow leaves. 'I really don't think it's safe, Alex. Could you pick up a stronger rope?'

She dropped to the ground, barely panting with the exertion. 'It's a fine knot,' she said to Sandy, 'but the rope is old. Dad'll get you another tomorrow; but until he does, I want your solemn promise that you won't swing on it or let any of your friends swing on it.'

'That goes for you, too, Chris,' Jill said.

'Well it doesn't go for me!' sneered a juvenile voice.

We whirled, and there was dear old Georgie, cocky in the security of knowing that we were too civilized to smack the impertinence off his face.

'Oh, yes, it does,' Angela contradicted coldly. 'If it isn't strong enough to hold the little ones, it isn't strong enough to hold you.'

Georgie flushed at this allusion to his weight. It seemed to be his only sensitive spot. 'You're not my mother,' he yelled, 'and I don't have to mind you!'

I took a step toward him, my civility rapidly retreating before a barbarous desire to flatten him, but Angela restrained me.

'It's dangerous, Georgie, so you'll just have to stay off of it,' she said, and took the end of the rope and tossed it up into the tree.

'I can still get it,' Georgie taunted, but he showed no inclination to do so, with me blocking his path.

At that moment, Mrs. Watson called him in for the evening. Jill suddenly remembered that she'd forgotten to take a steak out of the freezer and headed for home with Chris, while Angela, Sandy and I gave Matt a head start before racing to our own back door.

The prospect of a long summer spent coping with Georgie Watson, together with the usual mayhem of feeding, tubbing and bedding our two young acrobats, blotted out the interrupted conversation I'd been having with Angela until we were in bed ourselves. I remembered it with a jolt.

'Didn't the police suspect anything?' I asked in the semidarkness of our bedroom.

'The police were very sympathetic and nice,' Angela murmured sleepily. 'They could see he had locked the bathroom door himself. Actually, all I had done was balance the radio too close to the edge of the shelf and hope for the best.' As if that ended it, she rolled over and put the pillow over her head.

'Oh, no, you don't!' I muttered, lifting the pillow, for I had just recalled something else. 'What about "The Perfect Example"?'

'Sh!' she whispered. 'You'll wake the boys.'

'Well, *did* you?' I whispered hoarsely.

* * *

In that city neighborhood where we had spent our first two years of marriage, home had been a second floor walkup in a converted brownstone. Its age, dinginess and general state of deterioration were somewhat ameliorated by the low rent and large, relatively soundproof rooms, and it attracted several other young couples.

We were all blithely green at life and marriage, determined to succeed in both, and that old house would have exuded happiness had it not been for the constantly disapproving eye of our landlady.

She lived on the third floor of the house, and

every time the outer vestibule door opened she would appear on the landing, lean over the wobbly old mahogany railing and peer down the marble stairwell, hoping to catch someone sneaking in a forbidden pet or leaving a shopping cart in the vestibule.

She bullied her husband, tyrannized her three timorous daughters, and took a malicious delight in stirring up animosity among her tenants. 'I don't care what that snip in 2-D says,' she would confide to her innocent victim, 'I think your clothes are very ladylike.'

It was only after you had lived in the house a couple of months that you realized she was putting lies in your mouth, too. It was like an initiation to a fraternity, that first two months. Afterward, you would laugh with the more experienced tenants and compare the lies as they recalled, with amusing mimicry, how they knew by your icy expression exactly when she had slandered them to you.

She was such a perfect example of everything the young wives never wanted to become that we all called her 'The Perfect Example' behind her back.

It was bad enough when she pitted couple against couple, but it stopped being funny when she managed to slip her knifed tongue into a shaky marriage, as happened twice while we lived there. The first marriage probably would have crumbled anyhow, but the second was a couple of teen-agers deeply in love but handicapped by parental opposition and the sheer inexperience of youth.

When she discovered what was happening, Angela broke the rule of silence and tried to make them understand how 'The Perfect Example' was destroying them, but it was too late. The girl went home to her parents and the boy stormed off to California.

Never had I seen Angela so blazingly angry. 'She's like a big fat spider, leaning on that railing, watching us flies walk in and out, spinning her web for the defenseless midges!' she raged, almost in tears. 'Why aren't there laws against people like that?'

So it had seemed like divine vengeance when, two days later, the decrepit mahogany railing had finally pulled loose from the wall and collapsed under her weight, and 'The Perfect Example' had plummeted to the marble tiles of the vestibule three floors below. As soon as the police had declared her death a regrettable accident, her husband had put the house up for sale and happily removed himself and the three dazed daughters back to the corn fields of his native Kansas.

'What about "The Perfect Example"?' I repeated, shaking Angela.

'Oh, Alex,' she pleaded, 'it's after midnight.'

'I want to know.'

'She *knew* the house was old, but she was too miserly to spend a cent in repairs. That rail would have collapsed sooner or later—you heard the police say that—and I just helped it along a bit. And don't forget that I told her it wasn't safe to lean against all the time.'

'That was sporting of you,' I said bitterly. 'Just because you warned those two—that *is* all, isn't it?—you think that justifies everything!'

'Tell me something, Angela—*Angela!* Boy, your parents had some sense of humor when they named *you!*—how do you see yourself? As an avenging angel or Little Mary Sunshine scattering rays of joy through oppressed lives?'

'I'll tell you how I see myself, Alex Barrett,' she said in exasperation, propping herself up on one slim elbow. 'I see myself as the very tired mother of two boys who are going to be awake and wanting their breakfasts in about five or six hours! I see myself as the wife of a man who wants to hash over every petty little incident that happened *years* ago when I am exhausted!'

She fell back upon the bed and plopped the pillow over her head again. I didn't think it prudent to take it off a second time; she might decide to tell me it wasn't safe.

'Petty little incident,' indeed!

The night was broken by restless dreams in which I defended Angela before massed benches of irate judges and policemen who demanded adequate reasons why she should not be taken out and hanged. They were unmoved when I argued that she was a perfect wife and tender mother, and it only seemed to

292

infuriate them when I added that she in no way *looked* like a murderess. Through it all, a hooded hangman with a frayed clothesline rope looped around his shoulders swung back and forth on the chandelier chanting, 'We're going to give her the rope! The rope! We're going to give her the rope! The rope!'

Shreds of the dream clung to me all day. I couldn't rid myself of a feeling of apprehension, and when I stopped at a hardware store after work to buy Sandy's new rope, it seemed as if I were somehow adding to Angela's guilt.

As I drove into the carport late that afternoon, I saw Sandy rummaging in the toolshed. 'I got your Tarzan rope for you,' I called.

'Thanks, Dad,' he said, dragging out an old tarp, 'but we're going to play army men. Can me and Chris and Matt have this for a tent in the gully?'

'O.K., but aren't you afraid Georgie will tear it down?'

'Oh, we don't have to worry about *him* anymore,' Sandy said cheerfully, and disappeared around the corner of the house before I could find my voice.

Oh, no, I thought, and roared, '*Angela!*' as I tore into the house, nearly ripping the screen from its hinges. No answer.

'Surely Sandy would have thought it worth mentioning if the police had carted his mother

293

off to jail,' I jittered to myself, trying to look at the situation coolly. 'Angela!'

Then I heard her voice: 'Alex! I'm over here at Jill's. Come on over,' she called.

'Hi, Alex!' Jill caroled as I pushed open their screen. 'We're sort of celebrating. Want a drink?'

Women! Were they all so cold-blooded that they could murder a child, obnoxious as that child had been, without turning a hair? I sank down on the porch glider, unable to speak for the moment.

'Poor dear,' said Angela solicitously. 'Did you have a bad day? You look so drained.'

'What happened to Georgie?' I demanded, glaring at Angela.

'Didn't Sandy tell you?' asked Jill as she handed me the tall cool drink that I so desperately needed. 'He was swinging on the boys' Tarzan rope and it broke with him. He fractured both legs, one in two places,' she added with satisfaction.

'He wasn't killed?' I croaked weakly.

'Of course not, Alex,' said Angela. 'How could he have been? There weren't any rocks under the rope and that stretch of gully is mostly grass.'

'I hate to seem ghoulish,' Jill said, 'but it really does make the summer for us. By the time he gets out of those casts and off his crutches, school will be open again.'

She grinned at Angela. 'I just can't believe it!

A whole summer without Georgie Watson beating up every little kid in sight!'

'Just a lucky break for everyone,' I murmured sarcastically. There was no point in asking if the break had occurred up by the knot which Angela had examined last night.

'Well, it is,' Jill insisted stoutly. 'And as I told Mrs. Watson, it was his own fault. Angela very specifically warned him not to swing on that old rope till you could get a stronger one.'

'Angela's very thoughtful that way,' I observed.

At least she had the grace to blush.

The next day, a Saturday, even I was forced to admit that if it were any indication, it was going to be a very relaxed summer. The boys peacefully slaughtered the bad guys all day in the gully without once running in to us with tearful tales of Georgie's latest tyranny.

After all, I thought as I watched an afternoon baseball game undisturbed, maybe a summer of enforced solitude will be good for Georgie's character.

*　　*　　*

When I awoke early Sunday morning, my subconscious had completed the job of rationalizing the situation: don't some wives occasionally bring unusual talents to their marriages? If a woman loves to tinker with machinery, is it wrong to let her clean the carburetor on the family car? If she wants to paint the house herself, take up tailoring as a hobby, or learn how to fix the plumbing—if, in short, her oddball talents add to the comfort and serenity of her family—should her husband make an issue of it if it doesn't get out of hand?

That settled, I turned over in bed and began drifting off to sleep again when the loud spluttering roar of a lawn mower exploded on the morning quiet. I shot up in bed, examined the clock, and groaned: 7:02 A.M.!

I buried my head under a pillow, but the racket rose in volume. There was no way to escape it.

Sighing, I leaned over and kissed Angela's bare shoulder. 'M-m?' she murmured drowsily.

'Angela,' I whispered, 'do you suppose you could give Mr. Watson a reason why it isn't safe to mow his lawn before nine A.M.?'

THE JOKER

B. R. Wright

The tiny microphone just fit into a hollow in
the low terrace wall. Harry stepped back and
told himself, with a kind of anguish, that there
was no danger of its being noticed. Anyone
concerned about eavesdroppers would be
looking toward the door into the house, not at
the wall with its forty-foot drop to the sea.

He stared over the wall into the deep,
foaming pool that had undercut the cliff and
polished the walls of the cove to unmarred
smoothness. He was terrified by water—Greta
was, too—but the lashing of the waves suited
his mood tonight. There was the same uneasy
surge beneath the surface, the same sudden
furious thrusts. The water reflected a Harry
that no one—except perhaps Greta—had ever
seen.

He really had to smile a little at the idea of
Greta and his secret self. He had hidden his fear
of the water by building a house overhanging
the sea. He had hidden his fear of being
deserted, of being left all alone in an indifferent
world, by marrying the kind of woman who
would be desired and pursued by other men
always.

It was an interesting trick, he thought. One

of his best. And if Greta, more perceptive than most people, had recognized her limited role and resented it, he couldn't help that. Confidence, trust, frankness were expensive toys for a privileged few. He had learned to get along without them.

He shivered, and called himself a fool for being nervous. After all, no one would suspect him of malice in putting the tape recorder on the terrace. His jokes had never been vicious. This time it would appear that for once he had been caught in his own trap. People would talk about it for a long time and pity him, and though he regretted the pity he relished the talk. There were other ways in which he might have killed Greta (he'd use one of them if this didn't work out tonight), but in none of them would her friends have seen her so clearly for what she really was. That was important. He hated her now, with the same shattering intensity with which he had wanted her five years ago.

The doorbell rang.

'I'll get it.' Harry stood at the French doors and watched her come down the last few stairs and cross to the foyer. She was small, straight, auburn, like a fall candle, and tonight she would make all the cameo-skinned, elegant females at the party wish they had been born with red hair and freckles. He could be quite objective about her now—could marvel at what no longer belonged to him—had

298

apparently *never* belonged to him. (And that was the bad part—the wound that was not going to heal. She had been Peter Buckley's girl before their marriage; for the last six months she had been seeing him regularly again. The two facts invalidated all that had happened between.)

It was, predictably, Peter Buckley arriving first. Harry greeted him too loudly, toned it down, fixed him a drink, and went back to the door to meet the next arrivals. During the hour that followed he welcomed at least twenty more people, asked them how their work was going, whether their vacations had been exciting, how they liked their new houses, cars, and spouses. He showed first-time guests around—the fireplace made with not-quite-genuine fossils, the mirror that took your picture when you turned on the light over it, the mounted muskie that inflated while he described what a fight it had taken to land it. He mixed a great many drinks, told a great many stories. And all of this it seemed he accomplished without once taking his eyes from Greta and Peter. Every word they spoke to each other, every casual gesture, every smile was in some curious way a symptom of the disease that was destroying him. He felt like an invalid making bright conversation while at the same time he took his own pulse and found it dangerously irregular.

When Greta and Peter finally went out on

the terrace together, closing the door behind them, he was actually relieved. If they had *not* wanted to be alone, it would have proved nothing except that they were inclined to caution now, when caution was ridiculous. Harry thought of the overheard, whispered phone calls in which she had arranged to meet Peter, the times he had seen them driving together—the bitter afternoon when, coming home early along the shore road, he had seen them driving up from Buckley's beach cottage. Greta was supposed to be in the city that afternoon; when he asked her, she described in detail where she had eaten, whom she had seen, the antique sale at which, not surprisingly, she had seen nothing worth buying.

'—so marvelous,' a voice screamed in his ear. 'Like living in an eagle's nest. You two must adore the water!'

'Adore looking at it,' Harry corrected with a smile. It was Joe Herman's wife—a shrill, peevish kind of woman who embodied all the things Greta was not. Ugly, he thought, still smiling at her—ugly, malicious, domineering, and loyal. She might treat poor old Joe like dirt but nobody else had better try it.

June Herman's face turned red, as though some unexpected acumen let her read the thoughts behind his smile. 'A man with a wife who looks like Greta *ought* to keep her in an eagle's nest,' she said viciously. Harry turned, looking for an explanation for her anger, and saw Joe talking to Greta with obvious enjoyment.

The party dragged by, like a hundred others before it. He had been careful to add a few of the ingredients his guests had learned to expect: one of the 'gelatin' molds on the buffet was made of rubber; the woman in the painting over the fireplace smiled at people who stopped to admire her; the new bearskin rug growled when Joe Herman stooped to pat its head. 'Marvelous,' everyone said when they finally left, and he knew exactly what they were thinking. *Good old corny old Harry—he'll never change.* Not one of them knew he existed apart from his jokes.

Peter Buckley and the Hermans were the last to leave. 'Thank goodness,' Greta said when the door closed behind them. Harry looked at her sharply, but her expression was as innocent as her tone. She yawned and, as if on cue, crossed to the terrace door and went out into the silver light. He followed. As he crossed the room he seemed to leave his state of fevered alertness and enter into a kind of dull automatism. He did not have to think about what was going to happen next. It was set, inevitable.

'I'm tired,' Greta said. Her face was very white. The yellow dress was subdued fire against the darkness of the sea. Far below her the water lashed against the foot of the cliff.

'You had a terrible time tonight,' she said

when he walked over beside her. 'Why do you bother with jokes when you're feeling this lousy? Why don't you tell me what's worrying you?'

She had the knack, he thought. She should have gone on the stage; it was wonderful the way she delivered those small lines. *Tell the little woman all about it,* he thought savagely, aping the sense if not the tone of her plea. He moved a few steps along the wall, picked up the microphone, and waited until she looked at him.

'What's that?'

'Another joke,' he said and waited again, but she didn't seem to recognize what he held. 'It's the microphone of the tape recorder,' he said carefully. 'I had it set up out here to get an hour or two of private-type conversations. Ought to be good for some laughs.'

Awareness came slowly, just as he had imagined it would, in the long, painful night-hours of planning. And now, it was *her* voice that was careful, controlled, as she asked, 'You had it—out here?'

He nodded.

She took it well, considering the depth of the pit that had suddenly opened up before her. 'You ought to be ashamed of yourself,' she said. 'Funny jokes are one thing, but that— that's cheap and ugly.'

He pretended to be startled. 'You have a pretty poor opinion of our friends,' he said.

302

'What do you think we're going to hear, for heaven's sake? A lot of small talk about how pretty the ocean is in the moonlight and isn't it a dull party and wouldn't you think that joker would get tired of his little games after a while ... that's all it'll be. We can play it at the next party if things are slow ...' Without looking at her he lifted the tape recorder from behind the column of greenery in the corner and set it on the wall. 'Sit down,' he said. 'Might as well listen to it before we go to bed.'

She moved then, gliding along the wall so swiftly that he had only a fraction of a second to get ready. Her hands were on the tape recorder, pushing wildly, when he caught her around the hips and lifted her over the wall. One moment he was thrusting her away from him into space; the next his hands were empty. Her scream was cut short when she hit the water.

*   *   *

He had tried to prepare himself for the moments right afterward. Horror was what he expected, and it came, a wild trembling, a violent nausea as he stared down into the water. Doubt, fear, remorse because now he was a murderer and would know himself to be one forever. But he hadn't expected the overwhelming loneliness which, when it struck, drove every other feeling out of him. With his

303

own hands he had done it, had rendered himself alone in a world that thought he was a very funny man indeed. She was the only one who hadn't laughed.

Later he thought that he might have followed her over the wall in that moment, might have ended it right then, if the doorbell hadn't rung. After the third or fourth ring he recognized the sound. And he knew he had to go ahead with the plan.

When he opened the door Joe Herman stepped inside, pulling his wife behind him. 'Damn tire,' he snarled and grabbed the telephone in the entry. 'That's the second one this week—I don't even have a spare ...' He looked at Harry more closely. 'What's the matter—too much party? You oughtta cut out all that cute stuff.'

'Call the police,' Harry said. 'Call somebody. Greta just jumped off the terrace. She's killed herself.'

He didn't have to pretend the sobs that shook him when he actually said the words.

The Hermans stared. 'Look, funny boy,' Joe said, but something apparently convinced him it was not a joke, for he ran across to the terrace and his wife followed him.

'The cliff walls are smooth as marble for a hundred yards around the cove,' Harry said harshly from the terrace door. He watched them stare over the edge, seeing the churning blackness himself though he didn't leave the

304

lighted living room. 'That was one of the reasons we built here—privacy, no beach parties, nobody peeking in the windows.'

He went back to the phone and called the police himself. When he was through the Hermans were behind him, their faces white and curiously hungry as they struggled to believe the worst. 'You—you *wouldn't* joke about a thing like this,' Joe said uncertainly. 'I don't believe you would. But why would Greta—do that?'

Harry saw then that they were the right people to have here when the police came. They both knew him as The Joker; Joe had been involved in several of the best. They would believe the picture of the clown and the joke that backfired. They would want to believe it, would want the police to believe it. They would feel, in a way they would not even admit to themselves, that he had it coming.

'I don't understand it myself,' he said simply. 'We were just talking—you know, after-the-party talk. I mentioned that I had had the tape recorder turned on out on the terrace this evening. She looked strange—kind of sick—I asked her if she was feeling all right—she said yes, but then she started to cry and when I switched on the re-wind she started to moan and then she ran across the terrace and just—jumped.'

They looked at him.

'Poor kid,' Joe said. 'I wonder why...'

'What about the tape recorder?' June asked eagerly. 'Why don't you play it now and see if there was something on it that might have upset her?'

He knew he didn't have to let them hear the tape. June Herman knew the whole story already, or thought she did; he had watched her eyes widen when he mentioned the recorder, had seen the eager twitching of lips as she tasted the story she would have to tell.

'Greta never had anything to hide,' he said stiffly. 'That's a lousy thing to say.'

Joe shook his head and his wife made a small, protesting sound. 'Of course not,' she said soothingly. 'But just the same, Harry, you ought to listen to the tape before the police come. You just ought to.'

He thought it over, then shrugged as if he were too tired to argue. The recorder was still out on the terrace; he got it quickly and brought it back in. He knew he was taking a chance, but not a big one; there had been no doubt that Greta had not wanted him to hear the tape. And June Herman was the right one, the absolutely right one, to hear the whole story.

He pushed the re-wind button and waited, while the tape whirred innocently to the other spool. Then the room was full of the sound of waves. Loneliness came back as he listened; he was powerless before it, though he reminded himself that he had lost nothing, that he couldn't lose something he had never really had. Still he strained to hear Greta's voice, wanting the sound of it once more, regardless of the words it spoke.

Joe Herman leaned forward and turned up the volume of the recorder. There was the sound of footsteps on stone and then a giggle. Harry didn't recognize the voice but he could tell June was cataloging this, too, for future investigation. There followed a long pause with nothing but the splash of waves, and then, suddenly and sweetly, there was Greta's voice.

'It's more than a joke now, Petey,' she said. 'He hasn't trusted me from the very first, and lately we've been farther apart than ever. At first it just seemed as if it would be fun to turn the tables on him—once. Now it's much more. At first I had no intention of frightening him— now I feel as if shock is the only thing that might bring him back...'

'You're wonderful,' Peter said. 'I think I've mentioned that before. When are you going to do it?'

The Hermans frowned, trying hard to follow the conversation. As the tape whirled on, their faces seemed to move farther away, leaving Harry alone on a small island surrounded by Greta's voice.

'Soon,' the voice said. 'I'm not quite sure how I'll do it, but I can tell you this, Petey—I'll plan it so he thinks he's lost me. For a minute or two or maybe more he's going to face up to how much he needs me—he's going to value me as a person and not just as part of his pretty little stage set here on the cliff. I want him to wish to heaven he had one more chance to make our marriage work. I want him to know exactly what it's like to love someone terribly, as I love him, and not be able to reach him ...' She took a deep breath. 'And I do thank you, Petey, for making it possible.'

The entry door opened. Joe saw it first; with a real effort he tore his eyes from the tape recorder and got up clumsily. 'It's the police—' he said and then suddenly stopped.

Harry did not move. In the mirror over the couch he could see two figures neatly framed in gold, a picture to carry with him the rest of his life. Here the tall policeman, puzzled, frowning, and there, just beside him, the small, freckled, red-headed girl in a drenched yellow dress. They had come together in the darkness behind them; the policeman would have seen her somewhere on the beach beyond the smooth walls of the cove, walking slowly across the sand, trying to believe the thing that had happened.

Well, he thought, *I certainly found out what she wanted me to.* And then he began to laugh, because somebody's joke had backfired, and if he didn't laugh now he was going to cry. He laughed for himself, for the wife he had had, and for Peter Buckley who must have spent a good share of the last six months teaching

Greta how to swim. He was still laughing when the policeman put the handcuffs on him and led him out of the house.

THE MAN WHO TOOK IT WITH HIM

D. Olson

Bert Palm had courted Madelyn Hume in his spinsterish, doggy-devoted manner for fifteen years, not more than three of which had passed before Madelyn knew that Bert was not a marrying man, and that all he required of her was loyal companionship; in other words, an uxorial but strictly platonic relationship, an arrangement not without certain advantages or Madelyn would have rebelled long before she did.

In the past, Bert had been one of the Libya Chamber of Commerce's Young Men of the Year; now, at fifty-five, he was a successful realtor, a sober, corpulent man whom his neighbors called the 'Regent Street Aristocrat,' a Moose, a Mason, an Elk, a church deacon, a man with no hobby more depraved than tinkering with his blue 1932 Essex sedan, the age and appearance of which said more for Bert's character than any human testimonial. How many men of his age still drove the first car they had ever owned, and kept it looking exactly—yes, *exactly*—as it had looked in the showroom?

An achievement like this is apt to provoke a certain invidious resentment in most of us, who

310

watch helplessly as our two—or three-year-old hulks rust and depreciate before our eyes. Jokes were made about Bert and his Essex in the small town of Libya, and Madelyn knew that she was included in these jokes when she was seen riding beside Bert down Libya's main street on pleasant Sunday afternoons.

So why did she do it? Well, for one thing, boyfriends had never exactly clamored for her favors. As redheads go, she was pretty enough, but her sense of humor put them off. It was not a ha-ha sense of humor; its tongue was witty but its teeth were sharp. For another thing, Madelyn's brain was also sharp. She knew as well as everyone else that Bert must have built up a comfortable fortune over the years, he was not getting any younger and his relatives were not likely to reap the benefits of his frugality. Orphaned as an infant, he had been reared by an aunt who had two kids of her own and had never looked upon the unwelcome third with more than grudging affection.

So, while Madelyn was not unaware of the advantages of her position, she was nevertheless a warm-blooded young woman not that far from the brink of the hill herself, and she could scarcely be blamed for a certain wistfulness as she realized she could never be more to the one man in her life than the beneficiary of his life insurance, so to speak. While picnics at the Elks' summer cottage on Crystal Lake were pleasant enough, the

311

tameness of such diversions made her feel like a premature Golden-Ager.

Then along came Ralph Storrey. New at the office, a lissome young fellow with mischievous blue eyes, he found Madelyn's astringent witticisms amusing enough to invite her out. She thought about it and decided to accept. Ralph quickly made it plain that he was no more an advocate of the bliss that is marital than was Bert Palm, and though not a swinger by society's usual standard, neither was he a stick-in-the-mud like Bert.

When Ralph discovered that Madelyn, for all her free and easy way of talking, was no pushover, he began to look upon her as a challenge and he lost no chance to belittle the competition.

'Saw your sugar-daddy smoking a two-bit cigar in front of the Baldwin Building yesterday. You should tell him brown shoes with a blue suit is a no-no for a man in his position. Bad for the image.'

'So he's an individualist. Something not all of us can *afford* to be,' she retorted sarcastically.

Ralph winced, but he could tell Madelyn was annoyed and from then on he always called Bert 'old Blue-Suit-Brown-Shoes,' eventually abbreviating this to 'old B.S.-B.S.'

Offensive as he often was, Ralph also was fun, and Madelyn had been secretly hankering after a bit of fun for years. Moreover, there was something infectious about Ralph's mildly ribald humor, so that before she knew it Madelyn herself was referring to her more dignified admirer as B.S.-B.S., not with malice, but simply because the epithet was singularly appropriate somehow; even, in its way, rather endearing.

Instead of drifting through life, Madelyn now began to enjoy the bold, free strokes of a swimmer. Her job was not too boringly humdrum and now she had not only the old-shoe comforts of Bert's companionship, but the dancing-pump delights of Ralph's.

Along came July, and in came trouble. While using the phone one evening in Madelyn's apartment, Bert casually glanced at a note lying on the desk. He did not explode, but he did fume.

The note had been passed to Madelyn as she was leaving the office that afternoon, and it said: 'Mad, honey—Ditch old B.S.-B.S. tomorrow and we'll go for a romp at Crystal Dam Park. Kisses, Ralph.'

Bert stalked into the living room where he and Madelyn had been watching Lawrence Welk on TV—he in the easy chair, she on the sofa—and stiffly waved the note in front of her eyes. 'You can explain this, I presume?'

'Bert Palm! You've got your nerve snooping in my desk.'

Bert flung down the note and subsided glumly into his chair. 'It was *on* the desk, not in

313

it. But don't bother. I've known about your friend for weeks. We have the same barber, and Louie's a blabbermouth.' He glowered at the screen, obviously searching for the most cutting put-down. Finally, he said, 'I even saw him once. He's got awfully skinny legs.'

Madelyn roared, it was such a typical Bertism. 'I don't believe it,' she teased him. '*You*, jealous?'

'I won't be laughed at, Madelyn. Nor two-timed. Think it over. If you're here when I stop by for you tomorrow I'll take it to mean you've ended whatever liaison you may be enjoying with this—person. If not...'

If not. The meaning was clear, and a night's sober reflection left Madelyn with no doubt as to where her own best interests lay. She was waiting when the blue Essex arrived the following morning.

Later in the day, when they were sitting on a bench at the Elks' summer cottage watching the sailboat races, Bert was in the sort of magnanimous mood that female penitence often arouses in the male heart.

'You must understand by now, my dear, that you're every bit as important to me as a wife would be.'

'I said I was sorry, Bert.'

'I've been happy with our arrangement, Madelyn. It suits me. I'm sorry it doesn't suit you.'

'Oh, but I never said it didn't, Bert. I never

said that.'

'Your actions with respect to that—person—strongly imply it.' He watched a pair of snipes, bow to bow, cross the finish line below Point Stockholm. 'I'm wondering, my dear, if it wouldn't be wise for you to give up your job at the office.'

She suppressed a sharp retort. 'You don't trust me, you mean?'

For a moment she thought he might yield to an un-Bertish impulse to put his arm around her shoulder. Instead, he sighed. 'I trust you. But can you trust yourself?'

This dialogue, as between confessor and penitent, dragged on to the point where Madelyn was quite bored with it, until suddenly his remarks took an unexpected and more interesting course.

'You know, Madelyn, that I've been a very frugal sort of person. I'm neither a wastrel nor a spendthrift. I think I can say without exaggeration—and in strictest confidence, you understand—that my net worth is somewhere in the neighborhood of $150,000.'

Madelyn was unable to swallow this information without a slight gulp, for no matter how tight a man may be, if you see him day in and day out smoking cheap cigars and wearing scroungy old brown shoes and a shiny-seated blue serge suit, not to mention a tie of such vintage it had been out of style twice and back in again, well, you find it a bit hard to grasp that he's a man of such affluence as this lordly sum must imply.

'Why, Bert, honestly, I had no idea. I knew you were thrifty, of course, but I had no idea ...'

'I'm pleased,' he said, 'that you've always practiced more than a modicum of that virtue yourself.'

It would have been imprudent to point out that her thrift was imposed upon her by the skimpiness of her wages. 'That's the way I was brought up,' she declared modestly.

At this point the conversation grew even more interesting.

'You know, my dear, that all I have will someday be yours—on condition that you fulfill two promises. One, that you will never sell my Essex, and that you will always take as good care of it as I do myself. I know you aren't too impressed by antique automobiles, but this one will be worth a fortune to you someday.'

'Oh, Bert, let's not talk about such things.'

'Mortality whispers,' he said gravely, 'and we must listen.' He gave her hand a limp but fervent squeeze. 'And the money that comes to you with it, you must promise never to squander it, but to invest it safely and wisely. Promise?'

'Of course. But I *wish* you wouldn't talk like this. It upsets me. And on such a pretty day. Come along, let's walk down to the shore.'

All in all, it was a most illuminating day for

316

Madelyn. For the first time, she felt that the years of playing sister-mother-sweetheart to Bert had been justified. As for Ralph Storrey, away with him and his dangerous charms; let that dumb little blonde in Payroll have him. He was a nebbish and always would be, so forget him.

This change of attitude puzzled poor Ralph, and also intrigued him. Being a man of well-nourished ego, he stepped up his campaign to woo Madelyn away from old B.S.-B.S., at first with no luck whatsoever, but then gradually, as the weeks passed and Madelyn felt herself sinking once more into the dismal swamp of social neglect, she began to crave Ralph's lively company. Without meaning to she found herself sneaking dates with him and before long entertaining him in her apartment, after first telling him about that interesting conversation with Bert at the Elks' summer cottage and pressing upon him the need for absolute discretion in their relationship.

In spite of every precaution, she soon began to wonder if Bert had somehow found out what was going on; his manner became moody, almost sullen. Twice he called and broke a dinner date with her, pleading illness, and though he made no accusation, she fancied she could discern now and then the gray shadows of distrust in his somber glance.

On a Saturday morning not long after this, she was hanging new curtains in her kitchen when the phone rang. It was her mother, who asked her if she had listened to the noon news. Madelyn had not.

'Then brace yourself for a shock,' her mother said. 'Bert's dead.'

It was true. Bert had suffered a heart attack in his car while driving up to Forestview to show a piece of property. The Essex had gone off the road and struck a guardrail, damaging the fender and right headlight. Bert had died instantly.

Madelyn felt more like a widow than a widow would, even if she knew in her heart that her grief was tainted with the alloys of greed and guilt. She could not bear to have anything to do with Ralph. She owed Bert a decent period of mourning before resuming *that* relationship. Ralph was pleased to cooperate. He foresaw a brilliant future; he might even conquer his aversion to marriage.

After the reading of the will, however, there ensued a period of bereavement that was one hundred percent pure unalloyed grief, for although the beloved Essex was indeed bequeathed to his 'friend of long and loyal standing, Madelyn Hume,' the residue of Bert's estate went to the children of the aunt who had raised him.

Stunned and angry, Madelyn realized that Bert must have found out she had betrayed him. It was not sickness, as she had hoped, but jealousy that had accounted for his strange moodiness. She was so disconsolate she took to her bed, let the apartment go undusted, her hair unwashed, her phone unanswered. When Ralph came to the flat she was too despondent to conceal the truth. He didn't call again.

She blamed herself, but she also blamed Bert, for after all she had still given him the best fifteen years of her life, with nothing to show for them but that barbershop joke of a car! The Essex symbolized the loss of fortune and life's terrible unfairness. Once she took a hammer, intending to batter it into junk, but some ghost of common sense stopped her arm in mid-air. Then she thought it would be more gratifying to watch it slowly rust away out there in the drive, which was even more impractical since she had to get her own car in and out of the garage every day.

In the end, she advertised it for sale and sold it the very next day to a used-car dealer for much less than its true value.

It was her mother who first reported to her the strange rumors that were floating around—she belonged to the same garden club as Bert Palm's aunt—but Madelyn didn't put any stock in these rumors until one afternoon when she happened to run into the wife of one of the cousins who had inherited Bert's money. This young woman, who had always despised Madelyn anyway, was in a rancid humor. 'Oh, the rumors are quite true,' she admitted sourly in reply to Madelyn's outright inquiry.

'We *all* got fooled, it seems. You as well as the family. Of course, *we* never did expect anything. Bert never made any secret of how he felt about *us*. But when the assets were distributed we got less than five thousand. I suppose he was really a dirty old man with a lot of expensive, filthy vices. Of course, *you* knew him better than anyone, so I'm sure *you* would be the authority on that. Good afternoon, my dear.'

For several days Madelyn did nothing but ponder this astonishing enigma. She knew that Bert would never have told her he was worth $150,000 if he were not. She sifted through every recollection of those talks with Bert and as she weighed each bit of verbal evidence the awful truth became clear. Fantastic, preposterous, but inescapably clear—and she would have discovered the truth sooner had she interpreted Bert's remarks as literally as he had obviously intended them to be taken.

When he had spoken of the 'money that will come to you with the car,' he must have meant precisely that. When he had adjured her to take good care of the Essex because someday it would be 'worth a fortune' to her, that's exactly what he had meant. It should have occurred to her when he spoke of wise investments that the money must not at that time have *been* invested. Merely hoarded!

Yes, the answer was as clear as the water in Crystal Lake: Bert's money, the bulk of his

320

estate, was still in cash—and the cash was in the old blue Essex!

She got a bit hysterical when the full weight of this discovery fell upon her. Bert had had the personality of a miser; she might have known he would also have the eccentric habits of one. He had come as close as any man could to taking it with him when he went.

Naturally, she all but flew to the used-car lot, where her heart started pounding like the boxing glove on a one-armed pugilist when the used-car dealer informed her the Essex was already sold.

'But fret not, lucky lady. You like old buggies, I've got old buggies. Let me show you—'

She broke in to implore him to reveal the buyer's name, in hopes she might buy it back.

The buyer's name was Ralph Storrey.

Now, she had exchanged hardly a word with that ratfink since he had learned of her apparent disinheritance, and having seen him for what he was, she nurtured a genuine hatred for him, which was not diminished by seeing him several times with the blonde from Payroll.

Office grapevines being as efficient as they are, and with a new wardrobe and hairdo to lend credence to the rumor she began circulating, Madelyn was not surprised when Ralph stopped her in the cafeteria one morning with a facile compliment. Yes, she told him, the rumors were true: Bert had indeed left her his

321

money, employing certain legalistic maneuvers to circumvent tax complications; hence the misunderstanding. 'I'm giving up my job, of course,' she added. 'I'll stay on for another year, just to qualify for eventual pension benefits. Why sacrifice them, even if I don't need them?'

Ralph was impressed.

She looked away, sad-eyed. 'I have just one regret. I wish I hadn't sold the Essex. I had no right to. I'd give anything to get it back.'

'Anything?'

'Yes!'

'You know who bought it, don't you? I did.'

He said he thought he'd enjoy tinkering with it, maybe fix it up and sell it for a profit. She implored him to let her buy it back.

His blue eyes sparkled. 'Well, why don't you come over tonight and we'll talk about it over a drink.'

It was some relief to see the Essex and know it was safe, but how on earth was she going to reclaim it? Despite her pleas, Ralph would not agree to sell it back to her without 'thinking it over.' She was desperate. She was sure Bert wouldn't simply have hidden all that money under a seat or in the trunk. The car would have to be laboriously stripped down, and no matter how complex, difficult, and dirty a chore it would be she would have to handle it all by herself.

Ralph, meanwhile, pursued his own course

toward a fortune, but marrying one proved to be just as difficult. He bombarded Madelyn with flowers, took her to dinner at expensive restaurants, did everything but literally sweep her off her feet.

By then she would have married the Devil to get her hands on the Essex, and as there seemed to be no other way of doing it, that was exactly what she felt she was doing when she finally said yes to Ralph.

A simple wedding was followed by a short honeymoon, because Ralph made a great show of insisting they spend only his money. The act amused her and she wondered how soon he would begin to show a proprietary interest in her nonexistent fortune.

She did not go back to work after the honeymoon, and spent her first day at home examining the Essex, lifting out the seats, exploring the trunk, poking about under the hood, even crawling about underneath to study the undercarriage. All to no avail—one difficulty being that she had no notion what constituted an integral part of the automobile and what might have been added to conceal one-thousand or ten-thousand dollar bills. It was a dirty, tiresome, frustrating experience.

To make matters worse, Ralph would come home at night and spend hours tinkering with the car himself, as absorbed as a child would be with a new toy. She suffered agonies of suspense wondering if he might somehow blunder upon the hoard himself.

'It's *my* car,' he said angrily one night when she insisted he come away from it. 'I'll spend all the time I want with it.'

They began to have violent arguments daily on the subject.

'You're really jealous of that old heap, aren't you?' he sneered. 'Would you rather I played around with another woman?'

She would have given an honest answer to this if she thought it would send him off in pursuit of one. As it was, this trying situation continued until one evening at the dinner table when her nerves were already inflamed by the fatigue of trying to remove the crankcase that afternoon and having to spend hours washing away the oily, gritty evidence of her endeavor.

'Madelyn,' he said gently, 'we can't go on this way.'

'Meaning what, dear heart?'

'You know what I mean. All this bickering over that damned relic of a car. I'm fed up with it.'

'Does that mean you're going to stop neglecting me?'

He looked stern. 'It means I'm going to sell the car.'

She had to lean back very hard against her chair to keep from going to pieces. 'That's dumb, Ralph.'

'It's the only answer. I've even got a buyer.'

'If you insist on selling it you can sell it to me.

I'm the one who wanted to buy it, remember.'

'And what would that solve? No. I want it out of our sight.'

She began to sweat. 'I'll keep it in a garage. You won't even have to see it.'

'Madelyn, that's crazy. Only proves what I've known all along. You've got some sort of nutty fixation about that car. It's not healthy. It's sick. Just like your carrying on with old B.S.-B.S. It isn't natural.'

They argued, each becoming more heated. Finally he slammed his fist on the table. 'It's no use, Madelyn. I've told the fellow he can have it. He's stopping by on the way home from his office to look it over and go for a spin. He'll be here any minute.'

She went slightly crazy. 'Over my dead body!'

He made a fist at her. 'That can be arranged. Don't push me.'

Seeing that words had no effect on him she tried to calm down. She asked him how much the man had offered.

'Ten thousand.'

The thought of Ralph getting ten thousand for *her* car, with or without a fortune hidden in it, was enough to make her see red again, and she hurried from the room before she lost all restraint. Ralph's unexpected move had to be forestalled. Deciding there was only one thing to do, she went into the garage and stared tensely at the Essex, thinking first of puncturing the tires—but this wasn't drastic enough—the vehicle itself must be damaged in some way that would make any prospective buyer lose interest.

She picked up a claw hammer and slowly circled the car, knowing it had to be done, yet dreading the awful sacrilege. She thought of the hours poor Bert had devoted to the machine, the loving care he had taken of it. She looked at her watch; the man would be arriving any moment now. She wrapped a cloth around the hammerhead and, gritting her teeth, she swung at the back window. The breaking glass made more noise than she'd expected, but there was no time to be extra-cautious. She moved to the next window.

'What the hell are you doing?'

She turned and saw Ralph, simian-eyed with rage, looming in the doorway.

'You flaky broad! Have you lost your mind? Get away from that car!'

He walked around to the rear of the car and stared down at the broken glass. Muttering obscenities, he knelt to pick up the pieces.

Seeing his bowed head, Madelyn discovered the answer to her problem in a flash of inspiration. Only by getting Ralph out of the picture permanently would she ever find that money. Even so, if she hadn't been teetering on the razor-edge of panic at that very moment with a claw hammer clutched in her hand, it might not have happened. In fact, the hammer seemed to move downward of its own volition, cracking Ralph's skull like a walnut.

She dropped the hammer in horrified disgust, stumbling backward in her haste to avoid contact with the blood. She came very close to fainting; what kept her conscious may have been the awareness that every second now was crucial. She dragged Ralph's body into the corner and slung a paint-stained tarpaulin over it. There was a long smear of blood on the concrete floor. She opened the garage door, jumped into the Essex, and backed it into the driveway. Then she got out and shut the garage door.

Not more than a second later a yellow compact stopped at the curb, out of which stepped a bald-headed man in a raincoat. Madelyn tried to smile as he came towards her.

'Mrs. Storrey?'

She nodded idiotically, afraid to use her voice.

'I'm Gabriel Ives. Your husband is expecting me.'

How she may have looked needn't have bothered her: he had eyes only for the Essex, looking at it the way most men would look at a stunning woman.

'She's a real beaut,' he gloated. 'Ralph said so, but I didn't expect anything this fine. He inside?'

Ives started toward the garage. Madelyn flung out her hand. 'No. I'm sorry. Ralph had to go out.' She had to get her thoughts organized. She had to get rid of this nuisance.

The nuisance looked annoyed. 'Oh, shucks. He said he'd be here. Is it okay if I come in the house and wait for him?'

'Well...'

'He said he'd take me for a spin. I'm already sold, just looking at it. If it's in as good shape mechanically, I'll wrap up the deal tonight.'

'Ralph might not be back. Tomorrow. Come back tomorrow.'

'I'm flying to Boston tonight. I don't want this to slip through my fingers.' He looked at his watch. 'Listen. Suppose I drive it around the block a few times while we're waiting.'

Oh, no, she thought. *Not on your life, buster.* Never again was she letting this car out of her sight. She was somewhat more relaxed now; there was really nothing to worry about. Ralph was dead; he could never interfere again. She could do as she pleased. Only she mustn't let this man get suspicious.

'I'll give you a ride in it,' she said, forcing a smile. 'If you like it, we'll consider it sold. We'll close the deal when you get back to town.'

By then she would have found what she was looking for—perhaps without seriously damaging the car. An extra ten thousand was not to be dismissed lightly.

She told him to wait while she locked up and got her purse. When she came out he was already in the car, his fingers caressing the

328

pearl-gray upholstery. Madelyn was herself now, fully under control.

She carefully backed into the street and circled the block.

'Rides like a dream,' he said. 'Okay if I drive her?'

They changed places and Ives, after a grinding of gears that made Madelyn wince, soon got the feel of it. He drove slowly out Lancaster Road.

'Okay if I open her up a bit? Want to hear that engine.'

'This isn't a hot rod, Mr. Ives. Please slow down.'

It was almost dark now, and although she knew the house and garage were securely locked, she couldn't feel easy, thinking of Ralph's body under that tarpaulin.

'Mr. Ives, I think you'd better let me drive now.'

He stopped and they changed places. When she came to the first crossroad she started to turn around.

'Keep going,' he said.

'We can't get back this way. It's a dead end.'

'Keep going, Mrs. Storrey.'

'It ends up in an old quarry.'

'Don't argue with me, doll.'

His tone shocked her. She looked at him. He was taking something out of his pocket.

'What's that?'

'It's a gun, doll. What's it look like? Now

keep driving till I tell you to stop.'

'I don't understand. Who are you? What do you want?'

The man grinned. 'I want the five grand your hubby's paying me to make him a widower.'

*   *   *

The occupants of a run-down farmhouse not far from the quarry spotted the blazing auto and called in the alarm, but by the time the fire trucks got there nothing remained but charred metal and bone.

On the following day, the children who lived in the poor farmhouse were happily scavenging among the scorched fragments for 'treasures.' Little Ben found a radiator cap which still gleamed like silver. Sid found a piece of red glass. Poor little Polly found nothing but a few pretty little stones clinging to the inside of a torn leather pouch.

When they got home their mother scolded them for getting dirty. She was a toilworn woman with a tubercular cough who'd had more than her share of bad luck. Now her husband was out of work because the pulp mill had closed down, her father was bedridden, and her mother needed an operation they couldn't afford.

The children's father admired the radiator cap and smiled at Sid's pleasure over finding that piece of colored glass, but when Polly

330

showed him those pretty little stones his face got a funny look and his hands trembled.

A few minutes later, in the amber glow of sunset, every member of that family except the bedridden grandfather was combing the disaster scene. Polly enjoyed the new game they were playing: it was the first time in months that Daddy had seemed happy. Every time they found one of those pretty little stones he would give a strange, wild, joyful sort of cry.

THE PLURAL MR. GRIMAUD

J. Gillies

When Kennedy walked out into the glare of the patio, he could see a man sitting at the far end under a trellis of vines. Beside him a girl lay motionless in sleep on a foam mattress, a sea-green cordial glass at her elbow.

He said, 'Mr. Grimaud?'

He was about to take a step forward when the man said, 'No, stay there. I want to look at you.' He was a very tired man, with slow and careful English, and he tossed a silver coin in his hand as if it weighed a ton. The girl didn't open her eyes.

Kennedy's head swam in the heat. He'd only had a roll and coffee when he got off the train at Nice, in case he didn't get the job. He felt the sweat run from a crease in his face. Grimaud was still watching him. 'What do you weigh, Mr. Kennedy?'

'About a hundred and seventy pounds.'

'Mmmmm ... that's about right.'

In spite of himself, Kennedy swayed a little. He said, 'It's pretty hot, Mr. Grimaud. Do you mind?' He made a half-gesture towards the other chair.

Grimaud said, smiling, 'Just a minute more. Please. How old are you?'

Kennedy ran a handkerchief around his neck. 'I'm twenty-eight,' he muttered. The sweat had pleated his lashes together, he tried to blink it away. 'Look, this heat ... I have to ...'

'All right, Kennedy, sit down.' Grimaud had stopped smiling.

As Kennedy stepped into the cool of the bower, the slow voice went on, 'Well. I've seen a dozen men and you look more like me than most of them. You're in ... if you still want the job.'

'Thanks, Mr. Grimaud. Whatever it is, I'll do my best.'

'Of course we'll have to fix you up a little, darken your hair. But with some tinted glasses and a moustache like mine, you should pass. My lawyer said you'd been having a difficult time lately. What's an American detective doing in Paris anyway?'

Kennedy shifted uneasily. 'Well, I came over on a divorce case. After awhile it folded and I was stuck here ...' His voice died away in the breathless air.

Grimaud nodded without interest. 'I'll pay you twenty-five thousand francs a day. That's around sixty dollars.'

Kennedy's eyes widened. 'That's a lot of money. What do I have to do for it?'

'Oh, just take my place now and then.' With a great effort, Grimaud curled his hand to look at his faultless nails. 'You see ... somebody's trying to kill me.'

Suddenly, he threw something over the body of the inert girl and into Kennedy's lap. Looking down, Kennedy saw it wasn't a silver coin but a nickel-plated rifle bullet. The nose was slightly flattened. Grimaud said, 'The gardener found it yesterday ... by that border there. Someone must have tried a long shot from the olive groves.' As Kennedy turned it over slowly in his hands, he added, 'That's why I kept you standing out there in the sun, in case they were still around and wanted—'

'That was real nice of you,' Kennedy said bitterly. And he wondered if he had enough strength to stand up and walk away.

'Why not?' Grimaud laughed. 'You're working for me, aren't you? Or are you?' Kennedy let the bullet fall. He thought of the hot ride back to Paris, of the long drag around the agencies. The tired voice said, 'Well, are you working for me?'

He let his breath go and said, 'I guess so, Mr. Grimaud. I guess so.'

Grimaud stood up, cool and uncreased. 'Shall we go inside then? You may as well get started.'

The alabaster figure between them still didn't stir, as they moved around her and went through the grass cloth shades into the lounge.

* * *

Grimaud and the girl sat opposite him at dinner without speaking. Kennedy ate hungrily in spite of the sour smell that came from the bristle which Dominic, the manservant, had gummed to his upper lip. Dominic had also rinsed his hair a shade darker and set a small wave in the front like Grimaud's.

Afterwards Grimaud said to the girl, 'Is it a success, Anna?'

'It's great!' She opened her hands in a gesture of appeal. 'How will I know you apart?'

Grimaud had said without humor, 'I'll be the one who shoots you if you don't.'

Kennedy was still staring at the girl. Somehow she didn't look American; yet she was. Grimaud walked away from the table saying, 'Anna is taking you for a drive, Kennedy, before it gets dark. The scenery is agreeable. You'd better have this, by the way …' He was holding a small automatic in his palm.

It was a .22 Biretta and Kennedy was dropping it into a side pocket, when he saw the Jaguar sports at the entrance. He stood looking at it while Anna went on ahead, wrapping herself in a camel's-hair coat.

'Isn't this a little crazy? I'll be a sitting duck.'

'The agreement is that you take my place when I want you to.'

Exasperated, Kennedy said, 'Look, if someone's trying to kill you, let me protect you *my* way.'

'I'm paying you to do it *my* way.'

Kennedy hesitated, thinking of the check upstairs, for a week in advance, that would buy him a passage home. After a moment, he went on down the steps.

*   *   *

Anna drove fast, through olive groves ash-blond in the twilight. At the start, he was as tense as a coiled spring and then gradually he relaxed. Anna didn't speak. The wind agitated her hair and she only slowed twice, each time to light a cigarette, with the self-contained movements of someone used to doing things for herself.

Once he said, 'What are you doing here, Anna?'

For a moment, she looked at him with eyes as cool and vacant as warehouse windows. Then she said, 'Felix wanted a secretary and I liked Europe, so here I am.' She added calmly, 'He wants to marry me.'

She didn't speak again, and they went down through the old town, past the port, as far as the *Promenade des Anglais*. The bay was ringed with light and a moonpath divided it, and Kennedy thought it certainly looked like a wonderful place to die.

When they got back, Grimaud was waiting by the stairs. He said, 'You must be tired,

Kennedy. I won't need you any more tonight.'

Going slowly up the stairs, Kennedy looked over his shoulder into the lounge. It was full of smoke and there were three glasses standing on the breast-high bar.

*   *   *

In the morning when he entered the breakfast room, he could feel the tension in the air.

Grimaud said sharply, 'There's a parcel come by the morning post. Will you open it?'

It lay by his plate. Puzzled, he said, 'Sure,' and picked it up. It was only then he noticed that they had backed away and were standing by the open window. He stared down at the printed label addressed to Felix Grimaud. It had been posted in Cannes. That was all it revealed.

Suddenly, he turned angrily and threw it into the large empty fireplace. 'Listen,' he shouted at Grimaud, 'I'll do it! I'll open it, but I'll open it *my* way.' Then he went across and picked up the parcel. He unwrapped the brown paper, revealing a shoe box. He put it down on the table again. Then kneeling beneath the shelter of the table, he pushed the lid up gently with a knife. It fell away.

The silence was complete. As he straightened up slowly, Grimaud came to his shoulder. The celluloid doll had glasses and a moustache painted on it, but Kennedy was staring at the cocktail stick that was plunged through its chest.

Grimaud laughed. 'Crude ... don't you think?'

*   *   *

'Today you can relax, Kennedy,' he said, when they were sitting over their coffee cups in the vine-shaded bower. 'Tonight you are taking Anna out to dinner. I have reserved a table on a private terrace at the Casino Regale. It will not be as dangerous as it sounds. The head waiter has orders that you are not to be disturbed.'

Kennedy stared up at the bunches of Golden Chasselas grapes, which hung above their heads like gilt chandeliers. 'I think I'd like to go downtown today, Mr. Grimaud ... as myself, I mean.'

'I prefer you remain here.'

Kennedy shook his head. 'This is the sort of job that could end suddenly, and I want to let my family back in the States know where I am.'

'All right.' Grimaud unfolded himself and stood up slowly. 'But do not be long. Take one of the cars if you wish.'

He walked away languidly.

*   *   *

That evening while they waited for the car, Grimaud said, 'Your outing did you a lot of

338

good?'

'Sure,' he said non-committally. In his pocket where the check had been there was now a fold of thousand-franc notes. He put his hand in the pocket.

Grimaud was saying, 'If any of my friends should try and speak to you, Anna will explain that I am not very well tonight. Give me the gun, by the way. It's a little obvious in that dinner jacket, and they do not like firearms at the Casino Regale. Anna has a gun in her bag, should there be an emergency.'

A moment later Anna joined them, very attractive in shimmering black. They left at once, and Grimaud called after them from the portico, 'Enjoy yourself, Kennedy...It is very, very expensive.'

Driving down, he pieced together a few more little things about Anna. She'd come over to Germany in the WAAF, and originally met Grimaud on a Paris leave. Before that there'd been a boy back home in Ohio. She'd wanted him to come to Europe too, but he was working up a small transport business and wouldn't leave his partner. They were old air force buddies, she said resentfully.

They reached the table on the terrace without incident. The waiters came and went, but Kennedy couldn't taste the food. He was strung up again...waiting. At long last, a man in casino livery approached the table. 'There is a telephone call for you, *M'sieu.*'

Kennedy saw Anna's eyes widen with alarm. 'You're not to leave me. Felix was very definite about that.'

'Sorry, Anna. This is an emergency.'

He was away no longer than two minutes, and she stared at him curiously when he came back. 'Now listen to me carefully,' he said in a grim voice. 'We've got very little time. Right from the very start, I knew there was something wrong with this setup.'

He saw her breath catch. 'What do you mean?'

'I mean I had a hunch that first day when he threw me the bullet. You see, that bullet had never been fired, there was no rifling, and no powder burn on it. Also I figured that if he was really expecting me to be shot at, he wouldn't have sent you along. After that stale joke with the parcel, I was practically certain. If no one was trying to kill Grimaud, then there was only one reason why he'd want a double. *He* was going to kill somebody and he wanted an alibi! Tomorrow he'd have given the gun back to me, taken the alibi, and I would have been out in the cold. Who'd have believed my fantastic story about getting dressed up to look like him, if he'd denied it?'

'Felix would never...'

'Shut up! This morning I checked up on him at the commissariat in Nice, and Felix Grimaud has a record. The police were interested in my theory. So tonight they had a

340

squad car waiting at the villa and they tailed him as soon as he left. He was nabbed at the apartment of a big property owner on the Rue de Ste. Claire, but they weren't quick enough to save Dominic. Grimaud shot him down because he thought he was the one who'd sold him out.'

'I don't believe it.'

Her hands clenched around her evening bag.

'They're looking for you,' he went on quickly. 'They're interested in what Grimaud has been doing lately.' He felt in his pocket and pulled out the fold of thousand-franc notes. It hurt, but only a little. 'The Azur Express pulls out in twenty-five minutes, and the Caronia sails from Cherbourg the day after tomorrow. There's enough there to get you back to the States. You might do worse than take another look at that fellow in Ohio.'

'Why ... are you doing this for me?'

'Because this is going to be a nasty case and you don't want to be mixed up in it, and because we Americans usually stick together. Incidentally, you've got just twenty minutes to catch that train.'

She stood up. Her hand went to the money, stayed there. 'How will I get in touch with you again? I want to pay you back.'

'Forget it,' he said. 'There's plenty more.'

'I'll never forget it,' she said with serious eyes. And then she left. And he watched her go.

*   *   *

He sat on in the dusk, turning the brandy glass carefully in his hands. Some time later, a siren died outside and in a few minutes the Inspector with hard eyes with whom he'd talked that morning was sitting with him.

The Inspector filled in the details.

When he finished, he added, 'If there is ever anything we can do, *M'sieu* Kennedy, you have only to request it.'

Kennedy smiled wryly. He was thinking about something that had been bothering him ever since Anna left. 'Well,' he said, at last, 'I happen to be a little short of money. Do you think the Sûreté would okay this dinner check of mine?'

PSEUDO IDENTITY

L. Block

Somewhere between four and four-thirty, Howard Jordan called his wife. 'It looks like another late night,' he told her. 'The spot TV copy for Prentiss was full of holes. I'll be here half the night rewriting it.'

'You'll stay in town?'

'No choice.'

'I hope you won't have trouble finding a room.'

'I'll make reservations now. Or there's always the office couch.'

'Well,' Carolyn said, and he heard her sigh the sigh designed to reassure him that she was sorry he would not be coming home, 'I'll see you tomorrow night, then. Don't forget to call the hotel.'

'I won't.'

He did not call the hotel. At five, the office emptied out. At five minutes after five, Howard Jordan cleared off his desk, packed up his attaché case and left the building. He had a steak in a small restaurant around the corner from his office, then caught a cab south and west to a four-story red brick building on Christopher Street. His key opened the door, and he walked in.

343

In the hallway, a thin girl with long blonde hair smiled at him. 'Hi, Roy.'

'Hello, baby.'

'Too much,' she said, eyeing his clothes. 'The picture of middle-class respectability.'

'A mere façade. A con perpetrated upon the soulless bosses.'

'Crazy. There's a party over at Ted and Betty's. You going?'

'I might.'

'See you there.'

He entered his own apartment, tucked his attaché case behind a low bookcase improvised of bricks and planks. In the small closet he hung his gray sharkskin suit, his button-down shirt, his rep-striped tie. He dressed again in tight Levi's and a bulky brown turtleneck sweater, changed his black moccasin toe oxfords for white hole-in-the-toe tennis sneakers. He left his wallet in the pocket of the sharkskin suit and pocketed another wallet, this one containing considerably less cash, no credit cards at all, and a few cards identifying him as Roy Baker.

He spent an hour playing chess in the back room of a Sullivan Street coffee house, winning two games of three. He joined friends in a bar a few blocks away and got into an overly impassioned argument on the cultural implications of Camp; when the bartender ejected them, he took his friends along to the party in the East Village apartment of Ted

344

Marsh and Betty Haniford. Someone had brought a guitar, and he sat on the floor drinking wine and listening to the singing.

Ginny, the long-haired blonde who had an apartment in his building, drank too much wine. He walked her home, and the night air sobered her.

'Come up for a minute or two,' she said. 'I want you to hear what my analyst said this afternoon. I'll make us some coffee.'

'Groovy,' he said, and went upstairs with her. He enjoyed the conversation and the coffee and Ginny. An hour later, around one-thirty, he returned to his own apartment and went to sleep.

In the morning he rose, showered, put on a fresh white shirt, another striped tie, and the same gray sharkskin suit, and rode uptown to his office.

*　　　*　　　*

It had begun innocently enough. From the time he'd made the big jump from senior copywriter at Lowell, Burham & Plescow to copy chief at Keith Wenrall Associates, he had found himself working late more and more frequently. While the late hours never bothered him, merely depriving him of the company of a whining wife, the midnight train to New Hope was a constant source of aggravation. He never got to bed before two-thirty those nights he rode it, and then had to drag himself out of bed just four and a half hours later in order to be at his desk by nine.

It wasn't long before he abandoned the train and spent those late nights in a midtown hotel. This proved an imperfect solution, substituting inconvenience and expense for sleeplessness. It was often difficult to find a room at a late hour, always impossible to locate one for less than twelve dollars; and hotel rooms, however well appointed, did not provide such amenities as a toothbrush or a razor, not to mention a change of underwear and a clean shirt. Then too, there was something disturbingly temporary and marginal about a hotel room. It felt even less like home than did his split-level miasma in Bucks County.

An apartment, he realized, would overcome all of these objections while actually saving him money. He could rent a perfectly satisfactory place for a hundred dollars a month, less than he presently spent on hotels, and it would always be there for him, with fresh clothing in the closet and a razor and toothbrush in the bathroom.

He found the listing in the classified pages— *Christopher St, 1 rm, bth, ktte, frnshd, util, $90 mth*. He translated this and decided that a one-room apartment on Christopher Street with bathroom and kitchenette, furnished, with utilities included at ninety dollars per month, was just what he was looking for. He called the

346

landlord and asked when he could see the apartment.

'Come around after dinner,' the landlord said. He gave him the address and asked his name.

'Baker,' Howard Jordan said. 'Roy Baker.'

After he hung up he tried to imagine why he had given a false name. It was a handy device when one wanted to avoid being called back, but it did seem pointless in this instance. Well, no matter, he decided. He would make certain the landlord got his name straight when he rented the apartment. Meanwhile, he had problems enough changing a junior copywriter's flights of literary fancy into something that might actually convince a man that the girls would love him more if he used the client's brand of gunk on his hair.

The landlord, a birdlike little man with thick metal-rimmed glasses, was waiting for Jordan.

He said, 'Mr. Baker? Right this way. First floor in the rear. Real nice place.'

The apartment was small but satisfactory. When he agreed to rent it the landlord produced a lease, and Jordan immediately changed his mind about clearing up the matter of his own identity. A lease, he knew, would be infinitely easier to break without his name on it. He gave the document a casual reading, then signed it 'Roy Baker' in a handwriting quite unlike his own.

'Now I'll want a hundred and eighty

347

dollars,' the landlord said. 'That's a month's rent in advance and a month's security.'

Jordan reached for his checkbook, then realized his bank would be quite unlikely to honor a check with Roy Baker's signature on it. He paid the landlord in cash, and arranged to move in the next day.

He spent the following day's lunch hour buying extra clothing for the apartment, selecting bed linen, and finally purchasing a suitcase to accommodate the items he had bought. On a whim, he had the suitcase monogrammed 'R.B.' That night he worked late, told Carolyn he would be staying in a hotel, then carried the suitcase to his apartment, put his new clothes in the closet, put his new toothbrush and razor in the tiny bathroom and, finally, made his bed and lay in it. At this point Roy Baker was no more than a signature on a lease and two initials on a suitcase.

Two months later, Roy Baker was a person.

*   *   *

The process by which Roy Baker's bones were clad with flesh was a gradual one. Looking back on it, Jordan could not tell exactly how it had begun, or at what point it had become purposeful. Baker's personal wardrobe came into being when Jordan began to make the rounds of Village bars and coffee houses, and

348

wanted to look more like a neighborhood resident and less like a celebrant from uptown. He bought denim trousers, canvas shoes, bulky sweaters; and when he shed his three-button suit and donned his Roy Baker costume, he was transformed as utterly as Bruce Wayne clad in Batman's mask and cape.

When he met people in the building or around the neighborhood, he automatically introduced himself as Baker. This was simply expedient; it wouldn't do to get into involved discussions with casual acquaintances, telling them that he answered to one name but lived under another, but by being Baker instead of Jordan, he could play a far more interesting role. Jordan, after all, was a square, a Madison Avenue copy chief, an animal of little interest to the folksingers and artists and actors he met in the Village. Baker, on the other hand, could be whatever Jordan wanted him to be. Before long his identity took form: he was an artist, he'd been unable to do any serious work since his wife's tragic death, and for the time being he was stuck in a square job with a commercial art studio.

This identity he had picked for Baker was a source of occasional amusement to him. Its expedience aside, he was not blind to its psychological implications. Substitute *writer* for *artist* and one approached his own situation. He had long dreamed of being a writer, but had made no efforts toward serious writing since his marriage to Carolyn. The bit about the tragic death of his wife was nothing more than simple wish-fulfillment. Nothing would have pleased him more than Carolyn's death, so he had incorporated this dream in Baker's biography.

As the weeks passed, Baker accumulated more and more of the trappings of personality. He opened a bank account. It was, after all, inconvenient to pay the rent in cash. He joined a book club and promptly wound up on half the world's mailing lists. He got a letter from his congressman advising him of latest developments in Washington and the heroic job his elected representative was doing to safeguard his interests. Before very long, he found himself heading for his Christopher Street apartment even on nights when he did not have to work late at all.

Interestingly enough, his late work actually decreased once he was settled in the apartment. Perhaps he had only developed the need to work late out of a larger need to avoid going home to Carolyn. In any event, now that he had a place to go after work, he found it far less essential to stay around the office after five o'clock. He rarely worked late more than one night a week—but he always spent three nights a week in town, and often four.

Sometimes he spent the evening with friends. Sometimes he stayed in his apartment and rejoiced in the blessings of solitude. Other

350

times he combined the best of two worlds by finding an agreeable Village female to share his solitude.

He kept waiting for the double life to catch up with him, anticipating the tension and insecurity which were always a component of such living patterns in the movies and on television. He expected to be discovered, or overcome by guilt, or otherwise to have the error of his dual ways brought forcibly home to him. But this did not happen. His office work showed a noticeable improvement; he was not only more efficient, but his copy was fresher, more inspired, more creative. He was doing more work in less time and doing a better job of it. Even his home life improved, if only in that there was less of it.

Divorce? He thought about it, imagined the joy of being Roy Baker on a full-time basis. It would be financially devastating, he knew. Carolyn would wind up with the house and the car and the lion's share of his salary, but Roy Baker could survive on a mere fraction of Howard Jordan's salary, existing quite comfortably without house or car. He never relinquished the idea of asking Carolyn for a divorce, nor did he ever quite get around to it—until one night he saw her leaving a night club on West Third Street, her black hair blowing in the wind, her step drunkenly unsteady, and a man's arm curled possessively around her waist.

His first reaction was one of astonishment that anyone would actually desire her. With all the vibrant, fresh-bodied girls in the Village, why would anyone be interested in Carolyn? It made no sense to him.

Then, suddenly, his puzzlement gave way to absolute fury. She had been cold to him for years, and now she was running around with other men, adding insult to injury. She let him support her, let him pay off the endless mortgage on the horrible house, let him sponsor her charge accounts while she spent her way toward the list of Ten Best-Dressed Women. She took everything from him and gave nothing to him, and all the while she was giving it to someone else.

He knew, then, that he hated her, that he had always hated her and, finally, that he was going to do something about it.

What? Hire detectives? Gather evidence? Divorce her as an adulteress? Small revenge, hardly the punishment that fit the crime.

No. No, *he* could not possibly do anything about it. It would be too much out of character for him to take positive action. He was the good clean-living, midtown-square type, good old Howie Jordan. He would do all that such a man could do, bearing his new knowledge in silence, pretending that he knew nothing, and going on as before.

But Roy Baker could do more.

From that day on he let his two lives overlap.

On the nights when he stayed in town he went directly from the office to a nearby hotel, took a room, rumpled up the bed so that it would look as though it had been slept in, then left the hotel by back staircase and rear exit. After a quick cab ride downtown and a change of clothes, he became Roy Baker again and lived Roy Baker's usual life, spending just a little more time than usual around West Third Street. It wasn't long before he saw her again. This time he followed her. He found out that her lover was a self-styled folk singer named Stud Clement, and he learned by discreet inquiries that Carolyn was paying Stud's rent.

'Stud inherited her from Phillie Wells when Phillie split for the coast,' someone told him. 'She's got some square husband in Connecticut or someplace. If Stud's not on the scene, she don't care who she goes home with.'

She had been at this, then, for some time. He smiled bitterly. It was true, he decided; the husband was really the last to know.

He went on using the midtown hotel, creating a careful pattern for his life, and he kept careful patterns on Stud Clement. One night when Carolyn didn't come to town, he managed to stand next to the big folk singer in a Hudson Street bar and listen to him talk. He caught the slight Tennessee accent, the pitch of the voice, the type of words that Clement used.

Through it all he waited for his hatred to die, waited for his fury to cool. In a sense she had

353

done no more to him than he had done to her. He half expected that he would lose his hatred sooner or later, but he found that he hated her more every day, not only for cheating but for making him an ad man instead of a writer, for making him live in that house instead of a Village apartment, for all the things she had done to ruin every aspect of his life. If it had not been for her, he would have been Roy Baker all his life. She had made a Howard Jordan of him, and for that he would hate her forever.

Once he realized this, he made the phone call. 'I gotta see you tonight,' he said.

'Stud?'

So the imitation was successful. 'Not at my place,' he said quickly. '193 Christopher, Apartment 1-D. Seven-thirty, no sooner and no later. And don't be going near my place.'

'Trouble?'

'Just be there,' he said, and hung up.

His own phone rang in less than five minutes. He smiled a bitter smile as he answered it.

She said, 'Howard? I was wondering, you're not coming home tonight, are you? You'll have to stay at your hotel in town?'

'I don't know,' he said. 'I've got a lot of work, but I hate to be away from you so much. Maybe I'll let it slide for a night—'

'No!' He heard her gasp. Then she recovered, and her voice was calm when she spoke again. 'I mean, your career comes first, darling. You know that. You shouldn't think of me. Think of your job.'

'Well,' he said, enjoying all this, 'I'm not sure—'

'I've got a dreary headache anyway, darling. Why not stay in town? We'll have the weekend together—'

He let her talk him into it. After she rang off, he called his usual hotel and made his usual reservation for eleven-thirty. He went back to work, left the office at five-thirty, signed the register downstairs and left the building. He had a quick bite at a lunch counter and was back at his desk at six o'clock, after signing the book again on the way in.

At a quarter to seven he left the building again, this time failing to sign himself out. He took a cab to his apartment and was inside it by ten minutes after seven. At precisely seven-thirty there was a knock on his door. He answered it, and she stared at him as he dragged her inside. She couldn't figure it out; her face contorted.

'I'm going to kill you, Carolyn,' he said, and showed her the knife. She died slowly, and noisily. Her cries would have brought out the National Guard anywhere else in the country, but they were in New York now, and New Yorkers never concern themselves with the shrieks of dying women.

He took the few clothes that did not belong to Baker, scooped up Carolyn's purse, and got

355

out of the apartment. From a pay phone on Sheridan Square he called the air terminal and made a reservation. Then he taxied back to the office and slipped inside, again without writing his name in the register.

At eleven-fifteen he left the office, went to his hotel and slept much more soundly than he had expected. He went to the office in the morning and had his secretary put in three calls to New Hope. No one answered.

That was Friday. He took his usual train home, rang his bell a few times, used his key, called Carolyn's name several times, then made himself a drink. After half an hour he called the next door neighbor and asked her if she knew where his wife was. She didn't. After another three hours he called the police.

Sunday a local policeman came around to see him. Evidently Carolyn had had her fingerprints taken once, maybe when she'd held a civil service job before they were married. The New York police had found the body Saturday evening, and it had taken them a little less than twenty-four hours to run a check on the prints and trace Carolyn to New Hope.

'I hoped I wouldn't have to tell you this,' the policeman said. 'When you reported your wife missing, we talked to some of the neighbors. It looks as though she was—uh—stepping out on you, Mr. Jordan. I'm afraid it had been going on for some time. There were men she met in

New York. Does the name Roy Baker mean anything to you?'

'No. Was he—'

'I'm afraid he was one of the men she was seeing, Mr. Jordan. I'm afraid he killed her, sir.'

Howard's reactions combined hurt and loss and bewilderment in proper proportion. He almost broke down when they had him view the body but managed to hold himself together stoically. He learned from the New York police that Roy Baker was a Village type, evidently some sort of irresponsible artist. Baker had made a reservation on a plane shortly after killing Carolyn but hadn't picked up his ticket, evidently realizing that the police would be able to trace him. He'd no doubt take a plane under another name, but they were certain they would catch up with him before too long.

'He cleared out in a rush,' the policeman said. 'Left his clothes, never got to empty out his bank account. A guy like this, he's going to turn up in a certain kind of place. The Village, North Beach in Frisco, maybe New Orleans. He'll be back in the Village within a year, I'll bet on it, and when he does we'll pick him up.'

For form's sake, the New York police checked Jordan's whereabouts at the time of the murder, and they found that he'd been at his office until eleven-fifteen, except for a half hour when he'd had a sandwich around the corner, and that he had spent the rest of the night at the hotel where he always stayed when he worked late.

That, incredibly, was all there was to it.

After a suitable interval, Howard put the New Hope house on the market and sold it almost immediately at a better price than he had thought possible.

He moved to town, stayed at his alibi hotel while he checked the papers for a Village apartment.

He was in a cab, heading downtown for a look at a three-room apartment on Horatio Street, before he realized suddenly that he could not possibly live in the Village, not now. He was known there as Roy Baker, and if he went there he would be identified as Roy Baker and arrested as Roy Baker, and that would be the end of it.

'Better turn around,' he told the cab driver. 'Take me back to the hotel. I changed my mind.'

He spent another two weeks in the hotel, trying to think things through, looking for a safe way to live Roy Baker's life again. If there was an answer, he couldn't find it. The casual life of the Village had to stay out of bounds.

He took an apartment uptown on the East Side. It was quite expensive but he found it cold and charmless. He took to spending his free evenings at midtown nightclubs, where he drank a little too much and spent a great deal of money to see poor floor shows. He didn't get out often, though, because he seemed to be working late more frequently now. It was harder and harder to get everything done on time. On top of that his work had lost its sharpness; he had to go over blocks of copy again and again to get them right.

Revelation came slowly, painfully. He began to see just what he had done to himself.

In Roy Baker, he had found the one perfect life for himself. The Christopher Street apartment, the false identity, the new world of new friends and different clothes and words and customs, had been a world he took to with ease because it was the perfect world for him. The mechanics of preserving this dual identity, the taut fabric of lies that clothed it, the childlike delight in pure secrecy, had added a sharp element of excitement to it all. He had enjoyed being Roy Baker; more, he had enjoyed being Howard Jordan playing at being Roy Baker.

The double life suited him so perfectly that he had felt no great need to divorce Carolyn.

Instead, he had killed her—and killed Roy Baker in the bargain, erased him very neatly, put him out of the picture for all time.

Howard bought a pair of Levi's, a turtleneck sweater, a pair of white tennis sneakers. He kept these clothes in the closet of his Sutton Place apartment, and now and then when he spent a solitary evening there he dressed in his Roy Baker costume and sat on the floor drinking California wine straight from the jug. He wished he were playing chess in the back room of a coffee house, or arguing art and religion in a Village bar, or listening to a blue guitar at a loft party.

He could dress up all he wanted in his Roy Baker costume, but it wouldn't work. He could drink wine and play guitar music on his stereo, but that wouldn't work, either. He could buy women, but he couldn't walk them home from Village parties and make love to them in third-floor walk-ups.

He had to be Howard Jordan.

Carolyn or no Carolyn, married or single, New Hope split-level or Sutton Place apartment, one central fact remained unchanged. He simply did not like being Howard Jordan.

THAT RUSSIAN!

J. Ritchie

Ah, how Nadia could run—like a gazelle, like an antelope—for at least ten seconds; Mariska too.

For myself, I throw my weight around—which is the hammer.

On the upper deck of this Russian boat which travels to the sports meet in the United States, I stand and eat a sandwich while I watch these Russians at mass exercise, back and forth, right and left, and up and down.

It is not that we Hungarians do not exercise. It is simply that we are more individual about this. We do not want a loud-voice on a platform telling us what to do—especially if it is in Russian.

I observe the women's group down below and the overwhelming number of sturdy legs, but Nadia does not have sturdy legs. They are long and at a glance one sees that she can run and probably must, for she has lustrous black hair and violet eyes and one thinks of the ballet rather than the cinder track.

Mariska appears at my side. 'You are watching Nadia again?' she asks. 'That *Russian?*'

Mariska is the fastest woman in all Hungary.

This is true also for events in Poland and Italy. However, in Western Germany and France, she comes in second to Nadia in the 100 meter dash.

It is obvious that Mariska is very jealous of Nadia's running—fifty percent of the time, at least—and from the narrowness of her eyes, I have the feeling that in America they will settle this once and for all.

'We should have defected in Germany or France,' Mariska says. 'Or even Italy.'

I shake my head. 'No, Mariska. Since our ultimate goal is the freedom of America, does it not pay to remain with the team until it arrives there? In this manner we are assured free passage.'

We become aware that Boris Volakov has moved beside us.

Boris is a most unpopular man. He is commissar for the Russian team, plus in overall charge of the voyage. It is a rumor that his unfavorable reports have caused the disappearance of one high-jumper, one long distance runner, and one hop, skip, and jump.

'You are attending the All-Nations Friendship Party on board tomorrow night?' he asks.

With the Russians, we speak English. It is a beautiful language and besides it irritates them.

'I am sorry,' Mariska says, 'but I am developing a cold.'

'I have this trouble with my sinuses,' I say. 'This always requires forty-eight hours for the cure.'

Boris smiles like a shark and is not disturbed. 'I have talked to the leaders of all nationalities and they will see that medical problems of that nature are cleared up by the time of the party.'

He looks Mariska up and down. 'I have always admired the Hungarians. I have spent some time in Budapest.'

'Oh?' Mariska says with great sweetness. 'As a tourist?'

He clears his throat. 'Not exactly.'

Now, on the deck below, the exercises have come to a close and the group is dismissed.

Boris excuses himself and walks toward the iron stairs which lead to the lower decks.

Nadia looks up and sees that he is coming down. Very casually, but firmly, she begins to walk away.

It is interesting to watch—from my height—this pursuit and the evasion, this looking back over the shoulder, this increasing of the pace, this series of sharp right and left turns around lifeboats and funnels.

I study the situation and see that eventually she is about to be trapped—for this Boris is tricky and foresighted.

'I think I will go downstairs,' I say to Mariska.

She looks at me, but says nothing.

363

I go down the stairs and after five minutes, manage to intercept Nadia. 'This way,' I say, and take her arm.

'Oh,' she says, 'it is you again,' for we have met and talked before whenever I was able to create the opportunity.

She comes where I take her, which is to crouch behind a winch, and we wait. Soon Boris passes by, the yellow gleam of pursuit still in his eyes.

Nadia takes a deep breath. 'So far I have been saved by one thing or another, but I am running out of miracles and excuses.'

'Why are excuses even necessary?' I say. 'Is not a simple "no" in his face enough?'

She looks at me like I am a child. 'Life is not always that simple. Boris is a man of much influence.'

'Ah yes,' I say wisely. 'I understand that he has sent three men to Siberia.'

She smiles, but tightly. 'They were not men and they were not sent to Siberia. We are no longer that primitive in the treatment of our athletes. They were women who said "no" and they were simply dismissed from the team. Today they are teaching calisthenics to pre-school children in Kandalaksha, which is just beyond the Arctic Circle, but still in Europe.'

'Nadia,' I say, 'France is a nice country and free—in a capitalistic way, of course—and this is true also of Western Germany and Italy. Why did you not seek asylum in one of these

364

places? It is unlikely that Boris would have continued pursuit.'

She shakes her head. 'No. I could not do anything like that.'

'You have relatives in Russia? They would be liquidated?'

'We no longer liquidate relatives,' she says stiffly. 'However, I do not wish to leave the team. It is a great honor to be a member and this I would not willingly give up.'

I feel anger stirring. 'So remaining on the team is of greater importance than your honor?'

She looks frosty. 'I would prefer to have both.'

She thinks more on the subject of Boris. 'He is the commissar of the athletes,' she says bitterly, 'but in his life he has yet to run even the one hundred meter dash. He is greedy and opportunistic. He goes as the wind blows— wherever it is easiest, wherever he has the most to gain for himself. This is how he has come to his present position, after beginning as the custodian of the uniforms. Also, I think that in Russia he was a speculator in the black market, but has always been too clever to be caught.'

I rub my jaw. To me has come the expression that if a mountain does not come to the Mohammedans, then it is necessary for the Mohammedans to go to the mountain. 'Do not despair,' I say, 'I will personally work on this problem.'

365

That evening in the dining room, I sit at Boris' table—which is easy, for there is always room—and over tea I ask, 'Have you ever been to New York?'

'No,' Boris says. 'I know nothing about America except that the poor are exploited by the rich.'

'How true,' I say, and then sigh. 'It is unfortunate, but I will not be able to visit my cousin Stephen when we arrive there. He is one of these rich exploiters.'

Boris is interested. 'Rich? But why can you not go to see him?'

I smile sadly. 'Because he is a defector and as a loyal member of the party, I certainly would not want to be seen in his presence. He fled from Hungary two years ago.'

Boris' mind fastened on one point. 'A *rich* defector? Before he defected, did he somehow manage to—ah—transfer money to some Swiss bank? Hm?'

'No,' I say. 'When Stephen arrived in America, he was penniless.'

Boris thinks on this too. 'He defected but two years ago, but *today* he is rich?'

I nod. 'He has a large estate in Hoboken, a swimming pool, two limousines, three mistresses, and eight horses.'

Boris is impressed. 'Three? But how did this all happen?'

'It is all the responsibility of his agent, who has the strange American name of John Smith.

This John Smith had Stephen's experiences written into a book which has become a best seller. And also it will soon be made into a motion picture in which Stephen will hold a percentage.'

Boris is puzzled. 'But there are tens of thousands of defectors. Surely not every one of them could write a book and expect to make so much money?'

'Of course not,' I say. 'But Stephen was an important man behind the Iron—' I clear my throat '—in our country. He was a commissar overseeing the Fejer Building Institute. Perhaps you have heard of his book? *I Was a Commissar for the F.B.I.?*'

Boris frowns. 'It is somehow vaguely familiar.'

'People are extremely interested in Stephen,' I say. 'There is a shortage of commissars in America, for not many of them defect. They know when they have it good.'

Boris agrees. 'Good, yes. But riches, no.' He looks very casual. 'This John Smith agent, where does he live, this capitalist pig?'

'In Chicago at a place called State Street. Probably his name is in the telephone book.'

When I rise to leave Boris is still thinking about my cousin Stephen, who does not exist.

The night of the Friendship Party there comes a thick fog upon the ocean and it is necessary for the ship to slow almost to a halt and blow its horns often. Even so, we almost run into other ships, for we are now near New York and the traffic lanes are heavy.

In the dining room, I find that Nadia, Mariska, and I have been assigned to Boris' table.

He talks hardly at all. Mostly he is preoccupied and he drinks a good deal.

It is a yawning evening until ten when there is trouble in the bar among the united Czechoslovakians. The Czechs and the Slovakians begin to fight and the Ruthenians watch and smile.

When order is restored, I notice that Boris has left his previous thoughts and is now looking at Nadia.

His voice is thick with the drink. 'Nadia, let us, you and I, walk about the deck.'

'No,' Nadia says. 'The fog is bad for my throat.'

'You are not a singer,' Boris snaps and then he glares at her. 'How would you like to teach calisthenics to pre-school children?'

The band strikes up with dance music and I immediately sweep Nadia upon the floor.

'Nadia,' I say, 'this is not the moment to spill the soup in the ointment. You must cooperate with Boris for the time being.'

She is shocked. 'You, of all people, to say *that*?'

I explain hastily. 'I mean only for this walk on the foggy deck. You can come to no harm, for I think that he has drunk too much to be dangerous. I even wonder whether he can still walk at all.'

She studies me. 'Just what are you up to, Janos?'

I smile. 'I have a clever plan and I will tell you when it works. I have the feeling that soon you will never see Boris again.'

When we return from the dance, Nadia is more friendly and soon she and Boris rise and move toward the door. He walks much better than I anticipate and so I begin to worry.

Finally I too rise and walk out into the fog. I hesitate. Where have they gone? To the right or to the left? I listen, but I hear nothing.

I turn to the right and after a dozen steps I bump into two people who are much close together. I recognize the man as a Czech high-jumper and the woman as a Rumanian gymnast, which is bad politics at the present time, but they do not seem to care.

'Pardon,' I say. 'Did anyone pass this way recently?'

The man peers into my face and is relieved that I am not a commissar. 'No,' he says. 'Not that we notice.'

I go in the opposite direction, bumping into objects occasionally and listening. All I hear is the groan of horns near and far, and when there is no horn noise, it appears that I am in a vacuum of silence. I think that I may have taken the wrong direction after all, but then I hear the commencing of a scream. It is muffled by the fog and yet I feel that it is near.

I press on immediately and after only twenty feet I come upon Boris and Nadia, and I see that he is considerably less drunk than I had thought. When I see what could be impending, fury springs into my blood and I forget all about Mohammedans and their mountains. I spring forward shouting a nationalist war cry.

Boris is considerably surprised by my entrance out of the fog, but he becomes even more so when I immediately grasp him by one arm and one leg and swing him in a circle ... once ... twice ... and then I let go.

It is a great fling, perhaps a world's record for this type of event. Boris and his scream fly through a thin patch in the fog and over the ship's rail.

Nadia joins me and we look into the swirling white gray which hides the water.

'Was this your clever plan?' she asks.

'No,' I say sadly. 'There is many a slip between the cup and the ship.'

We are now silent and I try to think about this predicament.

'Nadia,' I finally say, 'I will surrender myself and confess. I will say that you were not even here. It was a personal quarrel.'

'Nonsense,' Nadia says. 'Since no one has rushed here, evidently the fog muffled his scream and he was not heard. We will simply walk away. Boris just disappeared, and we know nothing about it at all.'

'But you were seen leaving the ballroom with him,' I say. 'There will be questions asked. And there is no Supreme Court to throw out the confession that will inevitably follow.'

Nadia offers another idea. 'We will say it was an accident which we both witnessed. Boris slipped and fell overboard.'

I shook my head. 'I do not think we will be believed. It is generally established that commissars do not meet death by accident.'

We are silent again and then I sigh. 'Nadia, I do not worry for myself. If no one heard the scream, I do not think that Boris will be missed before tomorrow and we will have arrived in New York by then. Freedom is but a leap or a dash beyond.'

She is wide-eyed. 'You are going to defect?'

'Yes,' I say. 'We have planned upon this for a long time.'

The wide eyes become narrow eyes. 'We? Who is we?'

'Mariska and I.'

Her lips tighten. It is strange how these women athletes are so jealous of each other's ability to run. Among men, there is more sportsmanship.

'America is a big country,' I say. 'It is big enough for *two* runners of excellence.'

'I doubt this,' she says, but sighs. 'However, I do not think I have much of a choice.'

We arrive in clear weather at the Port of New York the next morning. Soon we descend the gangplank while the ship's loudspeaker calls out for Boris to report to his contingent.

There is a rumor—which Nadia and I have started—that Boris has drunk too much and fallen asleep in some corner of the ship.

We step without trouble onto American soil and are taken to the hotel.

I would have preferred to participate first in the sports meet before defecting—as would Nadia and Mariska—but to postpone our defecting could possibly be fatal. So at the first opportunity, the three of us join and find the nearest police station and declare ourselves to be political refugees.

It is something I have never regretted, and three months later—at my wedding—I see Bela, a pole vaulter on our team who also defected, but after the meet. Evidently he has heard that I was to marry and wished to attend the event.

We shake hands and he smiles. 'So it was you who threw Boris overboard,' he says.

Perhaps I pale a bit, for if this is made public information, I am ruined. The Americans would not shield a murderer, even if the victim is a Russian. 'Did you witness the event?' I ask quickly.

He shakes his head. 'No. But I have just heard that Boris himself maintains that this happened.'

I blink. 'Boris Volakov is alive?'

Bela smiles. 'You tossed him overboard just

as a small freighter glided past in the fog, and Boris landed unnoticed on the canvas top of a lifeboat. The length of the fall, however, rendered him unconscious for perhaps a half hour.'

I take a breath of relief.

Bela continues. 'When Boris awoke and ascertained that he was alive and on another ship, he rushed immediately to the captain on the bridge and announced that he was declaring himself a political refugee who wished to remain in the west, and he also wanted to send swiftly a radiogram to a Mr. John Smith of State Street, Chicago.'

I sighed. 'So Boris is now in America?'

Bela smiled again. 'No. Unfortunately for Boris, the ship upon which you tossed him turned out to be a Russian freighter.'

It was a successful wedding. I was handsome and Nadia, my bride, looked beautiful.

The maid of honor, of course, was Mariska, my sister.

THE VERY HARD SELL

H. Nielsen

The call came over the loudspeaker above the used car lot at 3:00 P.M.

'Mr. Cornell, you're wanted on the telephone. Mr. Cornell, telephone—please.'

It was a godsend, Cornell felt. Mr. Garcy was in a bad mood and so somebody had to take a beating. Here of late that somebody always seemed to be him. It wasn't fair and Garcy knew it. There were slack periods in the auto market when nothing moved. Sales were down in the new car show room, too. What was he supposed to do—hypnotize the customers? The woman hadn't wanted the blue Olds; she didn't like blue. Even Jack Richards, who was almost twenty years younger than Glenn Cornell and who always wore a perky little bow tie that charmed the feminine trade, couldn't sell a blue car to a woman who didn't like blue no matter how good a buy it was.

'Mr. Cornell, you're wanted on the telephone...'

Cornell took advantage of the chance to break away from Garcy and made it to the office before the girl on the switchboard could finish her second call. The voice on the telephone was masculine—young, definite.

'Is this Garcy Motors on Sutter Street? Mr. Cornell? You had a black Cadillac on the used car lot a few days ago—a '57 sedan. I think it had a card on it—$3750. Yes, that's the one I mean. Is it still there? It is? Good. I'm coming by to look it over as soon as I get off work. If it runs as good as it looks, you've got a sale.'

'It does,' Cornell insisted. 'It handles like a new car and carries a new car guarantee. What time will you be in? 5:30? Fine, I'll have her warmed up and ready. Say, what's your name so I'll know you? Berra? Okay, Mr. Berra, I'll see you at 5:30.'

When Mr. Berra hung up, Glenn dropped the telephone in the cradle. He raised his head and found himself eye level with the salesmen's rating chart Mr. Garcy always kept in plain sight. There had been six names on the chart, but the last two had lines drawn through them. Mr. Garcy never erased a name when he let a man go. He left it there, cancelled out by a chalk line, as a grim reminder of what could happen to anyone whose sales dropped too low. The name just above the last chalk line was Glenn Cornell. He turned around and saw Mr. Garcy standing in the doorway.

'A customer of mine,' Cornell said with forced brightness. 'He's been looking at the black Caddy. I'm taking him out on a demonstration ride at 5:30.'

It wasn't much of a lie. Cornell had never laid eyes on Mr. Berra; but Garcy didn't know that, and it was worth stretching the story a bit to see the way his expression altered from surprise to near disappointment and then to one of the leers he used for a smile.

'Good man!' Garcy said. 'He's really interested. Sell him, Cornell. Don't let him get away. He's on the hook. All you have to do is reel him in.'

It was more than a pep talk; it was an order. Cornell vowed then and there that he'd sell the black Caddy to Mr. Berra if it was the last thing he did.

Exactly one week later, at a few minutes before 11:00 P.M., a patrol car answering a neighborhood complaint found a black Cadillac parked in an alley behind a lumber yard, about two miles across town from Garcy Motors. A man was slumped over the steering wheel, his chin pressing down on the horn rim and the horn, according to the complainant, had been sounding for nearly an hour. The first officer out of the patrol car opened the right front door of the Cadillac.

'Hey, mister,' he called above the din of the horn, 'this is no way to sleep off a drunk. You're keeping people awake.' And then he paused and leaned forward, sniffing at the interior of the sedan. 'Bring your flash over here!' he shouted to his companion. 'I think this car's full of fumes!'

The second officer appeared at his shoulder and inhaled deeply.

376

'Not gas,' he said. 'Smells more like burnt alfalfa.'

But when the light from the flash caught the man slumped over the steering wheel, both officers fell silent. He wasn't drunk; he was dead. Glenn Cornell would never sell anything to anyone after what the .45 slug had done to the right side of his head.

Hazel Cornell was a nice looking woman in spite of the grief in her eyes. Twenty years ago, Police Detective Sommers decided, she must have been the prettiest bride of the season. Now she was a widow. She didn't cry—praise heaven for that! There were dark shadows under her eyes and a tightness about her mouth; otherwise, she might have been a typical housewife who had donned her best cotton dress and a small hat with blue flowers on the brim that was usually worn only to church, and come down to report a mischievous neighborhood child, or some other minor disturbance.

But Police Detective Sommers handled homicide cases.

'I know what I told the police officers last night,' she said, 'and I know how it all looks. But I knew my husband, too. It isn't true what was printed in the papers this morning. Glenn didn't kill himself. He was a religious man. He wouldn't take his life.'

Her voice was low but firm, the inner tension held in careful check. Sommers glanced down

377

at the Cornell file open on his desk. All of her statements of the previous night were there.

'But Mrs. Cornell,' he remonstrated, 'you admitted that your husband had been depressed and in ill health.'

'Not really ill health,' she said. 'His cough had been bothering him some. Glenn had bronchitis when he was a child. Ever so often, his cough came back. It was nothing new. He wouldn't have killed himself for that.'

'But you also said that he was worried about the prospective customer for the car he was trying to sell. He'd been working on the deal all week without getting a definite answer. He came home for dinner last night and refused to eat.'

'He had a headache,' she explained.

'He went to his room for about ten minutes and then came out again, saying that he was going to meet Mr. Berra and—' Sommers glanced down at the report again '—put an end to the indecision.'

' "I've got him on the hook," he told me. "All I have to do is reel him in." '

'Ten minutes,' Sommers repeated, ignoring the interpolation. 'Now, Mrs. Cornell, didn't you identify the gun found on the seat beside your husband's body as his own gun, which, you stated, was kept in his bureau drawer?'

'Yes, but Glenn—'

'And the ballistic test has proved that your husband was killed by a bullet fired from that
378

gun.'

'But Glenn didn't fire the gun!'

She wasn't excited; she was adamant. She hadn't come alone. Sprawled in the chair beside her, a teen-age youth stirred restlessly at her words.

'Mom, I wish you wouldn't get so worked up,' he said.

'I'm not worked up, Andy,' she replied quietly. 'I'm merely telling this officer the truth. Your father didn't commit suicide.'

It wasn't going to be easy to talk her out of such conviction. She was a firm woman. She must have been a devoted wife, and must be a good mother, an uncomplicated personality who was still in a state of semi-shock from learning that such an evil as violent death could happen in her orderly life.

Sommers tried again. 'Mrs. Cornell,' he said, 'do you realize what your statement means? If your husband didn't commit suicide, he must have been murdered. Do you know anyone who might have wanted to murder your husband?'

'Oh, no. Glenn had no enemies.'

'And yet you insist that he was murdered.'

'It might have been a hold-up. He was driving that expensive car. Someone might have thought he had money.'

She was grasping at straws, illusory straws.

'But you identified Mr. Cornell's personal effects at the morgue,' he reminded. 'His wallet, containing $17, his key case, his cough drops—'

'That cough of his,' she said. 'He was never without them.'

'—his wrist watch and his wedding ring. Nothing was taken. Men have been murdered for much less than $17, Mrs. Cornell, but your husband wasn't one of them.'

'Then it must have been a madman,' she said. 'One of those crazed fiends we read about.'

If she wasn't going to change her mind, Sommers could at least take the out offered him.

'It might have been,' he admitted.

'Or Mr. Berra. Have you found Mr. Berra?'

Her eyes were accusing him across the desk. But Sommers had never seen a clearer case of self-inflicted death. There had been no indication of a struggle in the car. He'd gone there himself as soon as the patrol car radioed in. No struggle, obviously. And there were no fingerprints on the gun except Glenn Cornell's. He opened his mouth to answer, but Andy beat him to it.

'Mom,' he pleaded, 'the police know what they're doing. Leave it be.'

'No, they don't know. Not when they tell the reporters that your father committed suicide. They should at least talk to Mr. Berra.'

She stood up, a small, determined woman without tears.

'Glenn Cornell did not kill himself,' she said.

She turned and left the office, and Andy scrambled to his feet to follow. He hesitated in front of the desk.

'Don't mind my mother,' he said. 'She's all upset, you see. She just can't believe it.'

He was a good-looking kid, ruddy-faced, short pale blond hair, broad shoulders encased in a school sweater with a huge S over his chest.

'But you can believe it, is that it?' Sommers asked.

'Sure, I understand. A man's confidence can go. His pride. I mean, maybe this customer he was trying to sell cracked wise, or maybe old Garcy was riding him too hard. Some bosses are like that. As soon as they smell chicken, they're like a wolf sniffing blood.'

'Chicken?' Sommers echoed. 'Are you trying to tell me that you think your father was chicken?'

Andy Cornell flushed red up to his close-cropped hair.

'Look, I didn't mean—Well, anyhow, I know he could be pushed around.'

'How old are you, Andy?'

'Sixteen.'

'And nobody pushes you around, do they?' Sommers asked.

'I'll say they don't!'

Sommers' eyes held the boy for a few seconds and then dismissed him. Andy went out, but long after he'd gone Sommers stared after him. At least the boy had inadvertently explained what was behind his mother's refusal to face the obvious. 'Chicken,' he repeated to himself. It wasn't much of an obituary. He could at least talk to Mr. Berra.

*　　*　　*

A row of red and white pennants dangled listlessly above the used car lot of Garcy Motors on Sutter Street, limp reminders of a sale that wasn't being patronized. Inside the showroom office, Mr. Garcy showed a similar lack of enthusiasm for his inquisitive caller. He'd already had to cope with a couple of reporters. Suicide. That was a bad subject to fool around with. Morbid. Could give a place a bad name.

'To be honest with you, Officer,' he said, 'and I am honest with everyone, I wasn't too surprised when the police called me down last night to identify Cornell's body and my Cadillac. Not surprised that he'd killed himself, I mean. The man was on the down grade—not up to par at all. A few years ago he topped the list on that sales chart month after month, slack season and heavy; but lately he'd lost his drive. Brought his problems to work with him. That's bad. When a man can't leave his problems at home, he's bound to hit the skids.'

'Problems? What problems?'

'Any problems. We all have them, don't we? Family problems, health problems, money problems; but we learn to keep them out of our work. Not Cornell. Excuses, always excuses. His boy stayed out too late at night so he couldn't get any sleep. His boy was getting in with a bad crowd at high school. He didn't want his boy going wrong. I tell you, Officer, if Glenn Cornell had had five or six kids he'd have been alive today. He'd have had to give up worrying long ago.'

Sommers thought of Andy Cornell—tall, blond, handsome.

'His son hasn't been in trouble, has he?'

'Andy? Of course not. Good kid, Andy. Wish I had a son just like him. My luck—four girls. But Cornell worried just the same. Maybe it was physical. He had headaches a lot—took pills all the time, and always had trouble with his throat. Never smoked. But he'd been with me for nearly eleven years, and I hate to let a man go.'

Garcy's eyes inadvertently strayed to the chart on the wall. Sommers' followed. 'Moroni, Taber—' he read aloud. 'What does the chalk line indicate, Mr. Garcy?'

Garcy scowled. 'I can't carry dead weight. I've got a business to run.'

Sommers nodded.

'Cornell,' he added, reading the next name above the discharged salesmen. Silence filled in for the things nobody said. 'So you think he

383

was sufficiently depressed to have committed suicide.'

'Depressed, unstable—use whatever term you want to use, Officer. The fact is still the same. He did kill himself, didn't he?'

Of course he'd killed himself. Nothing had ever been more obvious, and yet Sommers, irritated by one derisive word, had to keep asking questions.

'What about Mr. Berra?' he queried. 'Did you talk to him?'

Garcy's expression changed from bridled impatience to momentary bewilderment.

'Who?' he asked.

'Berra. Cornell's customer for the Cadillac. Mrs. Cornell has told us that her husband had taken the death car from the lot in order to close a deal with a Mr. Berra.'

Garcy met Sommers' gaze with unblinking eyes.

'I don't think there was a Mr. Berra,' he said. 'I'm serious, Officer. I know, I told your men the same story Mrs. Cornell told them last night; but I've had time to think it over, and I'm convinced the whole thing was a fabrication. I'll tell you why I think it. It began last Friday—a week ago yesterday. Cornell had muffed what should have been a sure sale—that was just before noon. I had a luncheon date at my club and had to leave, but I told him I wanted to have a talk with him when I returned. He was in trouble, and he knew it. It was almost three o'clock before I got back. I'd no more than gone out to the lot to speak with Cornell—he was in charge of the used car sales—than a call came over the loudspeaker for Mr. Cornell to go to the telephone. I followed him back to the office and got there in time to hear him making an appointment with a Mr. Berra to demonstrate the black Caddy at 5:30.'

'Didn't Berra show?' Sommers asked.

'He did not. At about 5:15 there was another call. I usually go home at 5, but I was staying around to see how Cornell would handle this sale. The second call was from Berra again. He couldn't make it down to the lot in time, but if Cornell would drive over to a service station at the corner of Third and Fremont he could pick him up and demonstrate the car from there. It sounded all right, so I let him go.'

'When did he come back?'

'I don't know,' Garcy said. 'I went on home. In the morning, the Caddy was back on the lot, but Cornell told me he had a sure sale just as soon as Mr. Berra raised the cash. I got after him about pushing for a low down payment, but he said Berra didn't want to finance—that he only did business on a cash basis and would have the money in a few days. I didn't think much about it at the time, but now, thinking back, I realize that Cornell was acting strange even then.'

'Strange?' Sommers echoed. 'In what way?'

'I don't know exactly. He didn't seem to want to talk about Berra, except to assure me that he was sold on the car and would raise the money. Usually the salesmen chew the fat a little about their clients, brag on how they handle them, or even have a few anecdotes; but Cornell was like a clam. I even tried to pump him. I asked him if Berra worked at the service station where he'd picked him up. He said no, he didn't think so, and that was all I got out of him. Three days later—no, four, Tuesday, it was. Last Tuesday I asked him if he'd heard from Berra and told him to get on the ball and not let the customer get cold. That afternoon he took the Caddy and said he was going to drive over to Berra's house. He came back about half an hour later saying that nobody was home and he'd try again.'

'And did he?'

'I don't know. I only know that on Thursday—day before yesterday—Mr. Berra called back. This time he said that he'd raised the money. His mother, who lived in Pasadena, was putting up the full amount on the condition Cornell would drive him over to her house and let her inspect the car first. I thought then that it sounded fishy, but a $3750 cash sale isn't something you toss in the waste basket, and I trusted Cornell. I told him to go ahead, but to—'

Garcy hesitated and a little color came up in his face.

'But what?' Sommers prodded.

'I was only kidding, of course.'

'But what, Mr. Garcy?'

'But not to come back until he'd closed the deal.'

The silence in the shop was broken only by the distant sound of voices in the back lot garage.

'And did he come back?' Sommers asked.

'No. He called in yesterday morning and said he'd run into a little difficulty, but would get it straightened out before the day was over. He still had the Caddy with him.' Garcy's face was no longer red; it was chalk white. 'Damn it, it was only a figure of speech! I didn't mean for the man to blow out his brains!'

Sommers let Mr. Garcy indulge in his anguish without interruption. The well-adjusted machinery of his own mind was tabulating and arranging certain facts. All of them led him to one question.

'Mr. Garcy,' he said, 'you've just told me that this man, Berra, telephoned Cornell here at the office three different times, and yet you started out by saying that you didn't think the man existed. How do you account for that?'

'Timing,' Garcy responded, grateful for a change of thought. 'I got to thinking about it this morning. Cornell got that first call just after I'd started dressing him down for fluffing the other sale—at a time when he knew I'd be talking to him because I'd told him as much

387

before I went to lunch. And then, there's the way he dragged out this deal for a whole week, all the time insisting the car was as good as sold. I think he'd already flipped, Officer. I think he'd so lost his confidence that he rigged up Mr. Berra out of his imagination and fixed it with some friend to make the calls just to make it look good. I never saw the man. Nobody on the premises saw him, and Cornell never told us anything about him. The switchboard girl heard his voice—a young man, she says. Maybe it was his son. But I still think Mr. Berra doesn't exist.'

Garcy could be right, but something stuck in Sommers' mind. No, not his mind; his senses. The senses absorbed and retained in an instant what the mind needed time to analyze. Some small thing. He scowled over the nagging thought of it.

'You say that Cornell took the car to Berra's house,' he said. 'Did he tell you where the house was?'

'No, he didn't. He said it wasn't far, and he was back in half an hour.'

'Could he have jotted down the address somewhere—in his sales book, for instance?'

Garcy shrugged.

'You can look through his desk if you want to. Believe me, if I could locate this Berra I'd have a few questions for him myself. Do you know how many miles Cornell put on that Caddy last week? Nearly two hundred. I

388

checked the mileage down at the police garage last night. I have to keep an eye on that kind of thing. Some of the young salesmen like to take a late model out on their dates at night and eat up the fuel. Little things like that can wipe out a businessman's profits. It only takes one leak to sink a ship, if it's neglected long enough.'

Sommers ignored the lecture and went to work on Cornell's desk. There was ample evidence of other customers—names, addresses and telephone numbers, but nothing concerning Mr. Berra.

'You see,' Garcy told him. 'He made up this customer out of the whole cloth. It's tragic when a man's so weak he has to resort to lies to keep up a front.'

Chicken. Garcy's vocabulary was thirty years removed from Andy Cornell's, but they were saying the same thing. For Sommers, it was just another goad to keep looking.

'Third and Fremont,' he mused aloud.

'What's that?' Garcy asked.

'The location of the gas station where Cornell was to meet Berra.'

'Oh, sure. That's what he said. Look, Officer—' Garcy's words stopped Sommers at the door. 'If you want to go on looking for Mr. Berra, that's your business. Selling cars is mine. I'd like to get that Caddy back on the lot in time for the Sunday display.'

'I'll have it cleaned up and brought over to you, Mr. Garcy,' Sommers answered. 'In the meantime, there's something you can do to jack up your sales force and keep them on their toes.'

'Yes? What's that?'

'Draw a line through Cornell's name,' he said. 'On that chart.'

* * *

According to the lettering on the canopy, the manager of the service station at the corner of Third and Fremont was a man named Max Fuller. It was a busy intersection and several minutes elapsed before Detective Sommers could command Fuller's attention. Even then it was hardly undivided. They stepped inside the office, but Fuller kept a wary eye on his assistant.

'New kid on the pumps,' he explained. 'Have to watch 'em the first few days. Police, isn't it? What's on your mind? Selling tickets to something?'

Sommers wasn't selling tickets to anything. He explained what was on his mind, and, as he did so, Fuller forgot about his pumps.

'Berra?' he echoed, at the sound of the name. 'Say, what's this guy done, anyway?'

It was an interesting response.

'What do you mean?' Sommers asked.

'Well, there was a fellow in here yesterday asking for the same man. Wanted to know if anyone of that name worked here, or if I knew where he could find him. I told him I'd never heard of the name, so he described him to me. A young fellow, he said. Twenty, maybe, but no more. Swarthy skin, dark hair and eyes, expensive looking clothes. The description didn't ring any bells, so he goes on to tell me a story about having picked up this Berra here at my station nearly a week ago. Craziest thing I ever heard.'

'Crazy,' Sommers echoed. 'In what way?'

'In every way. The way he picked up Berra. He drove over to the side of the building, see, so as not to block off my pumps. He cut the motor, figuring he'd have to come inside the office to find the person he was supposed to meet; but before he could get out of the car, the door of the men's room opened and Berra came out of it—running, he said, with his head ducked down. Berra pulled open the car door, asked if he was Mr. Cornell—'

'Cornell?' Sommers repeated.

'That's the name of the fellow who came in here yesterday asking about Berra. Cornell said he was, and so Berra got into the car. "Okay," he says, "let's go." Cornell is a car salesman, you see. The fellow who came running out of the rest room had called him about buying a black Cadillac—'

Max Fuller's voice broke abruptly. He'd been cleaning his hands on a wipe cloth as he talked. When he dropped it on the desk, his eyes caught the front page on the morning

391

paper that had been staring up at him all this time. One story had a black headline: Auto Salesman Suicide Victim. He followed the story for a few lines and then looked up, puzzled.

'Why, that's the guy,' he said. 'The same one who was in here yesterday.'

'The same one,' Sommers agreed. 'Tell me, did you see the man Cornell described—the day he was supposed to have come running out of the men's room?'

'No, sir, I didn't. Late in the afternoon—this was at 5:30, he said—things are really jumping around here. People coming home from work, you know. I don't have a chance to watch anything but the pump meters. To tell you the truth, I don't even remember Cornell driving in, but he sure could have without me noticing. You can see for yourself. There's plenty of area out there for a man to park a car clear of the pumps.'

Sommers moved back to the doorway. Fuller was right. It must have been thirty feet from the station office to the edge of the lot—an inner edge where a two-story commercial building rose up like a tall, windowless wall. A man could park his car clear of the pump area and not be noticed by anyone during the rush hours. By the same token, a man coming out of the rest room, which was in the rear end of the station building, would have been shielded from view.

'And you keep the rest rooms locked, I suppose,' Sommers said.

'Have to,' Fuller answered. 'Company orders. Sure wish I didn't. Those darned rooms give me more trouble than the rest of the business put together. I could write a book!'

'Mind if I look at it?'

'Go ahead. I've got to get back to my customers. If I can be of any help, let me know. I doubt it though. I couldn't help Cornell. He left here saying he was going to the other station.'

Sommers had started to leave. He paused outside the doorway.

'The other station?' he echoed.

'The other service station,' Fuller explained. 'The one down at Eighth and California. He told me that was where he left Berra after demonstrating the car. He sure seemed anxious to find that guy Berra. Crazy story, isn't it? Stories, when they're crazy like that, they stick in your mind.'

It was a crazy story. Sommers wondered how Garcy would have reacted to the tale he'd just heard. Would he still believe Berra didn't exist, or would he point out what was still an annoying fact: that nobody except the dead man had seen Berra? He went around the building and proceeded to inspect the men's room. It was exceptionally clean. The company could give the management a seal of approval for cleanliness. There wasn't a thing

393

out of order or out of place. Not a thing. The waste basket was in full view, the towel dispenser was filled, there wasn't so much as a leaky faucet or a dripping plumbing pipe. And there was no apparent evidence of Berra's having been in the room a week ago. Sommers made a careful inspection of the lavatory. It was an inexpensive casting with a hollow rim. He ran an exploratory finger along the under edge until it touched something unfamiliar. He squatted on his heels and examined the area by the flame of his cigarette lighter. There was a lump of something that looked a little like hardened chewing gum, but that scraped off on his fingernail into slivers of lead. Solder. Liquid solder. There were fragments of several lumps of it dotting the underside of the fixture. He didn't scrape off any more of it. He snapped off the lighter and stood up.

What did it mean? Chewing gum he would have understood, but not liquid solder. He left the rest room and went back to his car. For a few moments he sat parked in view of the spot where Cornell must have parked a week before his death. The door of the rest room was in full view. If it had been ajar when Cornell arrived, it would have been an easy matter for anyone waiting inside to see and recognize a specific model that had been requested to call for him. A very special form of taxi service—but to where? Max Fuller had told him. Another service station at the corner of Eighth and

California.

The station at Eighth and California was an independent—not so modern or so clean as the one Sommers had just visited, but twice as busy. The reason for that was the garage about twenty-five yards behind the pump area. It was there that Sommers located a stout, balding man in overalls whose name was Donnegan, and who owned the business. Like Max Fuller, Donnegan had a story to tell. Cornell had been in the previous day inquiring after the same party—a man named Berra.

'I don't know anybody by that name, let alone employ him,' Donnegan explained. 'All I've got on the payroll are relatives. I don't say they work, mind you, but they're on the payroll. Might as well be. I feed them anyway.'

'What did Cornell say about Berra?' Sommers asked.

'Just what I told you,' Donnegan said. 'Asked if I knew him. Told me how he looked—young, dark, well dressed. Said he'd dropped him off here a week ago after taking him for a demonstration ride in the '57 Cad Cornell was driving. Berra wanted to buy it, he said. Made him promise not to sell it to anyone else. Said he was going to meet his father here and put the bite on him.'

'Here?' Sommers echoed.

'Yeah. That's a good one, isn't it? The car salesman fell for it, too. You'd think those guys would get used to dead beats playing them for

395

suckers. Still, for a commission I guess a man will go a long way.'

'Two hundred miles,' Sommers said.

'How's that?'

Sommers didn't bother to explain, but it was hardly more than half a mile from Fuller's garage to Donnegan's. Allowing for a demonstration ride, there were still a lot of miles to account for to reach that two hundred total Garcy had complained about.

'Did Cornell tell you anything else?' he asked. 'Did he mention where he was going when he left here?'

'No, he didn't say anything about that,' Donnegan answered, 'but he did tell me one peculiar thing. He said this fellow Berra, when he got out of the Cad to meet his father here, ducked his head and ran for the men's room. "Maybe he was carsick," I cracked, but Cornell didn't laugh. He seemed worried or puzzled. Maybe that's a better word—puzzled.'

It was a good word because Sommers was puzzled, too. Something was beginning to take shape, some vague pattern—but of what? The man Garcy had insisted didn't exist was becoming more real. A young man—a young voice on the telephone. A perturbed salesman retracing his route a week after he'd first taken it, and a day after Berra's second call. He wouldn't have gone to those lengths to search for someone he'd put up to concocting a

396

prospective sale in order to get him off the hook with Garcy. Sommers had one more thing to do before leaving Donnegan's station, and after he'd inspected the men's room he was even more puzzled. On the underside of the lavatory he found several lumps of hardened liquid solder. There was a pattern, all right, but he needed more pieces before it could be meaningful.

Assuming that Mr. Berra did exist—why had he used Cornell for a chauffeur, and where else had they gone? Cornell had told his employer that he'd driven out to Berra's home, but that Berra wasn't in. Unless this was an outright lie, Berra must have given an address. It hadn't been in Cornell's desk, but there was a possibility that he'd jotted it down on a scrap of paper in his wallet. Sommers returned to headquarters and examined the dead man's effects. Nothing. A trail that had started out so promisingly had come to a dead end. There was only one other place to look.

Downstairs in the garage, Mr. Garcy's well-travelled Cadillac was ready to be returned to its owner. Cornell had been very neat with his dying. The upholstery wasn't bloodstained and the bullet had lodged in his skull, thereby saving the door's glass. Properly advertised, the car would make a quick sale to some morbid individual. Sommers wasn't morbid; he was determined.

The instant he opened the door of the
397

Cadillac, he was again aware of that sense of something known, but not recognized. He'd done this very thing not more than twelve hours ago—opened the door of the death car, to which he'd been summoned, and peered into the front seat. Was it something seen? No. Only Cornell and the gun that had fallen to the floorboards at his feet had been seen. But something smelled—yes, that was it: a pungent, smoky odor as if something had been burned. He opened the glove compartment. Nothing to explain the odor there—no oily rags or singed material of any kind; only one detailed price ticket from Garcy Motors and one city map.

One city map. Sommers was excited the instant he drew it out into the light. It was a new map, but it had been marked with a red pencil. Crosses, small red crosses at various locations. The more he studied the locations, the more interesting they became. One cross was at the corner of Third and Fremont; one at Eighth and California. There were three others at widely separated locations: two on corners and one in the middle of the block. Add the distances together and double for round trips and a good piece was gone out of the missing two hundred miles. Now, he had three more chances to locate the elusive Mr. Berra.

Sommers pocketed the map and closed the glove compartment. The car was ready to roll now—cleaned, vacuumed, the ashtrays pushed in. Ashtrays. Now there was something to be seen. Last night the ashtray on the instrument panel had been open. Sommers yanked it out and examined the contents, overlooked in the cleaning of the car, perhaps, because someone had pushed the ashtrays in. Glenn Cornell didn't smoke because of his delicate throat, and Garcy Motors would surely be more careful of a display model than to leave an ashtray full of stubs still faintly smelling of the weedy scent Sommers remembered from the previous night. And these were not standard cigarette stubs either; this was marijuana.

*   *   *

The pieces of the pattern were gathering fast. Sommers turned the contents of the ashtray over to the lab for analysis and got set for a tour of the city. There were three locations on the map to be identified. The first turned out to be a small independent grocery located across the street from a high school—the Charles Steinmetz High School. Sommers noted the name of the school with interest. He didn't linger at the grocery. Strolling in for a pack of cigarettes was enough to show him there was no one working inside answering the description of Mr. Berra. He didn't expect there would be. The second location on the map was even more interesting—an herb and health food shop operated by an oriental who, if not inscrutable, was at least self-possessed. Sommers didn't know what he was going to do with the wheat-germ flour he bought, but he did know the pattern was beginning to form a most interesting picture.

The third red cross on the map was in the middle of the block on a residential street, where aging bungalows were being replaced by modern multiple unit apartments. Without a house number, it would have been difficult to learn just what the third cross indicated except for the pattern in Sommers' mind. A man who didn't want to be found wouldn't give a correct address; he would give, if possible, an address where nobody lived. Vacant lots were the rule in such cases, but in this instance there was something even better. A house about to be moved stood like an empty shell with uncurtained windows and a collection of advertising throwaways cluttering the lawn and the front porch. *Nobody was home.* This is what Cornell had reported back to Mr. Garcy after calling on Berra. Nobody, certainly, was at home here. Sommers parked the car and began to examine the property for some sign of ownership.

At a casual glance, the building might have been only temporarily vacant; closer inspection showed the wreckers had already been at the porch foundations. Several brick pillars were in ruins and the brick fireplace just around the corner of the house was half-demolished. It was there that Sommers discovered the man with a wheelbarrow. The man looked up, surprised, a brick in each hand. These he promptly added to the growing pile on the wheelbarrow. When Sommers showed his badge, the man grinned.

'It's okay, Officer,' he said. 'I've got Mr. Peterson's permission to take these bricks. It's his house. We were neighbors for years. "Go ahead, take 'em when they move the building," he said. "Finish your patio." I don't know why I bother, to tell you the truth. One of these days, one of the buyers is going to offer me a price I can't resist and they'll be hauling my house away.'

'Where's Mr. Peterson?'

'Gone to Carmel. Retired. Suppose that's where I'll be going someday.'

'How long has it been since Mr. Peterson moved away?'

'From here, you mean? Oh, he hasn't lived in this old house for seven or eight years. Rented it out. The last tenants left about three weeks ago. Glad to see 'em go, too. Most people in this world are fine—just fine. All nationalities, all races. But once in a while you run across some bad neighbors. This Berrini family—'

'Berrini?' Sommers echoed.

'That's right. Not a family, really. Couldn't blame the mother so much. She was a widow who had to work. Three young girls in elementary school to support, and two sons who should have been a help and never thought of anything but hot-rods and flashy clothes. The older one—Bruno—even served time at one of those juvenile delinquent work farms a few years ago. I don't know about Joe. He's still in high school.'

'How about Bruno?' Sommers prodded. 'How old is he now? What sort of looking fellow is he?'

The man with the wheelbarrow stared at him thoughtfully.

'Is Bruno in trouble again?' he asked. 'He must be in trouble again. A man was here yesterday asking those very same questions. I don't think he was a police officer though. He was driving a big car, a big black Cadillac.'

Cornell again. A trail that had started with a trip to Third and Fremont was almost completed. Only one more location was needed to fill in the gap that stretched between an abandoned dwelling and an alley behind a lumber company.

'Bruno's a nice enough looking young fellow,' the man was saying. 'About twenty, I'd say, and a real flashy dresser. I don't know where he gets his money.'

'I think I do,' Sommers said grimly. 'Do you know the Berrinis' new address?'

'Couldn't tell you that, Officer, but I suppose the Post Office people could. Wherever they moved, they have to get mail.'

'That they do,' Sommers said. 'I've got

something for Bruno Berrini myself—special delivery.'

It was a very neat plan. Back at headquarters, Sommers conferred with Lieutenant Graves of Narcotics, and the little red crosses on the map found in the glove compartment took on significance.

'The way it looks to me,' Sommers said, 'the car salesman, Cornell, marked this map himself. Berrini—or Berra, as he called himself—would have been more careful. Cornell was used—that much must have been obvious to him yesterday morning when he called Garcy and said that he'd run into difficulty with the sale, but would have it straightened out before the day was over.'

Graves nodded agreement.

'The used-car routine is a new switch,' he admitted. 'We haven't run into it before. Berrini couldn't use his own car; if we spotted those delivery stations and watched them, it could be traced to him. The way he ducked his head and ran in and out of the rest rooms indicates how afraid he was of being seen. This scheme beats the stolen-car method where there's always a resulting investigation that might lead to an arrest. Who would think of reporting a reluctant car buyer to the police?'

'Exactly,' Sommers said. 'Cornell didn't even dare report him to his employer. Imagine his feelings when he realized he'd been tricked into chauffeuring a marijuana peddler on his rounds. He must have spent that last day of his life retracing the places to which the elusive Mr. Berra had caused him to drive: the station at the corner of Third and Fremont, the station at Eighth and California—that was the first day's route. Then he repeated the second trip: to the grocery store across from the high school and to the health food shop, checking the map as he went. By this time he knew what those locations meant. Berrini made one mistake. Maybe he was just too cocky, but on that second drive he smoked some of his own product. Cornell didn't smoke at all, and the fumes must have bothered his throat; in any event, something happened to draw his attention to the stubs I found in that ashtray.'

Graves had listened intently; now he asked, 'Why—?'

'Because Cornell was shot with his own gun, a gun usually kept in his room. He went home, according to what his wife said, just long enough to have gone into his room and taken the gun. By that time, he must have located Berrini. He told his wife that he was going out to meet Berra and "put an end to the indecision."'

' "I've got him on the hook," he told me. "All I have to do is reel him in." '

Mrs. Cornell's words intruded in Sommers' mind. They fit into the pattern too.

'A man doesn't go home to get his gun,' he added, 'if he's only going out to sell a car. The going was rough for Cornell, but not that rough.'

'That's one thing I don't understand,' Graves remarked. 'Granting that you're right and that Cornell did realize that he'd been used to deliver marijuana to the supply points on this map, why did he go after Berra himself? Why didn't he go to the police?'

There were alternative reasons. There was the possibility of attempted blackmail—that was the obvious one. Cornell had needed that sale badly enough to cling to it all week. He had enough on Berra to make him buy the car.

There was also the possibility of anticipating a reward if he nailed a marijuana peddler; Cornell could have used a reward. But to know why a man does anything, it is necessary to know something about the man himself; and everything Sommers had learned about Glenn Cornell suggested that he was a good citizen and a conscientious father. He was risking his life when he went after Berrini. He must have known that a hopped-up person was capable of anything. The only reason a man like Cornell would do such a thing was the kind of reason that stood tall and broad-shouldered in a high school jersey with a big S on the chest. S for Steinmetz.

Graves listened to that possibility spelled out, and then asked, 'Do you think Cornell's son is mixed up in this?'

'It isn't what I think that matters,' Sommers

said. 'It's what Cornell feared. I'm going to do a little checking at Steinmetz. Right now, I'd be willing to give odds that Andy Cornell and Joe Berrini are pals and that Glenn Cornell knew about it and worried about it. I'm not looking into a crystal ball when I say that, either. The man who called Garcy Motors asked for Cornell by name. If Bruno Berrini's kid brother pals around with Andy Cornell, chances are he knew Andy's father was a salesman at Garcy's. He might even have known that he was easy going—"he could be pushed around" was the way Andy put it. I think that's your answer, Lieutenant. I think Cornell took his gun and went after Berrini on his own because he was afraid police action might hurt his son. Guilt can rub off on the innocent, too, especially when the innocent is an adolescent with more bravado than brains.'

At least it was a reason, and there had to be a reason—even as there had to be a reason for the lumps of solder on the undersides of the two rest-room lavatories.

'You may be right,' Graves said. 'It shouldn't be too difficult to find out what happened last night. We know the deposit points for the marijuana—all we have to do is watch. Berrini's used them before, the multiplicity of the soldering lumps indicate that some kind of packet or container has been hidden under the lavatories more than once, and he'll use them again. Cornell's dead—a published suicide. What does he have to fear?'

Sommers was thoughtful. Lieutenant Graves' job seemed simple; his wasn't so easy.

'He may use the car salesman method of transportation again,' he suggested. 'You've got to admit, it's a good one. If it hadn't been for Cornell's curiosity and that marked map, we'd never have traced the black Caddy to him.'

'And Berrini knows nothing of the map,' Graves added.

'Of course not. He'd have destroyed it if he'd known. Lieutenant, I've got a request to make of your department. I want you to contact the used car dealers in this area and alert them to Berra's pitch. Chances are he'll be going through this same routine within the week.'

'Within the week?' Graves echoed.

'It's the football season,' Sommers said. 'What's a logical place to peddle marijuana— particularly marijuana that's been delivered to the pushers before Saturday?'

Graves grinned.

'You've been nosing around in my detail,' he said. 'You know we've been getting reports from the football games.'

'It's a report from a used-car dealer that I'm interested in,' Sommers said. 'You want Berrini for passing narcotics—that's an easy job. I want him for something that's going to take a little doing. I'm going out now and take some instructions in how to sell an

407

automobile.'

'You?' Graves asked.

'Who else, Lieutenant? I'm the man who wants Berrini for murder.'

* * *

Bruno Berrini was watched. Before the day was over, his new residence had been located in a stucco duplex within a few blocks of the house about to be moved. The school office was closed over the weekend, but on Monday it was learned that Joe Berrini, the younger brother, was a junior at Steinmetz High and a classmate of Andy Cornell. The two boys were seen together in the schoolyard on the day after Glenn Cornell's funeral, which was on Tuesday. It was the same day when Lieutenant Graves reported on the results of notifying the local used-car dealers of Berrini's routine. He'd wasted no time in trying his trick again. He used his own product, and that gave him more daring than sense. This time it was a salesman named Hamilton from Economy Motors who had the same story to tell that Sommers had already pieced out of interviews with Max Fuller and the man named Donnegan. A man who called himself Mr. Baron had telephoned in on the previous Friday and inquired about a '58 Buick displayed on the lot. Told it was still there, he expressed great interest and asked that a salesman pick him up for a

408

demonstration ride at a service station on the corner of Third and Fremont. From there on the story was the same. Baron's peculiar conduct had puzzled the salesman, but customers could be peculiar.

'Friday,' Sommers mused. 'That's the same day he used Cornell the first time. I was right. He works on a schedule. He should call back about the Buick on Thursday. He had to divide these trips up. No salesman would fall for making four stops on a trip. He'd be suspicious.'

'So Berrini divides his distribution points into two parts and services them a week apart,' Graves concluded.

They were right. On Thursday, Hamilton called in to report that Mr. Baron had decided to buy the Buick, but had to get the money—the full amount—from his mother, who insisted on seeing what he was buying before writing the check. Sommers and Graves went out to the lot together. By that time, Mr. Baron had called back to say he couldn't make it in, but would meet Mr. Hamilton in front of his home. The address given was the empty house.

Sommers got into the Buick.

'I'll be behind you,' Graves told him. 'Berrini will have the stuff on him, but I don't want to take him until he's made his deliveries. I want the receivers as well as the distributor.'

'I want more than that,' Sommers said. 'I want a murderer.'

He picked up Berrini in front of the house that still looked as if somebody had just washed the curtains and forgotten to pick up the throwaways from the porch. Berrini was a man of habit. He'd worked out a means of transportation to his delivery spots, but he wasn't prepared for a stranger behind the steering wheel. He balked at the curb.

'Where's Mr. Hamilton?' he demanded.

A young, dark, good-looking kid in a very sharp tweed jacket and slacks. He might have been all slicked up to go paying court to his girl, but Sommers knew a killer could look like an angel.

'Sick,' he answered, trying to sound convincing. 'He asked me to take his place.'

Berrini hesitated. Was the word 'cop' written all over Sommers' face, putting the lie to his story? If it was, he should be reaching for the holster under his coat. He didn't. He let the weight of the gun lean against his ribs, while Berrini's suspicious eyes passed judgment. The eyes were a little glassy. He was about ready to make that almost inevitable switch from reefers to something more potent. His judgment wasn't good. Almost a week had passed since Cornell's death, and there had been no public notice of anything but obvious suicide. Berrini felt safe. He crawled into the front seat and gave an address. He said very little during the half hour that passed before Sommers pulled up before a ranch-style home in one of the better districts. This was supposed to be where Berrini's mother lived. He waited for the story and it came.

'I don't see her car in the driveway,' he said. 'She must have gone to a little store a few blocks down the street. She buys a lot of this health food stuff. Let's drive down and see.'

'Maybe you should ring the bell,' Sommers suggested. 'She might have left the car in the garage.'

'She never leaves the car in the garage—never! She's at this store—I'll bet ten dollars. Just a few blocks—'

It was a thin story, but to a commission-hungry salesman eager for a cash sale it would have been convincing. Sommers listened to the directions and then proceeded to the herb shop. He pulled up to the curb and parked about half a block ahead of the unmarked car in which Lieutenant Graves was waiting. Berrini went inside alone. Through the front window, Sommers observed him in earnest conversation with the proprietor, after which they went into the back room for a few moments. When Berrini came back into view, Sommers knew the first delivery had been completed; but the lieutenant wouldn't make his move until they had proceeded on the delivery route. That was the agreement between them. Berrini's supply points were the lieutenant's concern, but Berrini belonged to Sommers.

411

Berrini returned to the Buick with another story.

'She was in here a little while ago,' he reported, 'but they were out of what she wanted. The clerk sent her to another store. If you don't mind driving a little farther, we'll catch her there. This car's what I've been looking for.'

So a man with a lagging sales record and a family to support would go along with the pitch. He'd come this far; he had to keep riding that sale. Sommers was beginning to get the feel of the part he was playing. Be pleasant, be nice, keep smiling. Pretend you don't know the next stop is a small independent market across the street from the Steinmetz High School. He glanced in the rear-view mirror as the Buick edged away from the curb. Lieutenant Graves was sliding across the seat to get out of the unmarked sedan. Within minutes, he'd have relieved the herb shop proprietor of his latest consignment. So far, everything was working out according to plan.

It was almost dark when they reached the store. The schoolyard was deserted and the streets empty. Berrini went inside and Sommers, as he had done before, watched from the Buick. Five minutes passed, ten minutes, fifteen. Nobody else went into the store or came out of the store. Little independents didn't do a volume business, particularly not at an hour when housewives were already preparing the dinners their families were waiting to devour. Twenty minutes. Sommers crawled out of the Buick and scanned the street behind him. Something must have delayed Graves back at the herb store; there was no sign of his sedan. By this time Sommers knew what Glenn Cornell had learned at the end of his long drive. Berrini, Berra, Baron—whatever he called himself—wasn't coming back. This was the end of the line. Thanks for the ride, sucker, but I don't need you any more. Sommers gave the lieutenant five more minutes and then went into the store alone.

The balding proprietor was adamant. The gentleman must be mistaken. A dark young man in a tweed jacket? Here, in this store? Nobody had come into the store in almost an hour. Business was slow; it was closing time.

'I don't think so,' Sommers said. 'I think it's opening time.'

He pulled the badge from his pocket and thrust it under the man's startled eyes.

'Open!' he ordered. 'Where's Bruno Berrini?'

The man's face reddened. 'Who?' he stammered.

'Bruno Berrini. He's in trouble—big trouble. You don't want to cover for a killer, do you?'

It was one thing to peddle marijuana to high-school students, one thing to twist young lives

413

so that they might never be whole again; but it was something entirely different to face a detective from Homicide and risk your own sweet freedom. One wild glance toward the rear of the store and Sommers had his answer.

'What's back there?' he demanded.

'Only the stockroom,' the man protested. 'Nothing else!'

There was only one reason for the man to scream the words. Sommers wouldn't listen to him, but Berrini would. There was no time to waste. The stockroom was dark, but beyond it a ribbon of light showed beneath a closed door. As Sommers moved toward it, the light disappeared. Now there was only a door— vague in the shadows—and behind it a man who knew why Glenn Cornell had died with his chin on the horn rim of a Cadillac he hadn't sold.

'Berrini!'

Sommers fired the word at the silence and dropped back against the wall beside the door.

He waited a few seconds and then—

'I'll give you to the count of three to come out, Berrini. If you don't want twice the trouble you've got now, you'll come quietly. We know you killed Glenn Cornell. We found a nice, clear print you forgot to wipe off his gun. One—two—'

It was a lie. There hadn't been a print on Cornell's gun that hadn't matched Cornell's own; but Sommers got no farther with his

414

threat. The first interruption was an undistinguishable oath, and then the walls seemed to split open with the sound of gunfire. But Berrini wasn't shooting at the door. Berrini wasn't shooting at all. Sommers discovered that when he jerked open the door and let the fading finger of light from the front of the store stretch to the place where Berrini crouched with his arms folded over his face as if they could stop the .45 leveled at the back of his head from splitting open his skull.

'Drop the gun!' Sommers ordered. 'Drop it on the floor!'

For about five seconds Berrini's life expectancy hovered at zero and then the barrel of the .45 drooped, lowered, and finally fell to the floor.

'Okay, kick it this way,' Sommers said.

The gun slid across the floor. Not until it was safely under his foot, did Sommers draw an easy breath. It was no small thing to have talked down the hatred blazing in the eyes of a tall, blond kid with a big S on his sweater.

*   *   *

Back at headquarters, Bruno Berrini made his confession. He hadn't meant to kill Cornell. Cornell had sought him out and insisted on one more demonstration ride. Not until they were under way did he reveal his knowledge of his brother Joe's use of him and demand

415

information about his brother's association with Andy. They quarreled then, and Cornell pulled his gun. It was self-defense, Berrini insisted. It was an accident. A guy has a right to defend himself, doesn't he? So the gun went off while he was struggling for it and killed a guy. It was self-defense. That was the story he would take into court, and whether or not he succeeded in selling it to a jury wasn't in Sommers' department. What was in his department, in his office, in fact, was a kid with a story to tell.

Andy Cornell was shaken and subdued.

'It was a crack Joe Berrini made the day after my father's funeral that made me suspicious,' he admitted. 'He was trying to be nice, I guess. "Your old man had to have a lot of guts to put a .45 to his head," he said. I got to thinking about it later. I even looked through all the old newspapers to make sure, but nobody had mentioned that my dad's gun was a .45. I didn't know it myself until the police returned the gun to my mother and I got hold of it. Dad would never let me near it. Too many kids got killed playing with empty guns, he always said. But it was a .45 all right, and how did Joe know that unless he knew a lot more? Then I got to thinking about this Mr. Berra and how much the name sounded like Berrini.

'I knew my dad didn't like me hanging around with Joe because of his brother's record. I didn't see what that had to do with

416

Joe, but it had worried him and so I got to thinking that maybe he'd had a fight with Bruno, or something. I knew Bruno was mixed up in what was going on at the grocery store across from the school. Kids know more about that kind of thing than cops, I guess. I just kept watching and waiting for my chance to talk to Bruno, which happened to be today.'

'A talk with Bruno,' Sommers repeated, 'at the point of a gun.' He was scowling when he said it. The kid might have been killed, taking that gun away from Bruno. 'Haven't you Cornells ever heard of going to the police?' he demanded.

Andy ducked his head. It was time for a lecture on the folly of a citizen taking the law into his own hands; but Andy Cornell had suddenly wilted, as if the excitement of his search for Bruno was all that had held back the grief of his father's death and now that barrier was gone. He would be remembering the warnings his father had given him about the Berrinis and picking up that burden, too. The kid had too much hard living ahead of him to be handicapped by additional crosses of guilt.

'Well, there's one thing I'll have to hand to you,' Sommers admitted, having decided to forego the lecture. 'You're not it any more than your father was.'

Andy looked up, puzzled.

'What's that?' he asked.

'Chicken,' Sommers said.

417

THE PRIVILEGES OF CRIME

T. Powell

Sheriff Alfie Abbott bounded from his rain-streaked official car as the headlights winked off. With his tall, lean deputy, Bud Smith, flanking him, Alfie ran across the dark street to the small, almost-deserted bus station. Like the tiny beaks of pecking chicks, the drizzle pattered on the tin roof over the concrete apron where the Cleveland bus was due to pull in at any moment for its brief stop.

Presenting shadows roughly in the shapes of a bowling ball and a tenpin, Alfie and Bud peered through the dingy window of the dim waiting room. A lone person was visible on one of the scarred benches, an ill-clad, dozing old lady with a battered pasteboard suitcase tucked under her seat. The ticket window was closed. Anyone wanting to catch a local out of Hoskinsburg at this hour had to pay a fare directly to the driver.

'Dad-burn,' Alfie growled in disappointment.

Then a door inside the waiting room opened. A man came out of the men's room, and Alfie's blue eyes lighted.

'Dad-burn!' he echoed in an entirely different tone. 'Believe we got him, Bud! He

418

sure fits the description.'

The man inside was short, stocky, swarthy, wearing tan poplin pants and a soiled zipper jacket. He looked at the dusty clock over the deserted ticket stall. The time was 10:53. The local, bound for Cleveland, was due to trundle in three minutes from now.

Alfie grabbed Bud's strong, wiry arm and yanked him away from the lighted window area.

'I guess we solved this one in a hurry,' Bud said. 'Lucky for us he's a real dumb crook.' Bud glanced toward the waiting room. 'Just a sitting duck. Like he wanted to get caught.'

'We ain't all the way caught him yet,' Alfie reminded. 'Got to be careful. Don't want to get the old lady in there hurt.'

Bud nodded, his long face grave. 'What's the plan, Alfie?'

Alfie's black slicker rustled. His eyes made a quick summation of the surroundings.

'We'll box him,' he decided. 'You cover the front door. I'll go in from the side where the buses come in.'

'Gotcha, Sheriff!'

'Keep a sharp eye through the front window,' Alfie cautioned. 'If he ducks back into the men's room, scat around to the alley.'

'You cut him off the rear, he won't get away,' Bud promised. His tone caused Alfie to look sharply at him. Bud's eyes had a glint that reminded Alfie of a blood-hungry bear dog.

419

Alfie stabbed a finger in front of Bud's hawkish nose. 'Now, Bud,' he ordered the deputy, 'you keep in mind all them court rulings about the treatment of suspects, arrestees, and criminals. Seeing as how we're the only law in this here crossroads community, we can't afford the time and taxpayers' money defending ourselves against charges of police brutality.'

Bud ground his teeth. 'All right,' he growled, 'but if he swings on me, I'm gonna bust him one!'

'Just so long as you don't use undue or inhumane force. He's got rights, you know.'

'Rights, hell! Downright privileges, I call it,' Bud snorted.

Alfie's attention was again centered on the bus station. He took a breath, hunched his shoulders in his moisture-laden raincoat. 'Well . . . here goes!'

As he barged around the corner of the building, Alfie figured he had a grade-A smart guy inside. In his book, a smart guy was a cluck so dumb he was convinced all other folks had even less sense.

The bird roosting in the waiting room with the hand of the law about to tap him must have sized up Hoskinsburg as a spot for easy pickings, with nothing more than a rube constable on duty.

But the yegg had botched his caper from the start, walking nervously into the Hoskinsburg

ServiCenter and Truck Stop where the night man, Jim Harper, was on duty alone. With no more aplomb than a wiggleworm feeling the first touch of a fishhook, the punk had tried to keep a lookout in all directions at once as he'd pulled a rusty revolver and informed Jim that this was a stickup.

Almost as scared as the would-be bandit, Jim had let out a bleat and dived behind a counter. The yegg had interpreted Jim's screech as a cry of wrath from a heroic man plunging toward a hidden weapon. He'd panicked, dropped his gun, took off. Hearing the sounds of flight, Jim had scrambled from behind the counter.

Short minutes later, Alfie and Bud had been on-scene, summoned by Jim's phone call.

'He hightailed it down Main Street on foot, Sheriff,' Jim had wound up his account of the event, sitting sickly on the counter. 'He was a loner, nobody waiting for him.'

'No car?'

'Not that I seen, Sheriff.'

'Hmmm,' Alfie had pondered. 'No train depot or airport ... just the Cleveland bus due....' He snapped his fingers. 'Dad-burn, Jim! That hooligan has cased our town. Timed his caper to the arrival of the Cleveland bus. Planned to leave you slugged unconscious while he made his escape with the loot, bold as brass!'

'That's it, Alfie!' Bud had grabbed his arm.

'You done deduced it!'

'Unless he had a car stashed on a side street,' Alfie said. 'Anyhow, rule number one is to cover all modes of exit, and in Hoskinsburg, the bus station is it. Come on, Bud. We got to beat the Cleveland bus to the station.'

Now it seemed that Alfie's efficiency and keen mind were about to pay off. Instead of covering the few miles to Cleveland and losing himself in the crowds before a dull-witted country constable got on the job and figured things out, the yegg was smack between the jaws of a trap. Alfie was sure he'd spotted the right man. It was unlikely that two strangers fitting Jim's description so closely would be in Hoskinsburg on the same night.

Alfie had reached the wide, swinging side doors. He peeked through the glass panes at the man in the waiting room. The man was younger than Alfie had first thought: about thirty, but hard looking, with heavy bones jutting against the swarthiness of the thick-lipped face, and a mane of black hair tucked like glistening feathers about the ears and bull neck.

Alfie gulped some of the sudden dryness from his throat, pushed open the door, and lumbered into the waiting room with the awkward grace of the bus that would arrive too late to do the punk any good.

The yegg threw an instant glance of suspicion at Alfie, then at the front door. He saw Bud's lank shadow out there, let out a wild breath, and took a step toward the men's room.

Alfie sidestepped to intercept him. The yegg rocked back on his heels. His mouth gave an ugly twist. 'What gives, pal? You trying to get in my way or something?' His voice reminded Alfie of sand spilling from a dump truck.

Alfie opened the collar of his raincoat to expose the small silver badge pinned to the lapel of his black suit. 'I'm sheriff of this county, and I got probable cause to hold you on suspicion.'

The yegg gave his head a bravado tilt. 'You nuts? I'm just waiting for a bus.'

'I know,' Alfie said mildly. 'But there will be others, if you're lucky enough to be innocent.'

'Yeah? Innocent of what?'

'Attempted stickup of the Hoskinsburg ServiCenter and Truck Stop less than twenty minutes ago,' Alfie said.

The yegg made a desperate assessment of Alfie's size and determined face. 'Listen,' he snarled, 'I got my rights...'

'Which will be respected,' Alfie assured him. 'Fact is, we'll start off by warning you that anything you say may be used against you.'

Although a sudden sag hit his shoulders, the yegg threw out a final threat. 'Okay, pal. But you go throwing a false arrest on me, I'll sue you until you can't afford a pretzel with your beer.'

'Beer's the drink on my salary,' Alfie said placidly. 'Now let's get going.' He turned his prisoner with a polite touch on the shoulder and frisked him.

Wedged between Alfie and Bud, who drove, the suspect was steeped in gloomy silence during the short ride to the small, drab building that housed Alfie's office and the four-cell jail.

When they had filed into the office, Alfie motioned toward a wooden armchair near the flat-topped desk.

The suspect eased into the chair, gripping the arms. 'I been thinking it over. Maybe I better level with you—'

Alfie jerked up a silencing palm. 'Whoa, now. We ain't taking any confessions from you under duress. The courts say it's the law.'

The suspect stared. 'Duress?'

Alfie stabbed a thumb at himself and then at Bud who had taken a guard position beside the door. 'Two police officers,' he said, 'holding you against your will, all alone, in a little room in the dead of night. Reckon you could claim it constituted duress, hence a violation of your rights.'

'You mean you're not going to listen to me?' the yegg said, slackjawed.

'Not until you got a lawyer,' Alfie said. 'The law says that's the rule.'

The yegg slumped back in the chair. 'What kind of sheriff are you?'

A sudden weariness flooded Alfie's eyes. 'I used to think I was a dad-burned good one. Now I don't reckon it matters so much. I got less than a year to go to retirement, and I won't have an outside punk using his rights to foul up the end of my career. I figure I'm due that pretzel with that beer.'

The suspect scurried a glance from Alfie to Bud, back to Alfie. 'That crack about suing you ... it was just that. Just a crack.'

'But a dad-burn good point,' Alfie said. 'No, sir. Law says you're not supposed to give me anything but your name, age, address whilst there ain't no lawyer present. Then if you got no lawyer and no means to hire one, I'm supposed to get one for you, even if we have to pay him with the taxpayers' money.'

The suspect sat in a stunned vacuum. His nervousness was gone entirely. 'I'll be a monkey's uncle,' he said at last. 'So even the hicks have heard the Supreme Court gospel.'

'Just going by the book,' Alfie said. 'You're the first thing approaching a major crime in Hoskinsburg in the past three years. Probably the last before I retire. I ketched you. I got a gun you handled, and a witness. My job is done, all the way by the book as she's written today.'

The yegg pulled himself upright. 'If you'll let me cop a plea, I'll tell you everything ... First time I tried a stickup and I—'

'Name?' Alfie said doggedly.

The suspect gusted a breath. 'Silvio Santos,' he said morosely.

'Age?'

'Thirty-one.'

'Address, Mr. Santos?'

Santos shrugged. 'No permanent address.'

'Okay. That'll do it for now. Take him back to a cell and see that the bed is clean, Bud.'

'Yes, sir.' Bud crossed the office, took Santos by the arm.

'Now wait a minute!' Santos held onto the chair. 'I got a few things to say about the caper in the truck stop—'

'When your lawyer arrives, Mr. Santos.'

'Who said I wanted a lawyer?' Santos yelled.

'Man, you *have* to want a lawyer,' Alfie jumped to his feet, yelling back. 'That's the way it is.'

'Who says so?'

'The law, you dummy! You got rights whether you know it or not. You have got to have a lawyer!' Alfie glanced down at his knuckles which had been thumping the desk. He pulled in a breath, lowered his voice. 'Now who is your lawyer?'

'I know a fellow in Cleveland, I guess...'

'What's his name?'

'Arnold Eman.'

'We'll contact him for you,' Alfie said. 'Part of our job. Part of the safeguards that have been erected to protect your rights.'

The attorney didn't arrive at Alfie's office

426

until ten o'clock the following morning. He swept in, introduced himself, shook Alfie's hand with a firm grip. Alfie's eyes were bugging. He'd expected a cheap shyster. Instead, Mr. Eman was a robust, expensively tailored individual who wore a diamond on his pinkie that weighed about nine carats. He exuded polished self-confidence and a waft of cologne that suggested Bond Street. Outside, a chauffeur waited in the limousine that had brought him here.

'Now if I may see my client, Sheriff.'

'Sure,' Alfie said. 'He's the only boarder we got in our jail just now. You'll have all the privacy you want. This way, please.'

When Alfie returned alone to his office, he rocked back in his desk chair, folded his hands across his girth, and gave himself to complex pondering.

After a time, he relaxed. With the rusty revolver, Silvio Santos' fingerprints, and Jim Harper's sworn eyewitness, he had an airtight case.

A smile tugged at Alfie's lips. Let Santos and the fancy lawyer go over it all they want, this was one case that wouldn't get thrown out on a technicality. The prisoner's rights had been protected to the final word, letter, and period.

In the sequestered quiet of Santos' cell, Eman was saying, 'Under the circumstances, I suppose it was best to call me.'

'Sure.' Santos sat on the comfort of his

spotless bunk enjoying a cigarette.

Eman sat beside his client and laid a reassuring hand on his shoulder. 'Just don't worry, Silvio. You'll go up—and then be out within a year.'

'With twenty-five grand waiting!' Silvio's dark eyes dreamed into the future.

'Shouldn't be a bad year,' Eman chuckled, 'except for the lack of women. Prisons are not what they used to be. Today you got rights, privileges—movies, ball games, libraries, inspectors who come around and taste the chow.'

'I'll make up for the woman part when I get out with my pockets full of payoff.' Silvio elbowed Eman in the ribs and laughed. Then the swarthy man leaned back and his face became serious. 'A year to decide on when and how to do it,' he mused.

'Check,' Eman said. 'Nobody will ever suspect you'd even heard of the mark. You'll never be connected with him.' The lawyer's face hardened. 'He's a lousy, dirty squealer who deserves no more consideration than a fly that needs stepping on. Between now and the trial I'll have plenty of time to brief you fully. Once you're inside and have everything sized up, we can smuggle in anything you need.'

Santos nodded. 'Imagine. Here I'd gone to the trouble of setting myself up for a parole-able penitentiary offense. Then it began to dawn on me that a legal jackass might be rung in who'd get me off completely.'

Eman lit an ivory-tipped cigarette, smiling at Santos through the curl of smoke. 'Exactly. Now for a few preliminaries about the creep the syndicate has decided to exterminate.' Eman cleared his throat. 'First, he is convict number 11802. His name...'

Eman's voice dropped to a confidential drone, and Santos listened, eyes half closed.

We hope you have enjoyed this Large Print book. Other Chivers Press or Thorndike Press Large Print books are available at your library or directly from the publishers. For more information about current and forthcoming titles, please call or write, without obligation, to:

Chivers Press Limited
Windsor Bridge Road
Bath BA2 3AX
England
Tel. (01225) 335336

OR
Thorndike Press
P.O. Box 159
Thorndike, ME 04986
USA
Tel. (800) 223–6121
(207) 948–2962
(in Maine and Canada, call collect)

All our Large Print titles are designed for easy reading, and all our books are made to last.